Undaunted

A Jessie Cole Novel

Rebekah Lyn

Real Life Books & Media
329 Cheney Highway #230
Titusville, FL 32780
www.rebekahlynbooks.com

Publisher's Note: This is a work of fiction. Names, characters, places, and incidents are a product of the author's imagination. Locales and public names are sometimes used for atmospheric purposes. Any resemblance to actual people, living or dead, or to businesses, companies, events, institutions, or locales is completely coincidental.

Undaunted/ Rebekah Lyn
ISBN: **978-0-9965926-3-5**

Originally published under the title *Jessie* in July 2014

Cover designed by LLPix Photography

OTHER BOOKS BY REBEKAH LYN

Seasons of Faith Series
Summer Storms
Winter's End
Spring Dawn coming
Christmas Vows

Coastal Chronicles
Julianne

Jessie Cole Trilogy
*Undaunted (*Previously sold as *Jessie)*
Destiny's Call

This book is dedicated to all of the men and women who bravely gave their lives for space exploration and all those who worked tirelessly to support them, especially my dad.

AUTHOR'S NOTE

This book was originally released in 2014 under the title Jessie. When the story grew from a single book to a trilogy, it seemed fitting to change the cover and title to match the overall storyline. Undaunted reflects Jessie's tenacity and determination despite his circumstances.

I've loved historical fiction for as long as I can remember. Eugenia Price and Morgan Llyweyln are two of my favorite authors and their stories, set in real settings with historical events, made deep impressions on me. When I started toying with the idea of writing stories set in coastal communities, a book about the space program seemed like a perfect fit. I grew up along side the Space Shuttle program and will never forget where I was the mornings Challenger and the Columbia were lost.

All of the details in this book that relate to the space program are accurate, based on the research I did on the NASA.gov website, archive.org, and video footage of the launches, including the moon landing and moon walk. Many of the videos are available on YouTube and can be found on my Jessie Pinterest Board.

While the locations in Titusville and Indian River City are real places, they were used fictitiously. The dream sequences with Gus Grissom are just that, dreams used by Jessie's subconscious to help him deal with his emotional turmoil. I have the utmost respect for Mr. Grissom and his family as well as all of the brave men and women who have been a part of our space adventure.

CHAPTER ONE

Rocket Launch

January 31, 1961

Jessie Cole raced out into the bright sunlight, heedless of the chill in the air. The other kids in his class flocked to the monkey bars or swings, a dozen or so started a game of kickball, but Jessie made his way to the edge of the schoolyard, to a spot where he had a clear view of the beach. The Air Force station had been launching rockets more often the past few months and Eugene Cole had come home the previous night grousing about another launch scheduled for the following afternoon.

"Why don't you like the rockets, Pop?" Jessie had asked over dinner.

"They're loud and cause traffic to snarl up," Eugene mumbled in between swigs from his glass of water.

"But don't you want to know what it's like out in space?"

"If we were meant to fly, we'd have been given wings." Eugene snorted. "I'm sure that monkey they're sending up wishes he could talk his way out of it."

When his father gave him a stern look, Jessie knew to drop the subject. Now he craned his neck, anxious for a glimpse of the missile, unsure when it was even scheduled for lift off. *If there's a chimp onboard that must mean they think they are ready to send up a man,* he thought. He bounced on the balls of his feet, raising one hand to shade his eyes from the sun and wishing his brothers could be there too.

Since the announcement of the *Mercury 7* astronauts in April of 1959, Jessie had been obsessed with becoming an astronaut himself. He saved every penny and bought as many issues of *LIFE* magazine as he could afford, scarfing up every detail printed about these new pioneers. He'd decided he liked Gus Grissom the best. He had kind eyes, unlike those of his father.

A low rumble rolled across the fields and Jessie's eyes scanned the sky for the sleek white machine. It rose above the trees, as the noise grew louder, vibrating Jessie's bones. He heard some of the kids on the playground shout but didn't take his eyes off the rocket until it disappeared, leaving behind a trail of smoke that was already dissipating in the breeze.

"Come on, children, recess is over, back inside," called his fair-haired teacher.

Jessie lingered a moment longer, silently agreeing with the murmurs of discontent from his classmates. Almost two years had passed since the astronauts had been named. It seemed like an eternity to Jessie, but he hoped this mission meant a man would be taking the pilot seat soon. The Russians had been first to launch a satellite into space, but Jessie was sure America would be the first to get a man there. He saluted the now empty sky before dragging himself away, back into the classroom.

After school, Jessie couldn't wait to find his brothers and tell them about the launch. He found the three of them waiting at the end of the long dirt road, already in an animated discussion about the size of the fish Max had caught over the weekend.

"I told you it was fifteen inches," Max insisted, glowering at Ricky.

Ricky shook his head, thick brown hair flopping into his eyes. "No way, it weren't more than ten."

Sam rolled his eyes as Jessie approached and Jessie smiled. Sam's tall, lanky figure was only half an inch shorter than Max but he never used his size to his own advantage. Jessie didn't understand why Sam so meekly followed Max who could be a real bully, mostly at school, but with his own brothers sometimes as well. Ten-year-old Jessie had been in his fair share of scraps with Max, and even had a few scars to prove it.

"I thought it was closer to twenty inches myself," Jessie interjected, causing Ricky to turn and look at him in disbelief.

"Why are you always siding with him?"

Jessie gave his brother a playful punch. "Because it's so much fun." Even though Ricky was a year older than Jessie, he was more like the baby of the family. Sometimes Jessie wondered if there was something wrong with him that made him act the way he did.

"Did you hear about the launch?" Jessie changed the subject as they started walking home.

Max kicked a stone out of his way. "Dumb teacher wouldn't even let us go to the window to look for it."

"I didn't hear any explosions so I guess it went well." Sam smiled.

Sam was the practical one of the group. Jessie didn't understand how Sam could spend so much time studying when there was so much more to explore around them. Jessie believed in learning from doing.

Jessie nodded. "Lucky monkey getting to go into space. Seems like a waste. It's not like he'll come back and tell them anything."

"On the contrary, he'll tell the doctors and scientists quite a bit." Sam scratched behind his ear. "I'm sure they have him rigged up with all types of devices to monitor things like his heart rate."

Jessie thought about this. "You mean a monkey's heart rate is just like ours?"

"I don't know exactly," Sam admitted. "They're the animal most similar to us, so the test results can probably give the doctors a good idea what the effects of launch will be on a human."

"Yeah, yeah, smarty pants, enough of that," Max broke in. "When are we going hunting again?"

Jessie grinned. "Anytime is fine with me. Why don't we skip school tomorrow?"

"You know mom wouldn't like that." Sam shot him a disapproving look.

Jessie shrugged. "It's not like I'm learning anything important."

Sam just shook his head. The boys arrived home ten minutes later, dusty and thirsty. They poured tall glasses of water and sat outside on the sagging front porch listening to the chatter of scrub jays and terns. When their glasses were empty and the sun had almost disappeared behind the house, Max rose.

"We should get cleaned up before Pop gets home." Max brushed sand off his pants and headed into the house.

CHAPTER TWO

Set Back

April 25, 1961

Jessie stood at the edge of the playground with two other boys, anxious for the next space launch. Recess would be over any minute. There would be no time for a hold in the countdown. Two weeks earlier the Russians had announced the successful launch of Yuri Gagarin into space. Once again the Americans had been left behind but today's launch would hopefully be the last before America put their own man into space.

Jessie held his breath as the rocket appeared above the trees. Then it happened. The plume of white smoke erupted into a fiery ball, debris flying in all directions. Jessie didn't wait for the teacher's frantic call to take shelter in the school. He shook his head and turned his back on the carnage. At the door, the teacher gently laid a hand on his shoulder and gave him a sympathetic look. Any other day and Jessie might have resented it, but he knew, today, it had nothing to do with his father and the reputation he'd developed for himself the past couple of years.

When school was out, Jessie dragged his feet along the familiar path home. He kept walking when he came upon his brothers, his head down, watching the sand shift beneath his worn-out sneakers.

"I heard the explosion." Max draped an arm over Jessie's shoulders. "Sorry."

Jessie nodded.

"Maybe we should go out to the beach, see if we can find any pieces," Ricky suggested.

The thought turned Jessie's stomach, but then he stopped. "That's not a bad idea. I'd like to have something to remember we at least tried to get to space."

"Don't talk like that," Sam said. "We'll get there, it's just going to take time."

Jessie knew Sam was trying to be encouraging, and so attempted a smile of thanks before shifting course across the large field of scrub grass.

The boys spread out when they reached the beach. The tide was low but turning. Jessie took the section closest to the water, knowing the rising tide would cover it in another hour. The salty tang of sea spray filled his nostrils and he inhaled, while his eyes and ears locked away every detail of the sand and surf.

He saw a flash of light ten feet ahead and quickened his pace, keeping his eyes on the spot. The ocean foamed up, then slowly retreated. Jessie squatted down to find a silver and black triangle, partially buried in the sand. Another wave rushed toward him, splashing over his feet and soaking the bottom of his shorts. He held onto the metal afraid the undertow would pull it out to sea. When the water receded, Jessie pulled the debris free of the remaining sand. It was five inches tall and three wide. Turning it over in his hands he noted scorch marks and part of what he thought might be the letter U or A from the USA painted on the side of the rocket.

"Guys," he waved to his brothers.

Max arrived first. "What'd you find?"

Jessie handed him the piece of metal.

"Cool." Ricky joined them and reached for the newfound treasure.

"Good job, Jess." Sam clapped his brother on the back. "I didn't think we'd find anything that big."

Jessie reached for the metal and traced the rough edges. "You don't think they will give up do you?"

Sam shook his head. "Since the Russians have gotten into space already, I don't see how we can give up now."

"I hope they don't." Jessie tore his gaze away from his find and looked at his brothers. "I want to be an astronaut."

Max laughed. "You can't be an astronaut."

"Why not?"

"Cause you gotta have money to be an astronaut. You don't think Shepard and Grissom and all those other guys are dirt poor do you?"

"Maybe they're not dirt poor, but they aren't filthy rich. They were chosen because they were in the military and had good records."

"So you gonna enlist when you turn eighteen? We'll probably still be in that dag gum Vietnam and you'll go and get yourself killed the first day in the jungle."

"Nuh-huh. I know how to take care of myself. I hide from you in the woods all the time." Jessie balled his hands into fists and planted his feet.

Sam stepped between them. "Cool it, Max. If Jessie wants to be an astronaut, then maybe he can be. Lots of things are changing."

Max snorted. "Yeah, and I could be President."

"If that happens, then I'm moving to Mexico," Ricky quipped.

Jessie laughed and unclenched his fists. Yet again Sam had brokered peace without anyone coming to blows. Maybe Sam was the one who would become President.

Sam stepped back. "Let's head home."

"Did you hear Mom and Pop got another letter from the government yesterday?" Max asked as they walked along the hard packed sand.

"About what?" Jessie asked, turning up the beach, shuffling through the soft sand to a well-worn path across the dunes. Thick saw palmettos, sea grapes, and sea oats grew on either side of the path, slowly thinning as the boys moved farther from the beach.

"About buying our land. They want to expand the missile complex more. They've been buying up all the land around here." Max swatted at a dragonfly buzzing around his head.

"But they already have so much land, what do they need more for?" Jessie ducked under the wispy needles of an Australian Pine tree, his brothers close behind.

"How'm I supposed to know? I didn't see the letter, I just heard them arguing about it after we went to bed. Mom wants to take their offer, but Pop doesn't want to move."

"I don't want to move either," Ricky agreed. "I like being close to the beach and huntin' in the woods."

"I don't think we have much choice. Sounded like the government letter said we take the offer or they'll just take the land away from us."

"They can't do that," Jessie cried. "We've lived here forever."

"Not forever, you moron," Max sneered. "Mom and Pop only moved here during the war, when Pop got assigned to the Banana River Naval Air Station."

"Still, that's practically forever." Jessie let his fingers run through the thin pine needles as they emerged from the copse of trees into a clearing.

"There are families that have lived here since the 1800s and they're being bought out too. I don't think the government is going to consider our twenty years here more important," Sam replied.

Jessie rolled his eyes. Leave it to Sam to know the history of the island.

"But they can't just take our land," Jessie insisted.

"Yes, they can, it's called eminent domain. If they can prove to the court that private property is needed for public use and fair compensation has been offered, the court will likely rule in favor of the government."

"But this isn't public use," Ricky interjected.

"Yes and no." Sam leaned forward, obviously warming to the subject. "A public park isn't being created, but the research being conducted and the satellites being launched are for the public good. Plus, the government will probably be able to make a pretty good case for public safety. Think about how close this piece of the rocket landed to our house. The government can use this incident and the others before as evidence of danger to the people still living on this end of the island."

"All right, professor, we get it, but it still doesn't mean I want to move," Ricky interrupted.

Up ahead, Jessie could see the orange grove that bordered their land, and glanced back over his shoulder. He couldn't see the beach through the trees, but it had taken less than five minutes to stroll home. Sam was right. This one had been a little too close for comfort.

CHAPTER THREE

A - Okay

May 5, 1961

The call of a blue jay screeched through the open window, jarring Jessie from a dream. He rolled onto his side, rubbed his eyes, and pushed up on his elbow to look out the window. The sun hadn't risen above the orange trees yet so he guessed it was about six. Spotting the offender on a limb not forty feet from the window, he wished he had his shotgun nearby.

"Jessie, you awake?" Ricky whispered from the upper bunk.

"Yeah," Jessie muttered, pushing the thin sheet back and swinging his legs over the side of the bed. Ricky dropped down from the bunk above, his eyes glittering.

"You think they'll really launch that Alan Shepard into space today?"

Jessie nodded, his own excitement growing. How had he forgotten today was the big day? He tugged on a pair of faded red shorts and a t-shirt, its neckline frayed from his nervous habit of chewing on it. Ricky wore similarly faded blue shorts and a t-shirt that had once been white, but was now an aging dirty grey.

"You know Mama isn't going to let us up on the roof today," Ricky said.

"That's why we got to get to the tree house." Jessie poked his head out the door and listened for any indication that his parents were awake, but the house was quiet. He took a tentative step toward the bedroom shared by Max and Sam. Its door swung open and the boys emerged, each boasting a huge grin. Jessie put a finger to his lips before they could make any noise and tiptoed down the short hall to the kitchen.

When he reached the front door, he turned the knob slowly, his heart stopping when the hinges gave a loud squeak. The three other boys raced out past him, as he stood frozen, waiting for the bellowing call of his father. After a minute that seemed like hours, the house remained silent and so Jessie too stepped outside, pulling the door closed as gently as he could behind him.

His brothers had already disappeared into the woods across from the house and Jessie quickly cleared the small yard and moved expertly through the dense underbrush and trees with barely a sound. In less than five minutes he plopped down next to Ricky in the tree house.

Max and Sam had built it two years before, collecting old boards and even a window from various abandoned buildings and miscellaneous junk tossed into the woods long ago. Built in one of the tallest trees on the edge of the forest, before the vegetation petered out into small scrub palmettos and marsh grasses, one side of the tree house was completely open, providing a clear view of the launch pad.

"How long you think we'll have to wait for the launch?" Ricky asked, fidgeting with an old conch shell.

"Hard to say since they're always delayed," Max replied, "but I managed to sneak Pop's transistor radio out last night." With a sly smile, Max pulled an old rag off the radio, dialed in to the local news station and turned the volume so they would be able to hear the launch countdown.

"I'm hungry," Ricky complained.

Sam smiled and emptied his pockets, producing four oranges, some boiled peanuts, and ten pieces of bubble gum. Max nodded then turned out his own pockets to reveal two apples, more boiled peanuts, and five candy bars.

Ricky eagerly reached for one of the candy bars, but Max swatted his hand away. "Those are for later. Have an orange."

Ricky frowned, but did as he was told. Sam handed an orange to each of his brothers before poking a hole in the top of his own and squeezing its sweet juice into his mouth. Jessie inhaled the aroma before puncturing his own fruit. When they had sucked them dry, the boys pulled the oranges apart and chewed on the tender meat.

The hum of an engine in the distance drew their attention. Jessie leaned out of the tree house and spotted a plane circling the launch pad. He knew, even at this distance, that it was an UH-19, patrolling the area to make sure no unexpected air traffic interfered with the launch.

The minutes ticked on agonizingly slowly as the boys watched the sun climb higher in the sky. They tossed their orange peels to the ground below and lay on their stomachs to watch a pair of squirrels scurry across the pine needles to investigate. After pawing at the peels and turning them over several times, the squirrels lost interest.

"Mama and Daddy were arguing again last night," Ricky said, breaking the quiet spell. Jessie rolled onto his back and sat up.

"I heard the government offered ten thousand dollars for our land," Ricky added. "That's a bunch of money. How can Daddy say no?"

"He's just stubborn," Max growled.

"He doesn't want to give up the still," Jessie grumbled, feeling his stomach tighten. "Then he'd have to buy his hooch and we certainly couldn't afford that, even with ten thousand dollars."

"You shouldn't talk about him that way." Sam gave Max and Jessie a stern look. "We don't know the whole story, so we don't have any right to judge the decisions he makes."

Max snorted. "What more do we need to know? The government letters only went out a couple months ago and already six families are gone. They're taking the money and moving on while that's still an option. Pop thinks he can be the last man standing and hold onto our land, which is right smack in the middle of the area the government plans to take over. He is a fool and we'll all end up paying for that before this is over."

Jessie listened to his brother's rant and quietly nodded in agreement. The family had suffered more than their fair share due to their father's drunkenness. Jessie tried to remember how many times he had been with his mother at the general store and seen other women's pitying looks directed their way. Mama had always smiled at them and exchanged pleasant words, but when she was behind closed doors he heard her cry.

Sam shook his head. "We don't know our land is in the middle of the area they want. It may only be on the edge, maybe they don't even need it."

"Look out there, Sam," Max said. "The launch site is ten miles away. Any plans to expand the program are gonna need this land."

Jessie looked across the expanse stretching between the tree house and the launch pad. He could make out a wild boar rooting in the dirt and a large hawk gliding smoothly in a circle. He knew there were deer bedded down for the day somewhere in the woods, along with the bobcats and panthers that still stalked the island.

For hundreds of years, Merritt Island had been a paradise for hunters and fishermen. The idea that all this land would be cleared and the animals pushed out angered him, but at the same time, the idea of a growing program of space exploration made his pulse race with excitement. Why couldn't the two things he loved so passionately exist together?

"Sixty seconds and counting." The voice of the radio announcer cut into Jessie's thoughts.

"T-minus thirty seconds."

Jessie stood up, his gaze zooming in on the tower.

"Three-two-one-zero-and ignition. Liftoff at thirty-four minutes after the hour."

A nearby hawk gave a loud screech, turned out of its whirling pattern and flapped it's wings in a furious flight away from the launch site.

"Look!" Jessie pointed toward the tower and his brothers all watched as a puff of smoke shot from the rocket.

The tall, needle-nosed rocket pushed off the ground, taking Jessie's gaze with it as the sleek Redstone climbed higher and higher.

Max turned up the volume of the radio and they all listened to the report as the rocket broke free of the earth's atmosphere.

"Freedom 7 reports the mission is A-Okay. Three point five g achieved and cabin pressure holding fine."

Jessie bent his head down and rolled the edge of his t-shirt into his mouth, chewing on the fabric.

"Flight trajectory is still A-Okay, the pilot is in good voice communication with Mercury control."

"I wish we could hear Shepard talking to control," Jessie muttered around the t-shirt. He closed his eyes, listening to the reporter sharing Alan Shepard's observations about the beautiful view and the cloud cover over three to four tenths of the east coast, up to Cape Hatteras.

"I can't believe he can see the whole coast," Ricky breathed in awe.

"The mission is now six minutes and forty seconds old. Astronaut Alan B. Shepard is still talking to us, working like a test pilot, reporting facts, figures, reporting procedures in the precise engineering manner of a test pilot," the reporter spoke in a calm tone. "Freedom 7 is beginning to roll into re-entry attitude."

"You think we will see it coming back down?" Ricky leaned out of the tree house, his eyes searching the horizon.

"No way." Max swatted Ricky on the back of the head.

"The Mercury space craft is beginning to re-enter the earth's atmosphere."

Jessie glanced at his watch, surprised that less than fifteen minutes had passed.

"The main parachute has deployed and the Mercury spacecraft Freedom 7 is now descending on its main parachute. The aircraft carrier Lake Champlain has reported visual contact with the capsule."

"That's it?" Jessie asked in disbelief. "That's what all the fuss was about? Fifteen stinking minutes?" With a disgusted shake of his head he climbed down from the tree house and stalked off.

Jessie ran through the marsh grass, its rough edges tearing at his exposed legs, stopping only when he reached the edge of a creek. He glowered at the launch pad, its metal beams reflecting the morning sun. What was the point of being an astronaut if you were back on earth so soon? He wanted to go out and explore space, to see what lay beyond the blue sky he saw every day. How far away were the sun, the moon, and the stars? Could they be reached in a day? He bent down, found a large stick and hurled it toward the tower. He knew it would never reach it, but it made him feel better all the same.

"I don't know what Mama is so worried about. This program will never need all this land if they can't get a man in space for more than a few minutes." Jessie looked around at the trees he knew so well. He'd grown up in this forest and had no doubt he'd live here forever.

CHAPTER FOUR

Eviction Day

July 22, 1964

"**C**ome on out, Eugene. Don't make us come in and drag you out. Think about your kids." Sheriff Stinson stood on the small front porch as Jessie and his brothers stood in the yard flanking each side of their mother. Eleanor stood rigid in front of their 1957 Bel Air, biting her lip, trying hard not to cry. Jessie could feel the tension of her body next to his, and every now and then a tremor ran through her shoulders. Although she managed to hold the sobs inside, a few tears slipped from her tired eyes. She quickly wiped them away and Jessie turned his gaze to the ground, so she wouldn't know he had seen.

Max shifted uncomfortably. "I told you we'd end up being the losers in this situation."

"Sshh," Sam hissed.

Jessie didn't turn to look at his brothers, but kept his gaze on Sheriff Stinson, who was now pounding on the door again. When Eugene didn't answer, Stinson waved a couple of other officers onto the porch. Between them, they held a thick section of tree trunk they had picked up from the back yard. Jessie watched as the two officers swung the wood back and forth, gaining momentum, until they swung it against the door.

The old wood splintered, but didn't give way completely. The officers tried again, and this time the door popped off its rusty hinges. Jessie could hear his father screaming obscenities at the officers as they pushed in through the doorway with guns drawn. Pop could be a real jerk, but Jessie didn't want these guys to kill him. He started to run forward, but someone grabbed his right arm as someone else caught him by the collar of his shirt.

He twisted his head around to find that it was his mother who clung to his shirt, tears now flooding her face, while Sam had hold of his arm. He tried to break free, but Max stepped in front of him and shook his head. There was fear in his brother's eyes and that stopped Jessie cold. He'd never seen Max afraid of anything, not even the seven-foot rattler they'd almost stepped on last summer.

Jessie reluctantly stepped back into line and Eleanor wrapped an arm around him, pulling him to her chest. He could feel her choked breathing as she tried to contain her sobs. Leaning into her, he tenderly rubbed a hand up and down her arm. She buried her face in his thick black hair and dropped a kiss on his head, the same way she had when he'd been little and had skinned his knee.

Jessie would have been embarrassed, had they not been the last people left on that end of the island. He thought about all of the families who'd already left. He and his brothers had watched as one by one the homes they had known were either torn down or loaded onto trucks and moved to the mainland.

Jessie and his brothers had spent many days in the tree house, watching the construction of a new launch pad, with rumors that another was scheduled to break ground the following month. The space program seemed to be kicking into high gear. Less than a year after that first, brief flight into space by Alan Shepard, another of the Mercury 7, John Glenn, had actually completed a full orbit around the earth.

The launch had been plagued with delays due to bad weather and a repair to the fuel tank, but on February 20, 1962, John Glenn took flight and spent close to five hours in space, orbiting the earth before splashing down near Bermuda. Jessie remembered skipping school once again, sitting with his brothers in the tree house watching the launch of *Friendship 7* and listening to the excited voices of reporters and mission control specialists. With each minute Glenn spent in space, Jessie's longing to be up there with him had grown. The box in his mind, that he'd consigned that desire to, after Alan Shepard's short-lived venture into space, had now crumbled, releasing Jessie's resolve once more to join Glenn and Shepard in space.

A gunshot rang out, jarring Jessie back to the present. After a few short moments of stillness, Sheriff Stinson stepped out onto the porch and walked toward Eleanor.

Her body stiffened against Jessie as he watched the sheriff cross the yard, the man's gaze passing over each face in turn before holding firm to Eleanor's. The sound of more footsteps on the wooden porch once again drew Jessie's attention to the door. The two officers who had rammed it in now emerged with Eugene between them, blood streaming from his right arm, his gaze refusing to leave the ground at his feet.

Eleanor's body went slack against Jessie and he had to wrap an arm around her to keep her from falling. He felt Ricky scoot beneath her other shoulder, to lend some extra support.

"I'm real sorry it had to come to this, Mrs. Cole," Stinson said.

Eleanor nodded and drew in a deep breath. "Can I go in and pack up a few things now?"

"Do you have some place to go?" Stinson's eyes softened.

"I made arrangements to rent a house up in Indian River City, near Eugene's brother, although Eugene himself hasn't known anything about it until now. Would you mind taking him to his brother's place? He can stay there until I can get things settled."

"Not a problem," Stinson replied, and Eleanor pulled a slip of paper from the pocket of her apron.

"Here's the address. They'll be expecting you." Eleanor pressed the paper into Stinson's hand.

The sheriff motioned for the waiting officers to tend to Eugene's wound. Jessie watched one of them pull a first aid kit from the trunk of his car, pour some alcohol on the flesh wound and wrap it in a white bandage that quickly turned red. With all that done, the officer pressed Eugene's head and ducked him into the back seat of the car before slipping behind the wheel and pulling out onto the rutted dirt road. They soon disappeared into the orange grove, leaving behind nothing but a cloud of dust. Not once, in all that time, did Eugene look up from the ground and acknowledge his family.

Eleanor straightened her back and firmly removed her sons' supporting arms. "Come on boys," she said, "we have work to do."

Max, Sam, and Ricky followed as she marched them into the house, but Jessie remained outside, his mind and body memorizing the trees, the smell of the nearby ocean, the straight rows of the orange grove, the sagging steps of the front porch – and the splintered doorway. He knew this day would be imprinted on his memory no matter how hard he might one day try to forget.

"Jessie!" He heard his mother calling. He plodded up the steps and made his way into the kitchen. Jessie looked around the familiar room, barely recognizing it. Gone was the framed print of the Eiffel Tower; gone were the pots and pans that had cluttered a shelf along the wall. How had his mother managed to pack all these things in the few minutes he'd hung back outside?

Jessie went into his bedroom and found his mother opening a suitcase on his bed. Ricky was already stuffing his own clothes into a similar bag. The beds had been stripped, revealing lumpy mattresses under their blue and white-stripped ticking.

"Pack up all your clothes," Eleanor told him, "and that infernal hunk of metal under your bed if you want to keep it, not that I understand why you hold onto it."

Jessie was surprised she knew about his piece of the ill-fated rocket. She'd still been at work the day he'd brought it home and hidden it.

Eleanor moved to leave, but then paused and reached out to caress Jessie's cheek. "I'm sorry this had to happen today. I'm afraid we won't be able to have much of a birthday celebration for you."

Jessie shrugged. It was just one more disappointment he could chalk up to his drunken father. He pulled a drawer out from the old wooden dresser and dumped its contents into the suitcase. A pair of socks rolled off the bed, but Jessie ignored them.

With his clothes packed, he lay down on the floor and pulled out the silver and black triangle. He traced his finger over the ridges in the metal, remembering the explosion, and the cold water washing over him when he'd discovered it on the beach. He'd been so disappointed when the rocket exploded, but less than a month later he'd come to understand how failures were only precursors to great success. He finally slipped it and its memories into the suitcase and secured the latches.

Outside, his mother and brothers were stuffing suitcases and boxes into the trunk of the Bel Air. Jessie added his to the pile and shoved his hands into his pockets. Gone were the days of sitting in the tree house watching the rockets. Gone was the freedom to hunt and fish to his heart's content. Gone was the childhood he had loved so well.

Without looking back, Eleanor put the car in drive as soon as the boys had piled in and the last door had been slammed firmly shut.

CHAPTER FIVE

The New House

July 22, 1964

Afterward a silent drive, away from the ocean, north along the Indian River, Mama pulled the car to a stop in front of a plain white concrete-block house with brown trim. Jessie didn't recognize the house and waited for his mother to explain, but she just slipped out from behind the steering wheel, opened the trunk, pulled out a box and carried it inside. The boys followed her, all four empty-handed, unsure what to expect.

Jessie stepped inside then stopped, startled to find the kitchen to his right was already set up with pots, pans, and even the toaster Mama had gotten with the Winn Dixie yellow stamps. The living room to his left held a small sagging sofa, the print of the Eiffel Tower, and framed family photos.

"Whoa, check it out," Ricky called from further back in the house.

Jessie followed the sound down a short hallway and found Ricky in a bedroom, slightly larger than the one they had shared last night. Instead of bunk beds, there was a twin bed on each side of the room, already made up with crisp white sheets and thin blue blankets. Under the awning-style window, several orange crates were stacked on top of each other, with their names written on them in bright red crayon.

In the next room, Jessie found a similar set up for Max and Sam. Continuing down the hall he found a bathroom and another bedroom for his parents. There was no bed in this room, but Jessie recognized the painting of a port village that had hung in his parents' bedroom for as long as he could remember. A small table, covered in a cloth embroidered by his grandmother back in West Virginia, held a bottle of perfume, his father's cologne, his mother's Bible, and a small, framed photo of Eleanor and Eugene on their wedding day.

Jessie remembered how bare the house had seemed when they left this morning and he realized his mother must have been slowly moving items here in preparation for the day they would be forced out. He wondered if Pop had been secretly counting on her to make sure they had a place to stay, once his stubbornness got them kicked out.

He heard his brothers moving through the house behind him, the sound of the front door opening and slamming shut. He went to the living room window and saw them grabbing boxes and suitcases from the car, their excited voices carrying through the thin glass. Ricky came running back and pushed the door open, flying down the hall to his bedroom. Max and Sam weren't far behind. Jessie waited until his mother was alone at the car before stepping outside.

"How did you do this?" he asked her.

Eleanor wrapped her fingers around a suitcase handle and pulled it from the car. "I started saving money after we received the first letter. Uncle Tommy knew the owners of this place and made the arrangements. I had enough for a couple months of rent a few weeks ago, and then the check from the government came in earlier this week. I started moving small things over every day when I went to work."

"But there isn't a bed for you and Pop."

"Uncle Tommy and some of his friends are going out to collect a few pieces of furniture tomorrow. I'll sleep on the couch tonight."

Jessie retrieved his suitcase and followed his mother into the house. In his room, he set the bag on his new bed and noticed Ricky had already placed shirts and shorts in one orange crate, socks and underwear in the other. Jessie did likewise. When he came to his treasured piece of metal, he debated hiding it under the bed again. But then, now that his mom knew about it, that just seemed pointless. He looked around, but there were no shelves. With a sigh, he dropped the metal back into the suitcase, closed the latches, and slid it under the bed.

Ricky turned the crank on the window, opening its three panes as far as they would go. A warm breeze drifted in, bringing the smell of a nearby barbeque.

"Mmm, I wonder what we are having for lunch," Ricky murmured.

"Humble pie would be my guess," Jessie snapped.

"Are there apples in that?"

Jessie turned to find a hopeful smile on his brother's face. "No, there aren't any apples. I can't believe you are hungry anyway."

"Why not? It's near about two o'clock." Ricky rubbed his stomach. "I haven't eaten nothing since breakfast."

Jessie fell on the bed and turned his back on Ricky. "Go ahead, ask Mama what's for lunch. I dare ya."

Ricky ran from the room calling, "Mama, what's for lunch?"

Jessie closed his eyes and soon drifted off to sleep.

CHAPTER SIX

Dreamer

July 20, 1964

S oft, warm sand scrunched between Jessie's toes. Waves rolled onto the shore, white foam racing up the hard packed sand toward him, receding just inches before it would have splashed over his feet. Jessie looked up and down the pristine sand, then back toward the dunes of waving sea oats and thick palm fronds. His roving gaze stopped at the sight of a man cresting the dune, seeming to float above the thick vegetation.

As the man drew closer, Jessie felt his stomach flutter with excitement, recognizing astronaut Gus Grissom.

"Good afternoon, Jessie." Grissom smiled down at him.

"Mr. Grissom, how did you know my name?" Jessie stammered in awe.

"I hear you want to be an astronaut when you grow up." Grissom started walking down the beach and Jessie fell in step beside him.

"I do," Jessie breathed. "I can't wait till I am old enough to apply." Jessie couldn't tear his eyes away from Grissom as they walked.

"That's good. We'll need lots of young men to carry on this mission. There is so much still to be learned and explored. I'm sure we'll face setbacks that will seem insurmountable, but as long as we have the faith and support of the country, I believe this space program can make a real difference. We can do things that others only dream of."

Jessie nodded solemnly. "I won't give up on you."

Grissom's eyes grew sad and he turned his gaze out to the ocean. "You were ready to give up on us once, after Alan's brief flight into space. You said it wasn't worth it for less than twenty minutes."

Jessie felt a stab of guilt. How did Grissom know about his innermost thoughts? "I was wrong then. After you and John Glenn made longer trips I understood Mr. Shepard was a pioneer, blazing the path, pushing the limits to see what could be done. I won't doubt again, I promise."

Grissom looked down at Jessie and placed a hand on his shoulder. "Remember that promise in the days and years to come."

Jessie nodded, thrilled by the faith and confidence Grissom's hand on his shoulder instilled in him. Just as quickly as he had appeared, Grissom was gone and Jessie was alone on the beach again. In the distance he could make out the upright shape of the launch tower.

"Wake up, Jessie," a quiet voice whispered in his ear, as a soft hand shook his shoulder.

Jessie rolled over and opened his eyes to see his mother standing over him, wearing the same pale blue dress she had worn that morning as they had been evicted. Jessie rubbed his eyes and looked at his watch, surprised only forty-five minutes had passed.

"Lunch is ready, sweetheart." Eleanor's eyes crinkled with her smile.

"I'll be right there," Jessie replied. When his mother had left the room, he sat up and studied his feet, surprised to see he wasn't barefoot, with sand between his toes, but rather wore the old sneakers he'd fallen asleep in. Did he only dream his meeting with Gus Grissom?

Of course it was only a dream. What chance did a kid like him have of actually meeting an astronaut? It was childish of him to have believed it for even a second, and yet... Jessie touched his shoulder, where Grissom's hand had rested, and he again felt that confidence. Dreams did sometimes come true, you know.

Not feeling hungry, and still bemused by his dream, Jessie meandered into the kitchen where he found his brothers sitting around the table, all eyes expectantly on him. With a start, he saw a cake standing there, decorated with fourteen brightly burning candles.

"Happy Birthday, Jessie." His brothers laughed and punched at each other.

Grinning, Jessie leaned over the table and blew out the candles in one giant breath, followed by the applause and cheers of his family. Eleanor sliced the cake and handed Jessie the largest piece. It was his favorite, chocolate with chocolate icing and strawberry jam in the middle. When had his mother had time to make this? Had it been in the box she'd first carried into the house?

He looked at his mother with a new appreciation for her strength. Despite all of the stress she'd been facing she hadn't forgotten her youngest son's birthday.

"Thanks, Mom." Jessie gave her an enthusiastic hug before sitting down between Sam and Ricky.

"Can we go out exploring after we eat?" Max asked, forking a large chunk of cake into his mouth.

"As long as you are home before dark." Eleanor was already moving about the kitchen, unpacking kitchen utensils and dishtowels from their boxes. The boys gobbled down the cake and set their plates in the sink before running out the front door.

Max took the lead to the end of the street, stopping at a wide ditch that separated them from a thick, almost jungle-like forest. They stood for several minutes, studying the ditch and the nearby trees, until Max found a long vine trailing down from an overhanging branch. He gave it a few good tugs before wrapping it around his wrist several times, taking a few steps back, then running forward. He swung out over the ditch and into the forest. Jessie heard his brother's laughter as he swung back toward them.

"Come on. You gotta try this," Max yelled.

Sam, Ricky, and Jessie searched among the trees for vines of their own, and with loud whoops, swung across the ditch several times before coming to a stop on the forest side. Max already had out his pocketknife, but they quickly learned the brush and vines here were far too thick for such a small blade.

"We need our machetes to get through here," Max announced.

"I bet we could make a swell tree house," Ricky shouted.

"We could have an entire fort and I doubt anyone would find it," Sam added.

Max scrambled up a thick oak tree. "Get up here, you guys."

The boys immediately obeyed and were rewarded with a view like nothing Jessie had ever seen before. Where their old tree house had looked out toward the ocean and missile facility, from their current perch in that old oak they could see miles and miles of trees in nearly every direction.

Jessie looked back toward their new home and saw the handful of nearby houses. In some ways, this area seemed even more wild and untamed than the land they had roamed on Merritt Island.

Ricky gave a long, low whistle. "Maybe this move isn't going to be so bad after all."

"This is a jungle. I bet there are plenty of panthers and bobcats roaming around." Sam spoke with that teacher-like tone that Jessie knew all too well. If they didn't do something fast, Sam was going to start in on a lecture about the habits of local wildlife.

"Bet ya I can make it to that pine tree over there, without touching the ground," Jessie jumped in before Sam could continue.

"No way," Max scoffed.

Jessie scooted out onto a broad branch of the oak, then reached for a vine. Pulling himself into a standing position, he leaned back as far as the vine would allow, then jumped out, swinging through the air toward the thick pine tree. Kicking out at it, he looped around its trunk, and landed on one of the branches facing his brothers.

"My turn," Max shouted. He repeated the same steps as Jessie, but when he approached the pine, instead of looping around he crashed right into its wide trunk. He pushed away from the tree, swinging back and forth like a pendulum. Jessie laughed hysterically until he saw the angry look Max shot him.

Max dropped to the ground and beat his way through the brush to the base of the pine tree. He tried to climb up but the bark peeled off whenever he found a hand or foothold. Jessie took his own vine and swung back to the oak tree, where Sam and Ricky were snickering at Max's unsuccessful attempt.

"I'm gonna get you," Max bellowed.

"What did *I* do?" Jessie called back. "I didn't move the tree. You must not've pushed out far enough."

A loud crash in the bushes below the boys sobered them immediately. "What was that?" Ricky whispered.

"I don't know." Jessie studied the ground below them, but the thick canopy filtered the sunlight, making it hard to see more than a few feet.

"Max, you might want to get off the ground," Sam called.

"Isn't that what I've been tryin to do?"

"Climb up the vine," Sam instructed. "Climb *now*."

Jessie was surprised by the urgency in his brother's normally studious voice, and Max must have been too, because he started pulling himself up the vine, hand over fist, as fast as he could. A low growl followed by a loud hiss rose from the forest floor.

"There must be a panther den down there," Sam explained.

"We don't need a lesson right now," Jessie snapped.

Max had climbed six feet off the forest floor and was now rocking back and forth, trying to gain enough momentum to reach the pine tree. When he did, he gave a mighty push off the flaky trunk and careened through the air toward his brothers. Jessie reached out, caught the vine and pulled Max to the safety of the oak tree.

"So, how long do you think we need to stay here before that cat moves on?" Ricky asked, with a nervous look below them. They could still hear the menacing growl.

"Panthers don't usually attack humans. Max must have been near a den with some kittens and the mother just wanted to scare him off. We should be fine if we head in the opposite direction," Sam assured them.

"*Should be?*" Ricky asked. "I'd prefer a little more guarantee than that."

"You afraid of a kitty cat?" Max taunted.

"About as afraid as you were when you were down there with it," Ricky shot back.

"I wasn't scared."

"Sure," Jessie smirked. "You just climbed up that vine like the devil was after you for the fun of it."

Max's face turned red and he stood up, ready to fight. Sam reached for his arm and gently tugged him back down.

"No fighting. Not today." Sam spoke softly. Jessie and Max glared at each other for a long minute, then Max reached out and cuffed Jessie on the shoulder.

"I'll let it pass this time since it's your birthday."

Sam peered up through the thick leaves. "It's gonna be dark soon. We should get home." He stood, reached for a vine, and swung back toward the ditch.

Crossing it was easier this time and in a matter of minutes they were shuffling up the short dirt road as the sun steadily sank to their right.

CHAPTER SEVEN

The Bully

November 18, 1964

Jessie and his brothers spent the summer exploring the nearby wild, tangled woods that extended for miles in each direction. Their bodies bore the scrapes and scabs dealt them by the saw-sharp palmetto fronds and a variety of briars. All too soon the summer ended and for the first time all four boys would attend the same school. Titusville High overlooked the Indian River, with an unobstructed view across it to the developing space center. On days when the humidity was low, and therefore crystal clear, Jessie found himself late to class, stopping to pick out what progress had been made on the new launch sites, and the Vertical Assembly Building.

"Hey, space boy, you think you got the nerve to ride one of those rockets?"

Jessie turned away from the river to find Alan Welty and two other boys glaring at him. The Cole boys had quickly learned that Alan considered himself king of the school and would happily beat up anyone who thought otherwise. JT Crawford and Dave Wheeler followed Alan everywhere, like little trolls. JT and Dave stood behind Alan now, cracking their knuckles, in what Jessie knew was supposed to be a menacing fashion.

"I got what it takes." Jessie puffed his chest out and stood taller, defying Alan to question him again. The summer spent climbing trees and building a fort had toughened up his lean frame and his biceps now gave a hint to his new strength.

Alan's eyes narrowed. "You think so? I think you're gonna run home crying to mommy in a few minutes."

JT and Dave moved to surround him, but Jessie stood his ground. His right hand gripped his math textbook, while his left remained in his pocket. Alan locked eyes with him and Jessie made sure not to blink. All of the other students were inside their classrooms by now. The air was silent and thick with humidity.

Jessie heard JT move behind him and ducked to miss the blow. Dave struck next, his leg swinging out to knock Jessie off his feet, but Jessie had already rolled beyond the bullies' circle.

Jumping to his feet, Jessie was ready when Alan charged him. As Alan's fist came flying at his face, Jessie lifted his math book, to block the blow, and then used it to smack Alan on the side of the head. The blow left him dazed. JT and Dave watched their leader stumble, but then returned their attention to Jessie.

Dave grabbed one of Jessie's arms and pinned it behind his back. JT's lips curled in a cruel smile as he raised his fist and swung it into Jessie's right eye. Jessie felt stabbing pain as the fist connected, but ignored it, reaching up with his free hand to grab and twist JT's wrist. JT spun around, his whole body trying to move in the same direction as the wrist. Jessie didn't let go until he felt the bone pop and JT howled in pain.

Dave released Jessie's arm and took a step back, holding his hands up in surrender. Jessie feinted to the left and Dave jumped, the sound of Jessie's laughter filling his ears.

An arm wrapped around Jessie's neck, choking him. It tightened, pulling his head back. He saw Dave rushing toward him, then felt the blows pummeling his stomach. Instinctively, his body tried to double over, but Alan's arm around his neck tightened in anticipation and kept him upright.

Through the rain of blows, Jessie heard the sound of racing footsteps. "Break it up," a deep voice demanded.

With a vicious push, Jessie was dropped to the ground and watched the feet of his attackers run off in the opposite direction. Splayed on the concrete, Jessie coughed and sputtered. He didn't move when he saw the polished black wingtips stop in front of him. He felt like he was going to puke.

"Stand up, young man."

Jessie struggled to his feet and looked into the face of Mr. Smith, his math teacher. Jessie gave a bemused glance down at the textbook on the ground and tried to laugh, but it came out as a cough instead. He felt Mr. Smith's eyes studying him.

"You're Jessie Cole, aren't you?"

"Yes, sir."

"You haven't been in this school a full semester yet and this is the fifth fight one of you boys has been in."

Jessie shrugged. "Guys aren't as friendly here as they are out on the island."

"Somehow I don't think that's the problem." Mr. Smith sighed. "How did this one start?"

Jessie shrugged. "That meathead Alan told me I didn't have the guts to be an astronaut."

Mr. Smith shook his head. "Guts or not, if you don't start studying your math you certainly won't become one."

Jessie started to argue then remembered the grade he'd received on his last test, a sixty-eight. Maybe Mr. Smith had a point. Jessie dropped his gaze to the ground and gave a disheartened nod. Mr. Smith waited another moment then gently touched Jessie's arm.

"Come on, we need to get to class." Mr. Smith turned and walked toward the low, white building with Jessie following.

Jessie felt all eyes on him as he entered the classroom and took his seat, but he didn't look up. He sank down in the hard wooden chair and opened his book to the chapter they'd had for homework the previous night. Mr. Smith went to the chalkboard and started the day's lesson.

Jessie listened to every word Mr. Smith said and jotted down notes on a piece of loose notebook paper. When the bell rang, Jessie slowly stuffed his notes into the spine of the book before closing it.

"Jessie, do you have a moment?" Mr. Smith asked when the classroom was empty.

"Sure."

"Do you really want to be an astronaut?"

"More than anything."

Mr. Smith rubbed his chin then his hand dropped to his side. "You'll have to bring your math grades up. If you're interested, I would be willing to do some after school tutoring."

A dozen thoughts rushed through Jessie's mind. What if the other kids found out? What about playing in the woods with his brothers? What if his mom found out he was failing math? What if he did fail math, would NASA still consider him?

"I guess. We could give it a shot." Jessie's words came slow as he continued to weigh out the consequences.

Mr. Smith shook his head, spearing him with an impatient look. "If you aren't going to take it seriously then I don't want to waste my time."

Jessie scratched his head and tried to look Mr. Smith in the eye, but the swelling in his own right eye made it difficult. "I do take it seriously."

"All right then. We can start tomorrow afternoon. Be here after your last class."

"Yes, sir." Jessie tucked his textbook under his arm and darted out of the room.

He drifted through the next three classes before lunch. When the bell rang, he made a beeline for the cafeteria, finding his brothers at their usual table. Max started clapping, and Jessie knew his brother had noticed the bruise forming around his right eye.

"Who was it today?" Max asked.

"Alan and his lackeys."

"You took on all three of them, alone?" Admiration shined in Ricky's eyes.

"Not intentionally." Jessie didn't feel like talking about the fight and shoved a piece of bread into his mouth.

"You look awful. What are you going to tell Mom?" Sam, always thinking ahead, dipped his napkin into a cup of water and handed it to Jessie. Jessie wiped his face with it, the cold water feeling good on his swollen cheek.

"I don't know." Jessie dropped the napkin on the table.

"If we go straight to the woods after school, you can tell her you fell or something," Ricky offered.

"I doubt she'll even notice," Jessie mumbled. "She works so many hours now that Pop isn't working."

"He's turned into a real bum since the move." Max's words were filled with a bitterness that Jessie understood all too well.

As the youngest and oldest, Jessie and Max seemed to bear the brunt of their father's drunken rages. Jessie didn't know where Pop got his alcohol from, now that he didn't have the still and he certainly didn't have any money, but he was drunker than ever.

"It'll be hard for her not to notice that shiner," Ricky insisted.

"Then I'll just have to avoid her for a few days. No big deal." Jessie stood and collected his garbage. "I don't feel like going to the rest of my classes. Who's up for a bit of cops and robbers?"

"Count me in." Max stood as well and crumbled his paper cup.

Jessie looked to Sam and Ricky, both of whom looked away.

"If I skip Ms. Peter's class one more time she is going to call Mama," Ricky replied.

Sam wiped his lips with the back of his hand, but remained silent.

"Yeah, I get it, professor," Jessie sneered then turned and marched out.

Getting off school property was easy, and in five minutes Jessie and Max had crossed the railroad tracks behind the school and were tramping through the woods.

"Someone really needs to teach Alan a lesson," Jessie grumbled.

"I don't get why the whole school is so afraid of him." Max tossed a stick through the trees.

"If we could just find a way to show everyone he's not as big and bad as he thinks he is." Jessie kicked a rock, but it didn't move. He paused and tried to pick it up, but it didn't budge. Jessie dropped to his knees and started digging.

"What is it?" Max watched without moving.

"I don't know. Help me dig it out."

Max squatted down and brushed at the dirt on his side of the stone. "Jessie, I don't think this is a rock."

Jessie scraped at the dirt some more and his fingers went through the object. Surprised, he pulled his hand back and looked at his brother. "What is it?"

Max moved around beside Jessie and brushed at the dirt where his brother had been digging. Gradually, the shape of the hole Jessie had pulled his fingers out of appeared. Max moved to the left and brushed the dirt some more until a similar opening became visible. The boys looked at each other then back at the object.

"I think it's a skull," Max whispered.

Jessie stared at the brown dome and empty eye sockets. His lips twitched upward as a plan formed in his mind. "I think I know how we can get back at Alan."

CHAPTER EIGHT

Plotting against Alan

November 18, 1964

"I wonder if there are any more bones," Jessie mused.

Max scanned the area and swept his hand around in the dirt. "It doesn't look like any of the other Indian burial grounds we've found."

Jessie scooped out several handfuls of dirt on either side of the skull, but didn't find anything more.

"What if it isn't an Indian?" Jessie asked.

Max shrugged. "How did it end up out here without any body?"

Jessie felt a mixture of excitement and fear ripple through him. "What if this guy was murdered and the killer chopped up the body, dropping parts all over town?"

"Who would do something like that?" Max scoffed as he stood and brushed dirt off his pants.

"It could happen."

"What are you going to do with the skull?"

"There has to be a way to use it against Alan. I bet he'd wet his pants if this turned up on his desk one morning."

"Nah, a thug like that isn't going to be scared of a hunk of bone."

"Yea? You got a better idea?"

A devious grin slid across Max's face. "I think we should find a way to set him up for the murder."

"Murder?"

"This guy couldn't have died of natural causes if the rest of his body isn't here."

"Animals could have dragged off the bones." Jessie's gaze swept around them. They were only a couple of miles from the high school but the woods here were thick and dark. After their recent encounter with a panther he didn't doubt there were predators that would love to feast on the bones of a dead man.

"You were the one suggesting he'd been murdered and chopped up," Max grumbled.

Jessie nodded reluctantly. "But setting Alan up for murder? Isn't that going a bit far?"

"Look at this thing," Max pointed at the skull in Jessie's hands. "I bet it's at least twenty years old. The cops will figure that out and Alan will be off the hook, but in the meantime he will be scared to death being investigated."

"How do we set him up? We can't just tell the police we found the skull out here."

"Of course not." Max rolled his eyes at his younger brother. "Come on, let's go to the fort and I'll tell you what I'm thinking."

The boys plunged through the dense underbrush, along trails meant for much smaller animals, until they reached the fort the brothers were still in the process of completing.

They'd found an area a mile from their house, where the trees didn't grow so close together yet still created a thick canopy overhead, keeping out the scorching sun. By gathering palm fronds and weaving them together, the boys had built three walls, five feet high. The fourth was under construction, and they expected it to be finished by the next weekend.

Within the walls of their fort, they planned to build several huts that they could use when it was raining or for storing the treasures they found during their adventures. Jessie wished those huts were done now so he could safely store the skull. Instead, he lifted an old palm frond that covered a shallow hole. He settled the skull in with a pile of broken arrowheads, Coca-Cola bottles, a couple of flashlights, and an old snakeskin, then returned the palm frond.

Max was already dragging several fronds to the end of the uncompleted wall and Jessie ran to join him.

"So what's your plan?" Jessie grabbed one of the fronds and striped a couple of strands to tie the branch in place on the wall.

"Pete Murphy's old man works for the police. Tomorrow, at school, we make sure Pete overhears us talking about Alan and how he was bragging about beating up some bum in the woods. Everyone at school knows Alan tries to take a souvenir from the kids he beats up, so we will play at guessing what kind of souvenir he could take from a bum."

"I don't know, Max. None of this sounds like anything the police would be interested in."

"That's because this is all just baiting the trap."

"What trap?" Sam asked, as he emerged from the undergrowth only a few feet from Max and Jessie.

"What are you doing here?" Max demanded. "You still have another class, professor."

"Substitute teacher today. So, what trap are you talking about?"

"It's nothin'," Max shrugged. "Just figurin' if we could trap that panther."

"Are you crazy?" Sam's eyes grew wide. "It won't bother us if we don't bother it, but if you try to trap it you might as well say goodbye now."

"You're such a chicken," Max taunted. "If we did it right, I bet we could kill it. It'd be nice to have a panther skin rug in the main hut when it gets done."

Sam shook his head. "I won't have any part of that." He turned to look at Jessie. "You better think twice about getting involved in such a crazy scheme. It'd kill Mama to lose two of her boys."

Jessie didn't reply, in awe of his older brother's ability to spin the lie so effortlessly. It was almost like Max had actually thought about trapping the panther. The idea jarred him and he stopped twisting the palm frond in his hand. He studied Max, who hadn't stopped working through the whole conversation and now had four more fronds added to his section of wall.

"What in the heck is this?" Sam yelled, causing Max and Jessie to turn to the interior of the fort. Sam was holding the skull in one hand.

"Found it on the way home," Jessie said. "Pretty cool, huh?"

"You don't pass any Indian burial mounds on the way here, and even if you did you shouldn't have taken this."

"Why not? It's not like he needs it anymore." Max laughed at his own joke but the others didn't.

Jessie hadn't thought about his other brothers finding the skull when they went to add their new treasure to the hollow. He hadn't thought he needed to hide it until Max lied about what they were planning. Why shouldn't Sam and Ricky be involved in the plan to get back at Alan? They'd all been in fights with him at least once since starting school.

"You need to take this back where you found it." Sam held the skull out and Jessie crossed the fort to collect it.

When Jessie took it, he glanced into the hole and saw the addition Sam had brought, a tattered army rucksack.

"Where'd you find that?" Jessie pointed at the bag.

"Out by Bum's Cave. I saw it a few days ago, but thought it may belong to one of the guys squatting there. They've been gone a couple days now, but it was still there. Not much inside, but it might come in handy carrying stuff out here once we get the place secured."

Jessie glanced at Max and saw a gleam in his eyes that he knew meant Max was planning something. He wondered if this bag might play into their plan for Alan.

"I'll take the skull back this weekend," Jessie offered. "Why don't you help us work on the wall? Maybe we can finish up by tonight."

Reluctantly, Jessie settled the skull back in the hole, before grabbing more fronds and returning to the wall.

For two hours the boys worked, weaving the fronds together and telling jokes they'd all heard a hundred times before. By the time Ricky showed up after school, the wall had extended another several feet in each direction.

"At least you made good use of your time playing hooky," Ricky congratulated them after inspecting their work. "Has anyone figured out what we are going to use for a door?"

"Still working on it," Sam replied.

"You better work faster. We're going to need it before too long."

"Did you see Alan any this afternoon?" Jessie asked.

Ricky nodded. "He didn't look too happy to see me so I kept my distance. I heard JT went to the hospital with a broken arm."

Jessie preened with pride at the admiring look he got from Max.

"You broke his arm," Max repeated.

Jessie shrugged like it was no big deal. "He wasn't as flexible as he thought he was."

"You could get suspended," Sam chastised.

"It was self-defense. Principal Gilroy can't fault me for that." Jessie's bravado faded a bit at the thought of being suspended, though. Would Mr. Smith still help him with his math? Would NASA hold a suspension against him?

"Self-defense or not, you know the Crawfords are going to demand the school do something."

"Stop being such a kill-joy, Sam. Our baby brother kicked butt." The pride in Max's words bolstered Jessie.

Sam looked from Max to Jessie and back. "You two are going to be the death of me."

"You sound like Mama." Jessie grinned and tossed a palm frond at his brother. "Tie this up for me."

All four boys worked until the sun dipped down so low they could barely see. Sam retrieved the flashlights from their treasure trove and led the way home.

The kitchen light was on when they arrived and a note was propped on the table against a plate of sandwiches covered with a dishtowel.

Sorry I couldn't be home for dinner, boys. I have to check on old lady Granger. Be sure to do your homework and get showers. I should be home before you go to bed.

Love,
Mom

"You certainly lucked out tonight, Jessie." Ricky smiled at his brother and the purple blossom around his eye.

Jessie had forgotten about the bruise, but at this reminder he opened the freezer, pulled out a bag of peas and held it over the swollen area.

"Lotta good that's going to do now," Sam said.

Jessie shrugged, grabbed a sandwich and took a bite as he headed to his bedroom. He kicked off his shoes and laid back on the bed, one hand holding the bag of peas, the other feeding the sandwich into his mouth. His stomach growled as the sandwich hit it and he debated getting up to get another.

He chewed slowly, thinking about the plan to get Alan, and wondered what Max had in mind. What he'd heard so far didn't inspire him with much confidence that Alan would get the message not to mess with the Cole boys.

"Brought you another sandwich." Ricky entered the room extending the sandwich to his brother.

"Thanks. I was too tired to get up." Jessie bit into the bread and mustard squirted out onto his chin. Ricky laughed and plopped onto his own bed.

"You got any homework tonight?" Ricky asked.

"Some math, but I don't feel like doing it."

"Want me to take a look at it?"

Jessie started to nod, but stopped. The memory of Mr. Smith's penetrating eyes when he'd asked if Jessie was serious about doing better made him sit up and toss the bag of peas aside.

"Maybe you can just help me out." Jessie reached for the math book.

Ricky turned on a lamp between the two beds and sat down next to his brother. Jessie felt Ricky looking over his shoulder as he flipped to the right page.

"I don't need you right on top of me." Jessie leaned back, pushing Ricky aside.

"I was just trying to see what you're working on," Ricky defended, but scooted to the end of the bed.

"It's these blasted equations. What do I need them for anyway?"

"They're not so bad. Let me show you a trick Sam taught me." Ricky took the book and started writing. Jessie watched his brother whip through several problems, taking note of everything he did.

"Now you give it a shot." Ricky slid the book toward him, so he reluctantly picked up his pencil and tackled the next equation.

Following the steps he'd watched Ricky go through, Jessie finished the problem and looked to his brother for approval. Ricky nodded. The two boys worked together for another twenty minutes until the worksheet was completed.

"Whew, glad that's done." Jessie closed the book with a loud thud.

"You think you can do it on your own now?" Ricky asked.

Jessie nodded. "I think so."

"Boys, I'm home," Eleanor called from the front door.

Jessie glanced at the bag of melted peas on the floor then looked at Ricky. In a flash, he pulled off his t-shirt and dove under the bedcovers. "Tell her I wasn't feeling well so I went to bed early."

"She'll just come in and check on you."

"Not if you guys keep her busy. Go on. Get out there and tell her about your day." Jessie waited until his brother turned off the light and closed the door before rolling to face the wall and closing his eyes.

CHAPTER NINE

Tutoring Session

November 19, 1964

A deep rumble shook Jessie's entire body. He rolled his head from side to side and caught a glimpse of the man beside him. A large helmet covered his head, but his face was visible through the glass visor.

"What's going on, Mr. Grissom?" Jessie asked.

Gus smiled, the corners of his eyes crinkling into fine lines. "The first time is always the scariest."

Slowly it sank in that Jessie and Grissom were in a rocket. "I'm not scared." Jessie tried to puff out his chest but felt the bite of the harness around him.

Grissom laughed. "You should be. We never know if they have put these things together right or not."

Jessie felt his throat tighten and hoped his face hadn't drained of color the way he imagined it had. "What do you mean? NASA's been doing launches for years now."

"Sure, kid, but there's always the chance of mistakes." Grissom shrugged. "But that's part of the excitement."

Jessie felt a weight on his chest as his entire body sank farther into the seat. He looked out the window and watched the crystal-clear blue sky race past. In a matter of minutes the blue turned to deep black and the weight lifted from his chest. He heard Grissom undo his own safety belt and reached to do the same.

"Beautiful sight isn't it?" Grissom pointed out the window.

Jessie floated closer to the glass and his breath caught. Below them was a blue and green ball with splashes of white.

"Is that..."

"Earth," Grissom finished with a nod.

Jessie rolled over, surprised to see the familiar surroundings of his bedroom. He rubbed his eyes and looked around again. Still his bedroom. Ricky snored in the bed across the room.

Swinging his feet onto the floor, Jessie pulled a fresh shirt from his crate and slipped it over his head. Early morning birdsong drifted in through the thin window, along with the scent of pine. He shoved his feet into his sneakers, grabbed his books, and crept out of the house.

On the front porch he stopped to look up and down the dirt road. The sky was tinged grey as night slowly receded into day. Jessie jumped off the porch and ran to the end of the road, then turned left toward the river. He slowed to a brisk walk and allowed himself to drift off back into the dream world he'd so recently awakened from. He could almost hear Grissom's words again.

"There's always a chance of mistakes," Jessie whispered.

When he reached the river, Jessie sat on the grass at the edge of the water and watched the sun rise. It was a clear morning, allowing him to see across the river to

Cape Canaveral. The towering structure of the launch pad was a dark silhouette against the orange ball of fire floating ever higher into the sky.

"No mistakes if I can help it," Jessie declared. He stood with a new determination and walked the remaining mile to school.

"Where were you?" Ricky asked when he found Jessie in front of the school.

"I didn't want to see mom before school." Jessie scanned the faces around them on the alert for Alan and his trolls.

"You didn't need to worry. She left before Max and Sam were even up. She works too much."

"Someone's gotta do it and Pop sure isn't." Jessie felt the familiar heat of bitterness warm his blood.

"Maybe I'll see if I can get a job after school, to help out. Oh, I almost forgot," Ricky held out a paper sack, which Jessie took without opening.

"If anyone should get a job it's Max. He's the oldest and should be the man of the house."

"Yeah, but do you think he could keep a job with his temper?" Ricky gave his brother a questioning look.

Jessie sighed. "You're probably right, and we can't expect the professor to take time away from studying his books. Looks like it's up to me and you."

"We can ask around this afternoon, see if anyone's hiring."

Jessie shook his head. "I can't today."

"Why not?"

"I have something I gotta do."

"What?"

"None of your business," Jessie snapped.

"Geez, you don't have to yell at me. I'll see if I can find something for both of us."

The bell rang and students started filing into the classrooms. Jessie and Ricky followed.

"See you at lunch," Jessie called as Ricky disappeared through a doorway.

"I don't think you will." An ominous voice called from behind Jessie. He felt his spine stiffen and prepared for the blow he knew was coming, but didn't turn around to face the oaf.

"There you are, Mr. Cole. I was hoping to catch you before class." Mr. Smith stepped out of a nearby classroom and beckoned to Jessie. Jessie crossed the distance between them in a few long but unhurried strides, and followed Mr. Smith through the doorway.

"Thanks," Jessie mumbled before slinking to a desk at the back of the room.

Mr. Smith stood at the front of the classroom, his gaze roving over the students for a long minute before picking up a piece of chalk and writing a long equation on the board.

"Who can tell me the solution to this problem?"

Several hands shot up right away. Jessie noticed the cute redhead in the front row had hers up first. She always seemed to know the answer. Mr. Smith waited, making Jessie feel like he should raise his hand as well, but he hadn't figured it out yet. He looked down at his paper and copied the problem to it, trying to remember all Ricky had shown him the night before. When he looked up again, his eyes locked with Mr. Smith's. Jessie gave a minute nod.

"Mr. Cole, did I see your hand?"

Several heads turned to look his way and Jessie saw the surprise on their faces. He cleared his throat and checked his work one more time.

"Five and five-eighths," Jessie managed to say around the lump in his throat.

"Very good." Mr. Smith nodded and turned to write another problem on the board.

Jessie exhaled and stretched his legs out in front of him. When he looked back at the chalkboard, he noticed the redhead looking his way, but she quickly turned away when their eyes met.

Mr. Smith went through a dozen more problems, calling on different students each time. Jessie concentrated on each answer, checking his own work for accuracy and was excited to find he was right every time.

"Tonight I want you to go through the examples on page fifty, and review all of the first five chapters. We will have a test on Friday." Mr. Smith wrapped up the lesson just seconds before the bell rang.

Jessie gathered his books and waited for the others to leave before stepping to the front of the class. "Do you want me to meet you in here after school?"

"You still want me to tutor you?" Mr. Smith seemed surprised.

"Yes, sir."

"Come by after school and we'll see what you need to work on." Mr. Smith turned and started erasing what was on the board.

Jessie stumbled out of the classroom and nearly fell into the arms of Alan.

"Well lookie here. If it isn't baby Cole." Alan locked his arm around Jessie's neck and pulled him away from the classroom.

"Leave me alone." Jessie struggled to free himself.

"What are you going to do? You think you can break my arm too? You know JT's had to be set in two places? You did a number on him." Alan squeezed harder as he spoke, cutting off Jessie's oxygen.

Jessie stopped struggling and allowed his body to go limp. With all of his weight now being supported by one of Alan's arms, the bully was thrown off balance. As he stumbled, he loosened his grip on Jessie, who took the opportunity to wiggle free.

A group of kids had gathered around them and started chanting. "Fight! Fight! Fight!"

Jessie looked at Alan, who had regained his balance and now glared at Jessie. With a shake of his head, Jessie pushed his way through the crowd, leaving Alan to stew on this new humiliation.

"Why didn't you hit him?"

Jessie turned to find the redhead following him. He stopped to allow her to catch up. "What good would it do? He's just gonna pick another fight tomorrow."

"But I heard you broke his friend's arm yesterday." She kept her gaze downcast, her arms wrapped tightly around a notebook pressed to her chest.

"That was self-defense. Three of them jumped me then."

"Looked like Alan jumped you today," she challenged.

Jessie shrugged. "One guy is easier to walk away from than three. Anyway, it's hard enough hiding one shiner from Mama. Two I think I'd have to explain."

The redhead giggled, a tinkling sound that reminded Jessie of the bell above the convenience store door.

"And I try to keep my arm breaking to one a week," he continued, hoping to make her laugh again.

She giggled and looked up. Jessie was sure his heart stopped when he gazed into the deep blue pools of her eyes, but then she blinked and dropped her gaze back to the ground.

"I'm Jessie, by the way." He wanted to shake her hand, but was suddenly conscious of the dirt and grease underneath his nails and so shoved his hands into his pockets.

"I know." She glanced over her shoulder. "I better get to class."

Before Jessie could speak, she sauntered off. Jessie watched her round a corner of the math building then ran to his English class, sliding through the door a split second before the bell rang.

The afternoon dragged and Jessie found himself more distracted than usual, mulling over the encounter with the redhead. Had she been impressed that he'd walked away from the fight or disappointed? His experience with girls was limited to what little bits Max shared about his dates with a couple of girls back on the island. Jessie wasn't sure he would call hanging out in the island tree house sipping cokes a date, but Max claimed to have gotten to second base, whatever that was. The tree house had been big, but not big enough to play baseball.

"Mr. Cole?"

Jessie felt a spit ball hit him in the neck and he looked up from his desk to find the students around him laughing and old lady Matthews glaring at him.

"What was the question?" Jessie stammered.

"I asked you if you could tell me where *The Old Man and the Sea* takes place."

Jessie scratched his head and tried to come up with a funny remark that would get him out of this jam. He hadn't read a single word of the story.

"Have you even opened the book, Mr. Cole?"

"Sure, sure." Jessie nodded. "I actually left it sitting next to the john last night. Good stuff."

Several kids laughed, causing Mrs. Matthews to turn her attention away from Jessie as she gave them a warning look.

"I'm so happy you are enjoying it. Then I'm sure you won't mind writing me a report on the first five chapters tonight. I expect it to be on my desk by the beginning of class tomorrow."

Jessie felt like he'd been punched in the gut. "Yes ma'am," he muttered and dipped his head.

Mrs. Matthews walked back to the front of the classroom and continued her lecture. When the bell rang, Jessie gathered up his books and made for the door.

"A minute, Mr. Cole." Mrs. Matthews held up one hand to stop him.

Jessie shuffled to a stop, a sense of déjà vu washing over him. Why did all of his teachers seem to want a minute with him all of sudden. At his old school he wasn't even sure his teachers had known his name.

"Mr. Cole, I know you may not find Hemingway very interesting now, but I assure you, one day in the future you will be glad I made you read it." Mrs. Matthews looked down her beak-like nose, her grey eyes boring into him.

"I'm sorry, Mrs. Matthews. I wasn't feeling well last night and I didn't get all my homework done."

Jessie thought he saw her eyes soften a bit. "Next time you aren't feeling well you might have your mother write a note."

"Yes ma'am." Jessie shifted the load of books under his arm.

"I look forward to your report tomorrow." Mrs. Matthews turned and crossed the room back to her desk. Jessie didn't wait for her to look back at him again. He darted out the door and found his brothers loitering in the courtyard by the library, tossing breadcrumbs to the sea gulls.

"Where ya been?" Max grumbled.

"Mrs. Matthews kept me after class."

"Well, let's get goin'. We should be able to finish the walls of the fort this afternoon." Max turned to leave.

"I'll catch up with you later. I have to go see Mr. Smith. I forgot to tell you at lunch."

Max spun around and faced his brother, studying him with hard eyes. Jessie didn't break eye contact. After a long minute, Max shrugged and stalked off. Ricky and Sam hesitated, then followed Max.

Two minutes later Jessie entered Mr. Smith's classroom and found the young teacher seated at his desk, grading papers.

"I wasn't sure you were going to show up." Mr. Smith put down his pen and focused on Jessie.

"Sorry, sir. I had to let my brothers know I'd be home late." Jessie rocked back and forth on the balls of his feet, unsure if he should take a seat at one of the desks or wait for Mr. Smith to offer the chair next to him. When Mr. Smith nodded toward a desk, Jessie dropped into the seat and opened his textbook.

"Where do you want to start?"

Jessie looked up from the book to find Mr. Smith leaning forward in his chair, elbows on the table and fingers laced together in front of his chin.

"I dunno. I kind of thought you would tell me." Jessie felt sweat building in his armpits.

"What do you have the most trouble with?"

Jessie could see Mr. Smith wasn't going to make this easy. He flipped through the book, realizing it all seemed like a foreign language to him.

"Which parts will I need to know to be an astronaut?"

Mr. Smith chuckled. "You'll need all of it and then some."

Jessie narrowed his eyes. "They got computers that do most of the work. I've seen it on TV."

"Yes, there are a number of computers that operate the space capsules, but what happens if those computers fail? What do you do then, when you need to figure out how long the oxygen you have onboard will last?"

Jessie shook his head. "That isn't gonna happen. The guys who built those computers are geniuses or somethin'."

"They are pretty smart, but that doesn't mean things can't go wrong. We're going places we never dreamed of twenty years ago and there is a lot of trial and error at the start of any new endeavor."

"I guess we oughta start at the beginning then." Jessie let out a deep sigh and opened the textbook to page one.

Mr. Smith pushed his chair back, the wooden legs screeching against the concrete floor. "Let's get started then."

CHAPTER TEN

The Cupboard is Bare

November 19, 1964

Jessie squinted as he walked west, following the path of the sinking sun. The tutoring session had run longer than he'd expected, but he wasn't in a hurry to meet his brothers. He knew they would ask where he'd been and he wasn't ready to tell them about the study sessions he'd committed to.

Instead of going to the fort, he went straight home. Approaching the house he slowed upon noticing the freshly mowed yard. When he'd left for school that morning, he'd noted how shabby the place looked compared to the neighbor's, but now it was neatly trimmed and some new flowers waved in the breeze.

Jessie pushed through the front door, took a cautious step inside and stopped to listen for any signs that his parents were home. He heard a loud snore from the living room. He set his books on the kitchen table without a sound, and crept across the small room to find his father stretched out on the sofa. A beer can had dropped from his dangling hand and spilled the last couple of ounces on the cool linoleum floor.

Jessie stood over his father, studying the man's rumpled clothes and matted hair. The paunch of his belly stretched the buttons on his shirt to near bursting. Blades of grass still clung to his pant legs and sweat stains ringed his armpits, the first signs of work Jessie had seen on his father since they'd left the island. With a shake of his head, Jessie kneeled down to collect the can and used the edge of his t-shirt to wipe up the stinking liquid.

Back in the kitchen, he dropped the can in the garbage before opening the freezer to look for a frozen dinner. Swinging the door open, he found a half empty box of ice cream sandwiches and two potpies nestled in three inches of frost.

Stunned, Jessie closed the door and opened the refrigerator. A bottle of milk, a carton of orange juice, three eggs, and a sparse collection of condiments greeted him. What in the world were they going to have for dinner? Jessie glanced at the clock, almost five-thirty. His brothers would be home soon. He scanned the counter looking for a note from his mother, but there was none. His stomach growled and twisted.

The front door opened and Max came tromping in with Ricky and Sam in tow. Their raucous laughter overlapped the animal-like snores of their father.

"What's so funny" Jessie turned away from the refrigerator.

Max stopped abruptly, causing Ricky to run into him. Max pushed back with a grunt.

"Ricky here thought he could catch a squirrel with his bare hands." Max chortled. "He fell on his face right in a pile of old panther crap."

Jessie could see the humiliation on his brother's face and tried not to laugh.

"The squirrel ran up a tree then turned around, and I swear it stopped to laugh at him," Sam added in between his own fits of laughter.

This image pushed Jessie over the edge and the guffaw he'd been holding in rolled out, doubling him over.

"Hey, did you mow the grass? That why you couldn't come to the fort?" Ricky stepped forward to change the subject.

Jessie shook his head. "Looks like Pop may have before he drunk himself to sleep."

"What did mom leave for dinner?" Max pushed around Jessie to the fridge.

"Nothin' that I can find." Jessie stepped to the oven and pulled open the door with a loud creak, but it was empty as well.

"What's all the racket?" Eugene's groggy voice preceded the sound of him struggling to get up from the couch.

The boys turned toward the living room to see their father stumbling around the small coffee table. Jessie felt the familiar mixture of fear and loathing that made him both want to run and beat the old man. His hands balled into fists and his body went rigid.

Eugene stepped into the kitchen, still rubbing his eyes with the palm of his right hand. "Where's your mother?"

Jessie shrugged but didn't speak, and neither did his brothers.

"I'm starving. Why don't one of you kids make yourself useful and find me something to eat?" Eugene plopped down at the table.

"It'll be close to an hour." Jessie reached into the freezer, removing the potpies. He read the directions and turned the oven on to heat.

"An hour?" Eugene roared. "Forget it. I'll go to Harold's." He pushed the chair back so fiercely it toppled when he stood. Without stopping to pick it up, Eugene stormed out. A minute later the boys heard the truck engine roar to life.

"This is all we got." Jessie held up the two boxes.

"I have some money saved. I'll walk down to Pantry Pride and pick up a couple more. I should be back before the oven is ready." Sam disappeared down the hall to his bedroom.

"It's not like Mama to miss dinner and not let us know." Ricky picked up the overturned chair and sat down in it.

"This is crazy." Max's eyes were flashing with anger and Jessie feared what his brother might do.

"She'll probably be home any minute." Jessie pulled a cookie sheet from the cabinet and set the aluminum potpie containers on it.

"It's time for Pop to get over the eviction and get a job. He's drinking us right out of this place and I'm sick of it." Max strode across the kitchen to the door.

"Don't go, Max," Ricky pleaded.

Max slammed the door behind him, leaving Jessie and Ricky staring after him.

"He's going to make trouble."

Jessie sank into one of the chairs across from Ricky. "It's been a long time coming."

"But what if Daddy kills him?"

"You don't think Max can take care of himself? Pop can barely stand up. More likely Max will kill him."

"He wasn't always so bad." Ricky looked at Jessie with such pleading in his eyes. Times like these made Jessie feel like he was the older brother instead of the other way around.

Ricky was sensitive and compassionate, much more so than Jessie or Max. Jessie knew Ricky tried to see the good in people no matter how bad they were. He'd even tried to find good in Alan and his trolls until they'd beaten him up several times.

"I don't remember a time when he wasn't a drunk." Jessie could hear the bitterness in his own voice and regretted it when he saw Ricky flinch.

"Don't you remember how he used to take us camping when we were little?" Ricky traced the paisley pattern of the faded vinyl tablecloth.

Jessie searched his memories then shook his head. "My first real memory of Pop is of him whooping me and Max for playing in the woodshed. I think I was four or five. I didn't understand for several more years that he'd been hiding his still in the shed, and had to move it after that."

Jessie watched Ricky's eyes grow large in alarm at this story. "That's your first memory?"

"Yep."

The door opened and Sam entered, out of breath, carrying a paper sack. Jessie stood, took the bag, added the new potpies to the cookie sheet, and slipped it into the oven. "Thirty minutes, boys."

"Where's Max?" Sam pulled plates from a cabinet and set them on the table.

"He went to confront Daddy," Ricky whispered.

Sam stopped, his hand hovering over the silverware drawer. "He did what?"

"You can't tell me you haven't been expecting this moment." Jessie reached around his brother and pulled forks from the drawer. "I'm surprised it took this long. Pop's saving grace has probably been our work on the fort keeping us out of the house so much."

"But, what if he's arrested? Why didn't you stop him?"

Jessie locked eyes with Sam. "Because I wish I had the nerve to go with him. Pop deserves what he has coming to him."

"You don't mean that. It's been tough for him to adjust to the move, to being told he doesn't own his land. He just needs more time."

Jessie smirked. "He didn't become a drunk after we moved. He's been making his own booze since before I was born. Maybe he sold most of it at one point, but he started drinking more when we still lived out there. What was his excuse then?"

"I'm sorry I'm late, boys. Mmm, something smells good." Eleanor bustled through the door with a paper bag in the crook of each arm.

"Mom, you have to stop Max. He's gone to Harold's to confront Dad." Sam's words came out in a panicked rush.

"Slow down." Eleanor sat her bags on the counter. "What are you talking about?"

"Pop got mad that dinner wasn't ready when he woke up from being passed out. He knocked over a chair and stormed out to the bar. Max went after him." Jessie's dispassionate synopsis was finished before his mother could pull a single item from the grocery bags.

"But why did Max go after him?"

"Come on, Mama. Wake up. Pop is a loser, and he's dragging this family down. There was no food in the fridge and only two potpies in the freezer. Sam had to go buy more so we could eat. You're working three jobs and still barely keeping the bills paid. What does Pop contribute? Ricky and I were talking this morning about finding jobs to help out. We can't continue this way." Jessie was shocked by his own impassioned speech. Avoiding any discussion of family affairs was his way of coping with Pop's failures.

Eleanor leaned against the counter, her shoulders sagging. Jessie noticed the tears pooling in her blue eyes and he felt a moment of shame for putting them there, but quickly shook it off. It was their father's doing not his.

Sam moved to his mother's side and wrapped an arm around her. "It's going to be okay."

Eleanor shook her head. "No, it's not going to be okay unless things change." Eleanor gave Sam's arm a gentle squeeze then quickly unloaded the two bags of groceries. When everything was put away she turned a determined face to Ricky, Sam, and Jessie. "You boys stay here. I'll be back soon."

When the oven timer went off, Max and his parents still weren't back. Jessie pulled the potpies from the oven and emptied three of them onto plates.

"Shouldn't we wait for them to get home?" Ricky asked.

"You can if you want, but I'm hungry now." Jessie used his fork to pierce the piecrust, causing steam to billow forth as he spread the meat, gravy, and vegetables around.

"Aren't you worried about what's happening?" Ricky pushed his plate away and crossed his arms.

"What's worrying going to accomplish?" Jessie swallowed several bites in silence.

"Jessie's right. We should eat and start on homework. I have a science project due next week." Sam rotated his plate twice before picking up his fork. With a loud sigh, Ricky pulled his own plate toward himself and started picking out all of the carrots, setting them aside on his napkin.

When Jessie finished eating, he took the plate to the sink and rinsed it off. "I have a book report to write." He grabbed his schoolbooks and retired to his room.

With the door closed, the conversation between Sam and Ricky was muffled, but Jessie knew they must be marveling at his announcement of writing a report without complaint. He wasn't looking forward to reading *The Old Man and the Sea*, but after his session with Mr. Smith, he was starting to understand why getting good grades in everything might be important in getting him into the astronaut program. He kicked off his shoes, picked up the thin paperback lying on the floor, and stretched out on the bed to read.

Fifteen pages in, Jessie was surprised to find he was actually enjoying the book. Sure it was a little slow, but he could relate to a man who fished for a living.

"Jessie, come quick," Ricky poked his head in the door and called out in a loud whisper.

Jessie looked up, startled by the interruption. "What is it?"

"They're back."

"So? I have work to do." Jessie waved his brother off and returned to reading.

Ricky entered the bedroom and pulled on Jessie's arm. "Come on."

Reluctantly, Jessie folded down the corner of the page, closed the book, and followed Ricky into the living room.

Eugene and Max were seated on opposite ends of the couch with Eleanor standing before them, her face an angry mask like nothing Jessie had ever seen before.

Eleanor looked up and waved for Jessie and Ricky to join Sam, standing at the end of the room, which they did.

"I want you all to hear this."

Jessie glanced at Max and Eugene. Both had several cuts and bruises on their faces and Max's right hand was wrapped in a bandage. It was hard to tell who'd gotten the worse end of the fight.

"I will not have any of you boys disrespecting your father." Eleanor's gaze swept over each of them. Jessie felt that she lingered longer on him than Sam or Ricky.

"What is there to respect?" Max snorted.

"He is your father." Eleanor raised a finger to stop Max's next outburst. "He's made mistakes and he will have to account for them one day, but you are not his judge."

"Mistakes?" The understatement stunned Jessie. "He's no better than the bums that pass through on the trains."

"Jessie." Eleanor's hard tone stopped him. "There are going to be changes in this family, starting tonight."

"You're a fool to think Pop is going to change." Max spat blood onto his bandaged hand.

Eleanor took several deep breaths. "Your father will start working again tomorrow. I made arrangements with Mr. Grant to take him on at the gas station."

Max chuckled. "Good luck getting him to show up."

Eleanor glared at her eldest son. "Things are going to change for you boys as well, Max. You are going to find a job after school. The fact that your baby brother was planning on doing it and you weren't shows me how selfish you have become. You graduate soon and will be on your own, it's time for you to get a taste of what that's like."

"But I have things to do, I don't have time for a job," Max whined.

"I don't want to hear it. I expect you to go out tomorrow afternoon and start looking for work. I'm sure you should be able to find a position as a bag boy or something similar by the end of the week."

"No more staying out past dark. You will all be here for dinner at five-thirty every night. There will be no more fighting at school and I expect to see nothing lower than a C on any of your report cards."

This last, Jessie knew, was directed at him. Any other day it would have made him angry, but after his experiences today, he knew he deserved the reprimand. Boy, would she be surprised if she knew he was already working to correct this issue.

"Nora, I'm sorry." Eugene at last looked up at his wife, but with a look Jessie had seen too many times before to believe it to be sincere.

"You're always sorry, Gene." Eleanor softened a bit. "Sorry isn't good enough anymore. You have to change. You have to be the man I fell in love with."

Jessie studied the wordless communication between his parents, as they gazed at each other for a long moment, before Eugene dropped his head to his chest. Jessie had never before thought of them as being in love. What had his father been like then? What had made Eleanor fall in love with him?

"Now, Max and Eugene, go get cleaned up. I will make us some sandwiches. The rest of you boys finish up your homework." Eleanor waited for Max and Eugene to shuffle out of the room.

Jessie turned to his brothers. "How long you think he'll last at that job?"

"It's not like he hasn't worked before. On the island he always had a job," Sam reminded them.

Ricky nodded. "Maybe having something to do all day will keep him from drinking so much."

Jessie shook his head. "You two are hopeless. Maybe we should call you Sally and Roberta."

Sam stuck his tongue out at Jessie. "I have work to do."

"Yeah, me too." Jessie left his brothers and returned to his bedroom. He was so engrossed in his reading he didn't hear Ricky when he entered a couple of minutes later.

"Jessie?"

"Leave me alone."

"But —"

Jessie lowered his book and snarled at his brother. "Leave me alone."

Ricky dropped onto his own bed and quietly pulled a book out of the pile on the floor.

CHAPTER ELEVEN

Ice Cream

December 4, 1964

T wo weeks had passed since the brawl between Eugene and Max and things had certainly changed. Eugene had started work at the gas station. Max and Ricky picked up jobs as bag boys at the Pantry Pride grocery store, a few blocks from the house, and Sam had two students he tutored in math and science nearly every afternoon. Jessie was relieved his mother hadn't insisted he get a job as well. He'd enjoyed her look of surprise when he told her he'd started after-school sessions with Mr. Smith.

Jessie nibbled on the end of his pencil as he reread the equation Mr. Smith had written on the board. It was slow going, but he was starting to understand some of the more basic principles of algebra. He scribbled out an answer and handed it to his teacher.

"Good." Mr. Smith smiled and returned the paper. "I've also noticed that you haven't been in any more fights lately."

"Yeah, Alan seems to have forgotten about us for the time being." Jessie folded the paper and shoved it in his textbook.

"I'm glad to hear that." Mr. Smith started erasing the blackboard. "Have you considered joining the ROTC program?"

"What's that?"

"It's the Reserve Officer Training Corps here on campus, sponsored by the Navy. It gives students the opportunity to learn how to become leaders, and what service to our country means. It could also be a way to help you get into college and pay for it."

Jessie considered this. He knew he'd need to go to college, but he also knew his family didn't have the means. The possibility of a scholarship was definitely appealing.

"Is it something I can start in the middle of the year or would I have to wait until next year?"

"I'm pretty sure you could start next semester. I'll talk to the instructor when I see him tomorrow and let you know."

"Thanks, Mr. Smith." Jessie stood. "I'll ask Mama about it."

Jessie thought about the ROTC program all the way home. He'd seen kids in the uniforms but had never given it any thought before. Now he tried to remember who those kids were, and if he knew any of them so he could find out what the program was really all about. He knew his father had been in the Navy for a few years; that's how Eugene and Eleanor had ended up in Florida.

By the time he got home, Jessie had decided to give ROTC a shot, despite his hesitation to do anything similar to his father. He could smell fried fish before he opened the door and his stomach growled. Mama must have stopped by the fish market today.

"How was school, honey?" Eleanor asked as she set the hot platter on the table.

"It was good. Mr. Smith says I'm catching up."

"That's good to hear." Eleanor smiled and untied her apron strings. "Dinner's ready," she called. Ricky ran down the short hall and plopped in his seat. Max and Sam were close behind but Eugene dawdled in front of the television.

"Gene, come on, the food's getting cold." Eleanor pulled out her chair and tucked a loose strand of hair behind her ear.

Eugene shuffled to the table, poured a glass of iced tea and took his seat without a word. Eleanor passed around the fish, grits, and coleslaw, as the boys caught up on all that had happened since they'd last seen each other at lunch. Eugene didn't talk much and Jessie noticed his hands were shaking as he ate, but it eased off by the time he'd finished the glass of tea.

"I'm proud of you boys," Eleanor announced as she started clearing the dishes. "You're all doing so well in school and at your new jobs. I thought we could celebrate by going out for ice cream tonight."

Jessie looked at his brothers, a large grin splitting his face. They'd heard the other kids talking about going to the Cutter Drug store for ice cream and daydreamed about saving up enough to go there themselves. They collected discarded Coca-Cola bottles on all of their exploring expeditions, usually gathering enough to turn them in at the convenience store, the collection normally earning around twenty-five cents for each boy. All their walking worked up an appetite, though, and looking at the display of candy invariably made them forget all about saving the money. Instead, they loaded up on bubble gum and chocolate bars, and split a cold Coke, each taking a long swig.

"Right on," Ricky cheered, bringing Jessie back to the moment.

"Jessie, I think it's your turn to do the dishes. After you clean up, we'll go."

Jessie bolted from his chair and gathered the empty plates. He washed faster than he ever had before.

"I'll help dry," Ricky offered, taking a plate from the drying rack.

Twenty minutes later they piled into the Bel Air, with Eugene behind the wheel. When they pulled into the parking lot, Max threw open the door as Ricky pushed him from behind. Inside the store, they leaned across each other, peering into the glass case at the vast array of flavors on offer.

"You can each have one scoop." Eleanor opened her purse and pulled out a worn, slender black wallet.

It took the boys five minutes to decide and place their orders. Jessie watched the man behind the counter, in his white apron and white shirt, reach into the display case. The metal scoop rolled through the pale pink cream, mounding it into a tight ball. The man was soon patting it firmly on top of the waiting sugar cone.

"Here you go, lad."

Jessie took it with reverence and studied it for a few seconds before taking a tentative lick. Strawberry flavor, as sweet as that of a fresh berry, now lingered on his tongue as he swallowed.

"Give me a taste." Ricky leaned over and licked a long swath of strawberry from Jessie's cone.

"Hey." Jessie pulled it away.

"Mm, that's good. You want to try mine?" Ricky held his cone toward Jessie.

He saw Ricky had chosen chocolate chip and nodded before sucking the point off the top of the cone. Sam and Max joined in with their own cones of chocolate and butter pecan. They all exchanged a taste and argued which was the best.

Halfway through his cone, Jessie noticed his parents sitting at the soda counter. Their backs were turned to the boys, but Jessie could tell they were arguing in hushed tones. Eleanor's back was ramrod straight, her head shaking from side to side. Eugene was slumped against the counter, head in his hands. Eleanor stopped speaking and Eugene lifted his head to look at her. Jessie saw Eugene's eyes flick to the boys then back to Eleanor. He gave a slow nod. She held out her hand and Eugene dropped his keys into it.

What had Pop done now? Jessie wondered. He hadn't missed a day of work and seemed to be drinking less.

"You boys ready to go?" Eleanor asked in a cheerful voice, but one that seemed strained to Jessie.

"Yes, ma'am." Jessie wiped his face with the back of his hand and started for the door. He heard his brothers sucking their fingers clean behind him, and his parents thanking the man behind the counter as they brought up the rear.

At the car, Eleanor opened the driver's door and adjusted the seat for her shorter legs. Jessie climbed in the back seat next to Ricky and leaned his head against the window.

"Why isn't Daddy driving?" Ricky whispered to Jessie, as their mother began to ease them out of the parking lot.

"I saw him give Mama the keys in the drug store. Don't know why." Jessie looked at his brother. Despite his own uncertainty, he felt his lips twitching upward at the sight of Ricky's face. "You're wearing as much ice cream as you ate."

Ricky stretched his tongue out and ran it around his mouth, as far as he could. Jessie giggled, for Ricky now reminded him of a frog.

"You missed some." Jessie pointed out, making Ricky repeat the action, wiggling his tongue back and forth at the corner.

Jessie cracked up, forgetting his concern about his parents and causing Sam and Max to lean forward, to find out what was so funny. Ricky looked at Sam and Max and showed them his tongue-waggle, causing them to join in with Jessie's laughter.

Eleanor pulled the car into the driveway and the boys tumbled out, still wagging their tongues and reveling in the day's rare treat. Jessie followed his brothers into the house but paused when he heard the door close behind him. He turned, expecting to see his mother's smiling face. All he saw was the door. He stepped to the window and pulled a corner of the flower-print curtain aside.

Eugene leaned against the front of the car; shoulders slumped, head down, arms dangling at his sides. Eleanor stood in front of him, but Jessie could only see the right side of her face. Dark lines of mascara mingled with the tears now running down her cheek.

The happy sounds of his brothers in the back of the house seemed so at odds with the scene he was now watching outside.

CHAPTER TWELVE

Separation

December 4, 1964

Eleanor pulled a tissue from her purse and blotted her face. Jessie dropped the curtain and ran to his bedroom, certain she wouldn't want him to see her when she came inside. He found his brothers in Max and Sam's room, sprawled on the floor, flipping through comic books.

"You haven't put that skull back where you found it," Sam chastised Jessie when he too dropped to the floor. "I thought you were going to do that weeks ago."

Ricky handed Jessie a Superman comic. "It creeps me out having it at the fort. What if his ghost is looking for it?"

Jessie fanned through the comic instead of responding.

Max tossed his gum wrapper at Ricky. "There aren't any ghosts."

"How do you know?" Ricky challenged

"When you die, that's it, end of story."

"How can you be so sure?" Ricky pressed. "I heard Pete Murphy talking about life after death the other day. He had a crowd of kids around him listening."

Max blew a large bubble. When it popped, strands stuck to his face, which he peeled off and pushed back into his mouth. "What does Pete know? I bet he's never seen a ghost either."

"He didn't mention ghosts. He was talking about getting a new body after you die."

"For real?" Sam put down the Spiderman comic he'd been reading.

"That doesn't make any sense." Max blew another bubble. "How can you get a new body when you are dead?"

"I dunno," Ricky admitted. "I didn't hear that part."

Jessie heard the front door open and the click of his mother's high heels. He waited, expecting to hear the heavy thud of his father's work boots. Eleanor then appeared in the doorway, her face pale, dark smudges under her eyes.

"I'm glad you boys enjoyed the ice cream. Do you have homework that needs to get done?"

"Yes, ma'am." Sam gathered the comic books lying on the floor and stood up. Jessie and Ricky stood as well. Eleanor kissed them on the cheek as they filed past her.

In their bedroom, Ricky sat on his bed and opened a book. "Did it look like Mama had been crying?"

"Why do you say that?" Jessie avoided his brother's gaze.

"She looked sad." Ricky kicked off his shoes and they bounced off the wall.

Jessie sat down next to his brother. "She and Pop were arguing."

"When?"

"At Cutters, and outside when we got home."

"How do you know?"

"I saw it." Jessie leaned back on the bed, his long legs hanging over the edge. He stared up at the ceiling and noticed peeling paint in one corner.

"What were they fighting about?"

"I couldn't hear them, but that's when Pop gave her the keys."

"You think he was drunk?"

Jessie sat up as if he'd been jolted with electricity. "He must've been. Why else would she take his keys?"

"He hasn't been to the bar since he started working."

Jessie hopped off the bed and left the room. He heard Ricky scurry after him. In the kitchen he opened the pantry door and shuffled the meager collection of canned goods, pasta, and beans. Not finding what he was looking for, he combed through every drawer and cabinet. When he'd finished, he flung open the refrigerator. There was little more in it now than two weeks ago. On the bottom door-shelf there was an unmarked bottle with what looked to be water in it. Jessie yanked it from the shelf and opened it. He sniffed but it didn't have a discernable odor. He lifted it to his lips, looked at Ricky and took a tentative sip.

The liquid burned the instant it hit his throat and he nearly choked. He leaned forward, coughing, his stomach threatening to return the ice cream he'd so enjoyed. Ricky rushed forward and grabbed the bottle before it fell to the floor. Jessie's hands dropped to his knees as he continued coughing.

"What in the world is going on?" Eleanor came into the kitchen and reached out for Jessie. She helped him to a chair and brushed his hair back off his forehead. "What's wrong, sweetheart?"

Ricky held up the bottle. Eyes flashing as hard as the emerald stones they reminded Jessie of, Eleanor snatched the bottle and clasped Jessie's chin, pulling it up so he was looking at her.

"I was looking for Pop's stash," Jessie managed, between ragged breaths. "He's been putting it in his tea at dinner, hasn't he?"

Eleanor released Jessie's chin and sank, like a deflating balloon, into the chair next to him. "Yes, I think he has."

"Is that why you drove home tonight?" Ricky stepped forward and placed a hand on Eleanor's shoulder.

"I was hoping to protect you boys from all this. Ricky, will you get Max and Sam please?"

Jessie watched as Eleanor took the bottle to the sink and poured it down the drain. When it was empty, she dropped it into the garbage, the thunk echoing through the silent kitchen. Ricky and his brothers filed into the room and Eleanor motioned for them all to sit down.

"I'm sorry this had to happen tonight, after you had such a good time at Cutters." Eleanor's voice was trembling and she paused to take a steadying breath.

"I was naïve to think your father could stop drinking right away. I found out he's been adding moonshine to his coffee in the mornings and to his iced tea in the evening. He says those are the only times, and it's only a drop, but I don't know what to believe anymore.

"At the drug store I could tell he was drunk, that's why I drove home. I couldn't risk your safety."

"He didn't seem drunk." Sam's brow furrowed.

"He wasn't as bad as he used to be, but something didn't seem right at dinner, and he was driving a lot slower than normal on the way to Cutters. When I confronted him about it, he admitted he'd added the moonshine to his tea."

"Where is he now?" Max demanded.

Jessie turned to his big brother and noticed his hands gripping the table.

"I told him he needs to stay with Uncle Tommy for a while."

Max pushed back from the table and started for the door.

"Come back here, Max." Eleanor didn't stand but her tone left no room for argument. Max stopped and looked over his shoulder. Jessie knew his brother had every intention of going down the street to Uncle Tommy's and pummeling their father. The pain on his mother's face made every ounce of his own being cry out to do the same.

"Sit down, Max." Eleanor shifted her gaze to Jessie. "And you stay where you are too. I know you both hold a grudge against your father. It's not fair that you have borne so much of his drunken behavior."

Eleanor reached a hand out to Max. Reluctantly he took it. With her other hand she cupped Jessie's face. She pulled Max closer and smiled at the boys. "It's no wonder you clash. You are so much like your father when he was young; strong and brave and stubborn."

Max yanked his hand away, his face growing red. "I'm nothing like him."

Eleanor reached for him but he stepped out of reach. "It's not bad to have similar personalities. That doesn't stop you from making your own choices, from choosing a better path than your father. He allowed his stubbornness to rule his life. You won't do that."

"Why are you making excuses for him?" Max's whole body was shaking and Jessie didn't know what to expect from his brother.

"I'm not making excuses. Your father has made many mistakes and he has to live with the consequences. I made a commitment when I married Gene and I take it very seriously, but I won't put my children in harm's way. If that means we have to live apart until he can pull himself together then that is what we are going to do, but I want to be clear, you are not to touch him. I won't have a repeat of your brawl at the bar."

Eleanor stood and stepped closer to Max. Jessie held his breath, afraid of what Max might do. Max was taller than Eleanor and for the first time Jessie noticed how small she looked. She wrapped an arm around Max's waist, though, and pulled him closer, laying her head on his chest. Gradually, Jessie could see the tension drain from Max's body. Jessie exhaled and stood, embracing his mother and brother. He felt hands on his back and glanced over his shoulder, to where Ricky and Sam now stood on either side of him.

Eleanor moved back, opening the circle to her two middle boys and the family came together, arms joined, heads touching briefly. Jessie couldn't remember them doing anything like this before. It felt like they were making a pact to protect each other.

"I love you boys so much. Don't ever forget that."

They all nodded then stepped back, breaking the circle.

"I have some reading to do." Jessie scratched his head, waiting to see if Ricky would join him in their room, but no one else spoke.

CHAPTER THIRTEEN

Mistakes

December 4, 1964

J essie picked up *The Old Man and the Sea* and opened it to the dog-eared page. He read it three times before flinging it aside, unable to focus. He crawled under the bed and retrieved the hunk of space metal. Turning it slowly in his hands he thought about what his mother had said about Pop making mistakes. He was hearing a lot about mistakes lately. This piece of metal he treasured so much represented a colossal mistake, but he'd come to see how it also represented possibility, courage, and adventure.

What were the mistakes his father had made to end up where he was now? How could Jessie avoid making those very same mistakes if his own personality was so like Eugene's? Would seeking direction from Mr. Smith, and listening to Mrs. Matthews, alter his path? Did the actions of a kid really matter?

"That was heavy stuff." Ricky entered the room and sat next to Jessie.

"Yeah."

"I really thought Daddy had changed." Ricky reached for the piece of metal.

"How do you suppose he started drinking?"

"I dunno. You think Max will leave him alone?"

Jessie shrugged. "I wouldn't mind getting in a few licks myself."

Ricky's face darkened. "You won't, though, will you?"

Jessie leaned back on his pillow. "Given the chance..." his voice trailed off as he contemplated.

"Whatcha guys doin'?" Sam stuck his head around the corner of the door.

"Talking about Pop. Where's Max?" Jessie asked.

"He's in our room. I think he needs some time alone." Sam stepped inside and made himself comfortable on Ricky's bed.

"I've got to finish reading three more chapters, but I can't concentrate." Jessie let out an exasperated sigh.

"When did you become so interested in school?" Sam teased.

"I'm in high school now. I gotta start getting serious so I can get a good job, maybe even go to college."

"Really?" Sam turned on his side to study his brother.

Jessie nodded. "I've been thinkin' about it."

"I'm impressed. If you need any help, let me know."

"Thanks." Jessie suddenly felt uncomfortable and reached for the book at his side.

Ricky scooted off the bed and grabbed a pair of pajamas. "I'm gonna get a shower."

"You guys mind if I sleep in here tonight?" Sam asked. Jessie grunted an approval and buried his head in his book.

When Ricky returned from his shower and dropped onto his bed, Jessie lowered the book and watched his brother pull back the bedspread and fold himself into his favorite sleeping position. "Do you mind if I keep the light on a bit longer? I'm almost finished."

"Sure." Ricky pulled the blanket over his head and turned his back to the room. Sam squirmed on the pallet he'd made up on the floor, fluffed his pillow and gave Jessie a quick wink before closing his eyes.

Jessie gazed down at Sam, imagining what it would be like to be as smart as his brother. Sam never seemed to have trouble in school; everything came so easy to him. Maybe if I work hard I can be as smart as Sam, Jessie mused, then returned to the book.

The next morning, Jessie awoke before his brothers and tiptoed out of the room. He showered and dressed, then quietly made his way into the kitchen. Eleanor entered the room as he finished his cereal and stood to wash his bowl.

Her eyes were red, with dark circles beneath them. She looked startled to see Jessie but didn't say a word. As he filled the percolator with water, she measured out the coffee. The pair sat at the table, waiting for the bubbly sound of perking coffee.

"Did you get your homework done last night?" Eleanor placed a hand on Jessie's.

"Yes, ma'am." Jessie thought of telling her about his determination to improve his grades and go to college, but he sensed her distraction and held back, sorry to have ruined her time alone with a cup of coffee. He wanted to get up and leave her to her own thoughts, but she still had her hand on his. She wasn't squeezing it, but he got the impression the feel of him there was comforting in some way so he remained still.

After the coffee had perked to a rich brown, she patted his hand and moved to the stove, spooned sugar into a cup and then poured in the fresh coffee. After a cautious sip, she gave a contented murmur. She handed Jessie a cup and they sipped in silence.

Eleanor ran a hand through her hair. "Why don't you go wake up your brothers?"

Jessie hesitated. He wanted to say something encouraging, something that would take away the sadness in her eyes, but he couldn't find the words. With a nod he went down the hall and flung open his bedroom door.

Sam was already sitting up, rubbing his eyes. "Morning," he greeted Jessie in a gravelly voice.

"Mornin'." Jessie crossed the small room and shook the foot of Ricky's bed. "Wake up."

"Five more minutes," Ricky mumbled from under the covers.

Jessie continued to shake the bed. "Come on, get up."

Ricky threw back the blanket and glared at his brother. Jessie laughed and grabbed Ricky's foot, pulling until it was hanging off the end of the bed. Ricky squirmed free before Jessie could start tickling him.

"I'm up," Ricky grumbled.

Jessie waited until Ricky's feet hit the floor before moving to his own side of the room, to make his bed and gather his schoolbooks. Sam dragged his blanket out of the room and could be heard waking up Max.

Jessie returned to the kitchen and found his mother arranging bowls and spoons for their breakfast.

"They'll be out in a few minutes. Can I help with anything?"

Eleanor shook her head. "I think they can manage pouring their own cereal. I'm going to run and get dressed." She kissed her fingers and placed them on his cheek as she passed him.

Jessie checked the clock, unusually anxious to get to school. A few minutes passed before Sam arrived, dressed in jeans and a pale blue t-shirt. He added the tiniest amount of milk to his cereal and woofed it down before the other boys appeared.

"How's Max this morning?" Jessie whispered.

Sam swallowed his last bite. "He hasn't said much."

Ricky shuffled into the kitchen, finger-combing his mussed hair. He poured a cup of coffee and reached for the cereal box. All three boys froze at the sound of Max's heavy footsteps coming down the hall.

"Morning." Max stepped into the kitchen and dropped into the closest chair. Ricky passed him the cereal box without a word and they all watched as he shook out the last crumbs.

"Want me to make you some toast?" Jessie lifted half a loaf of bread off the counter and pulled a couple of slices free.

Max looked up at his brothers. "Why are you all staring at me?"

Sam quickly turned to focus on washing his coffee cup, Ricky studied his hands, and Jessie dropped the bread into the toaster.

"You were pretty mad last night." Jessie spoke slowly, his gaze darting from Sam to Ricky, searching for support but finding none.

Max threw his head back and gave such a loud guffaw that Jessie jumped. "So you're worried I'm gonna be in a bad mood today?"

"It's hard to tell with you," Sam admitted.

"Are you gonna hurt Daddy?" Ricky lifted his gaze to meet Max's.

Jessie saw the laughter fade from Max's face, replaced by a dark scowl. "If he stays away from me there won't be any trouble."

"What about when he comes home?" Ricky pressed.

"Mom made it clear he wouldn't be home until he stops drinking," Sam interjected.

The toast popped up and Jessie handed it to his brother. Max folded one piece in half and crammed it into his mouth.

"Fat chance of that happening," Max mumbled as he chewed.

Jessie sat a glass of water on the table in front of Max and got a nod of thanks before Max washed down the toast.

Eleanor returned, one hand busy clipping an earring to her ear. Jessie noticed she wore one of her two nicest dresses, the brown one with red trim around the neck and hem.

"I have a job interview this morning at the F&S department store, then I'll be taking care of Mrs. Granger until seven tonight. I left a meatloaf in the fridge. When you get home, you need to heat the oven to 350 and cook it for an hour." She gave each boy a kiss on the cheek.

"I don't have any tutoring sessions today so I can take care of it," Sam offered.

Eleanor clipped the other earring on and gathered up her purse. "Thank you, Sam. You boys have a good day at school."

With a wave, she slipped out the door and Jessie heard the car start. He turned to his oldest brother and realized he was still in his pajamas. "You better hurry and get dressed, Max."

Max rolled his eyes and leaned back, tipping the chair onto two legs. "I think I'm going to stay home today."

"If you miss many more days this semester you're going to fail." Sam's stern gaze made Jessie feel guilty that he had considered joining Max, if only for the briefest moment.

Max seemed to mull this over while Ricky hurried back to his bedroom. Jessie was transfixed by the stare-off taking place between Max and Sam, sure Sam would look away first, giving Max unspoken approval to skip another day. To his surprise, Max dropped the chair onto all four legs and stood up with a loud exhalation.

Ten minutes later, all four boys ambled along the side of the road, kicking stones and the occasional beer can along the way. Jessie didn't pay attention to their idle chatter. He was already focused on the day ahead and the math test awaiting him.

CHAPTER FOURTEEN

Christmas

December 23, 1964

"Jingle Bells" played on the radio as Jessie and his brothers worked in the fort. The walls were complete and they'd started building some huts to protect them from the rain.

"I can't believe it's almost Christmas." Jessie stopped working and mopped at the sweat running down his face.

"Do you think Mama will let Daddy come visit on Christmas Day?" Ricky asked.

"I hope not. It's been nice not having him around." Max hammered a nail into the board Sam was holding for him.

"We always see Uncle Tommy's family, though. Do you think we won't go see them?" Ricky handed another board to Sam.

Jessie shrugged. "What do we really have to celebrate this year?"

"You're doing better in school." Sam smiled and Jessie felt a touch of pride.

Max rolled his eyes. "Yeah, that's something to celebrate. Less talk, more work."

Jessie glared at Max, but found another hammer and moved to the other side of the hut. Jessie allowed his mind to wander over the past six months; all of the fights at school, the progress of the space program, the cute redhead, his tutoring sessions with Mr. Smith, and Eugene's removal from their home. He was beginning to think the good things outweighed the bad.

"All we need now is a roof." Sam's voice intruded on Jessie's thoughts.

"We still have plenty of daylight, why don't we get started on it now?" Max took a step back and eyeballed the structure.

"Um, guys, did we figure out how we were going to put a roof on?" Ricky stared up at the walls that ended three feet above them.

"We have to weave together some palm fronds first, like we did with the walls." Sam laced his fingers together and arched them in front of his face, as if framing the hut. "Then we will figure out how to get them up there."

Jessie could tell from the look in Sam's eyes that his brother already had a few ideas. "All right. I guess we need to start collecting palm fronds again."

By the time the sun set the Cole boys had their roof ready to be attached. "Max and I can finish this up in a couple of days," Sam assured them as they made their way through the dark forest.

"You boys are a mess," Eleanor scolded when they traipsed into the house. "Go get cleaned up while I put together some dinner. We're having must-go tonight."

Jessie lingered in the kitchen, watching Eleanor pull covered bowls from the refrigerator, pouring their contents into pots already waiting on the stove. Must-go meant they were cleaning out all the leftovers and Jessie tried to remember what they'd eaten the past few days.

"Go on, get yourself cleaned up. Dinner will be ready in thirty minutes." Eleanor shooed Jessie away.

He found Ricky in their bedroom, his hands and face already scrubbed clean. Max popped his head in. "Bathroom is all yours, Jess."

Jessie washed up and returned to his room. All that dirt must have been holding him up because now he was beat. He dropped down on his bed and stretched out for a quick rest.

"Nice fort you and your brothers have built."

Jessie looked over his shoulder and smiled when he saw Grissom walking toward him. "It's a lot bigger than the tree house on the island," he answered, "but it doesn't have the incredible view."

"Times change and you have to be able to change with them. One day there may be a launch site where your tree house was. Would that be a fair exchange?"

"I guess."

"You don't seem very interested in the rocket launches tonight. What's bothering you?"

"Christmas is Friday. We don't even have a tree, and Ricky seems to be the only one who wants to celebrate this year."

"What has Christmas been like in the past?"

Jessie thought about this, pulling memories from a cobwebby recess of his brain. "They've actually been pretty nice. We never made a big deal out of it, gifts were small, but it seems like we were always happy."

"What's different this year?"

"Duh, Pop isn't here." Jessie shook his head.

"Isn't that a good thing, for you and Max at least?"

"Yeah, but Ricky is expecting to see him for Christmas."

Someone shook Jessie's shoulder. He opened his eyes to see Ricky standing over him. "Expecting to see who?"

"What?" Jessie sat up.

"You said I was expecting to see someone for Christmas."

"Oh, I must have been dreaming." Jessie rubbed his eyes and stretched.

"Well, dinner's ready." Ricky loped out of the room.

Jessie joined his brothers around a table loaded with bowls of left over cube steak and gravy, green beans, baked chicken and rice, garden peas, corn, mashed potatoes, and sliced tomatoes.

"We are going to be having Christmas dinner at Uncle Tommy's house like we usually do," Eleanor announced. She shot a stern look first at Max and then at Jessie. "I expect you *all* to be on your best behavior."

"Is Daddy going to be there?" Ricky asked.

"I'm not sure, but probably. You boys understand we won't have much for Christmas this year, right?"

They all nodded, but Jessie saw Ricky's look of disappointment.

CHAPTER FIFTEEN

New Clothes

February 26, 1965

A pair of black dress pants and pale blue dress shirt lay on Jessie's bed when he entered his room. He glanced at Ricky's bed and found a similar outfit there, only with a red shirt. In front of the orange crates the boys used as a chest of drawers he saw two pairs of identical dress shoes, polished to a shiny black. Setting his schoolbooks down, he reached for the clothes, surprised they had that crisp, never-been-worn feeling. Carefully folding the clothes, he returned them to the bed exactly as he'd found them. In Sam and Max's room he found the same surprise awaiting them.

Scratching his head, he headed to the kitchen where his brothers were pillaging the remnants of a bag of chips. They hadn't stopped talking about their plans for the upcoming spring break since starting the trek home from school.

"There are new clothes on our beds," Jessie interrupted their banter.

"What do ya mean?" Ricky mumbled through a mouthful of chips.

"Dress pants and a shirt, even shoes. I don't think they came from the thrift store either."

The front door opened and Eleanor bounced in. "There are my dear, sweet boys."

She put the sack of groceries she carried on the table and started to unload it. Jessie watched her, perplexed by her light-hearted manner, and even more so by the way she quietly hummed a popular tune. She opened the refrigerator and slid a carton of eggs inside then returned to the bag and pulled out a loaf of bread and a box of cereal.

"Did you boys see the new clothes I bought for you today?" Eleanor turned to look at her sons as she folded the paper bag.

Jessie nodded. "What are they for?"

Eleanor's face beamed. "We're going to church this Sunday."

Jessie couldn't have been more shocked if she'd told them they were going to a public execution.

Max dropped the bag of chips. "We're what?"

"Don't look so frightened, dear." Eleanor patted Max on the cheek. "You won't be struck down just for entering the doors."

"Are you sure about that?" Ricky snickered.

Eleanor paused for a moment and bit her lip. "Actually, no, I guess I'm not."

"What?" Max bellowed.

Eleanor giggled. It was such a girlish sound that Jessie had to turn to make sure it was coming from his mother. Her eyes twinkled and she looked younger, like she had when he was still a little boy.

"I think it's a good idea," Jessie agreed. "Which church?"

"The one right up the road. You pass it on the way home from school, well you would if you didn't cut through the woods nearly every day."

Sam nodded. "I know the one you're talking about."

"Good, now run and try on your new clothes. I want to see how handsome you all look."

Jessie, Ricky, and Sam obeyed leaving Max in the kitchen with their mother. Jessie could hear Eleanor's high heels clicking on the floor as she walked toward Max.

"This is going to be a good thing." Jessie heard Eleanor's soothing voice and tried to imagine Max's reaction. The heavy pounding of Max's feet down the hallway gave him his answer.

Ricky was stripping off his shirt before they even entered the bedroom, and Jessie did the same. They each went to their bed without speaking and picked up their new clothes. Jessie's fingers, unfamiliar with the buttons, fumbled as he unbuttoned the shirt and slipped his arms into the stiff sleeves. With a shrug of his shoulders, the shirt straightened across his back and he started the process of buttoning again.

"Why couldn't it have been a pullover," he grumbled, as he noticed the buttons weren't lined up correctly. Jessie glanced at Ricky, who was already pulling on his pants.

Five minutes later, Jessie and his brothers returned to the living room where Eleanor sat in a gold, velvet rocking chair, mending a pair of socks. Jessie felt himself stand taller when he saw his mother's face brighten at the sight of them. Each boy wore black pants and shoes, but their shirts were different. Max wore hunter green, Sam chocolate brown, Ricky fire engine red, and Jessie periwinkle blue. They stood before their mother allowing her to inspect them. Eleanor stood and ran her hands along their shoulders, tucking at the shirt where it tried to escape from Ricky's pants, and then knelt before Max studying the hem of his own, rolling it up then letting it back down until she was satisfied. She stood again and nodded.

"You look like perfect gentlemen. Now run and change, and I'll make some dinner." Eleanor crossed into the kitchen as the boys paraded down the hall.

Jessie was happy to get out of the foreign clothes and back into his t-shirt and shorts, but was careful to fold the shirt and pants just as neatly as he'd found them.

"You think Mama might let me wear these to school one day? I bet Mary Jane would look at me if I was all dressed up." Ricky held his shirt by the shoulders and struggled to fold it.

"Who's Mary Jane?" Jessie reached out to help his brother.

Ricky's face reddened. "A girl in my history class. She's real pretty, and smart too."

"I doubt she'll let you wear them to school, but there is a spring dance coming up." Jessie winked.

Ricky reddened even more. "I can't ask her to that."

"Why not?"

"She probably doesn't even know my name."

"So, introduce yourself, then ask her to the dance."

"Are you going?"

Jessie shrugged. "I haven't thought about it."

"Me either."

Jessie laughed. "If you haven't thought about it then why do you want Mary Jane to notice you?"

"Cause she's pretty."

"What were you going to do when she did notice you?"

"Ask her if I can kiss her."

Jessie grew serious. "Really? Have you kissed a girl before?"

Ricky shook his head. "Have you?"

"Nah. I bet Max has kissed a bunch of them. We should ask him."

Ricky looked up. "You think so? He's so mean, why would a girl kiss him?"

"I've heard a lot of girls say he's good looking. Maybe that's all they care about."

"I don't understand girls."

"Me either." Jessie patted his brother on the back. "Let's see if we can help Mama with dinner."

Ricky and Jessie found Eleanor at the stove, stirring a pan of ground beef. Ricky went to the cupboard and removed five plates, which he set on the table before returning for glasses and silverware.

Jessie stepped up beside his mother. "What can I do?"

"Would you get the large pot off the top shelf for me and fill it halfway with water?"

Jessie had to stretch, but he managed to get a finger on the pot and tip it toward him until it fell into his waiting hand. He took the pot to the sink and positioned it under the facet before turning on the cold water.

"You're getting so tall." Eleanor glanced over her shoulder at Jessie. "Before long you will be as big as Max."

With the pot filled, Jessie returned to the stove and set it on the back burner his mother had indicated. "You think I might one day be taller than Max?"

Eleanor tousled his hair. "Maybe. You are taller than he was at your age. Turn that burner on high, please."

"May I watch TV?" Ricky asked, already standing in front of the small set.

"For fifteen minutes," Eleanor conceded.

Max and Sam soon joined Ricky on the couch, watching the *Andy Griffith* show, but Jessie remained in the kitchen. He watched Eleanor brown the meat and drain the grease before setting it aside. She placed another pot on the stove and poured in a jar of spaghetti sauce she'd canned last summer, adding a bit of fresh green pepper and basil from the herb garden.

"Jessie, will you put some bread in the toaster please?" Eleanor wiped her hands on her apron then rubbed the back of one across her forehead, pushing aside a lock of damp hair.

Jessie dropped two slices in and watched them get sucked down as he depressed the button. He'd taken their old toaster apart when he was eight, determined to understand how it worked. Unfortunately, he hadn't been able to get it back together quite right and his father had been furious. Jessie cringed at the memory, as if he could still feel the sting of the belt as it lashed across his bare legs.

The popping toast ripped Jessie from his memories. He replaced the slices with two more and started the process again. Eleanor pushed a knife and a stick of butter toward him. Jessie took it without meeting her eyes and scraped it across the first piece of toast.

"Are you okay?" Eleanor asked.

Jessie nodded and slathered the next piece of toast.

"I know what you're thinking about. I'm sorry I let it go on for so long." Eleanor reached an arm around her son and gave him a gentle squeeze. She dropped a handful of spaghetti into the pot of boiling water, then stirred the sauce that was starting to burp plump bubbles.

Jessie felt his eyes burning and squeezed them closed. He'd stopped crying during the beatings years ago and refused to cry about them now. When the toaster popped again, he continued the process until there was enough for two slices per person.

Eleanor, wearing oven mitts Jessie had given her for Christmas, drained the noodles and transferred them to a round blue bowl that she'd placed in the center of the table. Jessie put two pieces of toast on each of the plates, then filled the glasses with ice and poured the tea. Eleanor found a ladle for the sauce then carried the pot to the table where a crocheted potholder waited.

Eleanor removed her apron and hung it on the peg by the door. "Go wash up, boys."

She took her normal chair and rubbed her temple, then reached over and placed her hand on Jessie's. "Thank you for your help."

The boys took their seats with much scraping of chairs and bumping of the table. Eleanor used two forks to serve out the spaghetti noodles but each boy spooned out their own sauce. Sam and Jessie each took enough to mix through all of their noodles while Max drowned his in sauce, and Ricky took only enough to add a spot of color to his plate.

The kitchen filled with the sounds of forks plinking against plates, dangling noodles being sucked up, and ice jostling as each boy drained their glass. This had long been one of Jessie's favorite meals and everything else faded away while he indulged himself.

After several minutes Eleanor broke the silence. "How was school?"

"Not half as stimulating as I expected it to be." Sam set down his fork and patted at his lips with a napkin.

Max guffawed. "You would say something like that. You couldn't just say it was boring."

"It wasn't boring. Mr. Wylie's history class can be quite fascinating, but there was a substitute today and she droned on and on about the Civil War, like we'd never heard of it before."

"I had a math test today," Jessie jumped in, hoping to prevent an argument between his brothers. "I think I did pretty good on it."

"Wonderful," Eleanor smiled at Jessie. "Studying pays off, doesn't it?"

"I got to dissect a frog in science class," Ricky announced before Jessie could say more.

Jessie caught his mother grimace before she spoke. "That sounds exciting. What did you learn about the frog while you were dissecting it?"

Ricky looked at the ceiling for a minute, his tongue slipping out the side of his mouth as he tried to concentrate, then he shrugged with the smile of a six-year-old imp. "I don't remember, but I pulled out his guts. None of the girls in the class wanted to do that."

His brother's triumphant announcement came as Jessie was taking a drink of tea, causing him to choke back his laughter. Jessie slid his gaze to his mother who looked like she was trying to keep from throwing up.

"What about you, Max? Did you have any excitement at school?" Eleanor asked after taking a long drink.

"Nope. I can't wait to get out of that place."

"What are you going to do when you are out? Have you been thinking about that?" Eleanor pushed back her empty plate and rested her hands on the table.

"I'll pick up more shifts at the grocery store until I find something better, I guess."

Jessie noticed Max's normally cocky air seemed to have deflated and wondered for the first time if his brother had any dreams for life beyond school. Sam talked about being a doctor or an archeologist and Ricky wanted to build things, but Jessie couldn't remember Max ever mentioning a job he wanted to do. Was it possible Max wasn't as confident about life as he acted?

CHAPTER SIXTEEN

Going to Church

February 28, 1965

essie awoke to the chirrup of cardinals outside his window and the smell of frying bacon from the kitchen. He pushed back the bedspread and shuffled into the bathroom then on to the kitchen. Eleanor was standing at the stove, turning bacon with a fork. Dressed in her worn housecoat, black with large pink flowers, and curlers in her hair, she leaned heavily on the edge of the stove.

"Morning," Jessie mumbled. Eleanor jumped a little and then turned, revealing dark circles under her eyes. Jessie reached into the fridge for a carton of orange juice.

"Good morning, sweetheart." Eleanor pulled another piece of bacon out of the sizzling grease and glanced into the oven at the pan of toast. "Did you sleep well?"

"I guess. What about you?" Jessie took his glass of juice to the table.

"Not really. I've had this headache since after dinner last night."

"We don't have to go to church." Jessie hoped he sounded concerned for his mother rather than seeking a way out for himself.

Eleanor gave a dismissive wave with the fork. "I can always lay down this afternoon."

Jessie gave an inward sigh. "What time does church start?"

"The service is at ten-thirty." Eleanor looked at her watch. "I'll have breakfast ready in another ten minutes. Why don't you go get dressed?"

Jessie polished off his juice before returning to his bedroom. Ricky was already sitting up, rubbing his eyes.

"Do I smell bacon?"

"Yep. I guess going to church means we get a big breakfast. It'll be ready in ten minutes." Jessie left Ricky and poked his head into the other bedroom. "Time to get up."

"Go away," Max growled.

"Breakfast will be ready in a few minutes," Jessie replied.

"I don't care. I'm not going to church." Max turned his back to the door and pulled the blanket over his head.

Jessie looked to Sam who swung his feet over the edge of the bed, then motioned for Jessie to leave them alone. Jessie stepped back into the hall, closing the door behind him. He hoped Sam could talk some sense into Max.

Back in the kitchen, Jessie found the plate of bacon already on the table along with a stack of toast. Eleanor now stirred a pan-full of eggs. Jessie set plates and silverware out before sitting at his usual place near the door. He felt his stomach growl and checked to make sure his mother's back was to him before sneaking a piece of crisp bacon off the plate. He broke it in half with a quiet snap and gobbled it up. Ricky arrived a moment later, pulling out his chair and dropping into it, sleep still in the corner of his eyes.

"Where are Sam and Max?" Eleanor asked when she turned around with the pan of eggs.

"They'll be here in a minute," Jessie assured her, hoping he was right.

"They better hurry or the eggs will get cold." Eleanor sat down with a cup of black coffee.

Jessie and Ricky spooned heaps of eggs onto their plates and each took several pieces of bacon.

Sam slipped into his seat and reached for the eggs. "Max isn't feeling well."

Jessie felt his body tense. He looked to his mother, but she didn't seem to have heard. Her gaze was far away, her hands wrapped around the hot mug of coffee. The boys quickly cleaned their plates, but Eleanor didn't eat a thing.

"Does anyone need to get in the bathroom?" Jessie asked after setting his plate in the sink. Sam and Ricky shook their heads. Jessie closed the bathroom door and turned on the tap, scrubbing his face and underneath his fingernails. He brushed his teeth until his gums ached, and spent five minutes combing his hair. When he emerged, he found Sam waiting by the door.

"About time." Sam pushed past Jessie, but Jessie grabbed his brother's arm.

"What happened with Max?"

Sam looked down the hall toward the kitchen. "He doesn't feel good. Probably needs to stay in bed all day."

"But he seemed fine last night," Jessie protested. Sam gave him a hard look then shut the bathroom door behind him. Jessie stood in the hall, wanting to barge into Max's room and demand he get up, but afraid of his brother's wrath.

"Whatcha' doin'?" Ricky appeared in the doorway of their bedroom, buttoning up his shirt.

Jessie shook his head. "Nothing. You almost ready?"

"I need to brush my teeth when Sam gets out. What do you think church is like?"

"I have no idea. I hope it doesn't last too long. I want to go out to the fort this afternoon."

Ricky's eyes lit up. "Me too. We haven't been out there all together in weeks."

Half an hour later Jessie, Sam, and Ricky followed Eleanor out of the house and piled into the car. Jessie was amazed at how pretty his mother looked in her long, dark-blue dress, and matching high heels. The circles under her eyes seemed to have vanished and her hair fell in large curls around her face.

It only took a couple of minutes to drive to church, but the boys were slow to get out of the car when they arrived. Jessie looked around at the other cars in the parking lot and recognized some of his schoolmates emerging from them. He hoped Alan Welty wasn't here. *There's nothing Christian about that bully,* Jessie thought with a grimace.

"Come on, boys." Eleanor's voice broke into Jessie's thoughts.

Jessie and his brothers followed Eleanor through the lines of cars, like a family of ducklings. When they reached the door, he hesitated, remembering Max's comment about being struck down. He hadn't been bad enough for that, had he? He'd been in fights and maybe he'd lied to his parents a few times, but he'd never stolen anything or smoked. He hadn't even kissed a girl. Surely he'd be fine to go inside.

Stepping across the threshold, it took a minute for Jessie's eyes to adjust from the bright sunshine to the soft glow of the church. Rows of long pews stretched from a center aisle to the outer walls. Eleanor quickly took a seat in one close to the back of the church and the boys fell in beside her. When they were seated, Jessie looked around him at the tall windows, spaced six feet apart. Several of them had stained glass, depicting scenes Jessie guessed to be from the Bible. One particular scene captured his attention, a man with long hair and a beard carrying a lamb in his arms, with several sheep around his feet. He was gazing at it when he heard his name.

"Hi, Jessie," said a shy female voice.

Jessie's gaze dropped from the window to find the cute redhead from math class standing in the row in front of him. "Hi," he managed to stammer.

"Is this your first time here?" she asked.

Jessie nodded and felt his heart rise into his throat when she sat down and turned to face him.

"It's nice to see you."

"Nice to see you too." Jessie felt something on his foot and looked down to see Ricky's own foot pressing on it. "Um, do you know my brothers?"

"I've seen them around school, but we don't have any classes together." She turned to look at Ricky and Sam. "I'm Virginia Benson."

Ricky and Sam introduced themselves, then music started playing and everyone stood. Virginia gave Jessie a smile and he felt his knees go weak, then she turned around to join in the song. Jessie tried to follow along in the hymnal he shared with Ricky, but he couldn't stop staring at Virginia. Her auburn hair fell to the middle of her back in loose curls. She wore a pale blue dress that matched his shirt and accentuated her tiny waist.

Jessie swayed on his feet a moment before Ricky tugged on his shirtsleeve and he realized the pastor had stepped up to the podium and the congregation was settling into their seats. Jessie sank down next to his brother and felt Ricky leaning closer.

"She's pretty," Ricky whispered. Jessie nodded, unable to believe his luck in his mother deciding to visit this church.

The pastor welcomed everyone and made announcements about upcoming events, but Jessie barely heard him. Instead, he found himself wondering what it would be like to hold Virginia's hand, touch her cheek, to kiss her lips.

"You should ask her to the dance." Ricky's soft words interrupted Jessie's daydreaming. He thought he saw Virginia's shoulders rise and fall in a small laugh.

"Be quiet," Jessie hissed. He tried to focus on the words from the pastor but they sounded like a foreign language. He spoke about someone named Jesus and how he sacrificed his life to save the world. Jessie didn't understand how one man dying could save everyone on the earth for all time. Why would anyone want to do that anyway? Did people like Eugene and Alan deserved to be saved?

After a closing prayer, the congregation broke up and greetings were called from row to row. Hugs were shared and many faces wore a smile of welcome. Several ladies approached Eleanor to introduce themselves and ask how she'd liked the service. Jessie milled around with his brothers, hoping for another chance to speak with Virginia. Her family had moved to the front of the church at the end of the service and he could see her now, talking with a couple of other girls that he recognized from school. One of them looked in his direction, giggled, and turned back to Virginia.

"These are three of my boys," Eleanor was saying, as she placed a hand on Jessie's shoulder. "I have another one at home, but he wasn't feeling well."

"What handsome young men," gushed a round woman with black hair, in such a poufy style it made her head look as round as her stomach.

A tall, thin woman with a narrow nose and straight auburn hair addressed Jessie, "I'm Mary. I saw my niece, Virginia, talking to you when you came in."

"Yes, ma'am. We have math class together." Jessie hoped his face wasn't as red as it felt.

"You must have your hands full with four boys," the round woman interrupted.

"They are good boys." Eleanor beamed with pride, making Jessie stand straighter, and he saw Sam do the same.

"Is your husband here as well?" the thin woman asked.

Eleanor's lips compressed into a tight line. "No, he couldn't make it either."

"Goodness, I hope he and your son aren't contagious," the round woman exclaimed, taking a step back.

"I don't think you need to worry about that," Sam replied dryly.

"Regardless, we shouldn't keep you from going home to tend to them." The round woman hiked her purse up on her shoulder. "It was nice meeting you. I hope we see you again next week." With a wave to another couple passing at the end of the row, she tottered off.

"Forgive Alma. She has a bit of a phobia about germs," Mary apologized. "Is there anything I can do to help out? I know how hard it can be caring for a sick man. I have two boys myself, but their father is as bad as either of them when he isn't feeling well."

"That's kind of you, but I'm sure they'll be better in no time."

Jessie knew Max would be fine as soon as they got home, but he wasn't so sure about his father. Did Eleanor know something she hadn't shared with them? Even though Uncle Tommy only lived a few blocks away, they rarely saw him or Eugene. Maybe he would try to sneak over there in the afternoon, to check things out.

"Well, don't hesitate to call me if you need anything." Mary leaned in and hugged Eleanor before slipping away and joining her husband who stood at the front door talking with the pastor. Jessie watched as she linked her arm through that of a man, only an inch or two taller than herself, with thinning brown hair and thick black glasses. They made an odd couple; she was sleek and polished while he seemed rumpled and worn.

Jessie looked around for Virginia, but her family had moved on from where he'd last seen them. There were only a dozen families still gathered in the church and cars could be heard starting up outside.

"Come on, boys." Eleanor ushered them out the door, pausing a moment to thank the pastor for a lovely service.

The boys clambered into the backseat and rolled down the windows. "It's only March and already hot," Ricky grumbled.

"It's warmer inland than we're used to on the beach," Sam informed them, in the tone they all knew meant a lecture was forthcoming.

"Why couldn't we have moved to another house on the island?" Ricky whined.

"It's not so bad. Maybe we can take a trip to the beach next Saturday." Eleanor looked at them in the rearview mirror.

"It's not the same," Ricky pouted.

"I think it sounds like fun," Jessie offered, hoping his support of Eleanor's suggestion would make Ricky more agreeable.

"Can we see some of our old friends too?" Sam asked hopefully.

Eleanor backed the car out of the parking spot and pulled onto the narrow road. "Maybe. I know where some of the families ended up after NASA bought their land. I'll make some phone calls and see what we can arrange."

This seemed to brighten Ricky's mood and he spent the rest of the short ride listing the friends he'd like to see again.

CHAPTER SEVENTEEN

Launch of Molly Brown

March 23, 1965

Highway 1 through town was jammed with Chevrolets and Fords. Jessie slipped between the polished chrome fenders, ignoring the angry honks of the motorists anxious to find a parking spot. A brisk breeze crossed the Indian River and caressed his face, as if trying to calm his excited nerves. All of the commotion surrounding the impending launch had made ducking out of school easier than usual. Cars were parked three deep behind a wall of people lining the river's edge. Jessie wriggled his way through the tightly packed crowd until he reached the front.

He hadn't been able to sleep all night, knowing Gus Grissom was making his second flight. This was the first manned mission of the *Gemini* program, with Grissom as Commander and John Young as pilot. Jessie hadn't understood the joke about calling their capsule *Molly Brown*, not until Sam had told him the story of the *Titanic*, and the brave woman of the same name who'd been onboard the ill-fated ship. She'd survived and while onboard the rescue ship, *Carpathia*, had managed to raise thousands of dollars in support of the other women and children who had lost everything. In an interview upon returning to the United States she had attributed her survival to the "Typical Brown luck. We're unsinkable."

Jessie liked the story and understood why Grissom had taken on her name after his scare with *Liberty Bell 7's* hatch blowing prematurely, and the capsule being lost in the ocean shortly after Grissom had been recovered from it. Jessie hoped Molly Brown's luck would be with his hero on this new mission.

Radio reports blared from several of the cars, with updates from Gemini Control explaining events taking place on site. When the countdown from ten started, Jessie heard the collective intake of breathe all around him and felt his own chest tighten.

"Ten-nine-eight-seven-six-five-four-three-two-one-zero, ignition. We have lift off at twenty-four minutes after the hour."

Jessie's screams of delight joined with those of the crowd, as they watched the cylinder shoot into the sky. He punched a fist into the air and jumped up and down. He felt hands clapping him on the back, but didn't take his eyes off the rapidly disappearing speck. He could sense the crowd breaking up around him and heard the spectators closest to him congratulating each other, as if they had been a part of making this launch happen.

"I thought I'd find you out here." A gruff voice preceded the meaty hand that dropped down on Jessie's shoulder and spun him around with ease.

Jessie looked into Alan Welty's cold black eyes. "What do you want, Alan?"

Alan sneered. "What I've always wanted. You and your brothers gone."

"We haven't done nothing to you."

"Nothin'? You broke my best friend's arm." Alan tightened his grip on Jessie's shoulder, but Jessie refused to flinch.

"If you hadn't picked a fight, he wouldn't have been hurt. Besides, you've been messing with us since we first arrived."

"You don't belong here," Alan growled.

Jessie tried to shrug off Alan's hand, but it didn't move. "We didn't want to move here, but there's not much we can do about it. What's it matter to you anyway?"

"That's none of your business." Alan's eyes narrowed.

Jessie laughed. "You just don't like new people do ya? Especially ones who show you aren't invincible. Are you afraid we've weakened your iron grip on the rest of the school?"

When Alan didn't respond, Jessie laughed even harder. He bent over to catch his breath, then drove his head into Alan's stomach. Alan stumbled back, dazed. Without any hesitation, Jessie straightened, bringing his fist up into Alan's chin. Alan's head flew back, causing him to lose the bit of balance he had just regained and fall on his back, with Jessie standing over him.

Alan rolled on his side and grabbed Jessie by the ankles, jerking his legs out from under him. In a flash, Alan was on top of him, fists pounding Jessie's face. Jessie raised his knee causing Alan to roll to the side. Alan jumped up and landed a swift kick in Jessie's side.

Jessie pulled himself into a ball and rolled away. He could hear the shouts of a man over the loud purr of hundreds of cars, then felt hands on him, trying to roll him over, but he resisted.

"It's okay, son. Let me have a look." The words were spoken in a soft, kind voice.

Jessie peeked through one half-opened eye and found a middle-aged man with thick horn-rimmed glasses kneeling beside him.

"Don't move too much. I'm going to check for broken bones." The man gingerly unwrapped Jessie's contorted body, pressing on each limb as he did so. When Jessie was laid out flat on the ground, the man ran his hands along Jessie's sides, causing him to cry out in pain.

The man sat back on his heels. "You probably have some bruised ribs, but other than that you seem fine."

"Thanks," Jessie managed through gritted teeth.

"Do you think you can stand up?"

Jessie nodded and allowed the man to help him to his feet. His head pounded and he could taste blood on his lips. He reached up and rubbed at his mouth and nose with the back of his hand.

"Here, use my handkerchief." The man handed him a starched, white square. Jessie hesitated, knowing the blood would ruin it.

"Go ahead, I have a dozen more at home." The man smiled and Jessie noticed a boyish glint in his pale gray eyes.

Jessie continued his exploration, patting around his mouth with the handkerchief. His gaze flitted around and he noticed a large group had gathered around them. Several women clung to their husbands. A group of tough guys stood, with cigarettes dangling from their thin lips. But Alan was gone.

"Is there someplace I can take you?" the man asked.

"I only live a few miles away."

"You should get some rest and put some ice on your face. By the way, I'm Dr. Weston."

Jessie faced the man again and accepted his outstretched hand.

"Jessie Cole."

"Sorry we had to meet like this, Jessie Cole."

Jessie tried to laugh, but pain shot through his chest.

"My car is right over there." Dr. Weston pointed at a burgundy Chevrolet Impala.

Jessie glanced at the road, still filled with unmoving cars. "I appreciate the offer, but I think I'll make it home faster on foot."

"At least let me bandage up your ribs. I have my medical bag in the car."

Jessie agreed and followed Dr. Weston who pulled a black bag from the rear seat. He set the bag on the trunk and rummaged through it until he found a long roll of elastic wrap. He helped Jessie remove his shirt then wound the material around his chest.

"It has to be tight to help immobilize the ribs in case they are broken, but let me know if it gets too tight."

Jessie gritted his teeth, searching the sky for any last glimmer of the Titan rocket.

"There you go." Dr. Weston stepped back. "You sure you want to walk?"

"Yes, sir. Thanks for helping me out."

Dr. Weston's eyes met Jessie's. "Do you mind me asking what the fight was about?"

Jessie felt his face flush with anger. "He's just a bully. Doesn't like that me and my brothers came to town."

"I see. When did you move here?"

"Over the summer. We had to leave Merritt Island."

Dr. Weston nodded. "I'm new in town too. My office will be open next week. If you need anything I hope you'll let me know." The doctor took a prescription pad out of his bag and scribbled something on it then handed the paper to Jessie.

Jessie shoved it into his pocket without looking at it. "How much do I owe you for the bandage?"

Dr. Weston waived his hand in dismissal. "No charge. We'll call it my good deed for the day."

Jessie wanted to protest, but knew he only had thirty-cents to his name.

"Maybe I'll see you at another one of these launches." Dr. Weston snapped his bag shut and returned it to the backseat.

"I never miss them." Jessie felt a twinge of regret. "We used to have front row seats on the island. This just isn't the same." He gestured toward the broad expanse of river separating them from the launch sites.

"It's closer than Kentucky, where I'm from." The doctor chuckled. "I look forward to being a part of this new exploration."

Jessie's eyebrows shot up. "You work for NASA?"

"No, I don't have that honor." Dr. Weston glanced toward the traffic that had started to inch along. "Why aren't you in school?"

"I had to see the launch."

"I would tell you to get back to class, but I think you'd better go home, and I better get to my office."

Jessie thanked the doctor again before weaving through the cars toward home.

When he reached the railroad tracks, he veered to the north. With a furtive glance over his shoulder, he pushed aside a curtain of vines and disappeared into the thick forest. Within minutes, the sounds of passing cars faded as he was enveloped in a world of birds flitting from branch to branch and squirrels chattering angrily. He moved by instinct and memory. Jessie and his brothers made sure to alter their route often so they wouldn't leave a trail.

He winced as he had to duck through a triangle created by two trees, bent by years of relentless wind into a melding embrace. He emerged into a small clearing, the sky still obscured by the far-reaching limbs of ancient oaks woven with vines. Dappled sunlight danced on the fallen leaves and sand, and reflected off a metallic surface. Jessie crept up to the object and sank to his knees with a sharp intake of breath. Before him lay the top of a goblet, tarnished by the elements. His heart raced as he scooped out the surrounding ground, pulling it free. He tipped it upside down and a large spider toppled out, ignored as Jessie turned the cup in his hands, brushing at the dirt caked into the crevices of what had once been ornate metalwork. With most of the dirt removed, he saw letters that appeared to be in a foreign language.

Jessie had heard stories of buried Spanish treasure in the area. He and his brothers had even explored some of the coquina caves, looking for it. He'd never imagined he could stumble upon it this way. He surveyed the area for any other items, but all he saw was decaying leaves and the occasional stubborn weed. With the toe of his shoe he made a large circle in the sand where the cup had been, then went back to the trees he'd come through and tied one of his shoelaces around a branch. After a final look around, memorizing every detail, he rushed on to the fort.

He was winded when he reached it, his chest burning as though Alan had just kicked him again. He gently dropped to the ground and lay on his back taking long, slow breaths until the pain subsided. His gaze traced the treetops and then turned to follow the hopping route of a cardinal, from tree back to fort wall to ground, pecking all the time at the leaves. When the bird took flight, Jessie sat up and studied the goblet again. It needed a good washing, but he didn't dare take it home. Ten feet away, he could see that the garbage can they'd sunk into the ground to collect rain water was now full. He moved over and squatted down by it, scooping water into an old army helmet, and dropped the cup in. He swirled the water around, watching the remaining dirt fall away.

After what felt like an eternity, Jessie dumped out the filthy water and dried the cup with his shirt. His fingers traced the engraving of two horses and what looked like a coat of arms set between a looping filigree pattern. The stem of the cup spiraled, with a leafy design, as if a vine were wrapped around it. A cracking twig tore his attention from the goblet, which he carefully set back in the helmet, before moving to the wall of the fort. He peered through one of the dozen slits they'd cut in the palmetto fronds, for keeping watch and for hunting.

He didn't immediately detect any movement, but there was another crack, drawing his gaze that way. He saw some bushes shake then a bearded man emerged, dirty gray hair awry around his shoulders, his clothes faded and worn. Jessie held his breath. They'd never seen anyone else this deep in the forest before. Most of the bums riding the trains stayed close to the tracks until they were ready to move on. The image of the skull he and Max had found flashed into his mind and a sense of foreboding washed over him.

Jessie scanned the fort's interior for a weapon, but they didn't leave their machetes or rifles out here. They'd erected two huts with a third near completion, but if the stranger came into the fort he would be sure to check those. His gaze dropped to the treasure hole they'd first dug. Since then they'd found a more secure way to hide their collections, but the old skull was still in there. Jessie raced to it, pulled back the cover and scooped up the skull. Moving silently, he placed it on its side near the doorway, but he hoped not close enough to look staged, then sneaked out through the fort's concealed back door.

Jessie listened for the stranger's movements, his ears attuned to all of the forest's noises. It was obvious the man wasn't a woodsman, what with the racket he made. Jessie heard the man approaching, poking at the doorway, and the rustle of dried fronds as he figured out how to open the door.

"What the devil?" the man cried a moment later.

Jessie grinned, trying to picture the look on the man's face upon finding the skull. The sounds of running footsteps told Jessie the man had been scared off, but he waited several minutes before moving, in case he came back with reinforcements. Jessie slipped back into the fort, and crossed to one of the slits, searching the forest. A blue jay squawked and lifted from a nearby branch, then all was quiet. Too quiet. The normal animal sounds had all stopped and that usually meant they sensed danger. Jessie retreated through the back door again. He desperately wanted to climb a tree, to watch over the fort, but the chance of crying out with the pain of his ribs was too high. Instead, he wiggled underneath a short palmetto bush. He bit his tongue when he rolled onto his stomach, his damaged ribs taking his weight. Maybe the tree would have been better, he thought.

Not a creature stirred for five minutes. Jessie was just about to give up and go home when he heard shuffling. He shook his head. Whoever it was sure didn't know anything about stealth. The bearded bum returned with a younger man wearing a couple days of stubble and standing a good five inches taller. While Jessie may have been able to take on the older man by himself, this younger one would be more difficult. Jessie watched as the men approached the fort and the older one pointed out the door.

"This ain't no Injun fort," the younger bum sneered.

"The heck it ain't. They's even a skull right inside." The older bum stood several steps behind the younger, keeping his distance from the door.

Jessie thought he saw fear in the dark eyes under their bushy gray eyebrows, and chuckled to himself.

"Even if there is a skull, don't mean it's Injuns. They ain't been no Injuns in this area for years." The young bum reached for the door and yanked so hard it came off in his hand.

Now Jessie was biting his lip to keep from screaming at the man. He could taste blood in his mouth and relaxed his jaw.

The younger bum stepped inside and disappeared from Jessie's sight. The older one stood outside, nervously stroking his beard.

"This is just some kid's fort," called the younger. "Come on, there's water here."

The older hesitated, looking around as if expecting some screaming Indian or angry ghost to come tearing through the trees. When nothing happened, he stepped inside.

"Not a bad set-up really," Jessie heard the younger one say. "We could make ourselves right at home."

"What if the kid shows up?"

The younger one laughed. "You think I can't handle a rotten kid?"

"What if it's a bunch of kids? One kid couldn't have done all this on his own."

"Who cares? You take off if you want, Joe, but I'm staying here."

"I don't know, Buster. What if this is on private property? Hanging out in the caves is one thing. All the bums do it, but this just doesn't feel right." The older man's voice trembled and Jessie hoped that young Buster would take Joe's advice.

"Private property?" Buster guffawed. "We're in the *middle* of the forest. Who you think owns land here?"

"What about that skull?" Joe insisted.

"The kid probably found it somewhere. Big deal."

"What if a kid didn't build this at all, but a killer, and that's why the skull is here."

There was a pause and Jessie hoped Buster was taking this into consideration. "I suppose that's possible. We'll take a look around and see if we find anything that can tell us who built the place. If it's kids we stay."

Joe didn't answer, but Jessie could hear the men moving around in the fort, gathering up the things the boys had left in the huts. Jessie tried to remember everything they had in there. There was the army helmet of course, and a rucksack with some tin cups and plates. He heard the rattle of the bag now. He remembered several carvings they'd done on rainy days, and their cane poles. As long as the bums didn't find the treasure chest then the items they found shouldn't betray their age.

"Hmm, hard to tell," Buster admitted when they had finished their search.

"Better safe than sorry." Joe now seemed to be pleading.

"Maybe. We'll clear out for now, but I'll come back in the morning and see if I can catch whoever is using this place. If it's a man I should catch him before he wakes up."

"And if he catches you instead?"

"Then one of us might have to die." Buster spoke with a cold calmness that made Jessie shiver.

Jessie watched as Buster leaned the door against the wall, trying to make it look undamaged, then he and Joe tramped back the way they'd come.

CHAPTER EIGHTEEN

Eleanor learns about the Bully

March 23, 1965

When the sounds of the bums faded into the distance, Jessie scooted out from his hiding place and quietly entered the fort. The helmet was where he'd left it, as was the skull, but after searching the huts, Jessie found that the rucksack was gone, along with all of its contents.

He felt his pulse increase as anger boiled in his gut. Obviously he didn't believe old Joe's theory that a killer might be using the area as a hideout. Grinding his teeth, Jessie moved to one of the huts still under construction. He removed the piled up palm fronds and thick logs until a dark blue metal box, buried up to the lid, could be seen. Dropping to his knees, Jessie fiddled with the combination lock. The pain in his ribs seemed to be making his fingers clumsy. Holding his breath to stop the pain, he tried once again. Success! He ran his hands over each item in the box, inventorying the collection of soda bottles, arrowheads, a jar of BBs, a box of ammunition, and seventy-five cents in loose change.

"I can't leave these things here now. If they come back and really start looking around they are sure to find them," Jessie whispered. Without the backpack he had no way of carrying everything, so he started shoving the arrowheads and change into his pockets. He managed to wedge the box of ammo and the neck of two soda bottles into his back pockets, grabbed three more bottles and set them, along with the goblet, on the ground until he could lock the box up again. He returned the fronds and logs to their pile, trying to make them look undisturbed, then collected his bottles and goblet, and with a final look around the fort, left through the back door.

He made a wide circle away from the fort back to his house; surprised to find it was almost three o'clock. He tried to remember if Max and Ricky had to work this afternoon, suddenly worried that they would go straight to the fort after school. He entered the kitchen and checked the calendar pinned to the wall, where he saw both boys had noted they would be working from three-thirty to seven that night. Jessie leaned forward, resting his head on the wall as relief washed over him. At the sound of a car in the driveway, Jessie made a beeline for his bedroom to hide the treasures, then ducked into the bathroom.

His face was bruised and dirty, his shirt was torn at the shoulder, where it had caught on the trunk of the palmetto, and dirt clung to his arms. He turned on the faucet and soaked a cloth in cold water. It felt good on his face and he held it there for a full minute before gingerly scrubbing at the dirt. With his face clean he wiped down his arms and rinsed out the now gray cloth. He heard his mother humming in the kitchen, apparently unaware he was home. He stole across the hall to his bedroom where he changed shirts, stuffing the torn one under his pillow. He'd have to ask Sam to mend it later.

"Hi, Mama. How was your day?"

Eleanor dropped several pieces of mail she'd been sorting through. "You startled me." She kneeled down to collect the envelopes and tucked a piece of hair behind her ear as she rose. When she looked up at Jessie, he saw the shock in her eyes.

"What happened to you?" Eleanor set the mail on the table and moved closer to her son, extending a hand to trace the bruise around his eye.

"It's no big deal."

"Who did this to you?" Eleanor demanded. Her eyes narrowed and Jessie could see a vein in her forehead throbbing.

"This kid at school." Jessie didn't want to worry her with Alan's continued attacks on the Cole boys.

"What's his name? I'm calling his mother." Eleanor took several steps toward the telephone on the wall by the door.

"You don't need to do that. I can handle it." Jessie had to think fast. If his mom called Alan's family she might find out about all of the other fights, the ones where Alan and his buddies hadn't fared so well.

"Young man, you are going to tell me this boy's name right now." The vein in her forehead was now pushing against her pale skin, and Jessie was afraid it was going to burst.

The front door opened and Sam stepped inside, his head buried in a book. He continued reading, oblivious to the presence of his mother and brother until he nearly ran into Jessie.

"What happened to you today? I didn't see you after the launch." Sam stuffed the book in his back pocket.

"Sam, do you know who did that to your brother?" Eleanor pointed at Jessie. Sam looked at his brother, their eyes met and Jessie hoped he gave him a pleading look that urged him to keep quiet.

"No, ma'am. It's going to be a real shiner, though, isn't it?" Sam gave a lopsided grin.

"You boys." Eleanor let out an exasperated sigh and shook her head. "Go study or something. Dinner will be ready at five." She dismissed them with a wave of her hand and turned back to the mail.

Jessie led his brother down the hall to his bedroom and shut the door. "You're not going to believe what happened."

"Alan kicked your butt again," Sam replied flatly.

"I would call it a draw, but that's not what I'm talking about." Jessie retrieved the goblet from under his pillow. "Look what I found."

Sam took the cup and studied it. "Looks Spanish."

Jessie nodded, barely able to contain his excitement. "I bet there's more where I found this. I marked the spot for us to go back and check it out. That's not all, though. There are a couple of bums trying to take over the fort."

"What are you talking about? The bums don't go that far into the woods." Sam handed the cup back to Jessie and sat down on Ricky's bed.

"I saw them. There was an old guy named Joe and a younger one called Buster." Jessie told Sam about trying to scare them off with the skull and their plan to take over the fort.

"We've worked too hard to let them have it," Jessie finished.

Sam was silent and Jessie could tell his brother was considering all he'd heard, but Jessie wanted action. Anxious for Sam's reply, Jessie tried to bounce up and down on his bed, but the first motion caused such intense pain his eyes watered.

"What are we going to do?" Jessie finally asked through gritted teeth when Sam didn't speak.

"We're going to tell Dad." Sam's matter of fact answer surprised Jessie more than if his brother had suggested they hold the fort with force.

"Yeah, right." Jessie laughed. "Really, what are we going to do?"

"Dad will deal with it."

"He can barely hold himself up much less deal with a couple of crazy bums." Jessie was growing annoyed with Sam. If this was the best that the smartest of the brothers could come up with then they might as well give up now and find a new place to start over.

"He's doing better. He hasn't had a drink in two months and he's got a steady job. We can't deal with this on our own, we need him."

Jessie rocketed off the bed, his arms outstretched, reaching for his brother's throat. "I don't need him for nothin," Jessie screamed, as he grabbed Sam.

Sam fell back on the bed with Jessie on top of him. Sam tried to pull Jessie's hands from around his neck, but couldn't get his arms past Jessie's elbows. Rolling onto his side, Sam pulled his knee up and rammed Jessie in the groin. With a howl of pain, Jessie's hands relaxed, and Sam was able to push Jessie away.

"What on earth is going on?" Eleanor cried. Jessie rolled off the bed onto the floor and glanced up to see his mother in the doorway, hand still on the doorknob.

"Haven't you had enough fighting for one day, Jessie?" She stepped into the room and pulled him off the floor where he'd fallen.

"We were just horsing around." Sam rubbed at his neck.

Eleanor released Jessie, her eyes slipping from one boy to the other. "I think there's something more going on here, and we're not moving until I get the whole story."

Jessie moved to his bed and perched on the edge, acutely aware of the burning pain slowly subsiding. There was no way he was going to tell his mother about the bums. She knew they spent a lot of time out in the woods, but they'd never told her about the fort, or any of the animals they'd encountered out there.

"Sam said Pop has stopped drinking. Is that true?" Jessie said, trying to deflect the conversation off the fight, but regretted the question when he saw his mother's face go even paler than normal.

Eleanor turned to Sam. "How do you know that?"

Sam squirmed, his gaze glued to the floor. "I see him every now and then."

"Where have you seen him?"

"At Uncle Tommy's. I've been tutoring Sally," Sam hastened to add. Their cousin Sally was six years younger than Jessie and very shy. None of the boys had spent much time with her. Jessie wasn't sure he'd even recognize her if they ran into each other at the store.

"Sally's only in fourth grade, how can she possibly need tutoring?"

"She's struggling with math and reading. I ran into Uncle Tommy a couple weeks after I started tutoring. Sally's issues at school came up and I offered to help out."

"And you never thought to tell me about this? To ask me if it was okay for you to be over there?" Eleanor was shaking, and Jessie was afraid she might collapse.

Sam didn't respond.

"Go to your room," Eleanor commanded.

Sam slid off the bed and shuffled past his mother. Jessie hoped she'd follow him out, forgetting about the fight she'd broken up. Instead, Eleanor sank down on the end of his bed. When she turned to face him, Jessie could see tears building in her eyes. She blinked several times, but one fell free anyway. She brushed at it with the back of her hand and took a deep breath.

"Maybe it's time your father came home."

"We don't need him, Mama. We've been doing fine without him." Jessie hated to see his mother cry. In the months since Eugene had been away Eleanor had hardly cried at all, and usually when she did it was because one of the boys had let her down.

Eleanor shook her head. "You boys need your father."

"We don't," Jessie insisted. "He'll just drag us down again."

Eleanor clasped one of Jessie's hands. "I've only seen him once, but he looked better, more like his old self."

Jessie watched a faraway look come into his mother's eyes. He wanted to say something that would make Eleanor believe the boys were fine without Eugene; that the family worked better without him, but then Eleanor raised her hand and caressed his face. Her touch was gentle, but pain still radiated through his cheekbone where Alan's fist had landed. They'd been in scrapes a time or two before moving to Indian River City, but they had been few and far between. Now he could think of more than a dozen encounters the Cole boys had had in the past eight months. Why was that?

"This isn't the first black eye you've had since we moved here." Eleanor seemed to be reading his mind.

"I check on you at night. I've seen the bruises." Eleanor's voice quavered, making Jessie feel guilty.

He and his brothers thought they'd done such a good job hiding their altercations. She'd never questioned them or shown concern, but she'd known all along.

"We're boys. It happens," were the only words that came to Jessie's mind.

Eleanor's lips turned up, but the smile didn't reach into her misty eyes. Jessie looked away. The anger that had boiled inside him was now chilled by sorrow and shame.

"I suppose some fights are inevitable between brothers, but these aren't all fights amongst yourselves, are they?"

Jessie shook his head.

"Whom are you fighting with?"

"It doesn't matter."

"It matters to me." Eleanor shifted on the bed, turning so that her leg was bent underneath her.

Jessie pulled at a thread in his jeans, watching as the small hole grew larger, until Eleanor placed a hand on his leg.

"I'm going to have to teach you how to patch those holes." Eleanor gave a half-hearted laugh followed by a sigh. "You don't have to tell me who the fights are with, now, but this is the last time. If it happens again, I'll have to do something about it."

"Yes, ma'am." Jessie kept his head down, eyes trained on the hole in his pants. Eleanor sat a moment longer, then pushed herself up.

She ruffled his hair. "Dinner will be in an hour. Why don't you get started on your homework?"

Jessie waited a minute before going to knock on Sam's door, pushing it open before Sam could answer.

"What do you want?" Sam grumbled.

"We still gotta figure out what to do about the fort."

Sam shrugged. "Not much we can do. We're just kids."

"So you're just giving up?"

"Wake up, Jess. It's only a fort. It's not like we were going to have it forever. There will be houses there in a few more years. Things are changing."

CHAPTER NINETEEN

Uncle Tommy's

March 23, 1965

Aﬆter dinner, with his brothers engrossed in *Rawhide* and Eleanor engaged with a basket of clothes needing repairs, Jessie ducked out the back door. The night air was cool, but still thick with humidity. Within five minutes he stood in front of a bright yellow concrete-block house. Two windows facing the street were illuminated behind thin white, lace curtains, through which he could see two children on the couch with their backs to him. Jessie watched for a moment, until the little girl jumped off the couch, excitedly pointing at the television across the room.

A tall, slender woman passed the window, her chestnut hair flowing in waves past her shoulders. She approached the little girl and bent down to say something. The girl returned to her seat on the couch, but scooted to the far end away from the other child. The woman turned and moved closer to the window. Jessie approached the house, lifting his hand in a wave. When he stepped into the light from the front porch, the woman smiled and hurried away. A moment later the door opened.

"Jessie, it's so good to see you." The woman pulled Jessie into a warm hug.

"Hi, Aunt Donna." Jessie stuffed his hands in his pockets, suddenly unsure of himself.

"Come on in." Aunt Donna stepped back and ushered Jessie through the doorway. Jessie followed his aunt into the living room.

"Tommy and your dad are on the back porch. Why don't you run on out there and say hi?"

"Thanks." Jessie glanced at the couch where Tommy Jr. and Sally were settling back in front of the television, envious of their easy smiles and laughter, then shuffled down the hallway to the back door. He could hear laughter through an open window, causing him to freeze a few steps from the door.

The back porch was dark, preventing Jessie from seeing the men. He tried to remember the last time he'd heard his father laugh, trying to match it to what he heard now.

"No, Tommy, I don't think Donna would appreciate you bringing home this mutt. Even she couldn't wash the stink off him."

Now Jessie was sure it was his father out there. Part of him wanted to run through the door and fall into his father's arms, but part of him wanted to beat the happiness out of Eugene. Memories long forgotten rushed back to Jessie. How dare Eugene be happy when his family had been struggling for so long?

"You want another Coke?" Tommy asked.

"Sure."

"No, stay there. I'll get it."

Jessie heard a board creak, then the door opened and Uncle Tommy stepped inside, nearly plowing into Jessie.

"Whoa, who do we have here? Too big to be Tommy Jr." Uncle Tommy flipped on the hall light. "Well, if it isn't little Jessie. Gene, your boy's here."

Jessie stood frozen, blood pounding in his ears. This had been a bad idea. He wanted to run, but Eugene appeared in the doorway. He wore a pair of threadbare jeans, a pale blue short-sleeve dress shirt, and twirled a baseball cap on his right index finger. His blue eyes were clear, with deep wrinkles at the edges. Jessie watched as those eyes raked over him and saw the twinkle fade away.

"What happened to you, son?" Eugene moved closer, cupped Jessie's chin and tilted his son's face up to the light.

Jessie had forgotten about the black eye and was surprised Aunt Donna hadn't mentioned it. "It's nothing," Jessie mumbled.

"Why don't you two go outside and catch up? I'll grab a couple of drinks." Tommy gave Jessie a slight push toward the door as he passed to the kitchen.

Jessie followed his father outside and looked around for a seat. In the glow from the hall light he spied a couple of folding beach chairs and an old wooden chair with a worn out cushion. Jessie opted for the wooden chair since it was farthest from the other two.

"I have to say, I'm surprised to see you." Eugene spoke slowly, in a somber tone that Jessie had to strain to hear. "I owe you and Max an apology, but even that ain't enough. I was real bad to you. I could make up excuses, but they don't matter. I know that now."

Jessie refused to look at his father. Instead, he gazed out into the darkness, listening to the crickets and an owl in one of the tall pine trees. He tried to imagine what Max would do if he were here. Jessie was pretty sure his brother would have taken a swing at Eugene by now, but he couldn't bring himself to do that. A memory from when he was four or five flashed before him.

Eugene and Jessie had been home alone, the older boys in school and Eleanor at work. Eugene had led Jessie through the woods, taught him how to make his first cane pole, and taken him to Banana Creek to test it out. They only caught one fish all morning, but Jessie remembered laughing the whole time. He'd been so proud to bring that fish home in the afternoon and show his brothers.

"Jessie?"

Eugene's voice returned Jessie to the back porch. He turned his gaze to his father and found an odd look on Eugene's face. He recognized it as concern, only because he'd seen it on Eleanor so often. All of the weight of the past eight months seemed to crash down on Jessie. All of the fights, the tension between Max and their mother, the bums trying to take over the fort, became more than Jessie could bear and he dropped his face into his hands.

Eugene moved awkwardly, kneeling before his son, wrapping one arm around his shoulder, cupping the back of Jessie's head and leaning his own against it. "I'm so sorry, boy," Eugene whispered.

The words bore through all of the emotions Jessie was feeling, crystallizing one. He shot up from the chair, pushing Eugene away. "You don't get to be sorry," Jessie screamed. "You don't get to be happy, like you were when I got here. You ruined everything!"

Jessie tried to run, but Eugene, still on the ground, grabbed Jessie's hand. Uncle Tommy appeared with three bottles of Coca-Cola and a look of confusion. Jessie shook off his father and jumped from the porch, running like a panther was chasing him.

"Jessie! Wait!" he heard his father call, heavy feet pounding behind him.

Jessie ran past his own house until he reached the woods. He ran until he could no longer hear Eugene behind him, until he could run no more. He stopped to look around, holding his aching chest, trying to catch his breath. Trees surrounded him, all light from the stars blocked by the thick canopy. He leaned against a broad oak until his breathing slowed. His ribs felt like they were sharp knives stabbing him with every breath. He listened to the sounds of the forest, realizing that he had no idea where he was. He turned to study the oak, searching for a way up into its branches. A large rock on the other side provided the boost he needed to reach a fork in the trunk. He scooted along the gently sloping arm until he reached another thick branch. He paused, searching the ground below for a landmark, but all he saw was darkness. Then he heard growling followed by a wild scream.

CHAPTER TWENTY

Night in the forest

March 23/24, 1965

Jessie, barely breathing, clung to the thick branch he was perched on. The growl sounded again, closer now. Jessie thought it was coming from his left, which he thought was east, but was so disoriented he couldn't be sure. A mosquito buzzed around his head, its insistent drone deafening in the silence. An owl hooted, then there was a rustle of wings. The air ruffled above him followed by the squeal of a mouse as it was scooped up in the predator's talons.

The Cole boys had camped out more times than Jessie could count, but this was different. Jessie's eyes darted from one shadow to the next, expecting danger to jump at him from all directions. He batted at the growing mist of mosquitos that seemed to sense there was fresh blood for the taking.

The panther screeched again, but farther away this time. Jessie briefly sagged onto the limb, his body relaxing the tiniest bit. The leaves around him fluttered as a soft wind passed through, causing him to shiver. Several minutes elapsed, in which all he heard were the familiar movements of night creatures - the crack of a twig, the crashing of a bush, the scampering of rats, and the occasional grunt of a wild hog. The sounds of the forest lulled him into an exhausted sleep.

The noise of anxious voices roused Jessie. Without opening his eyes, he turned his head in the direction the noise had come from.

"Are you sure you saw him run in here?" It was Eleanor's voice, tense and frightened.

"He had to. When I got to the end of the street, he was nowhere to be found," Eugene replied.

"Our fort is up that away."

At the sound of Max's grudging reply, Jessie pushed himself out of the tree's cradle, searching for any sign of light. The narrow beam of a flashlight bounced to his left, not fifteen feet away. He bit his lip, torn between anger toward his father and not wanting to worry his mother. He was about to call out to them when he stopped, worried he'd get in trouble for being here at all. Jessie watched the beam of light move farther away.

A few minutes later, a high-pitched whistle pierced the air followed by an expletive from Eugene. Jessie smiled, guessing that Max had led them to the fort.

"You boys built this?" Eleanor asked in disbelief.

"Yeah." Max's monosyllabic reply told Jessie just how angry his brother was about being out on this search. Max wasn't one to hold back when he had something to brag about and what they'd accomplished with the fort, Jessie thought, was certainly something to brag about.

"Nice place you got here," Eugene admired. "Why don't you check in the huts, make sure he isn't asleep?"

"You think he'd sleep through all the racket you've been making?" Max growled.

Jessie was enjoying being out of sight, but within earshot. He could picture Max's scowling face as he stomped through the fort.

"He's not here," Max reported.

"Oh, Gene, where could he be?" Eleanor wailed. "What if he's hurt?"

"He can take care of himself," Max asserted.

"I don't doubt that," Eugene agreed, "but I'd still feel better if we found him, especially after what Sam told us about those bums."

Max snorted. "Since when do you care?"

"Max," Eleanor admonished, but only half-heartedly.

"It's okay, Nora, I deserve it," Eugene sighed. "I can't expect them to forgive me right away."

"Or ever," Max barked.

"Why don't the two of you go back to the house in case he shows up there? I'll wander around a bit more and see if he got lost trying to find this place."

Max laughed. "More likely you'll get yourself lost."

"I was running the wilderness long before you were born," Eugene chuckled. "I think I know how to find my way around a bit of woods."

"I don't know, Gene."

"Come on, Mom. If he thinks he can take care of himself there's no need for us."

Jessie heard Max stomping, followed by the lighter steps of his mother, but the flashlight remained still. Jessie wasn't surprised by his brother's confidence in returning without any light; his loud movements would warn off any animals. When the sound of breaking twigs and crunching leaves faded, Jessie turned his attention back toward the fort.

The flickering light of a small fire replaced the flashlight beam. Jessie could hear the crack and pop of Eugene breaking limbs for the fire and whistling a tune. The song was slow and melancholic, with a vaguely familiar melody. Jessie strained to hear it, trying to place how he knew it.

"T'was Grace that brought us safe thus far, and Grace will lead us home." Eugene's rich baritone boomed through the still night.

Even with his lack of a church background, Jessie knew the song now, and couldn't believe what he was hearing.

Jessie climbed down from the tree, dropping to the ground with a faint thud, and remaining still as he tuned in to his surroundings. Eugene finished the song, applauded by the hum of cicadas. With painstaking effort, Jessie crept toward the fort. He hugged the wall until he reached the rear, where he waited, listening for any indication that Eugene sensed his presence. Slowly, Jessie rose from his crouch and peered in through one of the battle slits.

Eugene sat on a stump, his back to Jessie. The fire crackled and popped; the sharp aroma of pine rising into the air. Jessie watched the short, rhythmic movement of his father's arms and guessed him to be whittling. Jessie remembered the first time Max had taught him how to do that. They'd been in the old tree house on the island, hiding from Eugene, who had been on one of his binges and looking for trouble. Max had taken a beating that morning before the pair was able to escape to the woods.

"Here, you can have my old knife." Max had placed a small pocketknife in Jessie's palm, the wood worn smooth from years of use. "Pop gave it to me when I was about your age, before..." Max's voice trailed off and Jessie saw a frown tug at Max's lips.

"It's hard to believe he wasn't always like this," Jessie offered.

Max nodded and pulled another knife from his pocket. "Now, what you want to remember is to always pull the knife away from your body. You don't want to slip and stab yourself in the gut."

Jessie watched his brother shape a stick into a simple stake with a long, sharp point.

"Can you carve anything other than stakes?" Jessie asked.

"Course I can, but that is what you need to start out with, so you get used to the feel of the knife moving along the wood. You try."

Jessie chose a stick about three fingers thick and dug the knife into the bark, pulling the blade away from him, but it barely moved.

"You're cutting too deep. This is a slow process, peeling off a little at a time." Max took the knife and stick and showed Jessie again, angling the blade so that it shaved the first layer of bark, then repeating the step, removing the slightest bit more.

"Let me try again." Jessie grabbed for the knife, but Max pulled it back.

"You don't ever grab for a knife like that." Max gave his brother a stern look that reminded Jessie of their mother.

"Sorry," Jessie murmured.

Max handed the knife back and watched as Jessie tried again. Jessie furrowed his brow and slowly removed a thin strip of bark. He looked up and gave his brother a triumphant smile. Max nodded and indicated Jessie should finish his project. It took him ten minutes to create a point to Max's satisfaction.

"After you've done about a hundred more of those, I'll teach you how to make something like this." With a flourish, Max pulled a small deer from his pocket.

Jessie laughed. "You didn't make that."

"Better believe I did. Before I had you to hide out with I spent a lot of time out here alone. I've made a dozen of these animals."

Jessie reached for the figure, his fingers tracing the edges, marveling at how smooth and detailed it was. "Why do you suppose Daddy doesn't bother Sam and Ricky the way he does us?"

Max's face grew dark. "I wish I knew. Why don't you make a couple more stakes before we head back?"

"Well, well, well, what have we here?" The voice of a man on the other side of the fort wall jerked Jessie back to the present. Jessie rubbed his eyes, realizing for the first time how tired he was. He peered through the battle slit and saw Buster strolling through the front door.

Eugene didn't move, barely even looked up from his woodwork. "You don't want to come in here," he warned.

"What ya going to do about it, old man?" Buster moved closer to the fire.

"I don't want any trouble, but I'm going to have to ask you to leave."

Buster chuckled. "If you don't want any trouble, then I suggest you move on. I got a couple of buddies on their way."

The calculating way Buster spoke sent chills through Jessie. He knew he should run for help, but couldn't tear himself away from the scene playing out in front of him.

Eugene unfolded himself from the stump, his broad figure three inches taller than Buster. Jessie thought he saw Buster flinch for an instant, before a cruel grin slid across his lips.

"Don't say I didn't warn yo--" Buster drawled out his words, but the last was cut off by a piercing scream.

Jessie saw Buster, bent over, clutching something. Eugene returned to his stump, picked up a piece of wood, and startled whittling again. Buster straightened, and Jessie could see a wooden stake protruding from the bum's right forearm. His left hand clutched the injured limb, blood running between his fingers. Jessie had to bite back a cheer.

"I oughta," Buster growled, but stopped when Eugene looked up.

"You oughta get that taken care of," Eugene said, his knife still working. "I'd hate to have to put one in your other arm."

Jessie couldn't believe how calm and cool his father was, as if he did stuff like this every day. Buster didn't move for several minutes, but Eugene kept his head down, focused on his work. With a snarl, Buster turned and stumbled out of the open doorway.

CHAPTER TWENTY-ONE

Second Chances

March 24, 1965

At the first sign of light, Jessie crept from the fort, picking his way through the forest until he reached home. Pushing the door just wide enough to squeeze through, he tiptoed past the couch, down the hall to his closed bedroom door. He turned the knob; the squeaking of the hinges froze him in place, waiting to see if he had awoken anyone. He let out the breath he'd been holding when the house remained quiet. Not wanting to risk another squeak, he left the door ajar as he entered the room. Ricky sprawled across the tangled sheets of his bed, sleeping. Jessie crawled into his own bed, feeling each aching muscle as he sank into the mattress. It had never felt so good.

What seemed like a minute later, Ricky stood over him, shaking the bed. Jessie groaned and opened his eyes to find his brother fully dressed.

"What happened to you last night? Mama was worried sick. Does she know you got home?" Ricky's questions hit Jessie like a barrage of bullets.

Jessie pulled the blanket over his head. "Go away."

"Come on, tell me what happened."

"Nothing," Jessie mumbled.

Ricky tugged on the blanket, a tug of war ensuing, until it came free from Jessie's grip.

"I don't want to talk about it." Jessie grabbed for the edge of the blanket, but Ricky pulled it farther away. The bedroom door opened, drawing the attention of both boys. As Eleanor stepped into the room, Ricky dropped the blanket and put some distance between himself and Jessie, just in case.

"Go eat your breakfast," Eleanor instructed Ricky, who nodded and scurried out of the room.

Eleanor stood, hands on her hips, over Jessie's bed. Her eyes, etched by dark circles, captured him. "Do you have *any* idea how worried we've all been?"

Jessie couldn't tell if her voice trembled with rage or relief.

"I'm sorry," Jessie whispered, wishing the bed would swallow him.

"Where were you?"

"In the woods. I got lost." He wasn't sure if he wanted to tell her about the incident at the fort and why he hadn't let his father know he was there.

"You could have been hurt, out there all alone. Did you think about that?"

"It's not like I don't know how to take care of myself." The minute the words were out his mouth, Jessie knew they were a mistake. Eleanor's eyes narrowed to thin slits.

"I mean, I know how to avoid the wild animals, and..." Jessie tried to backpedal but his mother's look silenced him.

"You are grounded. Indefinitely." Eleanor turned on her heel and stormed out of the room, slamming the door behind her.

Jessie pulled the blanket back over his head and groaned. At least she hadn't mentioned him going to school today. He rolled onto his side with his back to the door, pain shooting through him from his bruised ribs. He gritted his teeth and closed his eyes. Despite the pain, sleep came quickly to his weary body.

"You sure managed to get yourself into a jam this time."

Jessie smiled at the voice behind him and rested the cane pole on his shoulder. He turned to see Gus Grissom walking toward him, carrying his own fishing pole.

"How did you know?"

Grissom chuckled. "This is a dream, so I know everything you know."

Jessie's smile faded. "Oh, yeah." He turned away from Grissom and cast his line into the St. John's River. The water reflected the deep blue of the sky like a perfect mirror. There wasn't a single ripple on this still day.

"Don't look so disappointed. I'm still a pretty cool guy." Grissom stepped up beside Jessie, set the end of his pole on the ground and released the hook that had been looped through one of the eyes. He wrapped a pink worm around the hook several times, making sure it was secure, then raised the pole and cast the line in a flowing arc, whizzing off the Zebco reel, into the middle of the river. He reeled in the slack and rocked back and forth on his heels a few times.

"You shouldn't be so hard on your old man." Grissom broke the silence between them.

Jessie could see Grissom out of the corner of his eye. The man gazed out over the water, turning the handle of the reel from time to time as the current of the river played with the line.

"Why not?" Jessie pulled in his own line and found the hook empty. Digging into a pail at his feet, he found a new worm and threaded it on the hook.

"We all make mistakes. Sometimes we get a second chance to make things right," Grissom paused and turned to look at Jessie, "and sometimes we don't."

The sadness in Grissom's voice made Jessie look up. The man he had built into his hero, all that he aspired to be, looked back at him, his eyes pleading.

"How do I get past everything he's done? Does one night of standing up for us make the past just disappear?"

Grissom shrugged. "That's a choice you have to make. You can cling to the past and all your hurt or you can let go and grab onto the future, all that is still to be written in your story."

"I thought I was chasing my future, with all the schoolwork I've been doing. Isn't that enough?"

"If all you want is to be an astronaut, it may be enough, but what about everything else in your life?"

Jessie thought a moment. "I have my brothers and my mom. What else is there?"

Grissom gave a hearty belly laugh. "You're still young. One day you'll be interested in girls and thinking about a family of your own."

"I guess." An image of Virginia floated through Jessie's mind. "That's a long ways off, though."

"Probably not as far off as you think." Grissom gave Jessie a knowing smile. "But you can't let other people into your heart as long as you are holding onto old grudges."

The pole in Grissom's hands jerked. He looked away from Jessie, focused on the dance of reeling in line, letting it out, reeling it in again, allowing the fish on the other end to tire itself without breaking the slender thread that connected man and fish.

It was exhilarating to watch and Jessie found himself holding his breath during the last minute of the struggle, until Grissom reached for the line and pulled a flopping bass onto the shore. The green and brown scales glinted in the sunlight like hundreds of colored diamonds.

Grissom held up his catch, twenty inches long and close to ten pounds. "What a beauty," Grissom exclaimed.

"Sure is. Another one that size and you can have a nice dinner," Jessie agreed.

"Nah, I'll let him go to fight another day." Grissom laid the fish out on the ground, placed his foot on the tail to keep it from flopping, and extricated the hook from its mouth. Cupping his hands around the fish, he crouched close to the water and gently set it free. Jessie watched the stunned animal float for a moment then swim off into the depths.

CHAPTER TWENTY-TWO

Eugene Comes Home

March 24, 1965

J essie rolled onto his back and opened his eyes. The fresh, earthy scent of the river lingered in his mind. He sat up and rubbed at his temples, reorienting himself. Footsteps sounded in the hallway. Jessie threw back his covers and walked to the door, opening it a crack, to peer out into the hallway. At the sight of Eugene carrying a battered blue suitcase, Jessie closed the door and leaned his back against it trying to control the swirl of emotions.

The footsteps passed by the cracked door and Jessie heard the plop of the suitcase on his mother's bed. Jessie crossed to the window and cranked it open. He was unclipping the screen when there was a knock on the bedroom door. Jessie turned to see it wide open, his father leaning against the frame.

"Going somewhere?" Eugene nodded toward the window.

Jessie took a step away from it, but didn't respond.

"We need to talk." Eugene sauntered to Ricky's bed and eased himself down. "You gave your mother quite a scare. I hope she hasn't had to worry like that the whole time I've been away."

Jessie's stomach roiled and he clenched his fists. "More like you're the one she's been worrying about."

Eugene spread his hands before him in a gesture of surrender. "I don't doubt that. I know I've made mistakes. Lord knows she's a good woman to have put up with it for so long, but that is between your mom and me. I'm here to talk about you."

"I'm sorry Mama was worried."

"She told me you and your brothers have been getting into a bunch of fights. Is that true?"

"A few. No big deal. We can take care of ourselves." Jessie moved to his own bed and scooted into the corner, farthest from his father.

"I know moving and starting a new school can be tough. I don't suppose I made it any easier, what with the way I handled the move and, well, you know." Eugene popped his knuckles then rubbed the back of his neck. "I know you don't want to hear how sorry I am, but it's true. I'm mighty sorry for all the trouble I've caused, not just this year. I don't know how my life got so out of control."

Jessie snorted. "Out of control is one way of putting it."

Eugene rose and paced the length of the small room. "I've cut you a bunch of slack here, Jessie, but you gotta cut me some too. I'm still your father."

"Some father," Jessie grumbled.

Eugene stopped pacing. The look of smoldering anger could have burned right through Jessie, but Jessie defiantly returned the gaze. It felt like an eternity before Eugene broke the connection and stomped out of the room. Jessie rewarded himself on winning that round by retrieving the Spanish goblet from the dress shoe he'd stuffed it in.

Sitting on the floor with his back against the bed, he turned the cup over and over, memorizing every detail. He tried to imagine the person it had once belonged to. Pictures from his history textbook of Spanish Conquistadors, in shining metal armor and thick beards, came to mind. He crawled to the end of his bed, where his schoolbooks were scattered, and grabbed the right one. He flipped through the pages several times before finding what he was looking for. The book talked about the traffic off the coast of Florida in the seventeenth and eighteenth centuries – English pirates, Spanish fleets, and cargo vessels from France. Jessie ran his finger under the words as he read about the storms, battles, and unseen sandbars that caused many ships to run aground, offering a bevy of loot like guns, iron tools, food, and treasure for the Indians. With each word, he grew more certain the goblet he'd found must be part of a larger treasure the Indians had recovered from one of these wrecks. He traded the book for the goblet and traced the twisting vine down the stem.

Ricky came barreling through the door before Jessie had a chance to hide the goblet.

"What's that?" Ricky dropped to the floor next to Jessie and grabbed for the cup.

Jessie pulled it back. "It's mine."

"I just wanted to see it," Ricky pouted.

"Well, it's none of your business." Jessie knew he would have shared this discovery with his brother under normal circumstances, but he was annoyed by the interruption.

Ricky stood with a loud hrmmph and stalked out of the room. Jessie returned his treasure to its hiding place and followed his brother to the living room. Ricky sat at one end of the couch with Eugene at the other, both watching television while Eleanor was busy in the kitchen.

Jessie touched his mother on the back. "Anything I can help with?"

Eleanor turned but didn't smile. "Set the table. Sam is tutoring and Max is working until six so it will just be the four of us."

Jessie pulled down plates and distributed them around the table. When the silverware and glasses were set out, he leaned against the refrigerator, at a loss for what to do next. Ricky and Eugene were laughing at something on television. The sound made Jessie's whole body tense. How could Ricky accept their father back so easily? Sure, he hadn't borne the brunt of Eugene's wrath the way Max and himself had, but he'd had to get a job to help pay the bills, had to give up things because of the hardships Eugene had brought on the family. How could he act like none of that had happened, like they were this big, happy family?

Jessie pushed himself away from the fridge and shoved his hands in his pockets. "How long 'til dinner?"

"About thirty minutes," Eleanor replied without looking at him.

"I'll be in my room." Jessie ambled down the hall before his mother could respond. The room felt small and cluttered when he stepped inside. He looked at the clothes, books, and shotgun shells haphazardly strewn around. He kicked a pair of sneakers to Ricky's side of the room, and tossed a t-shirt onto his brother's bed before tackling the items on his side. He stacked his books in a neat pile at the foot of the bed, stuffed the dirty clothes into the hamper they rarely used, refolded all of his clean clothes, found a box for the shotgun shells, and last of all made his bed.

He eyed the mess on Ricky's side, considered cleaning it up as well, but then thought better of it. Ricky was funny about anyone touching his stuff. One time he'd nearly broken Sam's arm when he had borrowed one of his slingshots.

Jessie flopped onto his newly made bed, staring at the ceiling, already despising the grounding punishment and the days of isolation awaiting him. How would he fill the hours after school, and especially the weekends, while his brothers went on with their own lives, playing in the woods, fishing in the river, even going to work? Jessie beat his fist against the bed several times, seething about this newest indignity he had to face because of his father.

CHAPTER TWENTY-THREE

Summer School Offer

April 6, 1965

When Jessie returned to school the following day, he asked Mr. Smith for extra math assignments and even asked Mrs. Matthews for ideas on books he might enjoy. Two weeks passed, with Jessie coming straight home from school, disappearing into his bedroom until dinner, then returning there until emerging the next morning. He immersed himself in the math work, barely noticing Ricky's coming and going, and found the problems getting easier.

"I'm impressed." Mr. Smith nodded in approval when Jessie turned in another assignment. "You're really getting the hang of this."

Jessie grinned. "I didn't know math could be fun, but these assignments are," Jessie's gaze roved around the room searching for the right word, "useful."

"Math does come in handy more often than we think. If you're interested, I'm teaching a physics class over the summer. Usually it's only for juniors, but I could make arrangements to get you in. You would learn a lot of things the engineers and astronauts are using, see if that career path is really what you want."

Jessie nearly hugged Mr. Smith. He couldn't believe his ears. "Yeah, that would be swell."

Mr. Smith patted him on the shoulder. "I'll get it set up."

"Oh, wait." Jessie felt like he'd been hit in the gut. "I have to check with my mama. I'm kind of grounded." He looked at the floor, embarrassed.

"No problem." Mr. Smith gave a small chortle. "Talk with her and let me know, but I have a feeling if you ask her if you can take a summer school class she'll probably say yes."

Other students were filtering in before the bell rang and Jessie took his seat in the back of the room. Virginia was one of the last to arrive, out of breath and her face flushed. Her gaze flitted to Jessie as she crossed the front of the room and slid into her seat. Jessie watched her smooth her skirt and run a hand through her curly hair. When Mr. Smith started speaking, Jessie dragged his thoughts away from Virginia, focusing on the equations on the blackboard.

After class, Jessie gathered his books, but hesitated when he noticed Virginia dawdling at her desk. They'd talked a few times since meeting in church, mostly about homework assignments or the cafeteria food. Taking a deep breath, Jessie moved toward her. Their eyes met the moment she looked up from her desk. The brilliant blue he'd always seen before appeared dull and reddened, though, as if she'd been crying.

"What's wrong?" Jessie stepped closer, resisting the temptation to brush a stray strand of hair off Virginia's forehead.

Virginia shook her head and dropped her gaze to her books. She shuffled them into size order before lifting them into the crook of her arm.

"You've been crying."

"It's just Alan." Virginia started for the door.

Jessie reached for her arm, causing her to turn to face him. "What did he do to you?" Jessie growled through clenched teeth.

Alarm leapt into Virginia's eyes. Jessie let go of her arm and stepped back.

"I didn't mean to scare you. I.. if.. if Alan hurt you..." Jessie's whole body was shaking.

"I don't want you to get in another fight with him. He's so big." Virginia's voice trembled.

"Everything all right?" Mr. Smith approached them.

"Fine." Virginia spun around to face the teacher. "We were just leaving."

Jessie followed her out of the classroom. "You could tell Mr. Smith if Alan was messing with you. He's cool for a teacher."

"It'll be fine." Virginia stopped abruptly. When he turned to her, she now stood rigid, her gaze going right through him. Jessie looked around for what had grabbed her attention. Alan was across the courtyard, pantomiming a rude act and pointing at Virginia.

Enraged, Jessie dropped his books and began to sprint for the boy. Alan laughed and started toward Jessie, who was preparing for the collision. Jessie then felt something grab at his shirt and pull him back. He fought, swinging his arms and twisting, until his arms were pinned.

"Let it go," Mr. Smith's calm words whispered in Jessie's ear.

Jessie fought a moment longer until Virginia came to stand beside him and took one of his hands. Slowly, Mr. Smith released his grip and Jessie stepped away.

"I saw what he did," Mr. Smith assured Jessie. "I'll take care of it. You two get on to class."

Virginia gave Jessie's hand a squeeze and a gentle tug. With a last look at Alan, that he hoped conveyed the disgust he felt toward the boy, he walked away.

The rest of the day, Jessie couldn't stop plotting ways he could destroy Alan. He was sorry that he and Max had never followed through on the plan to set the bully up for murder, using the skull they'd found. Even if the rap hadn't stuck, at least Alan would have been subject to scrutiny and humiliation for a few weeks. Maybe it would have put an end to his high and mighty reign over the school.

The final bell of the day rang, and Jessie raced out of the classroom. He weaved through the crush of laughing and talking students, milling about outside the classrooms, and searched for Virginia's face.

Students jostled each other as they made their way onto the waiting buses; smoke belching from their tail pipes. Jessie passed the last bus with not a glimpse of Virginia and his shoulders slumped.

When the rumble of the busses finally faded into the distance, the campus turned eerily quiet. Jessie kicked a stone, it's rolling sound the only noise to be heard. He paused at the door to Mr. Smith's classroom and peered in, but it was empty. Would Mr. Smith really do anything about Alan's obscene action? Maybe Alan would get detention or be suspended for a couple of days, but he deserved much worse.

"Watch it," a voice cried.

Jessie came to an abrupt stop, his face just inches from Virginia's. "I'm sorry," he stammered, taking a step back.

Virginia crumpled up a paper towel and tossed it into a nearby garbage can. "Do you always kick rocks at girls?"

"No. I wasn't. I mean, I didn't know anyone was still here." Jessie knew he sounded like an idiot and felt sweat beading on his forehead.

Virginia giggled.

Jessie dared to raise his gaze from the ground to be rewarded with a flirtatious grin.

"Can I walk you home?" he asked.

"You don't need to do that."

"I know, but I'd like to."

Virginia flipped her hair back over her shoulder and started toward the back of the school. They walked in silence through the grass beside the train tracks for several blocks. Jessie didn't have the slightest idea what he could talk about that Virginia might find interesting. When he could no longer bear the silence he ran ahead a few paces and jumped up onto the railway.

"What are you doing?" Virginia cried.

Jessie danced a jig on the narrow steel beam until he saw Virginia suppress a smile.

"Are you crazy? Get down from there before a train comes."

"Aw, don't worry about that. I'll feel the vibrations long before the train gets here. My brothers and I do this all the time." Jessie repeatedly jumped from one side of the track to the other, sometimes spinning in the air.

"Now you're just showing off." Virginia giggled, that tinkling sound Jessie had longed to hear again.

"Come on up." Jessie reached a hand out to Virginia. She shook her head and looked away shyly. Jessie hopped from one foot to the other, swinging his hands in large circles. Virginia glanced up at him and doubled over in laughter.

"You look ridiculous," she managed to get out when her laughs had died away.

Jessie didn't care how stupid he looked. He'd made her smile and that was all that mattered. He stepped off the track and stood close enough to smell her hair. It smelled of roses and fresh rain.

"Am I embarrassing you?"

Virginia suppressed another smile and started walking. Feeling like he'd conquered a giant, Jessie hurried to catch up.

CHAPTER TWENTY-FOUR

Heart Attack

April 6, 1965

"I just realized, I don't know where you live," Jessie said after another block.

"Over on Pritchard."

Jessie nodded.

"It's not out of your way is it?"

"Nah, I only live a few blocks over." Jessie glanced at his watch. He would usually be close to home by now, and he was still a mile away.

"Do you really think Mr. Smith will deal with Alan?" Virginia's worried question broke into Jessie's thoughts.

"He's a good guy. I trust him to do something about it, but I don't think it will be anywhere near what the creep deserves." Jessie glanced at Virginia out of the corner of his eye and saw her chewing on her hair. "Did he do something else? Is that why you were crying?"

"I don't want to talk about it. Tell me something about you. You moved here from Merritt Island, right?"

"Yeah, government wanted our land to expand the missile program." Jessie's face grew hot at the memory of their last day there.

"I saw an article in the newspaper a couple years ago about how upset people were about being forced to move. I can't imagine how hard that must have been, leaving behind everything you've ever known."

"We didn't have much choice. Mama took it better than the rest of us. I didn't know where we would go when we got kicked out, but she'd already arranged a rental and even moved some of our things."

"Didn't your Dad help?"

Jessie chortled. "Nah, Pop had to be drug out." Jessie noticed Virginia's startled look and knew she'd heard the bitterness in his words. "It's been okay, though. We've managed to find some neat places to hang out here. Nothing like being close to the beach, but not bad."

"You get along well with your brothers. That's nice. I wish my brother wasn't such a pain."

"I didn't know you had a brother."

"He's younger, only seven, and he drives me crazy."

"Mine do too, sometimes."

"You'd never know it, watching you guys together at school."

"Really? So, you've been watching us?" Jessie felt an excited flutter in his stomach.

Virginia blushed, her cheeks nearly as red as her hair. "It's hard not to watch when a couple of you are fighting with Alan and his goons."

Rebekah Lyn

Jessie dipped his head, unsure if he should be embarrassed or proud. Were he and his brothers known around school solely as the kids who fought a lot?

Virginia slowed and waved her hand toward a house. "This is me."

They stood in front of a robin's egg blue cottage with crisp white shutters. Neatly trimmed boxwoods ran along the front of the house behind cheery red and white petunias. A white Chevy Impala was parked in the driveway and a small red bike leaned against the corner of the house. The front door opened and a slim, brown Chihuahua bounded out, his bark belying his petite size. Virginia knelt down to scratch the dog's ears.

A woman stepped out of the house and greeted Virginia. Jessie recognized her as the woman from church, Virginia's Aunt Mary. He raised a hand to wave before turning back to Virginia.

"Would you like to come in for a glass of iced tea?" Virginia stood up and the dog scurried back to the front door.

"I should get going." Jessie rubbed his arm several times, surprised at the clamminess of his palm.

"Thank you for walking me home." She met his eyes, shyly.

Jessie gave an aw-shucks grin. "No problem."

"I'll see you tomorrow."

"Yeah." Jessie jogged back down the road until he was out of sight of the house, then slowed for the remaining six blocks. He thought about Mr. Smith's summer school offer. *Who would have thought I would be excited by the idea of summer school,* he marveled to himself. *Max is going to think I'm crazy, but at least Sam should be supportive. Maybe Mama will be so proud of me she'll shorten my restriction.*

This last thought made his step a bit lighter. He took the front porch steps two at a time and breezed into the house. In the kitchen he came to a screeching halt at the sight of his mother, hands on her hips, foot tapping impatiently against the floor.

"You should have been home twenty minutes ago." Her eyes bore right through Jessie.

"I...there was—"

Eleanor's look of disappointment cut him off. "I don't want to hear any excuses. You know you are supposed to come straight home from school. Have you been goofing off other days when I'm not here?"

"No, ma'am." Jessie knew he should drop his head in submission, but he held her gaze. "I was helping someone."

"And who might that have been?"

"You remember the redheaded girl who sat in front of us at church a few weeks ago?" Jessie paused and Eleanor nodded. His mouth was dry and he swallowed hard. "This guy was being mean to her all day. When I was leaving, you know I go through the back of the school, I ran into Virginia and offered to walk her home, to make sure he didn't mess with her anymore."

Eleanor's face softened a tiny bit. "And where does this Virginia live?"

"On Pritchard. I came home as fast I could once I left her house. I promise."

Eleanor removed her hands from her hips and reached for the coffee pot, pouring herself a cup. "I'll let it slide this time." She took a sip of the coffee, her face crinkling in distaste. Setting down the cup she looked at the clock across the room.

Jessie scratched his chin, trying to gauge his mother's mood. Should he tell her about Mr. Smith's offer now?

"There's something else." He hesitated, watching his mother's face, but she gave away nothing. "Mr. Smith, my math teacher, he offered to get me into a physics class he's teaching over the summer. It's supposed to be for juniors, but he thought I might find it interesting, help me decide if I really want to go into the space program."

"Are you asking permission to go to summer school?" Eleanor's eyes widened with surprise.

"Yes, ma'am."

"Well, I'll be," Eleanor exclaimed. She soon had Jessie in a tight hug. "I never thought you'd be volunteering for more school work."

Eleanor loosened her grip and held Jessie at arm's length, her face beaming. The moment was broken by the sound of coughing and heavy footfalls on the front porch. The front door opened and Eugene stumbled in, one hand on his chest, the other covering his mouth, as he continued to cough.

Eleanor raced to his side, easing him down to the couch, brushing wispy brown hair off his face.

"Jessie, bring a glass of water," she called.

Jessie stood rooted to the floor, unable to pull his gaze from his father's flushed cheeks. Unbelievable. His father had ruined the moment, probably drunk again, choking on a last gulp of vodka before entering the house. He felt his hands curl into fists and his legs tense.

"Jessie!" Eleanor yelled, her eyes frantic when they met his.

Jessie stepped to the sink, turned on the faucet; the water was tepid, but he didn't care. Eleanor took the glass and tipped it to Eugene's lips. He tried to take a sip, but blew it out in another fit of coughing.

"My…chest," Eugene whispered in between coughs.

"Jessie, dial the operator. Tell them we need an ambulance."

Eleanor was crying now; Jessie felt a tingle of fear streak up the back of his neck. He grabbed the phone from the wall and dialed. When the operator answered, Jessie didn't know what to say.

"Is anyone there?" the operator asked after several seconds of silence.

"My dad. He can't…he's coughing…his chest," Jessie stammered.

"Calm down, tell me your name," the operator coaxed in a soothing tone.

"Jessie."

"Tell me what's happening with your father, Jessie. Did he choke on something?"

Jessie shrugged.

"Jessie, I need you to talk to me so I can help."

"I don't know. He came in the house coughing and holding his chest."

"Is he having trouble breathing?"

Jessie craned his neck, trying to get a good look at Eugene. "I think so."

"Is your mother home?"

"Yes, she's with him."

"I'm going to send an ambulance. Can you tell me your address?"

Jessie rattled off the address and hung up the phone, after the operator had repeated it and assured him help was on the way. Jessie stayed by the phone, his hand still gripping the receiver, watching the struggle in the living room. When the coughing subsided, Eleanor tried to give Eugene some water again. He took a tiny swallow, gasped for breath, and sputtered, trying to suppress another cough. In a matter of minutes, strident sirens covered Eleanor's sobs and Eugene's labored breathing.

A knock on the door pulled Eleanor from her husband's side. She threw the door wide, allowing two men to enter. One of them carried a box, which he set on the floor while the other unbuttoned Eugene's shirt and pressed a stethoscope to his chest.

Eugene's face was ashen, his eyes closed, sweat running down his face. Jessie couldn't remember a time when his father had looked this bad before, even at his drunkest. The paramedics' lips moved, but Jessie couldn't hear their words. He felt like he was watching a silent movie. One of them wore a grim expression as he tied a band around Eugene's arm and thumped it several times before inserting a needle. A long tube coiled from it to a bag of clear liquid. The paramedic handed this to Eleanor and showed her how to hold it above Eugene's head, then the paramedics raced out the door, returning seconds later with a gurney.

They got it next to the couch, where they worked together to move Eugene onto its clean white sheet. One of them took the bag from Eleanor and hung it on a hook on the gurney, and then they carefully wheeled Eugene out the door. Eleanor followed, mascara tracks running down her cheeks. Jessie stepped to the door and watched his mother climb into the back of the ambulance. She glanced at Jessie as the door swung shut, an image that then stuck in his mind.

CHAPTER TWENTY-FIVE

The Hospital

April 6, 1965

As the ambulance pulled away, Jessie shut the front door and sank onto the couch, realizing the minute his rear hit the cushion it was right where Eugene had been sitting. He sprang back up and moved to the rocking chair Eleanor usually occupied. He rocked the chair back and forth in a mesmerizing rhythm.

Jessie didn't know how long he had sat there, dazed and appalled, when he felt a hand on his shoulder. He turned his head to see Sam standing next to him.

"What's wrong with you? I've been talking to you for almost five minutes." Sam removed his hand from Jessie's shoulder and dropped to the couch, slouching back into the corner.

Jessie flinched at the sight of Sam on the couch. He hadn't realized before how much his brother looked like Eugene, but in that position the resemblance was eerie.

"Don't sit there," Jessie said softly, dropping his gaze to the floor.

"Why not?" Sam leaned forward, elbows on his knees.

"I think Pop might be dead."

"What?" Sam leapt to his feet. "Where's Mama?"

When Jessie didn't answer, Sam wandered through the house, returning only a minute later and gazing out the window. "The car's out front. Is she at the neighbor's house?"

Jessie shook his head. "They went to the hospital."

Sam stepped in front of Jessie, grabbed him by the shoulders and shook. Jessie looked up into his brother's panicked face. Sam kneeled before him and squeezed Jessie's arms.

"What happened?"

After Jessie stitched together the events of the afternoon, Sam went to the phone.

"Uncle Tommy, it's Sam. Dad's been taken to the hospital. Can you take Jessie and me up there?"

There was quiet while Sam listened. Jessie went back to rocking, his vision blurring.

"Come on, Jessie."

Jessie struggled to focus until he recognized Uncle Tommy. Jessie felt unsteady on his feet and leaned against his uncle. Jessie's feet moved mechanically out the front door, across the porch, to his uncle's new Ford. The paint was still a shiny black, as clean as the day it had been driven off the lot. Jessie felt a rush of air as Sam ran past them and opened the back door. Sam ducked into the backseat and Jessie followed.

Jessie leaned his head back and closed his eyes. He was so very tired. The car backed up, turned, then pulled forward with a jerk. Jessie dozed off, but dreams of

Eugene's ashen face and retching coughs woke him with a start. He shook his head as if that would free him of the memory. Looking out the window, Jessie recognized the shops of downtown Titusville whizzing past.

They reached the hospital as an ambulance careened to a stop at the emergency room doors. Jessie knew it couldn't be the same rig that had collected his father, but he watched intently as a paramedic jumped out of the back. A chorus of guttural screams filled the air as the gurney was unloaded, the woman on it clutching the sheet in tight fists.

"Looks like someone's having a baby," Uncle Tommy commented as he ushered Jessie and Sam across the parking lot.

Jessie noticed the smile that played at his uncle's lips. Uncle Tommy and Pop couldn't be more different, Jessie thought. His uncle's face always looked soft and loving, the crinkles around his green eyes proof of his perpetual smile. His hands were smooth and neatly manicured, with the occasional paper cut from his job at the insurance office, but Jessie was sure they'd never been raised in anger toward Sally or Tommy Jr.

When they entered the hospital, they were greeted by a bright-faced teenage girl wearing a red and white-striped vest over a white shirt, red hair pulled back in a ponytail.

"Jessie? Oh my goodness, what's wrong?" she asked.

It took Jessie a moment to recognize the girl as Virginia. When he did, he straightened, stepping away from Uncle Tommy and flashing what he hoped was a charming smile. Virginia's gaze flitted from Jessie to Sam and to their Uncle Tommy.

"I believe my brother was brought in earlier this afternoon, Eugene Cole. Can you tell me where we might find him?" Uncle Tommy addressed the middle-aged woman next to Virginia whose horn-rimmed glasses hung from a chain around her neck. The lady slid the glasses up her nose and flipped through several pages.

"I don't see any new admissions. He may still be in the emergency room. It's right down—" the lady was turning to point when Virginia stepped around the desk.

"I can show them. Follow me." Virginia walked at a brisk clip that Jessie hurried to keep up with. They passed a cafeteria where the murmur of conversation wafted into the hall along with the smell of roast beef and broccoli. Jessie felt his stomach rumble and wondered what time it was.

Virginia led them to a desk and caught the attention of a man whose head was buried in a thick blue binder. "Victor, can you tell me if Eugene Cole is still down here?"

Victor set the binder aside and ran his finger down a list. "Yes, he's in bed thirteen, but the kids can't go back there."

Uncle Tommy looked from Jessie to Sam. "Will you boys be okay out here for a few minutes? As soon as I have information I'll come right back."

"I can stay with them, Mr. Cole," Virginia offered.

Victor stepped out from behind the desk. "Follow me."

"Why don't we sit down?" Virginia led Sam and Jessie to three vinyl chairs the color of split pea soup that made a farting sound when sat on. Virginia giggled and blushed at the noise.

"Jessie, are you okay? You look, funny." Virginia sat between the two boys and had to turn slightly to look at Jessie.

Jessie gazed into her blue eyes and thought about how they reminded him of the St. John's River on a clear day.

"I think Pop's dead," Jessie whispered.

"Oh, no, he's not dead." Virginia's voice was filled with such tenderness it reached through the swirl of regret and fear Jessie was battling. "Victor wouldn't have taken your uncle back there if your dad was dead."

She slipped her hand into Jessie's, her fingers lacing with his as if they were meant to be there. Jessie looked down at their entwined hands and felt something stir within him.

"But he was so gray," Jessie murmured. He gazed out the window at the construction underway to expand the hospital. Scaffolding rose above the level of the window and hammers could be heard beating on metal.

The click-clack of running heels caught Jessie's attention. He looked toward the hallway where his uncle had disappeared and saw Eleanor running toward them. She threw her arms open and cried, "Boys!"

Jessie and Sam stood and rushed to meet her. Eleanor wrapped her arms around them both and buried her face between their heads. She stroked their backs for a long minute before lifting her head and looking at each of them.

CHAPTER TWENTY-SIX

Third Chances

April 6, 1965

Eleanor walked the boys back to where they had been sitting. Jessie looked around for Virginia, but she had disappeared. His hand still tingled where her fingers had held his. He looked at Eleanor. Although her face still bore the tracks of mascara, her eyes were no longer wild and frightened, but tired and maybe a bit relieved.

"I called the house, but you didn't answer. Are you okay, Jessie?" She caressed the back of his head, twirling her fingers in the longer hair at the nape of his neck.

"He was sitting in the rocking chair when I got home. I don't think he'd moved from there or heard anything since you left. What happened?" Sam asked.

"My poor, sweet boy," Eleanor murmured. "It was terrible." Eleanor told Sam about Eugene's traumatic entrance into the house, how they couldn't get him to stop coughing, and leaving in the ambulance.

"Wow, and Jessie saw all of that?" Sam looked at his little brother.

Eleanor nodded. "When we got here, they did an electro cardiogram, drew some blood, put him on oxygen, and did another test, I don't remember what they called it. They don't think he had a heart attack, but something called angina. They're going to keep him overnight for observation. We were just getting ready to go to his room when Tommy showed up, so I sent them on. Would you like to see him?"

Sam stood right away, but Jessie didn't move. He looked from his brother to his mother, and with a sigh he stood as well.

"Sure, which room?" Jessie mumbled.

"Thirty-seven." Eleanor led them down several halls, following signs until they reached the right room. The scents of antiseptic and bleach assaulted Jessie as he followed her into the room.

Uncle Tommy sat in a chair next to Eugene's bed. Jessie retreated into the far corner of the room, near the head of his father's bed, taking shallow breaths in through his mouth. Jessie glanced at his father, still pale, a plastic tube wrapped around his face with two prongs going up his nose. A mess of emotions tore through his gut as he watched the sheet rise and fall in a steady rhythm. Eleanor leaned close to Eugene's head, gently brushed her fingers through his hair, and spoke quietly. Jessie guessed she was telling Eugene that the boys were here. His eyes fluttered open and roamed the room until catching sight of Jessie.

Eugene tried to raise his hand. Jessie watched it move in slow motion, rising only a couple of inches off the bed before falling back like a lead weight. Eugene tried again, but this time holding his hand up those few inches, long enough to crook a finger and motion for Jessie to come closer. Jessie shook his head, pushing farther back into the corner, wishing he could melt into the wall.

"It's all right, Jessie." Eleanor waved her son over.

Jessie took a hesitant step forward, then another, until he stood a foot from the bed. His body was rigid, ready to jump back should Eugene reach out to him. He looked up at his mother, who gave him an encouraging nod.

"I'm...sorry... you...had...to...see...that." Eugene's words were hoarse, spread out by deep breaths.

Jessie didn't respond, didn't look into his father's face, but kept his gaze glued to the hand that was already bruising around the needle inserted there.

"Is there anything you need?" Sam stepped forward, placing a hand on his father's foot. Jessie saw the bed move slightly under the heaviness of Sam's touch.

Eugene cleared his throat. "No, son, and I don't want you to worry." He rasped then swallowed hard.

"Don't talk, Gene. You need to rest." Eleanor caressed his forehead and kissed it lightly.

"Why don't I take the kids home?" Uncle Tommy stood, placing a hand on Eleanor's back.

"Thank you, Tommy." She looked at her watch. "Oh no," she gasped. "Max and Ricky should be home from work soon. They don't know what's happened."

"Don't worry. I'll stay at the house until they get home and explain everything. Give me your keys and Donna and I will drive your car up here."

Jessie watched his mother reach for her purse before realizing she'd left it at the house. "Sam, will you give your uncle the keys when you get home?"

"Yes, ma'am." Sam moved around the bed and gave his mother a hug then leaned down and awkwardly hugged Eugene.

Jessie shuffled around the bed without acknowledging his father. Once he was clear of the bed, he rushed out the door and hurried down the hall. He barreled past an elderly man with a walker, nearly knocking him over.

"Watch it!" the man called.

"I'm sorry, sir." Jessie heard Uncle Tommy apologizing behind him.

Jessie continued on, past the front desk and outside into the warm night. At a hedge of bushes he leaned over and puked. He heaved again and again until there was nothing left, then still bent over the bushes, he started to cry.

He felt an arm slip over his shoulders and gently lead him away to a concrete bench. A tissue was handed to him, and he wiped his mouth and nose. His t-shirt clung to the sweat on his back. He watched a trail of ants scurry around his feet, some carrying pieces of a broken candy bar. Then he noticed a pair of well-polished Mary Janes disturb the ants. He looked up to see Virginia, a plastic cup of water held out to him.

He hated that she was seeing him so weak and childish. He wished she would go away, but reached for the cup and drank it down in one long gulp.

"Thanks," he mumbled.

Virginia took the empty cup back. Her lips moved as if to speak, but Jessie looked away. A second later, he heard her footsteps retreating.

CHAPTER TWENTY-SEVEN

Telling Max & Ricky

April 8, 1965

T he house was dark when Uncle Tommy pulled into the driveway. Jessie followed Sam and his uncle in, but didn't stop in the living room. He went straight to the bathroom, stripped out of his clothes and jumped into the shower. He scrubbed his body fiercely, as if doing so would erase all that had happened. When he stepped out and wrapped a towel round himself, his arms and stomach were red.

In his bedroom, he pulled on a clean t-shirt and underwear and crawled into bed. He could hear the television playing the theme song for *Wild, Wild West*. Max and Ricky should be home in ten minutes, Jessie thought.

Just as he was drifting into an uneasy sleep, haunted by his father's hacking gasps, the front door opened to the sound of Max and Ricky laughing. Jessie held his breath as the sound stopped abruptly. The television was turned off and Jessie pictured Uncle Tommy standing up from the couch, asking the boys to sit down. Sam would be sitting by quietly, letting their uncle do all the talking. Uncle Tommy's words were too soft for Jessie to make out, he could only hear the steady pace at which his uncle spoke, probably calm and matter of fact like always. When Uncle Tommy finished, there was silence, then the television came back to life. Slowly he let out his breath, releasing muscles he hadn't realized were tense. Footsteps came down the hallway and the bedroom door opened.

Ricky didn't turn on the light, but crept to the edge of Jessie's bed. "Are you awake?"

Jessie rolled over to face the wall, dragging the sheet over his hunched shoulders.

"I'm sorry you were here alone for that. I didn't need to pick up the extra shift today," Ricky whispered. When Jessie didn't answer, Ricky left, closing the door behind him.

In the darkness, Jessie chewed on the collar of his t-shirt, his fingers slowly rubbing the fabric over his teeth. He listened until Uncle Tommy's car started, a low and steady purr, followed by the choking and sputtering of Eleanor's before the engine finally caught, the exhaust releasing a mighty pop. The engine noise faded down the road and Jessie heard the door to Max and Sam's room open and shut. Still the television played. A gentle rain started to patter on the window, a slow steady beat that lulled Jessie to sleep.

In his dream, Jessie walked along the beach, the surf rushing over his feet and swirling around his ankles. Sandpipers played tag with the foaming water, running away as it flooded toward them, then chasing it back out into the depths. Jessie could smell the tang of salt on the air as he inhaled deeply, feeling at home.

To his right, the dunes were covered in thick palmetto bushes and sea oats bent by the light breeze. A shadow fell on the ground beside him, and Jessie looked over his shoulder to see Gus Grissom jogging toward him. Jessie stopped, waiting for him. Barely winded, the astronaut stopped in front of Jessie and offered a lopsided grin.

"Nice of you to invite me back. I wasn't sure if you would after our last meeting." Grissom pulled at his gray t-shirt, fanning himself with it.

Jessie shrugged and the pair walked down the beach.

"You've had a rough day," Grissom broke the silence first. "You want to talk about it?"

"I don't know, Mr. Grissom."

"Call me Gus. As often as we meet, and since you are creating me, I think we can be less formal."

Jessie smiled. "A'right, Gus. What was it like orbiting the earth?"

"It was amazing," Grissom admitted, his face breaking into a grin, "but we aren't here to talk about me."

"Can't you just tell me a little bit?" Jessie begged.

"Maybe after you tell me about your day."

Jessie sighed. "How can a guy go from being the hero in a girl's eyes to the biggest loser and in just a few hours?"

"I'm sure that's not the case. What happened?"

"Virginia is the prettiest girl in school. I don't know why some of the other boys are so mean to her. I'd like to wring Alan's neck for making her cry."

"Some boys do stupid things to the girls they like, even some grown men do those same stupid things."

"Eww, no way Alan likes her. You don't make a girl cry if you like her. Even if he does, she thinks he's a creep. She let me walk her home today."

"Is that the hero part you were talking about?"

"I don't know. I went after Alan at school. I would have beaten him bad if my math teacher hadn't stopped me. Maybe that's why she let me walk her home. But then, tonight, I was such a mess."

Grissom walked on without comment.

"I thought Pop was going to die today," Jessie spoke just above a whisper, "and I wasn't sure if I wanted him to live or not."

"That's tough," Grissom agreed.

Jessie bent down to collect a perfect sand dollar. He held it in the palm of his hand, the edges extending onto his fingers and wrist. He traced the flower-like shape in the center several times.

"I hate him, but when he was choking, I felt so scared. When the paramedics loaded him into the ambulance, one of them looked back at me. His eyes told me he didn't think Pop was going to make it. Instead of fear, I felt a relief that finally it was over. Mama wouldn't have to worry about him and his drinking anymore. But then I saw Mama's face through the back window as they drove away. She looked at me, like she knew what I was thinking, but instead of being mad at me, she just looked sad."

Jessie tossed the sand dollar out into the surf.

"I'm not surprised you had such conflicting thoughts." Grissom paused to pick up a small conch shell, causing Jessie to stop as well. When Grissom straightened, he held up the shell for Jessie to see.

"You know why there are so many of these in different sizes washing up on the beach?"

"When the conch outgrows one shell it sheds it and grows a new one," Jessie replied.

Grissom nodded. "We don't outgrow our skin, but we do outgrow our clothes, and we outgrow our toys, and we even outgrow our thoughts and habits. You've had a terrible relationship with your father for most of your life. It's only been a few weeks that he's been back in your home, trying to show you that he has outgrown his old habits."

Jessie snorted. "You mean the drinking and beating?"

"Now listen," Grissom coaxed. "People do change. Sometimes people change because they have a turning point moment in their lives, a near-death experience, losing something important to them, but more often than not, the change coincides with finding faith in God, and a real desire to turn their lives into something that is pleasing to Him."

"Eugene didn't find God," Jessie interjected.

"Do you know that? Have you had a real conversation with him since he came home?"

Jessie scratched the back of his neck and rubbed his hand up and around his head then started walking again, forcing Grissom to follow.

"Whether or not he's found God isn't the point. The point is, you're in a period of transition. Everything in your life is changing at a rapid pace. You're getting interested in school and what you'll do when you graduate. Girls, especially one, are becoming important to you too. You're watching Max, as the school year winds down, and wondering what he'll do, if he'll stay in the house or go out on his own. Yet deep down, despite all of these changes, there is still a little boy who used to enjoy going fishing with his daddy, and roasting marshmallows over a campfire in the woods."

Grissom stopped and turned to Jessie, waiting until their eyes met. "That little boy and the man you are becoming collided in those minutes you watched your father struggle. Now you have a chance to meld those two parts of you together. You can soften your heart towards your father, give him the benefit of the doubt that he has changed, or you can bury that little boy deep inside, beneath all your anger and bitterness, hoping he won't ever surface again."

CHAPTER TWENTY-EIGHT

Extravehicular Activity

June 3, 1965

Early morning summer heat greeted Jessie and his brothers as they stepped out of the house. Jessie ran his hand over the short fuzz on his head, still entranced by the way it felt like a Brillo pad. The boys had gotten buzz cuts the previous weekend to help beat the heat.

"Where are we going to meet for the launch?" Jessie directed at Max, who carried a small radio in his back pocket.

"As soon as you get out of class, we'll meet at the entrance to the school." Max swept his brothers with his gaze, like a general assessing his men for battle, eyes steely with purpose and determination.

"I can't believe we're finally going to get our man out to walk in space. The Russians may have beat us again, getting that Leonov guy out on a space walk in March, but I can feel it. We're about to take the lead," Jessie crowed.

"I don't know," Sam warned. "The Russian space program has a big head start on us."

"Not so big, They only got a man in space a month before us."

"Yes, but they are now nearly three months ahead of us with their spacewalk. Who knows what they have planned next."

"Hrmph." Jessie glared at his brother and walked even faster.

The school grounds were all abuzz when the brothers arrived. They joined a group of boys who greeted them.

"Did you hear?" One of the boys asked. "They found a dead body out by the railroad tracks."

"Near Bum's Cave?" Max inquired.

"No, it was closer to the woods than the tracks," another boy said.

"Does anyone know who it was?" Jessie's interest was piqued, thinking of those bums, Buster and Joe. He'd never told his brothers about Eugene's run in with Buster at the fort, and since he'd been grounded he hadn't been back. He wasn't even sure if his brothers had been out there. Between work and school there wasn't much free time anymore.

"I ain't heard anyone say who it was. Look, there's Pete Murphy. I bet he knows." The group of boys moved toward a beanpole of a boy with thick brown hair and equally thick glasses, tape wrapped around the bridge.

"Hey, Pete! What'd you hear about the dead man?" Max spoke for the whole group who had gathered around, eager to get the story.

Pete shrugged. "Pa left early this morning. I guess he was called out to work the scene."

Jessie could feel the crowd deflate at Pete's words. What good was it having the kid of a cop in class if he couldn't tell them any of the juicy details, seemed to be the feeling they all had.

The crowd scattered and Jessie drifted off to class, still thinking about Buster and Joe, wondering if the dead man was one of them, and if so, who had done them in.

The hours before the *Gemini 4* launch dragged, broken only by eager questions as everyone sought updates between classes. Jessie wished his classes were near Max, maybe he'd been allowed to turn on his radio.

When the time finally arrived, he jogged across the parking lot, joining Max and Ricky who were already waiting at the entrance. He looked over his shoulder and saw Sam making his way toward them as well.

Jessie was thankful his high school was located on US 1, almost directly across the river from the Space Center. The highway was filled with cars and the banks of the river were crammed with spectators. The boys wormed their way to the front and Max pulled the radio from his pocket. Several people around them cheered when he turned it on. Max gave a mock bow to the crowd and turned the volume up as high as it would go. With rapt attention, the boys and the crowd near them listened to a commentator from Houston control provide a rundown of the morning's activities of astronauts Jim McDivitt and Edward White, advising that things were actually running ahead of schedule and the weather looked perfect for a launch.

Seagulls whirled overhead, spying on the people below, looking for their next easy meal. Jessie scanned the crowd, searching for anyone who might have a sandwich or apple in their hand, unaware of the gulls' skill at scooping those items up in a blink of an eye. A pretty young woman, her blonde hair in dozens of braids, wearing tiny round sunglasses, a tie-dyed t-shirt and cut-off shorts, dangled a bag of chips in one hand, while her other was busy holding a pair of binoculars. She didn't see it coming.

A gull, that had been gently riding the currents a second before, dove like a bomber, its beak clamping around the bag and yanking it from her hand. "Hey," she cried, nearly dropping her binoculars. Jessie snickered and turned his attention back to the tower across the river, barely visible through the haze of humidity.

The tension mounted as the commentator announced T-minus 90 seconds and counting. The crowd grew quiet; the cars still on the highway came to a standstill. Jessie waited for them to say the vehicle had gone to internal power, which came as soon as he thought it.

"All eyes at Cape Kennedy, and the world, are watching this by Early Bird satellite on pad nineteen," a newscaster cut in over the flight control commentator. "The bird stands in magnificent glory in its last seconds on earth."

Jessie desperately missed their tree house on the island, but knew it was no longer there. From what he'd heard, a blockhouse had been built in that area for this very mission. If only he were close enough to see the "bird" himself. He almost wished he'd stayed home to watch the launch on television, but nothing compared to the thrill of standing here, amongst a crowd of equally excited individuals, all waiting to see the trail of smoke rising from across the river.

"Coming down to T-minus 30, half a minute to go," the newscaster cut in.

Jessie rose on his tiptoes as if that would put him closer to the action.

The commentator was counting down in a serious tone, "Ten-nine-eight-seven-six," the man's voice never changed, never showed a drop of excitement, "five-four-three-two-one-zero-ignition."

"Lift off, we have a lift off," the newscaster said. Now a multitude of voices were chiming in with comments like "climbing nicely," "looks like a beauty," and "oh baby."

Jessie seconded the "oh baby" and punched his right fist into the air, while keeping the fingers of his left firmly crossed.

"One minute into the flight she looks to be going well, very well," the newscaster seemed to be congratulating himself, which annoyed Jessie. He wanted the newscaster to be quiet so he could hear mission control.

Then he heard the words he'd been waiting for.

"Safely through Max Q, safely through the first dangerous point after liftoff."

Jessie gave a sigh of relief and uncrossed his now aching fingers. He gazed at the sky until the trail of smoke started to dissipate. The crowd had already started wandering off, the traffic again moving on US 1, but Jessie didn't move. He wanted to hear more from mission control, a check-in from the astronauts, but now the radio announcer was only recapping everything he already knew, the goals of the mission and when they were expected to return. He motioned for Max to turn it off.

Amazed at how fast the crowd was able to dissipate, Jessie looked around, catching sight of the chick that had lost her bag of chips. He chuckled. She was climbing into the back of a yellow Volkswagen van along with half a dozen other people. A man's hand hung out the passenger side window with an odd-shaped cigarette smoking between his fingers. The last girl to get in the van took the cigarette from him and took a long drag. Jessie was surprised when she didn't exhale right away, but seemed to hold her breath for nearly a minute, before blowing out a large smoke ring.

"Don't even think about it," Max said, over Jessie's shoulder.

Jessie turned to his brother. "What are you talking about?"

"Those guys at the van, they're doing drugs."

"How do you know?"

Max shook his head. "I'm older, I've seen things, and trust me, you don't want to get messed up in that."

"Why'd she hold her breath for so long?"

"By holding the smoke in your lungs for a longer period, it increases the high you experience." As always Sam had the answer, but Max shot him a questioning look. Sam shrugged. "I tutor a couple of football players. They get high. I asked them about it."

"You haven't tried it, have you?" Alarm was written all over Max's face.

"Of course not. Have you seen how stupid people get when they're high? These jocks have come to tutoring sessions a couple of times when they don't even know their own names. I don't even bother to teach them anything on those days. I let them go to the convenience store and eat their weight in junk food."

Max relaxed. "I guess we should get back to class."

Ricky groaned, but they all started across the field, until they heard someone calling Jessie's name. He tensed for a moment, remembering the last launch and the beating he'd received from Alan, but this wasn't Alan's voice. Jessie scanned the remaining crowd and recognized Dr. Weston. Jessie waved and jogged toward the doctor, who was leaning against his Impala.

"I'm glad I caught you." Dr. Weston offered his hand and Jessie shook it like he did that kind of thing all the time. "How are your ribs?"

Jessie unconsciously touched his side. "Much better. They only hurt for a couple of weeks. How did you get out of your office for the launch?'

Dr. Weston's eyes twinkled. "I schedule all of my appointments around them. Becomes a real problem when they get cancelled because of weather and whatnot."

Jessie's brothers approached and he turned to introduce them.

"What a mighty fine looking bunch of young men."

"Thank you, sir," Sam answered for them.

Dr. Weston bowed his head. "I should let you boys get back to school. I'm glad to know you are doing well, and it was nice to meet all of you." He opened his car and slipped inside. Jessie waved then followed his brothers across the street.

CHAPTER TWENTY-NINE

The Body

June 3, 1965

On his way to English class, Jessie heard running feet behind him, turning to see Ricky hurrying to catch up. His face was red and sweat glistened on his forehead. Jessie waited for him.

"You heard anything more about that body?" Ricky asked.

"Nope. You?"

Ricky shook his head. "I think we should skip the rest of the day and head over to the tracks, see what we can find out."

Jessie considered it for a moment. "I don't know."

"Come on, it's the end of the year. Nothing is going on in class."

Ricky was right. Jessie had completed most of his exams earlier in the week. What if Mama found out he'd skipped class, but then she'd never found out before. Had she? He remembered her words about knowing the boys had been in fights, but she'd never said anything about it.

"Nah, I'm in enough trouble with Mama as it is. Max would probably go with you, though. Why don't you find him?"

Ricky looked crestfallen. "He's got a test next period. Forget it. We can stop on our way home, I guess." With stooped shoulders and head down, Ricky loped off in the direction of the gym.

Jessie hurried on to class, the rest of the day a boring blur of tic-tac-toe and word search games. When the final bell rang, Mrs. Matthews handed him a slip of paper. "Here are some books you might find interesting. In case you get bored this summer."

"I don't know how bored I'll get, but thanks." Jessie took the paper without looking at it and stuffed it in his folder. As much as he hated to admit it, she'd gotten him to enjoy reading. Not that he'd give up going hunting or fishing in order to do it, but if the weather was too bad, he might consider picking up a book now.

Outside, Jessie meandered along the walkways, past the cafeteria and gym, to the back of the school. His brothers were waiting for him, rather impatiently from the look on Max's face. Jessie hurried to join them and the boys crossed the street without a word. Max led them along the railroad tracks, Sam, Ricky, and Jessie walking abreast behind him.

"Where do you suppose they found the body?" Ricky asked.

"I reckon there will be some police tape or something when we come to it." Max didn't turn around as he spoke.

Jessie and Sam exchanged a look. Jessie didn't think Sam had mentioned the bums to Max or Ricky since neither brother had brought up the possibility that the body could be one of them. Half a mile from the school they came to the site. Pete Murphy and a handful of other kids from school were congregated across the railroad tracks from an area marked off with police tape.

"You found out anything yet, Pete?" Max called as the brothers approached.

"I ain't even been home yet," Pete replied.

Jessie craned his neck, trying to see around the cluster of students. Unable to see much, he crossed the tracks, careful to stay a few feet away from the police tape. The tall grass was depressed within the marked off area, including several trails the police officers had made. Jessie thought he saw blood on the ground, but it was such a small amount it was hard to be sure.

"See, we should have skipped and come out here while the police was still working," Ricky grumbled. "There's nothing to see now."

Jessie rejoined his brothers, just as disappointed as Ricky. He'd hoped at least to get an idea about who had been killed, or how. Now he'd just have to wait and see if there was anything in the paper about it. Something in his gut told him the dead man was Buster and that Eugene had something to do with it.

CHAPTER THIRTY

House Call

June 3, 1965

"I don't have to work today. Want to go to the fort?" Max asked when the boys left the crime scene.

Sam and Ricky eagerly agreed, although Ricky shot Jessie a sympathetic look. This grounding really stinks, Jessie thought, as he trudged on along the tracks, head down, watching his feet moving from one railroad tie to the next. Lost in his thoughts, he didn't notice the other boy until a fist connected with his lower back. Jessie dropped to the ground, his head narrowly missing the thick steel of the railroad track. He looked up in time to see a fist coming toward his head and rolled to the side, using his leg to trip his assailant. With a loud thud the boy fell to the ground. Jessie hurried to get himself up, not surprised to find Alan lying at his feet.

When will this kid learn? Jessie thought. He pushed aside the stabbing pain in his back and balled his fists, ready to rain down all of the rage and bitterness bound up inside him. He took a swing only to have his wrist grabbed, an inch from Alan's face. Jessie looked up to find Eugene holding onto his wrist. Jessie tried to shake his father off, but Eugene's grip was tight. Jessie looked back to Alan who now wore a sneer as he pushed himself off the ground.

"You get on outta here," Eugene barked.

Alan looked from Jessie to Eugene. "This isn't over, Cole," Alan growled before running back toward the school.

"You okay, son?" Eugene let go of Jessie's wrist.

"I could have taken him," Jessie hissed.

"I'm sure you could have. From what I hear, you two have had a number of dust ups this year."

Jessie picked up the folder he'd dropped and limped away, his heart still pounding. Jessie ignored Eugene, who fell in step beside him.

"You want to tell me why that boy has it in for you?"

Despite the pain in his back, Jessie picked up his pace, but Eugene matched him. Sweat now ran down Jessie's back and face, burning his eyes. He lifted his shirt to wipe his face.

"Fighting isn't the answer to your problems," Eugene offered when Jessie didn't answer his question.

"Fighting is all Alan understands," Jessie shot back.

"Maybe, but I'm sure his folks can be talked to."

Jessie laughed. "You want me to tattle on the biggest bully in school? Yeah, that will go over well."

"Maybe his parents don't know the kind of trouble he's getting into."

Jessie stopped and turned to his father. "If they haven't seen the bruises he's gone home with or heard about the broken bones of his friends, they're idiots. We've given him as good as he's dished out. More often than not we're the ones who've come out on top. Maybe that's why he has it out for us, no one else has ever stood up to him, and I don't plan to stop until he understands he can't push us around."

Without waiting for a response, Jessie started walking again, cutting through the yards of several houses until he reached his street. He banged through the front door and tossed his folder on the kitchen table. The air in the house was hot, like walking into a broiler. Jessie cranked open his bedroom window, but not a breath of air stirred. He flopped onto the bed, forgetting about the blow to his back, and crying out in pain as he hit the mattress. He rolled onto his side, barely breathing, teeth clenched as the stab echoed throughout his entire body.

"You need to see a doctor." Eugene appeared in the open doorway.

Jessie shook his head. "I'm fine."

"No you're not. Has your mother found a new doctor here in town?"

Jessie shook his head again.

"I'll call her at work, see if she knows—"

"Don't bother Mama." Jessie pushed himself up on his elbow, gritting his teeth, and reached for a tin box on top of his orange crates. "If you gotta call someone, call him." Jessie handed Eugene the prescription page with Dr. Weston's phone number on it.

Eugene took the paper and left the room. Jessie lay back down, the pain receding from a sharp stab to a burning throb. He closed his eyes, trying to think of anything to take his mind off the ache. He didn't know how much time passed before Eugene returned.

Jessie opened his eyes when Dr. Weston spoke. "Where does it hurt?"

Jessie rolled onto this stomach and pointed at his back. Dr. Weston lifted Jessie's shirt and let out a long whistle.

"He did a number on you this time."

"No kidding," Jessie mumbled into the pillow.

"You got a nice bruise started and it's going to hurt for several days. If you have any blood when you urinate we'll need to run some tests." Dr. Weston lowered the shirt.

Jessie turned back onto his side.

"It's a good thing school's out. You need a break from fighting."

Jessie gave a weak laugh. "Thanks, Doc."

Dr. Weston looked over his shoulder at Eugene. "He can have some aspirin for the pain every four hours, and have him drink plenty of water."

"Yes, sir. Thank you for coming so quick."

"You take care of yourself." Dr. Weston gave Jessie a wink before turning to shake Eugene's hand. "It was nice to meet you, Mr. Cole."

When Dr. Weston was gone, Eugene returned to the bedroom with a glass of water and a couple of aspirin. Jessie sat up to drink the water and take the pills.

"Where are your brothers?" Eugene asked when Jessie had finished.

"Out in the woods."

Eugene stiffened. "Did they go to that fort of yours?"

Jessie nodded, studying his father's reaction.

"Quite a place you boys have built out there. Max didn't want to show us that night you run off, but your mother was worried sick." Eugene took the empty glass. "Why don't you try to get some sleep? I'll come get you when it's time for dinner."

Jessie eased himself back onto the bed, squishing the pillow up under his head. He heard the front door open and close, knowing Eugene was heading for the fort, and wondering what his father was afraid his brothers would find there. Part of him wanted to follow, to see if his suspicions about the dead body were right, but he was just getting comfortable and all of the adrenaline had drained from his body, leaving him exhausted. I'll close my eyes for a minute. Ricky will tell me if Pop did anything.

The smell of onions and peppers teased Jessie from his slumber. His eyes fluttered open and swept around the dim room. He pushed himself up, grimacing at the dull ache in his back. The window was still open, showing gray clouds hanging low in the evening sky, offering the hope of rain. Jessie found Eleanor standing at the stove, tending a large skillet and humming a tune Jessie didn't recognize. He pulled a glass from the cabinet, the noise of the door falling shut causing Eleanor to turn her head in his direction.

"Did you have a nice nap?" she asked as she stirred the vegetables in the pan.

"I guess." Jessie filled the glass with water, dropped in a couple of ice cubes, and took a long sip. "Where is everyone?"

Eleanor shook her head. "You were the only one here when I got home. I guess your brothers are off in the woods somewhere celebrating the end of the school year." She stopped stirring and gazed at the pan for a minute. "Your father should have been home hours ago, though."

From where Jessie stood, he could only see Eleanor in profile, but he was sure he saw a frown turn down the corner of her mouth. Was she worried Eugene was out drinking? Had Eugene's trip to the hospital made her doubt his claims of sobriety?

"I was planning on steak for dinner. Would you mind starting the grill?"

"Really?" Jessie scrambled to the drawer where the matches were kept.

"Don't put too much lighter fluid on," Eleanor warned as Jessie ran around the corner.

Jessie threw open the back door and stepped onto the back porch, proud that his mother trusted him to get the grill going. When Eugene hadn't been around, only Max had been allowed to use it. Jessie hadn't understood why his mother hadn't given any of the other boys a chance, considering they had all built campfires numerous times.

A spider web tethered the bag of charcoal to the house, reminding Jessie how long it had been since they'd had a barbecue. He pulled the bag free of the silky strands and shook coals into the grill, piling them in a pyramid shape. With a little squirt of lighter fluid around the middle and a strike of a match, the fire came to life. Jessie stood back and watched the coals heat, flames reaching up above them a foot or so. The sound of their crackling joined the hum of cicadas and a pair of cardinals chirping back and forth. Jessie's gaze drifted from the flames to the woods at the end of the street, expecting to see his brothers any minute.

The sun sank lower and lights appeared in the windows of the neighbor's house, but there was no sign of Max, Sam, or Ricky. Jessie turned back to the fire and found the coals were now an ashy white, perfect for cooking the steaks. He ran inside to get the meat, but stopped dead in his tracks at the end of the hallway.

CHAPTER THIRTY-ONE

The Police

June 3, 1965

Eleanor held the front door open for a tall broad shouldered police officer. He stepped inside, his head swiveling around to take in the kitchen and living room, until he stopped on Jessie at the end of the hallway.

"Would you mind talking in the kitchen?" Eleanor gestured to a chair at the table. "I have dinner on the stove."

"The grill is ready for the steaks." Jessie stepped forward, trying to read the name on the officer's shirt. "Hey, are you Pete Murphy's dad?"

The policeman nodded but didn't smile. Jessie reached for the plate of steak sitting by the sink.

"Maybe we should wait until your brothers get home to start those." Eleanor placed a hand on Jessie's shoulder.

"I bet they'll be here any minute." Jessie hoped he sounded more confident then he felt.

Eleanor hesitated then let her hand slip off his shoulder. "Make sure the large one is well-done for your father."

"Where is Mr. Cole?" Officer Murphy asked.

Jessie looked from Office Murphy to his mother and saw anxiety tighten her features. "I think he went to meet my brothers," Jessie offered.

"Hmm, when did he leave?" Officer Murphy pulled a pad of paper from his shirt pocket.

Jessie scratched his head. "Maybe three-thirty or four o'clock. It was after I got home from school."

"Can anyone else verify that?"

Jessie ran a finger around the edge of the plate, avoiding his mother's gaze. "Dr. Weston can verify Pop was here."

Officer Murphy's eyebrows shot up in surprise. "Is that the new doctor in town? How would he know?"

Jessie risked a look at his mother. "Pop called him; asked if he would stop by and check on me." Jessie paused, trying to frame his next statement.

"Did you get in another fight?" Eleanor's words seemed to surprise the police officer, whose attention had been focused on Jessie.

"He punched me from behind," Jessie protested. "I would have taken care of Alan once and for all if Pop hadn't interfered."

"That wouldn't happen to be Alan Welty would it?" Officer Murphy's eyes bore into Jessie.

Jessie returned the gaze without blinking, defiance burning within him. "Yes, sir. He's nothing but a bully."

"That's what Pete tells me too. He thinks you boys are some kind of heroes that you and your brothers are the only ones who haven't cowed down before this kid."

Jessie didn't like the tone Officer Murphy was using. It gave him the impression there was a big "but" coming and wondered what kind of trouble Alan was causing now.

"Mr. Welty contacted the police station this afternoon." Officer Murphy turned to Eleanor. "Said his son saw Eugene carrying a body out of the woods last night. The body we found, out by the tracks this morning." Murphy looked from Eleanor to Jessie. "Either of you know anything about that?"

Eleanor grabbed for the back of a chair as she slumped forward. In his haste to reach his mother, Jessie dropped the plate of steak, the ceramic making a loud crash when it hit the floor. He helped her into a chair then filled the empty glass he'd left beside the sink and handed her the water, while shooting an angry look across the table at the policeman.

"Pop may be a lot of things, but he *ain't* no killer." No sooner had Jessie bit out those words than the front door opened. Max, Sam, Ricky, and Eugene stepped inside, each of them sweaty, dirt sticking to their skin. They stood, lined up along the back of the couch, all eyes staring at the scene in the kitchen. Jessie looked at Eugene, not sure why he'd said what he just had, not when he'd immediately thought of Eugene that morning after the boys had learned of the body.

"Bob Murphy, well I'll be," Eugene bellowed, stepping forward to shake the officer's hand. "How've you been? I haven't seen you in, what's it been, six years? How's that lovely wife of yours?"

Officer Murphy shook Eugene's hand, his face reddening at the mention of his wife. "Pam's doing well. She's been getting on me for not inviting you over for dinner since you moved up from the island."

"We'd love to come for dinner sometime. Got a lot of catching up to do."

Jessie watched in bewilderment. How did his father know Officer Murphy? Why hadn't his mother had a similar welcoming response when she'd invited the policeman in?

"Eugene," Officer Murphy looked around the now crowded kitchen, "is there someplace we can talk privately?"

Eugene's face clouded and his eyes narrowed. "Sure, Bob." Eugene turned to his sons, "Why don't you go get cleaned up for dinner? Jessie, pick up those steaks, I smelled the charcoal heating up when I came in, wash them off and get them on the grill. I'll come check on them in a few minutes."

Sam, Ricky, and Max shuffled down the hall and Jessie scooped up the steaks, running them under the faucet for a long minute, hoping to hear what his father and Officer Murphy had to talk about, but the men remained silent until Jessie finished cleaning up and the back door had closed behind him. The coals were fading, and Jessie leaned down to blow on them, ash swirling in the grill pan before a flicker of light danced to life. There were sizzles and pops as he laid each steak on the grill, water still dripping off them onto the hot bricks.

Jessie watched the steaks, fat slowly melting off and dropping into the low flames. Did Alan really see Pop carrying the body, or did he make it up after Pop broke up our fight? Was it just another way for Alan to get even with the Cole boys?

"What's going on in there?"

The words startled Jessie. He turned from the fire to find Ricky standing there.

"How did you—"

"I crawled out the window. So, why are the police here?"

"Alan told his father he saw Pop carrying that dead body out of the woods last night and they called the police."

"What?" Ricky yelled, quieting at a gesture from Jessie. "That's not possible," Ricky whispered.

Jessie stabbed one of the steaks with a fork and flipped it over. "I don't know."

Jessie wasn't sure if he should tell his brothers about the night Eugene had spent in the fort, when he'd warned Buster to stay away. If they didn't know about it then they wouldn't have to lie if the police asked them any questions.

The back door opened and Eugene came lumbering out. "How are those steaks coming?"

Jessie glimpsed Ricky duck back into the shadows and creep around the corner of the house. "Just flipped them for the first time. Probably need about five more minutes."

Eugene reached for the fork. "Let me take a look." Poking at the meat, he pried a chunk from the center of the largest piece, blood oozing from the opening.

"Five more minutes for you maybe, but I like mine good and dead." Eugene pressed the fork against the meat, juices falling onto the fire making the flames jump higher. Jessie cringed at the word "dead".

"How do you know Officer Murphy?" Jessie flipped over a five-gallon bucket, creating a seat for himself.

"Bob? He and I were in the service together." Eugene looked around the porch then crossed to a pile of lawn chairs resting near the corner. He pulled a red and yellow striped one from the heap.

Jessie knew most of the chairs needed some kind of repair; simple oil to the hinges, rivets replaced, or new fabric webbing for the seat. This particular chair needed it all. The hinges groaned in protest as Eugene struggled to open it, and a length of striped fabric unraveled from missing rivets in the seat, fluttering in the breeze. Eugene tossed the chair aside and reached for another, which also groaned against opening, but at least its seat was intact. Setting the chair across the grill from Jessie, Eugene cautiously settled his weight into it. When the fabric didn't immediately break, he relaxed.

"I was surprised to hear you tell Bob I wasn't a killer."

Jessie stiffened. He hadn't been sure if they'd heard him when they arrived. "Yeah, I was surprised to be saying it too."

Eugene rubbed his chin. "Do you think I had something to do with that man they found this morning?"

"I don't know enough about it. Did Officer Murphy tell you who the guy was?"

"There wasn't any identification on the body. White guy, about six-feet tall, blonde hair, probably homeless, looked like he'd been beaten to death."

"Did he have a gash in his arm about a month old?" Jessie met his father's gaze across the fire as he spoke.

Eugene's face didn't betray any emotion, not the slightest flinch of surprise or shadow of fear. Jessie almost wondered if his father had even heard him. The steaks sizzled between them. Eugene leaned forward, flipped two of them then moved the other four to the plate before standing up.

"Why don't you take these in to your mother? She can keep them warm in the oven while I finish the others. Bring back a new plate for them."

Jessie took the plate from his father, their hands brushing as Eugene held onto it a second longer than necessary. Jessie expected him to say something, to answer the question or scold him for hiding that night in the woods, but Eugene let go of the plate and turned his focus back to the grill.

Inside, Jessie could smell the onions and peppers now ready to be served with the steak as well as baked potatoes and bacon. They hadn't had a meal like this since moving to Indian River City. What made tonight special? Jessie's head hurt from all of the unanswered questions, and it pounded some more when he met the curious gazes of his brothers. Ricky had slipped back in through the window and clearly had told Max and Sam what Jessie had shared with him about Officer Murphy's visit. Max mouthed something at him, but Jessie looked away.

"The other two should be done in a few minutes," Jessie announced, handing the plate to his mother.

"Good, the potatoes should be ready then." Eleanor covered the plate with tin foil and set it on top of the stove, the heat rising from the oven more than enough to keep them warm.

Jessie noticed the table had already been set and there were even flowers in the center. He reached for another plate from the cabinet and retreated to the back door before any of his brothers could pull him aside for a private word.

On the porch, Eugene sat in the chair with his back to the door, which Jessie allowed to slam shut behind him, but Eugene didn't turn. Jessie returned to his five-gallon bucket and took a seat, holding the plate on his lap.

"What were you guys doing in the woods this afternoon?" Jessie asked.

"We rebuilt the door to the fort, put out a few squirrel snares, stuff like that."

"How many times have you been out there?"

"Since the night you ran off? Today was the first time. It's your spot, if you wanted me out there I guess you would have invited me."

Jessie considered this. If Eugene hadn't been checking on the fort periodically, and his brothers hadn't been out there very much, in all probability Buster had moved in. How could anyone who didn't know the forest have found the fort and taken Buster down if he had been living there? Instead of getting answers, he was only finding new questions.

Eugene stood and gave a long stretch before reaching across the grill for the plate. Jessie offered it up to him, without moving from his seat. Eugene speared the remaining steaks onto the plate.

"Why don't you cover that up? I'll come out after dinner and make sure it's all out." Eugene strode to the door and stepped inside.

Jessie watched the flames that had risen from the melting fat flicker and fade into the embers. He found a nearby stick and stabbed at the brittle coals, watching them fall apart in orange and white flakes, flashing with their exposure to the air, then fading with nothing left to burn. He reached for the grill cover, set it in place with a metallic clink, and returned to the kitchen.

Everyone was gathered around the table, a seat between Eleanor and Ricky left open for Jessie. He sat on it and unfolded his napkin on his lap. Reaching for his fork, he was surprised to find his mother's hand held out to him on one side and Ricky's on the other.

"Your father is going to say a blessing before we eat," Eleanor explained, taking his hand.

Jessie looked at Ricky who awkwardly took his hand as well.

"Our heavenly Father, thank you for this day," Eugene spoke reverently, "and thank you for this wonderful family. I know we've had some rough times, Lord, and I am grateful that you have given me a second chance to show them how much I love them. Lord, I ask that you will bless this food before us, may it nourish our bodies so we may bring glory to you. Amen."

Jessie hadn't closed his eyes or bowed his head. He'd watched his father through the entire prayer, unable to comprehend what was taking place. His gaze had dropped from Eugene's face to the space between his father's hand and Max's. They hadn't clasped as the others around the table had, but Max had placed his hand next to Eugene's. That was more than Jessie could have imagined possible a day ago, but now he felt like something had happened that afternoon that had changed the family dynamic once again, and he hadn't been a part of it.

With Eugene's closing, hands were released and eyes opened. His brothers dished onions and peppers onto their steaks, crumbled bacon into their baked potatoes, and chattered about their plans for the summer. Jessie took the bowls when they were passed to him, but he didn't hear any of the summer plans. He was watching the faces of his mother, his father, and most importantly, Max.

Eugene and Eleanor shared several glances when the boys were planning amongst themselves. Glances that gave Jessie the impression they had a secret, something they were conspiring to keep from the boys, but about which they could barely contain their excitement. Max was quieter than Sam and Ricky, but not sullen like he had been since Eugene's return.

"Jessie?" Eleanor touched his hand and he realized she'd been speaking to him for the past minute.

"I'm sorry, what was the question?"

"Is everything all right? You've barely touched your dinner."

Jessie looked at his plate, surprised to see she was right. His potato was churned up with bacon, cheese and melted butter, but not a bite had been taken, and his steak, while cut into small pieces, still filled most of his plate.

"I'm fine," he managed to reply.

"When do you start summer school?"

"I have two weeks off before the session starts." Jessie scooped up some potato and filled his mouth.

"I can't believe you volunteered for that class," Max sneered. "If I didn't have to redo English to graduate I wouldn't step foot in that school again."

"We all know how anxious you are to work full-time at the grocery store," Sam mocked, in a weary tone.

"Now boys," Eleanor broke in before an argument could start, "your father and I were thinking about spending the weekend at the beach. I talked with Jan Maisey last week and she said we could stay with them. She said Harry and Jim have missed you terribly."

Jessie brightened at the thought of seeing friends from the old neighborhood. Harry and Jim were the same age as Ricky and Sam, and had run in the woods with the Cole boys for years. Jessie realized he hadn't thought about them in months, he'd been so caught up in their new life in town.

Ricky bounced in his chair. "When are we going?"

"We'll head out around lunchtime tomorrow." Eleanor dabbed at the corners of her mouth then pushed her chair back and started clearing the empty plates.

Jessie hurried to finish his dinner, barely noticing how cold it had gotten. There was a scraping of chairs as his family rose from the table around him. Max plopped himself in the center of the couch, while Sam moved to help Eleanor at the sink and Eugene went outside to make sure the fire in the grill was out. Jessie was left alone at the table when Ricky scampered off to the bedroom.

Within minutes the dishes were put away and everyone was in the living room, Eugene, Max, and Sam on the couch, Eleanor in her rocking chair, Jessie and Ricky lounging on the floor. Ricky reached up to turn on the television, the theme song for *Daniel Boone* already playing. Jessie looked around at his family, all in the same room without an angry word or a single scowl of contempt. This was what family was supposed to be, right, but how did we get here?

CHAPTER THIRTY-TWO

The Beach

June 4, 1965

"Don't forget to pack clean underwear," Eleanor called down the hall. Ricky snickered. "Does she think we're animals?"

"Probably, since you haven't bathed in three days," Jessie retorted.

"We're going to the beach, who needs a bath?" Ricky shoved his swim trunks into a paper sack, grabbed a couple of t-shirts and dropped them in as well.

Jessie had packed his own bag before going to bed the previous night. He couldn't wait to get back to the beach, to feel the salt on his skin and the water on his toes. He tried to remind himself that they weren't going back to the old neighborhood; that Orsino didn't exist anymore. There wouldn't be acres of woods to run through or private untouched beach.

The Maiseys had moved to Cocoa Beach when the government bought their land. Jessie knew the astronauts stayed at a hotel on Cocoa Beach when they were preparing for a launch, and was disappointed there were no launches scheduled in the next week. Maybe some of them had come to watch the *Gemini 4* launch and were still in town.

Jessie picked up his bag of clothes and wandered into the kitchen where he found his mother putting together peanut butter sandwiches. A plate, stacked five high, already waited on the table. He snagged one and took a bite before he dropped his bag by the front door and paced from the living room to the kitchen, munching on his sandwich.

"Oh for heaven's sake, sit down," Eleanor cried when he bumped into her for a second time.

"I'm too excited to be still," Jessie whined.

"Then go outside and help your father check the car." Eleanor flicked her dishtowel at him, but Jessie jumped back out of reach.

Outside, the hood of the Bel Air was raised with Eugene bent over the engine. Jessie watched him pull out a dipstick, study it, wipe it with a dirty rag, and drop it back into place. He couldn't remember a single time he or his brothers had checked the oil while Eugene had been staying with Uncle Tommy. *We weren't doing such a good job taking care of things after all.*

Eugene wiped his hands on the rag and lowered the hood, making sure it clicked into place. "Morning, son. You want to help me out?"

Jessie nodded and took a step closer. Eugene pulled a tire pressure gauge from his pocket.

"Go around and check all the tires." Eugene tossed the gauge to Jessie who fumbled it before gaining control. "You know how to use it, right?"

Rebekah Lyn

Jessie looked at the long, round piece of metal in his hand. There was a threaded hole on one end that he assumed went on the valve stem. "Sure, how hard can it be?"

He kneeled beside the right, back tire, unscrewed the valve cover, and attached the gauge. When a white measurement bar popped out the end, Jessie flinched, yanking the tool off the tire.

Eugene laughed and made his way around the car, kneeling beside Jessie. "Not bad, but don't yank it off like that." Eugene took the tool, attached it to the tire, and when the bar popped out again, he checked it with a satisfied nod.

"See, this right here," Eugene pointed at the measurement, "marks how many pounds of pressure is in the tire. These tires need to be between thirty-two to thirty-five pounds." Eugene handed the tool back to Jessie, who moved to the front tire.

After a couple of attempts, Jessie attached the gauge properly, studied the reading and nodded, before moving to the other side of the car. When he finished the last tire, he stood and held out the gauge to his father.

Eugene pushed the tool back to Jessie. "You keep it. You'll have your own car before you know it."

Jessie held onto the gauge, his gaze glued to the warm smile on his father's face. *How can Pop look at me like that when I have been so mean to him? I've told him how much I hate him.*

The front door opened, Ricky and Sam pushing each other out, paper bags in each arm. They ran to the car and drummed on the trunk until Eugene opened it. After dumping the bags in, the boys ran back into the house, emerging seconds later with more bags. Max followed, his head down, carrying several pillows, which he dumped into the trunk before slipping into the backseat. Ricky and Sam, too excited to sit or stand still, raced around the car until Eleanor stepped out of the house. Jessie watched her pull the door shut and lock it, a bulging grocery bag on her hip. When she reached the car, instead of putting the bag in the trunk with the others, she set it on the front seat.

"Come on, boys," she called to Ricky and Sam.

Jessie climbed in the back seat, next to Max who had claimed the passenger side window. Ricky and Sam joined them, arguing over which one should have the other window. Eleanor and Eugene slipped into the front seat and he gave the gas pedal a couple of quick punches so that the car started with a roar.

In less than five minutes they were on the highway, windows rolled down and wind whipping through the car. Jessie was glad they all had crew cuts so hair wasn't flying in their faces. Sam had won the battle of the other window, but Ricky leaned forward so he could peek out toward the river, leaving Jessie with only the windshield or back window to look out. He opted to look forward and rested his chin on the back of the front seat. Eleanor reached back and ran her hand over his fuzzy head.

By the time they reached the beach, all of the boys were antsy. Eugene had barely put the car in park before the back doors flew open and Jessie followed his brothers out into the rough grass of the Maiseys' front yard. The front door opened, Harry and Jim bursting forth. Ricky and Harry instantly fell into a tussle, wrestling each other to the ground, their laughter mixing with the squawks of nearby seagulls.

"Can we go to the beach?" Jim called to his mother, who stood on the porch hugging Eleanor. Jessie stopped running after Harry and Ricky long enough to watch Eugene and Dan Maisey shake hands before disappearing into the house.

"Let the Coles change into their swimsuits first," Jan Maisey replied.

"I'll get the keys from Daddy," Ricky offered, untangling himself from Harry and dashing into the house. Jessie and Sam had already stripped off their shirts when Ricky returned.

"Come inside to change," Eleanor instructed. The sternness in her voice caused Jessie to look at her. He took in her red cheeks and Mrs. Maisey's hand covering an embarrassed smile. A quick glance at Sam, holding the waistband of his already unbuttoned shorts, and Jessie understood his mother's concern. The boys grabbed bags from the trunk and ran into the house, following Harry and Jim to their bedrooms.

Ten minutes later, warm sand covered Jessie's feet and he relished the feel as it filled the space between his toes. He watched Harry and Jim run out into the water, not slowing down until it reached their thighs and they fell forward into the water. Ricky and Sam were close behind. Sam dove into an incoming wave, his head popping up behind the rolling foam. Max joined Jessie in the thick sand above the water line.

"It's good to be back, isn't it?" Although Max didn't sound very happy.

"We aren't quite back, though, are we?" Jessie understood his brother's lack of excitement. Max would never be able to visit the places they had known growing up. It was bittersweet for Jessie, knowing his home was now a missile launch site. When he became an astronaut, he could be launched into space from the very site where they used to hunt bobcats or from the clearing where they had camped every summer, but his brothers would never have that experience. Maybe it didn't matter as much to Ricky and Sam. Maybe just returning to the beach with old friends was all they needed.

Max looked to the north, along the stretch of sand dotted with fishermen, children building sandcastles, and couples lounging on blankets. Jessie knew his brother was thinking of the stretch of beach miles from here, where they'd found an old boat, battered and broken, washed onto the shore after a hurricane.

Max shook his head. "If you really do get to be an astronaut, will you find Smitty's grave?"

Jessie had forgotten about Smitty, a mangy mutt the boys had adopted ten years before. Smitty had run with them in the woods, waited faithfully below the tree house, and collected the ducks the boys had shot down. He'd died three years before the move. Max had buried him near the dunes, with a whittled dog bone as his marker.

"Yeah, I'll find Smitty," Jessie whispered.

"Race you to the water." Max smiled and took off without a count. Jessie followed, laughing when Max tripped in the sand, allowing Jessie to take the lead. He reached the water a second before Max, who rocketed himself onto Jessie's back, pushing him down into a deep wave.

The boys came up sputtering. Max grinned, looking more like the mischievous brother Jessie had known on the island. The hurts of the past year, all of the fights, the adjustments to life in town, washed away with the falling tide.

When the sun sank behind the three-story hotels and the sky turned a pale purple, the boys slogged out of the surf, falling, exhausted, onto the hard packed sand. Harry rose first, running up to the dunes and gathering driftwood. Jim found a few broken boards that were probably once part of a boat hull. In no time, the Maisey brothers had built a fine bonfire. All that was missing was some hot dogs.

CHAPTER THIRTY-THREE

Bonfire

June 4, 1965

At the thought of food, Jessie's stomach growled. He looked toward the dunes, but didn't want to leave the camaraderie of the fire. As if on cue, the silhouette of a woman crested the dune. Before she entered the glow from the fire, Jessie knew it was his mother. He jumped up to meet her.

"I thought you boys might be hungry." Eleanor held up a paper bag, which Jessie took before pulling her into a tight hug.

Eleanor laughed. "All right now, no need to get half the beach on my clothes." She stepped back and brushed sand off her skirt and blouse. "Your father and the Maiseys will be down in a few minutes. They were loading up a cooler with some drinks."

"You're the best, Mama." Jessie kissed her on the cheek and raced back to the fire.

Sticks were found and sharp points whittled, to spear the hot dogs. Each of the boys had a stick in the fire by the time the other adults arrived, Eugene and Dan lugging the ice chest between them. Jessie leaned back on his elbows, gazing up at the sky. It was filled with stars, more than he'd seen in the past year.

He imagined what it would be like to be up there, among the stars. Would he look back to the earth or out farther into space? It had been a little over four years since President Kennedy had challenged the nation to put a man on the moon. It felt like time was slipping away and the space program falling behind. Would NASA be able to meet the challenge or would the program fall apart before Jessie even finished school?

"Your wiener is burning," sputtered Ricky through gales of laughter.

Jessie dropped his gaze from the sky to the fire, where the other boys were pointing and laughing. Jessie had forgotten all about his hotdog, now blazing at the end of its stick, swelling until it burst out of its casing and dropped into the fire pit. With a nonchalant shrug, he reached for a new dog and set it over the fire again.

They ate all of the hot dogs and an entire bag of marshmallows before the fire died back to a pale glow. Jessie felt his eyes grow heavy and could hear Ricky snoring on the other side of their circle. A warm wind rattled the grass behind them. Dan Maisey stirred first, pushing himself off the ground with a quiet grunt. Eugene, Jan, and Eleanor followed suit, gathering up their bag of garbage, emptying the melted ice and kicking dirt on the fire. Gradually, the boys stood, brushing sand off their now dry swimsuits.

No one talked as they made their way back up the dunes. They paused when they reached A1A, the sound of revving engines growing louder. Jessie looked to the north where the noise was coming from, and saw two Corvettes racing toward them. Jessie forgot his fatigue, waving wildly and cheering as the cars whizzed past.

"Did you see that?" he cried, excitement coursing through his veins. "Those had to be astronauts! I bet it was Grissom and Shepard."

The other boys were jostling to look down the road for a glimpse of the sports cars. Jessie ran down the street in the direction they had disappeared until he heard his mother calling after him. He stopped, his eyes searching for any sign of his heroes, but they had disappeared. Glumly, he followed the rest of the group back to the house where a tent had been pitched in the back yard.

Jessie tried to join in the excitement of camping out, but couldn't stop thinking about how close he'd been to meeting an astronaut, to telling them how much he admired them, and wanted to be like them. The boys ducked into the tent, where pillows and folded blankets awaited.

Harry flicked on a flashlight while they each grabbed a blanket and pillow, settling into a circle. Jim and Max told ghost stories, to which Jessie only half listened. When all quieted down and he was sure the others were asleep, Jessie slipped out of the tent, his bare feet squishing into the thick grass. He looked to the sky and felt his heart leap at the sight of a shooting star. When it burned out, he closed his eyes and made a wish.

CHAPTER THIRTY-FOUR

Max's Birthday

June 20, 1965

The weekend at the beach had provided much needed relaxation for the whole family, but had flown by too fast. In the days leading up to summer session, Jessie noticed Max retreating into himself, growing more sullen, all of the closeness they had shared at the beach disappearing. He'd picked up more shifts at the grocery store, barely spending any time at home. The day before summer school started was Max's eighteenth birthday.

As soon as Jessie's eyes popped open that Sunday, he rolled out of bed, and bounded into Max's room. Max and Sam were still hunkered down under their sheets, bedspreads kicked to the floor, but that didn't stop Jessie from flying to Max's bed and shaking it until his brother rolled over and glared at him.

"Happy birthday," Jessie shouted, disregarding the evil eye directed his way.

"What's so happy about it?" Max grumbled, yanking the sheet up over his face.

"Aren't you excited?" Jessie was puzzled by Max's reaction. Mama had always made sure their birthdays were special. They didn't have to do any chores that day, they got to eat whatever they wanted, and she never failed to make sure they had one gift that would leave them speechless.

"Leave me alone," was Max's muffled reply. He rolled to face the wall, his back arching out until it pressed against Jessie's leg on the edge of the bed, forcing him back.

Jessie looked toward Sam's bed, but his brother hadn't moved, as if he'd slept through the whole exchange. Jessie knew Sam was awake, he could tell by the shallow breaths he heard coming from him. *Nice of him to join in the celebration,* Jessie inwardly grumbled as he stomped out of the bedroom.

The living room and kitchen were dark, causing Jessie to check the clock. It wasn't quite seven yet. Maybe that was why Max had been so grumpy. With a shrug, Jessie opened the coffee tin and set up the percolator, turning the burner on and sitting down to wait for the coffee to boil. It didn't take long for the scent of fresh coffee to lure Eleanor out of bed, shuffling into the kitchen in her housecoat.

"Aren't you sweet to start the coffee?" She went to tousle his hair out of habit, giggling at the fuzzy cut. "It reminds me of your butt when you were a baby."

"I didn't have this much hair on it did I?" Jessie ran his own hand over his head.

Eleanor nearly choked on the glass of water she had started drinking. "No, I don't suppose you had that much hair, but the same soft feeling, that's what I meant."

"What's the plan for Max's birthday?" Jessie jumped from his chair and opened the refrigerator, pulling out a bottle of milk.

Eleanor leaned back against the counter and crossed her arms over her chest. "I don't think he wants to make a big deal out of it this year. We'll just have a nice dinner tonight; cube steak and gravy, green beans, mashed potatoes. That reminds me, I need to pick up some potatoes after church."

Jessie set the milk on the counter, gaping at his mother. "But it's his birthday. We always make a big deal."

Eleanor reached one hand up to rub her temples. "He'll have to register for the draft tomorrow, remember."

"Oh, yeah," Jessie whispered, feeling like an idiot for not having thought of the significance of this day. Several boys from Max's class had registered in the spring, when their birthdays had come. Jessie had heard about one guy who'd been called up only last week.

The lid on the percolator started to jiggle. Eleanor turned to it, but didn't cut back the heat right away. Jessie thought he heard her sniff. He beat his fist against his forehead then reached out and touched her back.

Eleanor turned to face him, her eyes watery, but she offered a brave smile. "Ready for some coffee?"

They drank in silence, Jessie trying to figure out how he could apologize to his brother for being so stupid. They were still sitting at the table, their cups now empty, when Eugene stumbled down the hall, his eyes only half-open.

"Do I smell coffee?" His voice was thick with phlegm and he gave a mighty cough.

"Sit down, I'll get a cup, dear." Eleanor hurried to pour a fresh cup, spooning in two scoops of sugar and stirring it before setting it in front of Eugene.

"Why don't you go wake Ricky and get dressed? I'll get Sam and Max up in a few minutes." Eleanor patted Jessie's back as she passed his chair.

Jessie rinsed his cup out in the sink before sidling back to his room. Ricky was sitting up in bed, his back against the wall, the sheet pulled up to his shoulders, allowing his feet to peek out.

"You're up early," Ricky observed, when Jessie entered the room.

"Mama said we need to get dressed for church." Jessie found his dress pants and shirt, shook them out, hoping they weren't too wrinkled, and left for the bathroom. He hung his clothes over the shower curtain rod, turned on the sink faucet and dunked his head under the cold water. Without looking up, he fumbled for a washcloth and scrubbed his face. After he toweled off, he leaned in close to the mirror, checking to see if any facial hair had grown overnight, but only found smooth skin. Regardless, he splashed a tad of Max's aftershave on his cheeks and proceeded to dress.

Back in his bedroom, he found Ricky had already dressed and was shoving his feet into his shoes. "I think I need new ones," Ricky complained when he stood up.

Jessie could see his brother's toes bulging at the end and sides. "Maybe Mama can take you shopping for some next week while Max and I are at school."

The word "school" caught in his throat as he said it. Now that he'd been out of school for a couple of weeks, the idea of going back so soon made Jessie feel sick to his stomach. He hoped it would be as interesting as Mr. Smith had promised. Jessie heard a door open and glanced out into the hall as Sam passed by.

Whomp! Whomp! Whomp!

Jessie jumped at the rapid noises. He ran into the hall, where he found Eugene and Eleanor standing in front of the door to Max and Sam's room. Their mother's eyes were wide and she stood a step behind Eugene, her knuckles white where they gripped his shoulder so tight. Jessie darted past and into the bedroom, sliding to a stop in the middle of the room. Max sat on the end of his bed, elbows on his knees, head in his bloodied hands. A quick glance revealed three fist-sized holes in the wall.

Eleanor crept into the room, kneeling before her son, gently reaching for his hands and pulling them down to her lips. Jessie watched her kiss each of the scratches on his hands, tears falling down her face and mixing with the blood. Eugene stepped forward, handing Eleanor his handkerchief, which she used to dab at the blood.

"I'm sorry, Mama," Max whispered.

"It's okay, baby. Don't you worry about a thing."

"It's nothing I can't fix." Eugene rested a hand on Max's back, slowly massaging the neck muscles.

Jessie stumbled back, until he felt Sam's bed behind him and sank onto the crumpled covers. He hadn't seen Max cry since they were little, after the first time Eugene had beaten them both. Even then, Jessie didn't think Max had been crying for himself, but more for the beating Jessie had taken. Now, he watched as Max's shoulders shook and wretched groans escaped his tight lips. Max looked up and their eyes met. Jessie couldn't look away.

"I'm sorry, Max," Jessie stammered. "I didn't think…"

Max nodded, gave himself a shake, and stood up. "I better get dressed."

Eleanor pulled Max to her, his head resting on hers. She held him close for a long time. When she let go and turned away, she held her arm out to Jessie, who eagerly slipped into it, the two supporting each other into the kitchen. Jessie didn't realize Eugene had stayed behind until he seated Eleanor in a chair and turned to ask his father a question.

"Leave them," Eleanor instructed, as if reading Jessie's mind.

Sam and Ricky joined Eleanor at the table, an uneasy silence settling between them. Jessie found a box of cereal and set it on the table before grabbing bowls and spoons. By the time Eugene appeared, all of the boys were slurping down their breakfast. Eugene poured himself another cup of coffee and drank it over the sink, gazing out the window.

Ten minutes later, with the breakfast dishes washed and the last cup of coffee sitting in front of Eleanor, Max emerged, dressed in a new pair of black pants and a crisp white shirt. His eyes were bloodshot and his knuckles were scraped, but other than that, no one could have guessed the events of the morning.

"Are we ready to go?"

"Do you want some breakfast?" Eleanor reached for a bowl.

"Nah, I'm fine."

Eugene pulled keys from his pocket and tossed them to Max. "Why don't you drive today?"

Max caught the keys. "Thanks, Pop."

Jessie led the family out the door, taking a place in the back seat, making sure Eleanor sat next to the window.

CHAPTER THIRTY-FIVE

Secrets

June 20, 1965

Only a dozen cars were in the parking lot, allowing Max to nose their own into a spot near the front door. Jessie couldn't wait to get inside, out of the already oppressive heat. He could feel sweat trickling through his short hair and reached into his pocket for the red-checked bandanna he always carried with him. A pair of ladies broke away from a group when the Coles entered the church, enveloping Eleanor in gentle hugs. Pleasantries were exchanged as Jessie scanned the church. He allowed himself a sigh of relief when he saw no sign of Virginia or her family.

Sundays had been the hardest time to avoid her since the incident at the hospital. A couple of times, Jessie had convinced his mother he was either too sick or too busy studying to go to church. The other weeks, he'd dragged his feet getting ready, making them late, so that the service had already started when they arrived. After the service he'd gotten at least one of his brothers to run outside with him to toss a football or play tag, while Eleanor and Eugene finished socializing. This was the first week Virginia hadn't been in attendance.

"A lot of people must be on vacation," Eleanor commented as they took their normal seat.

Empty pews were scattered throughout the church, yet the building seemed warmer than usual. Jessie reached for a paper fan in the back of the pew in front of him, and fanned his face. After the singing and some announcements, the pastor set his Bible on a podium, loosened his tie, and scanned the sparse crowd with his clear, gray eyes.

"Those are some powerful words. 'And He walks with me, and He talks with me, and He tells me I am His own.' We sing songs like this every week, but do we really live them out? Do we have a true relationship with God, conversing with him on a daily basis or are we just putting on a show for our neighbors?"

Jessie shifted uncomfortably, waving the fan faster.

"In Luke, chapter eleven, verses thirty-seven to forty-two, we see Jesus being invited into the home of one of the Pharisees. Now, we know the Pharisees prided themselves on being strict observers of the Jewish Law. This Pharisee, however, was surprised when Jesus sat down at his host's table without washing up first and what did Jesus say to him? 'Now then, you Pharisees clean the outside of the cup and dish, but inside you are full of greed and wickedness. You foolish people! Did not the one who made the outside make the inside also? But give what is inside the dish to the poor, and everything will be clean for you.'"

The pastor paused, placing both hands on the podium. Jessie looked up at the stained glass window. The waving limbs of a nearby tree made sunlight dance through the thick panes.

"Jesus wasn't talking about how well his host cleaned his dishes, he was talking about the man's heart. The Pharisees prided themselves on knowing the scriptures better than anyone else, and carrying out all of the tenets of the law, yet they failed to recognize Jesus as the Messiah. How often are we like the Pharisees, proud of our knowledge and accomplishments, yet oblivious to the gift right in front of us?"

Jessie felt a pinch on the back of his arm and pushed his elbow into Ricky's side. Ricky tried to squirm away from his brother, but Max was on the other side, not moving. Eleanor placed a firm hand on Jessie's leg and he could feel her glaring at him. He sat up straighter and folded his hands in his lap, trying to focus on the words of the pastor, but he didn't see how any of it related to him. He didn't have any garden to walk in, and well, yeah, he was proud of a few things, the fort they'd built, standing up to Alan, breaking JT's arm, but who wouldn't be proud of those things? It was Max's birthday so Jessie knew there weren't any gifts for him that he was missing out on. What was this preacher talking about?

"There is a difference between religion and relationship that I want you all to understand." The pastor stepped out from behind the podium, unbuttoned his suit coat and slipped it off his shoulders, draping it neatly on the piano bench. "There are many people who are wrapped up in religion, appearing to do all the right things, going to church, tithing, praying, giving to those in need, but those are just outward actions. When you have relationship with God, though, wow, what a difference that makes."

The pastor smiled, and the passion Jessie could see in the man's eyes drew Jessie's attention.

"When you truly accept and appreciate the sacrifice Christ made on the cross, for our sins; when you recognize the power of that unconditional love, you are changed. You recognize that you are the cup that God made, and he knows you inside and out. You may talk to your best friends about struggles you are going through, but do you tell them everything? Do they know every secret about you?"

The pastor looked over the room and Jessie felt like the man was looking right through him. He thought about the secret he was keeping from his brothers, about Eugene's encounter with the bum at the fort.

"God knows all of your secrets, no matter what you do to try to hide them from the world. When you have a relationship with God, you have the freedom to talk to him about everything; you have the comfort of knowing that there isn't anything too big for Him to handle and that He will walk with you through any struggle."

"Amen," Eugene whispered. Jessie looked past his mother to where his father sat. Eugene's eyes were closed and his lips moved soundlessly.

"Having a relationship with God means you are in communication with Him not just for a couple of hours on Sunday but every minute of every day." The pastor's words swelled, his arms reaching out to encompass the whole congregation. "You praise and worship Him; you know that you are under His protection; you are filled with His peace and love."

The pastor paused, dropping his hands to his side. A reverent silence filled the church. Jessie's gaze slid across the profiles of the people around him. Some were stone-faced, apparently unmoved by the pastor, while others wore broad smiles and nodded their heads.

"When you have a true, right relationship with God, the world will see it in the way you love others. You will forgive, serve, and accept out of love rather than obligation. If you don't have that kind of relationship with God right now, you have the chance to invite Him into your heart."

Softly, the piano started playing. The family in the row in front of him bowed their heads as Jessie picked up the fan he'd dropped in his lap and started fanning himself again. He felt Ricky poke him in the side once more, but ignored it, his thoughts still lingering on the pastor's words. A man walked down the aisle and kneeled at the front of the church. Two ladies walked forward as well and the pastor placed a hand on each of them. The man at the piano started a second verse and then Jessie felt the pew shift under him. He turned to see Eugene and Eleanor rising. Eugene took his wife's hand and walked with her to the pastor who welcomed them with open arms. They talked through the whole verse and chorus before returning to their seats. Eleanor patted Jessie's leg when she sat down again, then rested her head on Eugene's shoulder.

CHAPTER THIRTY-SIX

Long Wait

June 20, 1965

After church, the boys filed out into the bright summer afternoon. The asphalt was hot under Jessie's feet, causing him to hurry to the car, but when he opened the door, a blast of air as hot as a furnace poured out. He leaned over to roll the window down, waiting for Eleanor and Eugene to emerge from the church.

"How long you suppose they're gonna be in there?" Ricky asked, leaning against a pine tree.

Jessie shrugged and joined his brother in the shade, while Sam and Max walked down the sidewalk toward the convenience store, two blocks away.

"You haven't heard anything more about that dead body have you?" Jessie peeled at the tree bark.

"Nope. I still can't believe Alan tried to pin that on Daddy."

"Maybe that's why Pop stayed after the service. Maybe he's telling the pastor all about killing that guy." Jessie was confused by the sermon and his parents' actions.

"The police would've come back by now if they believed Daddy had anything to do with it."

"Not if they didn't have any evidence."

Ricky shook his head. "Daddy didn't kill anyone. You got any money? I want to go get a Coke."

"No, I don't got no money," Jessie barked. "Use your own."

"I left it at home. Surely you got a quarter."

Jessie turned out his pockets to prove he wasn't carrying any cash. "Do you think Pop really has changed? That he won't go back to drinking and hitting?"

Ricky glanced toward the church then back at Jessie. He sucked on his lower lip, then nodded. "I don't think he'd be in the church still if he hadn't changed."

Jessie thought about that, reviewed the folks he'd seen in the church since they'd started coming. He could name half a dozen regular attendees he'd heard were hotheads or gamblers. One man he'd even seen firsthand kicking a dog in the street. Did simply going to church make you a better person? He'd been going there for three months now, but that didn't mean he would hold back come fall, when Alan Welty tried to beat him up again.

Sam and Max came into sight at the end of the road. As they got closer, Jessie could see they carried a bottle of Coca-Cola. Ricky must have seen it too, because he pushed off the tree and jogged to meet them. Max handed the bottle to Ricky, who took a long drink, nearly emptying the contents.

Jessie waited for them in the shade, still pondering what going to church meant. When Ricky reached the tree again, he handed the half-empty soda bottle to Jessie. The glass was still cold and he held it up to his face for a minute before tilting it to his lips, allowing the fizzy liquid to cascade down his throat. He hadn't realized how thirsty he was until that first gulp went down. Before he knew it, the bottle was empty. He shook it, his tongue searching for any drops clinging to the rim.

"Thanks." Jessie wiped his mouth with the back of his hand.

"Are Mom and Pop still inside?" Max took the empty bottle from Jessie's hand and set it at his feet.

"Yep. Wonder what they're talking about." Jessie studied Max, equally curious about the reconciliation between him and their father.

"I'm gonna see if we can walk home. I want to get out of these clothes." Max crossed the parking lot and pulled open the church door.

Jessie expected his brother to appear again in a minute at the most, but after five passed, he started getting antsy. "What *are* they doing in there?"

"I don't know, but I'm getting hungry," Ricky groused.

Jessie rolled his eyes. "I'm going to find out what's going on."

He marched off, determined to drag his parents out of there whether they were ready or not. Before he could reach the door, though, Max stepped out, followed by Eugene and Eleanor. Eleanor was beaming and Eugene even seemed to have a glow about him, but Max walked slowly, head down, hands stuffed into his pants' pockets.

"Come on, boys," Eleanor called in a sing-song voice. "Time to go."

Sam picked up the empty bottle and raced Ricky to the car. The ride home was quiet. Max kept his head out the window, back turned to his brothers, and jumped out as soon as the car stopped in front of the house. The sound of his bedroom door slamming greeted the rest of the family as they entered the house. A minute later, as Jessie reached his own bedroom, his shirt half unbuttoned, he caught sight of Max in shorts and a t-shirt darting out the back door.

Jessie started to follow him, but a gentle hand on his shoulder held him back.

"Let him go," Eleanor said, removing her hand and opening the door to her bedroom. "He'll be back for dinner."

CHAPTER THIRTY-SEVEN

Lazy Afternoon

June 20, 1965

Jessie looked through the window, back toward the woods, but Max had already disappeared. Eleanor sent the boys through the house to open all the windows and turn on the few fans they had.

"Prop open the back door, too," she called.

Jessie did so before sitting down at the table.

"What took so long at church?" Jessie leaned his head on the palm of his hand, his eyes following Eleanor around the kitchen.

"Your father had some questions he wanted to ask the pastor." She kept her tone light, but Jessie noticed a shadow pass across her eyes.

"But you were in there forever." Jessie dragged the last word out, then realized he sounded like Ricky.

"You're being dramatic." Eleanor waved her hand dismissively.

"What about when Max went to ask if we could walk home? He was in there a long time, and he didn't seem too happy when you all came outside."

Eleanor poured flour into a long white pan. "There are some things that are private. If your brother wants to talk to you about it, he will, but I don't want you asking him."

"Yes, ma'am." Jessie knew there was no point trying to argue or push the issue. He watched Eleanor a few minutes longer, but then got bored and so wandered to the bedroom.

Ricky was lying on his stomach, feet in the air, arms hanging off the end of the bed, a comic book open on the floor. "I bet we could give Daniel Boone a run for his money."

Jessie looked down at the comic book, open to the story of "The Murder's Cave." It reminded him of Bum's Cave and the dead body that had been found three weeks ago now. Officer Murphy hadn't come back, nor had any other policemen, and Jessie hadn't seen anything more about it in the newspapers.

"Why do you say that?" Jessie motioned for his brother to scoot over so he could sit on the bed as well.

Ricky wriggled closer to the wall before pointing down at the comic. "I think we've lived in the wilderness as long as he has. Between the four of us, we probably have more experience."

Jessie laughed. "Yeah, but he'd be about two hundred years old by now."

"You're no fun." Ricky closed the book, burying his face in the blanket and wrapping his arms around his head.

Jessie chuckled, patting Ricky on the back. "You're right. I'm no fun." He scooped up the abandoned comic book and carried it to his own bed where he opened and read through it.

Having eventually read it cover to cover, Jessie wandered back out to the kitchen where Eleanor sat at the table, a tall glass of iced tea in front of her. He noticed her hair was wet at the temples and her cheeks were flushed from the heat. The oven made the kitchen and living room at least ten degrees warmer than the rest of the house.

Jessie turned one of the chairs backward and straddled it. Eleanor frowned, but said nothing. Jessie crossed his arms along the back of the chair and rested his chin on them. He'd been grounded to the house for three months, but he'd never been as bored as he was now. Maybe it was the anticipation of Max's birthday dinner and presents that made the day seem to drag on.

"Where is everyone?" Jessie asked.

"Your father had to run an errand, but I don't know what Sam's up to. Isn't Ricky in your room?"

"He's asleep." Jessie stood and poured himself a glass of tea. "How long until dinner?"

"Another hour." Eleanor stood and opened the oven a crack. "Do you want to help me ice the cake when it cools?"

"I dunno. May I go outside until then?"

"What are you going to do?"

Jessie took a drink of his tea. "Maybe I'll see if we have any oil for the lawn chairs. They all need it bad."

Eleanor nodded. "As long as you don't get yourself all dirty."

Jessie finished his tea before going out to the back porch and rummaging through a cabinet there, until he found a can of oil and an old rag. He spent the next half hour oiling the joints of the chairs, until they moved smoothly.

"Mama says it's time to get cleaned up." Sam appeared in the doorway as he finished speaking.

Jessie grinned. "I got them all working again."

"Great," Sam drawled. "Now come on in, I'm hungry."

"Where you been anyway?" Jessie returned the oil to the cabinet, wiping his hands on the rag.

"Around." Sam turned without another word, leaving Jessie to follow him in.

After washing up, he found the rest of the family in the kitchen, with the exception of Eugene. Max, Sam, and Ricky sat in their normal seats, while Eleanor was pulling a pan of biscuits out of the oven. A large red bowl, filled with fresh black eye peas, and a skillet of cube steak and gravy already sat in the middle of the table. Eleanor plucked the biscuits from the pan onto a serving platter before carrying it and a bowl of mashed potatoes to the table.

Outside, an engine rumbled to a stop, and a door shut before footsteps could be heard. The front door opened and Eugene strode in, mopping sweat from his face.

"I was afraid I might be late." Eugene gave Eleanor's waist a squeeze and dropped a kiss on her cheek.

"You almost were," Eleanor scolded. "Now say the blessing."

"Heavenly Father, thank you for this food, and thank you for giving us Max on this day eighteen years ago. Lord, keep your hand upon him and guide him as he continues to grow into a fine young man. Amen."

The dinner was the most subdued birthday celebration Jessie could remember. Even those days after Eugene had been sent to Uncle Tommy's had been livelier. No one mentioned Max's birthday until the dinner dishes were cleared and Eleanor set the cake on the table. She lit the candles and they sang "Happy Birthday", but Max didn't blow them out at the end.

"Open my present first," Ricky insisted, holding out a poorly wrapped box.

Max took the gift and pulled at the newspaper wrapping, revealing a box of shotgun shells. "Thanks, Ricky, those will be great for hunting."

Sam went next, giving Max four new comic books. *"Batman, The Green Lantern, Richie Rich*, and *Billy the Kid.* Those will keep me busy for a while. Thanks."

Jessie handed Max a box wrapped in the morning cartoons section of the paper, anxious for his brother's reaction. Max pulled the paper away and opened the long, narrow box. A smile crossed his face and his eyes lit up as he pulled out a shiny knife.

It had taken Jessie five months to save enough money for it. The knife came with a sheath that could be attached to a belt. Watching Max admire it made Jessie feel proud of his choice.

"This is great, Jess." Max worked the knife into its sheath.

Eugene stood and helped Eleanor to her feet. "Well, now it's our turn. Would you get the blindfold for him, my lovely wife?"

Eleanor giggled as she wrapped a dishtowel around Max's eyes before helping him to his feet.

"Now, you boys stay here until Max has seen his gift." Eugene stepped out the front door with Eleanor guiding Max outside.

"No way," they heard Max exclaim, sending them all running outside.

In the front yard sat a slate gray, 1951 Chrysler, with the roof and fenders cut off, perfect for driving in the woods or on the beach. Max didn't bother with opening the door, simply jumping into the driver's seat and gripping the steering wheel.

Eugene handed Max the key. "Why don't you take your brothers for a spin around the block?"

Sam and Ricky jumped in, but Jessie hung back, looking to Eleanor for permission. "Go on," she waved.

Max cruised to the end of the street, turned left, then went down two blocks before turning right, soon on the return approach to their house. Jessie grinned at Ricky in the back seat with him. Max looked back briefly, his smile brighter than any Jessie had seen this past year. Jessie knew it was a moment he and his brothers would look back on in years to come as one of the happiest times in their lives.

When the boys pulled up, Eugene and Eleanor were still standing in the yard, arms wrapped around each other, Eleanor's head resting on Eugene's chest. Jessie saw the contentment on their faces as the car came to a stop and the boys jumped out.

"Happy birthday, baby." Eleanor caressed Max's cheek and he turned his head to drop a quick kiss in the palm of her hand.

CHAPTER THIRTY-EIGHT

Summer School

June 21, 1965

"Are you going to drive to school today?" Jessie and Max sat across the table from one another, finishing their breakfast. Jessie cast a hopeful look at his brother, wanting very much to show up in Max's cool new car.

"Nah. Pop said I should use it when we go out to the river or back in the woods more than regular street driving." Max tipped his bowl to drink the last drop of milk, pushed back from the table, and placed the bowl in the sink. "You ready to go?"

Jessie exchanged his own bowl for a notebook and pencil. "Ready."

At the school, a couple dozen kids were huddled in tight groups, waiting for the classrooms to open. Jessie saw Mr. Smith open his door and whistle to get everyone's attention. Seven boys broke away from their groups and filed into the classroom.

"See ya later." Jessie left his brother's side. Max grunted a reply and joined one of the remaining cliques.

"Good to see you, Jessie." Mr. Smith greeted him with a nod.

Jessie stepped inside, his eyes scanning the room. He recognized a couple of the faces, but didn't really know anyone. He took a seat on the far side of the room, third desk from the front.

"Good morning, boys. Welcome to summer school. I know a couple of you have already seen this material once, so try not to ruin the surprises for the rest of the class."

One of the boys snickered, but Jessie didn't turn to see who. His plan was to keep his head down and not draw attention to himself. Mr. Smith picked up a stack of books from his desk and walked around the room handing them out.

With the books distributed, Mr. Smith moved to the blackboard and started writing. "Please turn to page five."

Jessie opened his book and read over the short paragraph at the top of the page. For the next three hours, Jessie scribbled furiously in his notebook, trying to capture everything the teacher said. When Mr. Smith released them for the day, Jessie was reluctant to leave. The other boys seemed to linger as well.

"I'm Randy." A lanky boy, hair the color of a carrot and freckles dusted across his cheeks, stepped over to Jessie's desk.

"Jessie."

"You're Sam's younger brother, right?"

Jessie nodded.

"He and my sister had a few classes together. I think she has a crush on him." Randy chuckled. "Of course, she'd kill me if she knew I'd told you that."

"I won't tell him," Jessie replied with a wink. "Have you been through this class before?"

"Nah, I'm a freshman like you, well I guess technically we're sophomores now. I want to go into engineering and Mr. Smith told me this would be a good class to take. Why are you here?"

"I want to be an astronaut." For the first time, Jessie didn't feel shy talking with a fellow student about his dream.

"Right on." Randy gave him a high-five. "I better run, see you tomorrow.'

Randy jogged out of the room, leaving Jessie alone with Mr. Smith. "I sure am happy you talked me into taking this class."

"I think you'll learn a lot and make some good friends." Mr. Smith smiled and closed the book on his desk. "Now you better get home before your mother thinks you are out having fun."

"Where ya been?" Max griped the minute Jessie joined him in the courtyard.

"Look, there's Pete Murphy." Jessie pointed to a boy at the edge of the courtyard, heading for the street. Without waiting for his brother, Jessie jogged off to catch up with him.

"Pete! Hey, Pete, wait up."

The boy turned, but didn't stop. Jessie caught up with him on the sidewalk outside of the school.

"What do you want?" Pete grumbled.

"I was wondering if anything new turned up on that dead guy. Your old man said Alan accused my Pop of having something to do with it." Jessie hadn't meant for the words to come out as harshly as they did, but they had the desired effect. Pete came to a stop and Jessie gave him his meanest stare.

"Alan accused your dad and so mine had to follow up on it. That's his job. Word around Bum's Cave, though, was that the guy was a big talker, seemed to think he was better than everybody else. A couple of the regulars down there tried to get him to move on, but he wouldn't so Pa figures they moved him on to the next life."

Jessie's shoulders sagged. "So the case is closed?"

"Pretty much. There wasn't enough evidence to prove who was involved. Sounds like several guys wailed on him pretty good then left him to die." Pete started walking again.

"Thanks, Pete. I knew Alan was trying to get to me."

"He's a real loser," Pete agreed. "I told Pa as much when he asked me about him."

Jessie looked over his shoulder, expecting to see Max behind them. "I wonder what happened to Max."

"Maybe he cut through the woods." Pete kept walking, leaving Jessie alone on the side of the road.

The house was empty when Jessie got home. He poured himself a glass of tea and turned on the television before sinking onto the couch. The television droned without him noticing what was on. His thoughts were still on Pete's words, exonerating Eugene. The idea of some of the other bums beating Buster to death made sense. Based on what Jessie had seen of the man, he was an arrogant jerk, unlike most of the drifters Jessie had come in contact with who were quiet and tried to remain unseen.

Jessie turned at the scrape of the front door opening. Eugene ducked through. "I really gotta do something about that. Oh, hey, Jessie. I didn't realize you'd be home yet. How long has this door been sticking like this?"

"I dunno, a while I guess." Jessie joined his father by the door, studying a spot around the lock. The metal plate was scratched, the wood swelled up around the edges. "Looks like the wood needs to be shaved down some."

Eugene grunted. "Run get me some sandpaper."

Jessie collected the sandpaper, a chisel, and a hammer, and returned to the living room. Eugene was kneeling by the door, rubbing a finger over the lock plate. He took the sandpaper and scrubbed the swollen wood, a large splinter breaking off almost immediately.

"Hmm, we may need to replace the whole casing here." Eugene picked at the spot and more wood crumbled into his hand. "Well, gosh darn if we don't have termites."

"That's bad isn't it?" Jessie leaned forward to inspect the area himself.

"You bet your britches it's bad." Shutting the door, Eugene stood, stretching his back, a loud pop sounding as he rolled his neck. "Good thing I ran into Fred Mayberry at the produce market this morning. He offered me a job on his crew. Pays almost twice what I'm making now."

"Really?" Jessie was skeptical. Eugene had been working at the produce market for four months, making a little over minimum wage.

"Fred said his construction company got a contract to clear a bunch of land, to make way for new houses; the city's expecting close to a hundred houses this year for folks moving in to support the space program. I think that's a bit of a stretch, myself."

"What are you going to be doing?"

"Driving a bulldozer around, tearing down trees."

"Oh." Jessie couldn't hide his disappointment. The idea of the space program growing had consumed him for years now, but he'd never thought about the impact that growth would have. They'd lost their land on the island, now the land around them in town was going to be changed too?

"Fred still has a place on his crew for one more person. I didn't know if any of you boys would be interested."

"Max and Ricky have their jobs at the grocery store, but Max might be interested in the change."

"What change?" Max pushed through the front door.

"I was telling Jessie about my new job, clearing land for houses. There's one more spot on the crew if you're interested."

Max shrugged. "Maybe. It'd have to be part time 'til I finish summer school."

"I'll call Fred tonight and let him know." Eugene gave Max a jovial slap on the back. "Now, what do you suppose your mother has planned for dinner?" Eugene went to the kitchen, leaving Jessie and Max in the living room.

"What happened to you after school?" Jessie dropped back onto the couch, leaving room for Max.

"I went by the post office, registered for the draft." Max sat on the opposite end of the couch, slouching into the corner.

"You don't think you will get called, do you?"

Max stared vacantly at the television. "Why don't you take the job with Pop? That way, if I do get called up…"

"Don't talk like that," Jessie insisted. "You take the job. Maybe you can talk to the manager at the grocery store and I can take your place there. It would be nice to have some extra money."

"Sure. I'll talk to him tomorrow."

CHAPTER THIRTY-NINE

Drafted

August 3, 1965

The family spent almost a week with Uncle Tommy, while their house was treated for termites, and Jessie had to walk within a block of Virginia's house to get to school. He glanced down the road as he passed every morning and afternoon, unsure of what he would do if he saw her, but she was never outside. Maybe her family had gone away for the summer.

Before Jessie knew it, summer school came to an end and he started picking up more hours at the grocery store. It was easy work, bagging groceries, helping folks out to their cars. The older ladies would tip him a quarter and one woman, with a set of screaming twins, had even given him seventy-five cents when he loaded her car and made a funny face that got the kids to stop crying.

"Thank you," she sighed. "I don't know how much more I can take. Their daddy shipped off to Vietnam a week ago and it seems like they haven't stopped crying since."

Jessie looked at the two-year-old boys in the back seat, now sucking their thumbs and watching him through the open window. Their blonde hair was curly at the ends; their noses were red and snotty from crying. Jessie made another face, which caused the boys to giggle, and brought a tired smile to their mother's face.

"I'm here just about every afternoon. Bring them by again if they need a laugh," Jessie offered before wheeling the shopping cart back to the store.

That evening at dinner, Jessie was about to tell the story of the twins when Max tossed an envelope on the table. Jessie looked from his brother's tense face to his mother whose cheeks drained of color. Eugene reached for the envelope and clasped Eleanor's hand as he pulled out the letter. It took him only a second to scan the contents, his gaze flicking to Max for a moment. Eugene gave Eleanor a grave nod.

A strangled cry escaped from Eleanor's throat before she raised a hand to cover her mouth. Max met her gaze and Jessie watched in silence, suppressing his own cries of outrage.

"What is it?" Ricky asked. His words were so naïve. Jessie didn't understand how his brother didn't comprehend what everyone else at the table knew.

"He's been drafted, you moron," Sam hissed.

"But he's only been eighteen for two months," Ricky stammered.

"It doesn't matter." Eugene's words were gentle.

"I have to report for evaluation in two weeks." Max took the letter from his father.

"Maybe you won't pass the physical." Eleanor looked hopeful.

"I haven't been sick in years and I'm strong. I don't have much hope of my health failing me."

Jessie was surprised at how calm his brother seemed. Max didn't sound scared or angry. He sounded resigned, as if he'd thought of all the ways out without finding a viable option. What would it be like without Max around? Jessie wanted to get up and shake his brother, tell him there had to be another way, that Max should run away to Canada, anything but give up.

"It's going to be okay," Max assured them. "I've survived gators, bears, and panthers since I was seven. I've learned how to take care of myself in the wilderness." He tried to smile, but his mouth only twitched.

Jessie saw fear, like that of a cornered animal, in his brother's eyes. Who would protect Max in that jungle? Sam, Ricky, and Jessie would be left behind, unable to watch his back. Anger gripped Jessie's heart as he pushed out of his chair, toppling it, and headed for the door.

It had been months since Jessie had run into the forest. The smell of pine needles, animal scat, and decaying leaves filled his lungs, welcoming him home. He darted around trees and jumped over ditches. He crashed through a clump of bushes, sending a pair of doves flying. A blue jay screeched overhead, warning other animals of Jessie's rampage. He ran on, blindly, coming to a stop only when he reached the outer walls of the fort.

He stared in disbelief. A tall new structure rose in the middle of the fort, built of rough planks with a tarpaper roof. Jessie pulled open the fort door and crept closer. The two huts the boys had constructed stood to the right of the new structure. They looked unchanged since the last time Jessie had been out here. The new building was two stories with a large window on the upper level. On the left side of the building was a wooden door, which Jessie pushed open. The room he entered was dark. A shaft of light fell in the far corner and Jessie could make out a ladder. He stumbled forward, hands out, feeling for any obstacles.

When he reached the ladder, he looked up. The shaft of light came through a hole in the floor. Jessie climbed to the second story where windows at the front and back allowed in light and a nice cross-breeze. A small coffee table sat in the middle of the room with an assortment of carved animals scattered on it. Wood shavings littered the floor. Jessie stepped to the window and looked out. There wasn't much of a view; the woods were thick all around the fort, unlike their old tree house with its view of the original launch sites.

"Not bad, huh?"

Jessie turned to see Max's head rise through the opening in the floor.

"You guys have been busy. I didn't realize you all came out here that much."

"I may have said I was working extra shifts when I was really coming out here," Max admitted. "Pop helped out some too."

"What?" Jessie leaned back against the wall.

"Yeah, he actually found the lumber." Max scratched his head. "He never did mention where."

"So you and Pop worked on this together? When did you two become so chummy?"

Max sat down, pulled his pocketknife out, and reached for a small log from a pile Jessie hadn't even noticed. "I don't know. It happened slowly. He came out here one afternoon, a week or so after you were grounded. I was the only one here and I was working on the third hut. Pop didn't say anything, he just started helping. A week later he showed up with the coffee table.

"I don't know how he got the lumber out here. I came by on the way home from school one day and it was lying here along with a bag of nails and a couple of hammers. Next day, Sam and I came out and started building. Pop would show up every now and then, lend a hand, bring something new."

Jessie eased down the wall until he was squatting on his heels. "Pop said he hadn't been out here since the night I ran off. Why would he lie?"

Max looked up in surprise from his whittling. "Why were you asking him about that?"

"I thought he might have killed the bum."

"Why'd you think that?"

"It wouldn't have been the first time Pop hurt him. I saw him throw a stake through the guy's arm."

"When?"

"The night I ran away and you showed him this place," Jessie grudgingly admitted.

"You were here?"

"I was in a tree and could hear you guys. After you took Mama home I came closer. I was crouching back there," Jessie pointed, "when Buster showed up."

"Pop did mention he thought you were out here that night. Maybe that's why he didn't tell you about his trips to help us."

"So, now you're best buds 'cause he came out and helped you build this place?"

Max picked up his knife and started carving again. "No, it's not like that." Max looked Jessie in the eye. "Don't you get tired of being angry at him?"

Jessie held his brother's gaze for a long time, searching for the answer he thought Max wanted, then nodded. "I don't know what I'm supposed to feel. When he went to the hospital, I was scared and relieved. I hoped he would die then I felt awful. I hoped he killed the bum and would go to jail. But I told the police there was no way he'd do that. Every night I expect him to walk in the door stinking of booze and ready to beat on me."

"I know what you mean. I didn't buy his changed man speech when he gave it to me the first time or probably the fifth. When he comes home late, I study him to see if he's been drinking. We've done that most of our lives. It's hard to believe it's only been a year since we left the island."

"Now you're leaving," Jessie whispered.

Max leaned back against the wall. "Yeah, now I'm leaving."

The sunlight coming through the windows danced as the trees around them swayed in the breeze. The air moving through the room was hot and whirled the wood shavings across the floor. A cardinal landed on the edge of the window, where its head turned sideways before sounding a high-pitched metallic, whoit, whoit, whoit. An answering call came from the other side of the fort sending the cardinal flying between Jessie and Max, out through the opposite window.

"Remember going to church on my birthday?"

Jessie nodded.

"Mom and Pop stayed late, they told the pastor they were afraid of sending me to war. When I went in, they sat me down and circled around, placed their hands on me, and prayed. They prayed I wouldn't get called, they prayed for my safety if I did get called, they prayed for each of you, and they prayed for strength for all of us. That's when I knew Pop really had changed. Now it's time for you and me to change, to let go of our fears and our anger. I'm still struggling with the whole God thing, though. It's hard to believe God would allow us to have been beaten on for so long and now He's going to send me to war."

"I don't want you to go, Max."

"I know, Jess. I don't want to go, but I don't see any way out."

Two weeks later, before the sun rose, Jessie lay awake in his bed, listening to the song of a whippoorwill. He could smell fresh coffee and heard the clink of a fork against a plate. Careful not to wake Ricky, Jessie crawled out of his bed, tiptoed to the door, which he eased open enough to slide through.

Eleanor sat at the table, her hair still in curlers. She watched Max sop up the last of his eggs with a piece of toast. Eugene was pouring coffee into a thermos. Jessie stayed in the shadows of the hall, watching, chewing on the collar of his shirt.

"This trip is just for his physical, Nora." Eugene squeezed his wife's shoulder. "He'll be home before you know it."

"Is there time for him to drink another cup of coffee before you go?" Eleanor's voice shook.

"No, he has to be on the bus in Cocoa in less than an hour."

"I don't know why you have to drive him down there, when the bus comes right through town to get to Jacksonville."

"That's just the way the government does things." Eugene bent down and kissed Eleanor's forehead. "I'll be back in a bit."

Max pushed back his chair and took his plate to the sink before leaning down and kissing his mother. Max looked back over his shoulder before stepping outside and his eyes met Jessie's. Jessie held up a hand and Max waved then pulled the door closed behind him.

CHAPTER FORTY

Looking Ahead

August 19, 1965

Max passed his physical with flying colors and returned home to await his orders. A couple other boys from his class had been on the bus to Jacksonville and they'd requested to be placed together, but he certainly wasn't holding his breath.

"It was humiliating," Max told his brothers one afternoon at the fort. Jessie had been released from his grounding and was trying to enjoy his last week of freedom before school started again. "They stripped us down to nothing, lined us up and had a doctor walk down the line inspecting us. Then they ran us through a bunch of obstacles and gave us some tests. Half the guys were stoned out of their minds; they didn't even know their own names. Those are the guys they should be sending over there if you ask me."

"Did they say when you'd get your orders?" Sam pushed his glasses up on his nose.

"Just sometime soon." Max popped a piece of Bazooka bubble gum in his mouth.

"At least you will get to see the launch tomorrow," Jessie reminded him. "Assuming the weather doesn't push it back again. *Gemini 5* is going to be the longest manned flight yet."

"I guess that physics class didn't deter you from your career in space." Max grinned.

"Nope, made me even more sure that's what I want to do."

"I think I've decided I want to work in construction, like Daddy," Ricky piped in.

"There will be plenty of that going on for the next few years," Sam agreed.

"I can't believe school starts again on Monday. Seems like we just finished," Ricky moaned.

"Yeah, yeah, let's not talk about that. Let's talk about the launch. *Gemini 4* accomplished the first space walk, but failed the rendezvous portion of the mission. You think *Gemini 5* can make that rendezvous?" Jessie couldn't contain his excitement.

Sam peered over the top of his glasses instead of pushing them up again. "I wouldn't give them good odds since they already had those problems with the fuel cell."

Jessie blew out an exasperated breath. "If they don't rendezvous then how can we ever build a space station?"

"What do we need a space station for?" Ricky's eyebrows had knit together and his brow furrowed.

"Lots of reasons. We can base astronauts up there for experiments, and use it as a jumping off point for exploring farther into space."

"Whoa, cowboy," Max held up a hand to stop Jessie's excited chattering. "We haven't even made it to the moon yet."

Sam nodded. "Max is right. We're a long way from missions to other planets. Heck, we're still a long way from the moon."

Jessie crossed his arms and narrowed his eyes. "We'll be on the moon before you know it and I want to be the first man to go beyond it."

Max spread his hands before him. "Maybe you're right. You follow the program more than I do."

The conversation turned to the start of the new school year and Jessie's thoughts drifted. He'd kept up his subscription to Life magazine for the past six years, read every newspaper story he could find about the space program and sometimes, at the convenience store, he would meet men who worked out at the Cape. A couple of them were happy to talk with him and encouraged him to keep studying.

"Come on, we better get home for dinner." Max stood and brushed dirt off his legs. The rest of them followed suit, with Jessie bringing up the rear. He watched his brothers and tried to imagine just Ricky and Sam walking there ahead of him.

CHAPTER FORTY-ONE

Eight Days or Bust

August 21, 1965

The angry caw of a blackbird woke Jessie the next morning. He checked his watch and found it was already seven-thirty. He threw back the covers, grabbed a clean t-shirt and pair of shorts from the piles next to his bed, and changed in a flash.

"Ricky, wake up," Jessie whispered in his brother's ear.

Ricky squirmed then pulled the sheet tighter around his shoulders. Jessie shook the bed until Ricky opened his eyes.

"What is it?"

"The launch, it's in an hour. Get up." Jessie grew more impatient every second. When Ricky didn't jump right out of bed, Jessie gave him a shove and left the room. He peered into Max & Sam's room and found both brothers getting dressed.

"Do you mind?" Max threw a shoe at the door, causing Jessie to duck.

Jessie went to the kitchen to wait, glancing at the percolator on the stove, wishing for the first time that they had an electric coffee pot.

"What are you waiting on?" Max teased as he and Sam scooted past. The three boys then jogged several blocks, until the humidity brought them to a stop.

"It's like trying to breathe under water," Jessie complained.

"I bet we have a hum-dinger of a storm this afternoon." Max looked to the sky where a few wispy clouds were forming in the west.

"As long as it doesn't interfere with the launch." Jessie fanned his shirt, trying to cool down some. They were only a block from the river and could already hear the car radios. Most were tuned to the local news, but a few blared the newest Beatles song.

"I don't know why girls go so crazy every time the Beatles come on the radio." Max pointed to a car full of women in their early twenties, stuck in traffic, all giggling and singing along to the song.

"You don't know much about girls, period." Jessie nudged his brother in the ribs.

"More than you," Max shot back.

As if on cue, the girls in the car looked in their direction and Max waved, offering a lopsided smile and a wink. Jessie watched one of the women untangle herself from the car and walk toward them. She had long bronze legs, accentuated by the hot pink shorts that barely covered her bottom. A white mid-riff top exposed her flat stomach and slender arms. A sleek sheen of brunette hair fell to the middle of her back.

"Hello there," she purred.

Jessie noticed Max swallow hard. "Hi."

"My friends and I would love for a local to show us the best place to watch the launch. Can you help us out?"

Jessie had never been so jealous of his brother. He barely cared about the launch, yet this gorgeous babe wanted Max to show her to a prime viewing area?

"Sure. I'd love to help you." Max took the woman's hand and walked her back to the car. The back door opened and Max climbed inside, the babe sitting on his lap.

Jessie knew they wouldn't get far in this traffic, but he got the impression the women really didn't care. Even the driver had turned in her seat to talk with Max, only focusing on the road again when a truck sounded its horn and inched up on her.

"How does he do it?" Sam's question had more admiration behind it than jealousy.

"I have no idea." Jessie's gaze followed the car another hundred feet until it stopped again. "Let's go. Launch is in thirty minutes."

Sam and Jessie zigzagged through the cars on the highway until they reached the field on the river's edge where cars were parked haphazardly. Some of the spectators had climbed onto their roofs, others had set up lawn chairs in the back of pickup trucks, and the rest were pressed together on the edge of the river.

When Jessie and Sam had wormed their way to the front of the crowd, Jessie eyed the water. It looked cool and inviting, not quite glassy, the barely imperceptible breeze rippling its surface. Without a word to Sam, Jessie waded in. His shoes filled with water and squished into the mud on the river bottom. By the time he had waded in up to his knees, Jessie could hear Sam behind him.

"Are you kids crazy?" A panicked woman yelled.

Jessie looked over his shoulder and easily picked out the woman, one hand over her mouth, the other clutching the collar of a young boy's shirt. Her son, Jessie guessed.

"Come on in, the water's fine," Jessie smiled and offered an inviting wave to the crowd. A few men chuckled, others kicked off their shoes and followed Jessie's lead.

Sam joined Jessie and the two continued on out until they were waist deep. The car radios were now only a distorted drone at this distance, but Jessie knew the countdown sequence well enough to play it out in his mind.

"You sure know how to start trouble," Sam teased.

"What trouble? It's cooler and, " Jessie looked back over his shoulder, "we're fifty feet closer to the action than anyone else."

"Great idea, kid." One of the men who'd followed splashed water up on his chest then briefly dunked his head under. "How do folks down here stand this heat?"

"You get used to it," Sam replied.

"Where ya from?" Jessie squinted, trying to get a better look at the man.

"Michigan. We drove down a few days ago for the launch. When it was pushed back we decided to stay on, but I tell you, I can't wait to get back to cooler weather."

"Whoa, you came all that way just for the launch?" Jessie felt his eyes go wide.

"I've been following all the news. After Ed White completed the first space walk I knew I had to come see at least one launch."

Jessie nodded. "I haven't missed one yet. You know the slogan for this mission is eight days or bust? It's going to be the longest flight yet."

"You sure know your stuff, kid."

Jessie checked his watch. "Almost time."

Everyone's attention turned across the water. Jessie played out the launch sequence in his mind, hearing the familiar launch control voices. He closed his eyes to block out all of the sounds around him. When he opened them again, his focus was trained south, across the water. A cloud of smoke rose into the sky and cheers erupted from the shore. Jessie watched the rocket rise, passing the sun only two hours above the horizon. Jessie waited until the smoke melted away into the clear blue, leaving no remaining trace of the rocket.

"That's it?" The guy from Michigan sounded disappointed.

"What were you expecting?" Jessie went on the defensive.

"I don't know, a bigger show I guess."

"We are north of the launch sites here," Sam explained. "Out at Cocoa Beach you would have been closer, may have seen it come right over you there."

"Why didn't anyone tell me that?"

"Did you ask?" Jessie countered.

"Well, no, I guess I didn't, I just followed all the other cars."

"The launch sites are moving farther north. They're just about finished with a new pad right over there." Sam pointed across the river, where the skeleton of the Vertical Assembly Building was rising against the horizon.

"Huh. Guess I'll have to come back another time." The man splashed his face again. "At least I got to cool off some. You kids have a good day." He turned and started slogging back to the shore where cars were already backing into the flow of traffic.

CHAPTER FORTY-TWO

Sophomore Year

August 23, 1965

J essie's reflection in the bathroom mirror was not being cooperative. He splashed more water on his comb and ran it through his hair one more time. The crew cut had grown out, but now he couldn't get his hair to lay flat. He'd spent the previous evening studying a photograph of The Beatles in one of his *LIFE* magazines. No matter what he did, Jessie couldn't get his hair to go as straight and flat as in that photo.

"Come on, we're going to be late." Sam pounded on the bathroom door.

"Yeah, I'm coming." Jessie ran the comb through one more time.

Stepping out of the bathroom, Jessie found Sam leaning against the opposite wall, legs crossed at the ankles. Sam burst out laughing when he saw his brother. Jessie felt like he was looking in the mirror again. Both boys wore black t-shirts and jeans. Where Jessie's hair had a slight curl to it, Sam's was completely flat, the look Jessie had been trying to create for himself.

"No fair," Jessie moaned at the sight.

"You better go change. We can't show up looking like twins."

"Why should *I* change? You go change." Jessie demanded.

"I'm older, so I get to tell you what to do." Sam pointed at the bedroom. "Put something else on."

"What's going on," Eleanor appeared at the end of the hall. Jessie saw a smile tug at her lips, but she suppressed it and placed a hand on her hip. "You're going to be late for school. Jessie, why don't you go put on that nice blue and white checked shirt I bought you?"

"Yes, ma'am." Jessie hung his head and marched into his room, emerging a minute later buttoning up his new shirt. "Come on."

The school campus buzzed with students reconnecting after the summer break. Girls squealed with delight as they ran to greet each other and boys exchanged high-fives. Jessie saw at least a dozen guys wearing the black shirt and jeans combo and was grudgingly thankful he'd changed.

Across the courtyard he spotted a face he recognized and couldn't tear himself away. She had grown at least an inch over the summer, and stood with her shoulders and back perfectly straight, head held high, but not in a snooty way. The hair that had been a riot of tangled curls last year was now smooth and curled at the ends to frame her face. She wore a tan and green plaid skirt that skimmed her knees and a white button-up blouse that hinted at her curves.

"Go talk to her." Sam nudged Jessie with his elbow.

"I can't." Jessie forced himself to look away.

"She's prettier than I remember." Ricky gave an approving whistle.

"Yeah, she is," Jessie agreed, glancing in the direction he'd last seen her, but Virginia was gone. "I better get to class."

"Me too." Sam and Ricky followed several students to the other side of the school, while Jessie crossed the courtyard and opened the door of his science class.

"Oh, excuse me." Jessie stepped back, apologizing to the student he'd bumped into. His gaze met Virginia's.

She offered a demure smile as she straightened the wide, tan belt around her waist. "Nice to see you."

"You too," Jessie stuttered. Without thinking, he ran his hand back through his hair, ruining the flattening effect he'd struggled all morning for, then rushed to plaster his loose curls back flat against his forehead.

Virginia giggled. "Did you have a good summer?"

Jessie stepped further into the classroom, Virginia staying by his side. "It was all right. How about you?"

Virginia's gaze shifted to the desks. She chose one in the second row and sat down. "I went to visit my aunt in Boston."

So that's why she wasn't in church. Jessie took the desk beside her. "You spent the whole summer there?"

"Mostly. We took a couple of trips to Cape Cod and Nantucket."

"Neat." Jessie had no idea where she was talking about, but thought he remembered something about Cape Cod being a place where the rich folks up north spent time in the summer.

"How's your dad doing?"

Jessie felt his cheeks turn red. Of course she remembered the scene at the hospital. It was too much to hope she'd forgotten. "He's good."

"All right, class. Quiet down." A hefty woman with brown hair and three chins stood at the front of the class. Rolls of fat swung from her arms as she clapped her hands together to get their attention.

Jessie had to choke back a groan of disgust at the sight of the teacher, but he welcomed the end to the awkward conversation. He opened his notebook, deciding he wouldn't look up from it for the rest of the class, not unless Ms. Smathers, as she introduced herself, was writing on the blackboard.

Throughout the lesson, on why plants need sunlight to thrive and make chlorophyll or chloroform, or some other chloro word Jessie couldn't spell, he stole glances at Virginia. She didn't slouch in her seat, making him adjust his own posture. Her gaze followed the teacher back and forth across the room, making notes from time to time.

Class came to an end all too fast. Jessie waited for Virginia to leave the room first and stepped out behind her. "Can I walk you to your next class?"

Virginia batted her eyelashes at him. "Last time I checked you were able to walk fairly well. If you're asking permission to escort me, yes, you may."

Jessie wasn't sure what she meant, but it sounded like a yes to him. "Where are you headed?"

"English with Mr. Cunningham. You?"

A nervous laugh escaped Jessie. "Same."

"Lead the way, then."

Jessie moved in the direction of the English and history classrooms, searching for something to say, maybe some way to explain why he'd avoided her the last weeks of school, but she didn't seem to show any anger about that. Maybe they could have a fresh start. Max would know what to say, why didn't I think to ask him for advice last night?

"Isn't this it?" Virginia's words brought Jessie to a stop. He saw her pointing to a door a few steps behind him. A piece of paper was taped to the door with the name Alex Cunningham on it.

"Uh, yea, you're right."

That tinkling-bell laugh floated from Virginia's mouth. Instead of embarrassing Jessie, the sound lifted his spirits. He stepped forward and held the door open, again taking the seat next to her.

Jessie took a deep breath. "What are your classes for the rest of the day?"

Virginia listed off the subjects and teachers. Much to his dismay, they didn't share any more classes and they were often at opposite ends of the school.

"That's too bad," she frowned. "Maybe you would like to walk me home after school."

Maybe? Was she kidding? Play it cool man, don't seem too excited. "I could probably work that out."

Virginia's eyes darkened at his words, but then she smiled. "I'll wait for you by the gym."

"I hear you walked Virginia Benson home from school today." Max sauntered into the bedroom where Jessie was working on his math homework.

Jessie closed his book and made room on the bed for his brother to sit down. "Ricky and Sam aren't even home yet, how did you know?"

Max waggled his eyebrows. "You know what mom always says. It's a small town and people are always watching."

"Uh-huh. Who told you?"

"I'll never tell. So, did you ask her out?"

"Ask her out? I could barely carry on a conversation with her for the fifteen minutes it took to walk her home."

"That's easy. Just tell her how pretty she looks. Girls love to hear that. The more you talk about them the happier they are."

"I don't know." Jessie fanned the pages of his textbook back and forth, considering Max's advice. "How many compliments can you pay a girl before you run out of things to compliment?"

"There're plenty of things to compliment: her eyes, her hair, her smile, her clothes, her shoes. Girls love it when you notice their shoes. It's kind of weird actually."

Jessie looked down at his own shoes, lined up by the bed, a pair of dirty sneakers and a pair of black loafers in dire need of a shine.

"I'll give it a shot, but Virginia is smart. She even reads for fun. Over the summer she read two books by Charles Dickens and one by Jane Austen. Those are *old* books."

Max chuckled. "And all you read was Beetle Bailey and Superman comics."

"I read Ricky's Daniel Boone comic too."

"Oh, yeah, be sure to tell her that." Max stood. "I can see I have my work cut out for me. I gotta teach you how to talk to girls before I get shipped off. Finish your homework then we'll get started."

CHAPTER FORTY-THREE

Orders

September 14, 1965

Augugust faded into September, the first three weeks of school were behind them and Jessie spent every free minute with Max. Between school and work, though, there wasn't much free time, an hour or two after dinner and homework. Every afternoon he wasn't working, Jessie walked Virginia home from school.

"I've complimented everything from her hair to her toe nail polish. What am I going to say to her tomorrow?" Jessie moaned when Max got home from work.

"Tell her about your brother shipping off to Fort Benning." Max dropped down on the bed next to Jessie, covering his eyes and forehead with one arm.

Jessie felt his throat constrict. "You got your orders?"

"Came in the mail this afternoon. I have to be there in ten days."

"There's still time to get out of the country." Jessie knew what Max's answer would be, but had to give it a shot anyway.

Max lifted his arm and shot Jessie an angry look. "You know how I feel about that. What happens if the war is still going on when Sam turns eighteen and he gets drafted? Is he supposed to high tail it to Canada too?"

"I don't see why not. Maybe the whole family just needs to move up there."

"And what does that do for your chances of becoming an astronaut?"

"Oh." Jessie bent his head down and popped the collar of his shirt with his teeth. "I'd rather have you and Sam home safe than be an astronaut."

Max sat up and moved closer to Jessie. "No kidding? You'd give up going to space to save me and Sam?"

Jessie gave his brother a solemn nod.

"That means a lot, Jess, but I can't have you giving up on your dream."

"Maybe you can shoot yourself in the foot or something during training."

"I've heard of guys doing that, but it only delays the inevitable. I've heard rumors some of the rich kids have bought their way out of service," Max shrugged, "but I certainly can't afford to. Don't worry. I'll take care of myself."

That night, Jessie lay in bed, staring at the ceiling, unable to sleep. He listened to the crickets and cicadas outside the window, the crescendo of their song rising until it seemed the bugs would explode, then throttling back to a soft hum. He heard the distant scream of a panther and wondered how much longer the big cats would be able to survive in the area.

In only a couple of months, hundreds of acres had been cleared for new houses. Jessie and his brothers had seen more deer carcasses along the roads, as they traveled west to the St. Johns River or south toward Cocoa in Max's modified buggy. Would Max come home again before all the woods were gone?

"Lot of big changes going on, huh?"

Jessie blinked and found himself on the beach again. He swiveled his head looking for the familiar voice. "Gus? Where are you?"

A booming laugh rose from the water. Jessie looked into the waves and saw Grissom walking out of the surf toward him. "You didn't know I could throw my voice like that, did ya?"

"Well, as you have so aptly pointed out in the past, it's my dream so I can make you do pretty much anything." Jessie grinned.

"Touché. So, you're willing to give up space to keep your brother safe? That's mighty noble of you."

"I don't know about noble. Although, you think Virginia would find it noble? Should I tell her?"

Grissom's eyes crinkled at the corners as he chortled. "She'd probably find it irresistible. That is if she knows how much you want to be an astronaut. Have you talked to her about that?"

Jessie kicked at the sand. "Not really. I don't want her to laugh at me."

"Why would she laugh? It's a respectable career path."

"You're biased."

"Darn tootin I am!" Grissom stood up straighter, striking a heroic pose.

Jessie couldn't help laughing. "I bet a shrink would have a field day with these dreams."

Grissom looked crushed. "All right, let's get back to the reason you brought me here."

"I don't know why, you're supposed to tell me."

"You wanted to talk about Max and that cute girl, Virginia. Doesn't seem so long ago you were telling me thoughts of girls were still a long ways off for you."

Jessie remembered the dream several months ago when he and Gus had been fishing. They'd talked about second chances, how Jessie needed to give his Pop another shot. "Seems like a lifetime ago."

"A lot has happened since then. I'm glad you and your father are getting on better."

"He's different. He even had the pastor pray over Max the day before he registered for the draft." Jessie pursed his lips. "Fat lot of good that did."

"You can't blame the draft on the pastor, or on God."

"Why not?" Jessie demanded.

"What good does it do blaming anyone? Does it change the situation or make you feel any better?'

"I guess not." Jessie shoved his hands into his pockets and walked a few steps away.

"I wish I could tell you Max will be fine, but you know I can't see the future any more than you can."

"Gee, you're ever so helpful. What can you tell me about Virginia?"

"I like her. She's pretty and smart. I'm fairly sure she could do better than you, though." Grissom winked.

"Swell, if you're my subconscious then I really don't need any enemies, do I?"

"I said she was pretty and smart."

"She is that, but you're right. She could do way better than me. I don't know what I'm thinking."

Grissom clasped Jessie's shoulder and brought him to a stop. "She likes you. If she didn't then she wouldn't want you walking her home and she certainly wouldn't have brought those homemade cookies for you last week."

Jessie nodded. "Those were good. I don't even remember telling her how much I like oatmeal cookies."

"There you go. She managed to find that out on her own. Why would she do that if she didn't like you?"

"Good point. Thanks, Gus."

"Anytime kid. Now you better wake up or you'll be late for school."

"Five more minutes."

"I already gave you five minutes." Eleanor shook Jessie's shoulder.

Jessie opened his eyes, his mother's face just inches from his. She smiled and stood up.

"You must have been having some dream. Breakfast is on the table."

Once Jessie sat up, Eleanor left the room. "Ricky, you awake?"

"Yep," Ricky mumbled around his toothbrush.

Jessie rubbed his face until his eyes were no longer sticky, then he shuffled through the clothes on the floor until he found an outfit that wasn't too wrinkled or stinky. Time to do laundry.

CHAPTER FORTY-FOUR

Shipping Out

September 23, 1965

"Hi, Jessie." Jessie didn't look up when Virginia stopped in front of his desk. Instead he opened his science book, thumbing through the pages until he found where they'd left off the previous day. Virginia stood over him a second later, then with a swish of her skirt, she walked on to her own seat. Out of the corner of his eye he glimpsed Virginia's disappointed face. If only she knew how hard it was to be sitting here right now. *I shouldn't be in school today.*

Mrs. Smathers grunted as she heaved herself from her chair and reached for the chalk. "I know how much you all look forward to the dissection portion of biology." The girls groaned. "Yes, I know, you young ladies aren't so fond of it, but it looks like there are enough gallant young men in here for you to pair up and keep your hands clean. Before we start dissecting, though, we're going to learn about the organs we'll find in our test subjects."

Jessie stole a glance toward Virginia. She didn't wear the grossed out expression he'd expected at the mention of cutting an animal open. In fact, she didn't look like she'd heard Mrs. Smathers' announcement at all.

Mrs. Smathers went on to talk about how the organs in many animals were the same in humans, but Jessie only caught snatches of what she said. His mind felt like a beehive, thoughts buzzing so loud he was sure the students around him must hear. It took several seconds at the end of class for Jessie to realize it was time to go. Virginia hesitated in front of his desk, but when he didn't look up, she sashayed out. Jessie didn't miss the way her hips swayed as she passed through the door. He gathered his books and hurried after her.

"Virginia!" he called. She slowed and looked over her shoulder, but didn't smile. Jessie took a step toward her, watching as her eyes grew wide a second before a large figure stepped between them.

"I haven't had a chance to welcome you back to school, Cole." Alan sneered down at Jessie.

Jessie was startled by the growth spurt Alan had experienced over the summer. He now stood two inches taller and had added at least twenty-five pounds to his beefy frame.

"I'm not in the mood today, Alan." Jessie tried to step around the bully, but Alan matched his step, keeping his body between Jessie and Virginia.

"Now, that's no way to accept my welcome. Why don't we shake on a new year?" Alan stuck out a stubby hand.

Jessie eyed it warily, knowing there had to be a catch. Unwilling to be seen as afraid, he slowly reached out to take Alan's hand, his entire body tensing. Alan squeezed hard when their hands met, causing Jessie to grit his teeth.

"I'll see you around," Alan promised as he let go.

Jessie nodded and stepped around Alan, refusing to show any sign of the pain he felt. Virginia still stood on the other side of Alan, concern written in her tight lips and questioning eyes. When Jessie joined her, the pair walked in silence toward their next class. Outside the door, Jessie stopped and touched Virginia on the arm. She looked at him with those eyes that filled him with such longing.

"What's wrong?" Her words were so soft he wasn't sure if she'd actually spoken them, or if he had wanted her to so badly he'd imagined it. He looked around them. A handful of students were still standing around, taking advantage of every second they didn't have to be in a classroom.

"Max," Jessie started, surprised by the crack in his voice. He cleared his throat, his eyes clinging desperately to Virginia's. "He left for Fort Benning this morning."

Virginia's hand flew to her mouth but then reached out to touch Jessie's arm. "I'm so sorry."

"Come on, it's time to start." Mr. Cunningham stood at the door, ready to pull it closed. Virginia entered the room first, leaving Jessie alone. Jessie heard Mr. Cunningham shuffle his feet and jiggle the door handle. The reprimand Jessie expected for dawdling didn't come and he turned to notice the pitying look on the teacher's face.

"I wish I could say your brother's going to be okay, but…" Mr. Cunningham trailed off. Jessie nodded, grateful for the teacher's honesty.

The rest of the day was a blur, moving from classroom to classroom on autopilot. At lunch, the three remaining Cole brothers picked at their food in silence. At the end of the day, Jessie found Virginia by the gym, as she'd been every day since the beginning of the year. The sight of her both cheered and depressed him.

She threaded her arm through his, something she'd never done before. Even if it was out of pity, Jessie liked the feel of her so close to him. He'd learned to take small steps to accommodate Virginia, but today they walked even slower than normal. A slight hint of fall could be felt in the breeze coming off the river and Jessie found himself wondering what the weather was like in Vietnam.

"Do you think Max has reached Fort Benning yet?" Virginia asked after they'd walked several blocks.

Jessie shrugged. "I know it's somewhere up in Georgia, but I don't know how long it will take to get there or if the bus he's on was stopping to pick up more guys along the way."

"Why didn't your parents let you and your brothers stay home today? Did you have a chance to— " Virginia stopped herself.

"To say goodbye?" Jessie finished. "We stayed up all night, the four of us. Pop drove Max to the bus at six this morning."

Jessie thought about the conversations from the previous night, Max's last words of wisdom on girls, Sam's tips for Max on what to expect in the jungle, Ricky's assurances that all would be fine.

Before he left, Max had taken Jessie aside. "I know you won't miss a launch while I'm gone so you should hold on to this for me." Max placed the transistor radio he'd bought years earlier in Jessie's hands.

"I couldn't." Jessie tried to push his brother's gift away.

Max looked at the ground. "I won't be able to use it in combat. It's better if you have it."

Jessie wrapped his fingers around the cool metal box. "As soon as you come home you can have it back."

Virginia's arm squeezed Jessie's tighter and she leaned her head against his shoulder. Jessie returned the squeeze and leaned down to inhale the scent of her shampoo. When they turned onto her street, Virginia straightened and released Jessie's arm, taking a step away from him.

"I'll keep Max in my prayers."

Jessie struggled to hold back the snort of disgust he immediately felt at her words. He saw the sincerity in Virginia's eyes and knew she believed prayer would help. She had no way of knowing of Jessie's cynicism about God. On the outside he looked like the perfect believer, attending church nearly every Sunday, walking a pretty straight path the rest of the week. How could she know about the failed prayers to keep Max from being drafted?

"Thanks," he mumbled.

The front door opened and Virginia's mother stepped outside. Jessie waved and forced a smile for the woman.

"I'll see you tomorrow." Jessie took a step back toward the road. Virginia brushed at a strand of hair that had blown into her mouth. She looked like she wanted to say something, but she remained silent, taking a small step toward the house. Jessie turned and walked back down the road, feeling her eyes on his back until he turned the corner.

Instead of going home, Jessie plowed into the woods, ducking under branches and climbing over fallen limbs. The tangled refuge seemed to welcome him as he moved deeper. He needed to surround himself with the familiar smells and sounds, to push away the nagging fear in his belly. When he reached a triangle created by two trees, he stopped short, recognizing his shoelace tied around one of them.

Being grounded most of the summer, he hadn't had a chance to come back here to search for more treasure. He thought of the goblet he still had hidden under his bed, forgotten for the past several months, and an idea struck him.

What if there is treasure out here? Could I buy Max's way out of the army?

CHAPTER FORTY-FIVE

Treasure Hunt

September 23, 1965

J essie pulled a box out from under his bed and removed the Spanish goblet he'd found six months earlier. He studied the engravings, looking for anything he may have missed before. Not finding anything new, he took the goblet into Sam's bedroom.

"You remember when I found this?" Jessie asked, handing the cup to his brother.

Sam nodded. "About the same time you got grounded."

"You think it's worth anything?"

"Probably, if you could find the right buyer."

Ricky strode into the room. "You still have that?" he asked, nodding at the goblet Sam was now studying.

"Yeah, I'd forgotten about it with everything that's been going on."

"Why'd you remember it today?" Ricky was now stretched out on Max's bed.

"I was out in the woods and came upon the spot where I found it." Jessie reached for the cup. "I thought if we went back and found more, maybe we could buy Max out of the army."

Sam guffawed. "He's not a slave."

"Isn't he?" Jessie retorted, his face flushing with anger and embarrassment.

"He's kind of right," Ricky agreed. "Max didn't volunteer and didn't have the option of saying no."

Sam sobered. "Never really thought about that."

"Max said he'd heard rumors of rich guys buying their way out of service, so if we got rich…"

Sam tugged on his ear. "Any idea how much it costs to buy your way out?"

Jessie shook his head. "We've all heard the stories of Spanish treasure buried around here, though. Surely there's enough to get Max back and save the rest of us if this blasted war doesn't end soon."

"You know those are only stories. There isn't any proof that there is treasure. In fact, the Spaniards came to Florida *looking* for gold."

"Ugh, why do you have to be such a smarty pants," Ricky groaned.

"I didn't say it wasn't worth checking out. Even if we can't buy Max out of the army finding treasure would be cool."

"Are you guys free after school tomorrow?" Jessie looked at each of his brothers in turn, waiting for their nods.

"Good. Meet me at the corner of Capron and Coquina."

"You're still going to walk Virginia home?" Sam raised a quizzical eyebrow.

"Well, yeah." Jessie squirmed under his brothers' intense gazes.

"Jessie and Ginny sitting in a tree—" Ricky cut his taunt short at Jessie's angry look.

"Okay, we'll meet you there, but don't take as long as you usually do." Sam stood. "I have to go do some homework."

The next day, Jessie couldn't wait for school to be over. Every class felt twice as long as normal, and even Virginia's great smiles every time they passed couldn't calm his nerves. After his last class, he raced to the gym. Virginia was leaning against the wall, her blue knee socks leaving only a couple of inches of exposed skin before the hem of her yellow skirt, but Jessie noticed for the first time how brown her legs were. He found himself trying to imagine her in a bathing suit. She must have spent the whole summer in one to be so tanned.

"You ready?" Virginia interrupted Jessie's daydream and he felt himself flush, sure she knew what he'd been thinking.

"Yep." He smiled and expected her to take his arm, as she had the previous day. He was disappointed when she didn't and started walking almost a foot away from him.

"You seemed to be in a better mood today," Virginia commented.

Jessie didn't know if he should tell her about his plan. "I'm still worried, but Max wouldn't want me to stop living until he comes home." Feeling bold, knowing what he said was true, Jessie reached out and took Virginia's hand. It took a second for her fingers to relax and twine around his own. A smile played at the edge of her lips, sending Jessie's heart soaring. If it hadn't been for his brothers waiting for him, Jessie would have dragged his feet to make this moment last as long as possible.

Approaching Virginia's house, she released his hand and put distance between them yet again. Was she ashamed of him? He wanted to ask her, but Mrs. Benson was already waiting at the front door. Jessie didn't linger, hoping for a smile or a word from Virginia. He gave her a curt nod and turned in a huff.

"That didn't take as long as I expected." Ricky pushed off the tree he'd been leaning against; Sam a few steps away.

"Let's go," Jessie ordered, cutting across the street into the pine and oak trees. It only took him five minutes to find the spot. Ducking through the embracing trees, he stepped into the small clearing and waited for Sam and Ricky to catch up.

"The goblet was right here." Jessie pointed at a small depression in the ground. He was surprised to find the area barely looked disturbed from his digging. The wind and rain had nearly erased all trace of his previous visit.

Sam scanned the clearing. "Odd place to find treasure."

"Where would you expect to find it?" Ricky countered.

"Spread out and we'll see if we can find anything else." Jessie wasn't in the mood for a lecture from Sam. "The goblet was only partially buried."

The boys went in separate directions, kicking at the dirt and dead leaves. Jessie moved slowly, searching for the glint of metal in the irregular shafts of sunlight. From time to time he'd kneel for a closer look, usually finding only a gnarled root.

"We need one of them metal detector things," Ricky called from the other side of the clearing.

"Well, we don't have one so keep looking," Jessie shot back. He was growing frustrated; beginning to think the goblet had been a random find, maybe even dropped there by someone only a few years ago.

"Cool," Sam drew out the word. Jessie saw his brother rising from a crouch.

"What'd you find?" Jessie jogged over to his brother's side. Sam held up a small dagger. The blade was a dull gray, the tip broken off, but it was the hilt that caught Jessie's attention.

"Is that a ruby?" Jessie's eyes grew wide. At the top of the hilt, just before the blade, was a stone almost an inch in diameter.

Sam brushed at the dirt until the stone was completely uncovered. Stepping into a shaft of light, he held up the dagger, the deep red stone catching the light.

"I think it is," Sam agreed.

Jessie dropped to his knees and started brushing at the dirt, searching for anything else. Several shards of colored glass and broken pottery turned up.

"Don't just throw those away," Sam cautioned. "This could be an archeological find."

"I don't care, professor. I'm only interested in things we can sell." Jessie started digging deeper, feeling the dirt packing under his fingernails.

"But you could be destroying evidence of an old Spanish settlement." Sam grasped Jessie's shoulder, but Jessie shook him off.

"What's more important? Alerting the historians that some old dead guys might have lived in this spot or saving Max from becoming a young dead guy?" Jessie looked up at Sam, waiting for a response.

Sam tugged at his ear, looked at the dagger in his other hand, then nodded and joined Jessie on the ground. Jessie looked to Ricky who wasted no time kneeling down and digging before Jessie could say another word.

For half an hour the boys dug shallow trenches, uncovering more pottery and the occasional glass bead. Jessie wiped at the sweat pouring into his eyes, determined not to give up until he found something more. Surely there were three or four gold coins. Wouldn't that be enough to get Max home safely? The woods grew darker as the sun dropped in the west and still they searched.

Sam leaned back on his heels and let out a tired sigh. "We better get home soon."

Jessie punched the ground. "There has to be more here."

"We'll come back this weekend with some shovels." Sam stood and brushed at the dirt on his pants.

"And maybe we can find a metal detector," Ricky added hopefully.

Jessie shook his head. "We can't wait until the weekend. We have to find more treasure now." He clawed at the ground desperately until he felt Sam's hand on his back.

"It's going to be dark soon. We won't be able to see what we are digging up. Come on." Sam gave Jessie's shirt a gentle tug.

"What if someone else finds this spot?" Jessie couldn't bring himself to give up yet.

"Look around," Ricky spun in a full circle, hands outstretched, "who's going to find this place?"

Jessie relaxed a tiny bit. Ricky was right. As much time as the boys spent in the woods, this was only the third time Jessie had been here. With a resigned nod, Jessie stood and led his brothers home

"My goodness," Eleanor exclaimed when the boys entered the house. "You look like you've been working in a coal mine. Go get washed up."

Jessie was thankful she didn't ask what they had been up to. He didn't think she would understand their treasure hunt, even if it meant they could get Max back home.

CHAPTER FORTY-SIX

Disappointment

September 25, 1965

"There's not enough." Jessie leaned on the shovel, his whole body drenched in sweat. He and his brothers had spent all day digging up the clearing, but had only found trinkets from an era long past.

Sam nodded in agreement. "Even if we could find someone interested in the glass beads and pottery shards, I don't think we've found anything worth more than a couple hundred dollars."

Jessie swayed unsteadily, gripping the shovel for support. "At least we gave it a shot."

"It was a good idea." Ricky dropped an arm around Jessie.

Sam and Ricky gathered up the artifacts they'd uncovered, dropping them into a small bag. Jessie heaved the shovel onto his shoulder, and together they began their silent trek home.

The boys tromped into the house, greeted by the smell of fried chicken. Jessie felt his stomach growl.

"Max loves fried chicken," Jessie muttered. "You think he will get any while he's in training?"

"I doubt it," Sam replied.

"You will just have to eat an extra portion for him," Eleanor gave Jessie a strained smiled. "Go get washed up."

Stepping in front of the sink and looking into the mirror, Jessie saw the dirt streaked across his face and sweaty hair matted to his forehead. He reached for a washcloth and soaked it in cold water. Dirt and sand filled the sink as he scrubbed at his face and arms.

He pulled on a clean t-shirt and a pair of threadbare sweatpants before returning to the kitchen to find Eugene already at the table. Jessie plopped down in his own chair and reached for a piece of chicken.

Eleanor swatted at his hand. "Wait for your brothers."

Sam and Ricky appeared a few minutes later and Eugene said a prayer. Jessie gritted his teeth at his father's request for protection.

"What were you boys up to today?" Eugene asked before taking a bite of his chicken.

Jessie saw his brothers look to him. "We were just out exploring," he replied before they could speak.

"I can't believe there is anything left for you to discover." Eleanor passed a plate of biscuits around the table.

"There's a lot less swamp here than on the island," Ricky explained. "Plus there are the caves."

"Caves? What caves? Is that safe?" Eleanor looked to Eugene.

Eugene gave them all a stern look. "You boys need to stay out of any caves."

"What do you know?" Jessie spat. "We went into the caves all the time before Max left. Nothing's ever happened to us."

"Well, I'm telling you now. I don't think it's a good idea, so stay out of them from now on." Eugene's tone was even and calm, but Jessie felt a menacing tingle and remembered the look Eugene had always given right before a whipping.

Jessie dropped his fork with a clatter and stomped down the hall to his room, slamming the door behind him.

"Eugene, wait," Jessie heard his mother plead. He expected the door to open any minute but it didn't.

Jessie pulled out his hunk of rocket metal and scrunched himself up in the corner of his bed. He turned the junk over and over, wondering if he could find a way to talk to Grissom without being asleep.

There was a knock on the door, but Jessie didn't answer. He knew his brothers wouldn't knock and he certainly didn't want to see his father. The knock sounded again before the door slowly opened. Jessie watched Eugene enter the room and sit down on the end of the bed. He didn't look angry, though; he looked defeated.

"Sam tells me you found some treasure out in the woods. Would you mind showing it to me?"

Jessie studied his father for a clue to his interest before setting aside the metal and reaching for the bag, between his bed and the crates. Eugene pulled each item out, inspecting them in great detail.

"I know how much you want Max home, but now that he's been called, I don't think we can buy him out. However, we can see if there is any value to these items and set up a nest egg to help him get started on his own when he comes home. I think he'd like that."

Eugene reached over and cupped the back of Jessie's head. "We're going to get through this."

CHAPTER FORTY-SEVEN

Rendezvous

December 15, 1965

"Hey, Doc." Jessie jogged up to his friend.

"Shouldn't you be in class?" Dr. Weston gave Jessie a wink.

"You know they do fire drills for the launches. We're supposed to stay on school property, but that's just too far away." Jessie looked over his shoulder at the buildings.

Dr. Weston chuckled. "It's nice to see you, and twice in less than two weeks. This rendezvous mission sure has been a problem, though, hasn't it?"

"Yeah, but I knew they'd figure it out. It's a shame that Shirra and Stafford won't get to be up there for long this time."

"As long as they've had to wait to get this rocket launched, I think they'll be happy if all goes well."

Jessie nodded, wondering how he would handle it if he were in their shoes. *Gemini 6* had been scheduled for launch in October, but the Agena target vehicle, that was to be used for the rendezvous attempt, had failed to go into orbit. Then, just three days ago, another launch had failed due to a minor hardware problem. Now, after months of waiting, only a few hours remained until the world would know if the American's had the capability to maneuver two spacecraft together.

"How's Max doing?" Dr. Weston's question broke into Jessie's thoughts.

"He made it through boot camp and started infantry training. He might get some leave around Christmas."

"That would be nice. I'm sure it would make your mother happy."

Jessie nodded but didn't voice his fear that it would only make things harder. He pulled Max's radio from his pocket and twisted the knob until he could hear the calm announcer counting down. Seconds later, the familiar pillar of smoke rose into the sky followed by the rumble of the engines. Jessie watched the rocket speed through the blue expanse, longing for the chance to sit in the pilot seat.

"Don't worry, you'll make it up there." Dr. Weston patted Jessie on the back.

"Thanks, Doc." Jessie looked around at the dispersing crowd. "I guess I better get back to class."

"If I don't see you before, I hope you have a Merry Christmas, and I hope Max does get to come home."

Jessie weaved his way through the cars crawling along the road and joined the last of the students returning to class. He took his seat and opened his book, but barely heard a word the teacher said.

"Are you coming, man?"

A hand waved in front of Jessie's face and he realized Randy had been talking to him. "Oh yeah, is class over already?"

"You're out of it. The bell rang a couple minutes ago. We're about to be late for English."

Jessie scooped up his books and followed Randy out of the room. "Can I borrow your notes?"

Randy grinned as they made their way to the next class. "Sure. When I noticed you had zoned out, I made sure to write as much down as I could. There's going to be a test Friday."

"Great." Jessie pushed through the classroom door and made his way to a desk on the other side of the room.

"Is everything all right?"

"Yeah, I was just thinking about the launch," Jessie hesitated and looked at the floor, "and the war."

"You heard from Max?"

Jessie nodded but before he could say more the bell rang and the teacher closed the door.

CHAPTER FORTY-EIGHT

Surprise

December 23, 1965

Cold rain pelted the window, waking Jessie from his dream. He rolled over to find Ricky still sound asleep, his blanket pulled tight over his head. The heavy clouds made it impossible to tell what time it was, so Jessie crawled out of bed and padded to the living room. The smell of stale coffee let him know his parents had already been up. He flipped on a light to see the clock in the living room. It was almost nine thirty. He couldn't remember the last time he'd slept so late.

Moving to the refrigerator, Jessie poured himself a cup of orange juice and dropped a couple of slices of bread into the toaster. While the bread toasted, he went to check on Sam.

"You finally woke up?" Sam asked when Jessie pushed the door open.

Jessie wasn't surprised to find his brother lying on his already made bed, reading a book. He was surprised, though, to see a large lump under the covers of Max's bed.

"Sshh." Sam raised a finger to his mouth before Jessie could speak. "He got in late last night."

"Does Mama know he's here?"

Sam shook his head. Jessie could barely contain his excitement. He had so much he wanted to talk to Max about. Sam closed his book and stood, shooing Jessie from the room.

"How did he get here?" Jessie whispered as they moved down the hall.

"He took a bus and started walking from the station. When a train came through he hopped on the back."

"How long is he staying?"

Sam took a seat at the table while Jessie slathered butter on his toast. "I don't know. He was beat when he got in so we didn't talk much."

Jessie chewed thoughtfully, wondering why Max hadn't let them know he was coming home. What can I give him for Christmas? Will he be here long enough for us all to go hunting or visit the beach, one last big adventure?

"Maybe dad is right about miracles happening every day," Sam said.

"What?" Jessie abandoned his mounting questions and turned his attention to Sam.

"You know, Dad is always talking about God watching out for us and providing, even when we don't know where things will come from."

"Are you jumping on the religion boat too?"

"I've been doing some studying and Jesus was a historical figure. That's beside the point, though. It's kind of a miracle that Max got leave just in time for Christmas, don't you think?"

Jessie shrugged. "It's just the way the timing worked out. If he'd gotten his orders a few weeks earlier or later, his leave would have fallen at a different time."

"You really are stubborn, aren't you?"

"The kid's right." Max shuffled into the room, rubbing his eyes with one hand and scratching his stomach with the other. "Luck of the draw that I got to come home now."

Jessie jumped up from his chair and wrapped Max in a hug. Max gave him a gentle squeeze before pushing Jessie back.

"Why didn't you let us know you were coming?"

"I didn't know for sure I was until yesterday." Max dropped into a chair and rolled it up onto its back legs. "And I didn't want a big fuss."

"How long are you staying?" Jessie filled the coffee pot with water.

"Five days."

"But I thought you got a whole month off."

"There was an earlier jungle training slot open that I was able to get into." Max shrugged. "This way I can get my time in and get back to the States a few days earlier."

Jessie studied his brother. Max had always been in good shape, but now his arms bulged with muscles and his bare stomach was flat as a board. Jessie was starting to ask about training, but the front door opened and he turned to see Eleanor entering with bags of groceries in each arm. Jessie moved to help her and caught one of the bags just in time as she gasped and let them fall from her arms.

"Hi, Mom." Max stood and hugged Eleanor.

Jessie gathered the spilled groceries and took them to the counter, the sound of his mother's sniffles and hushed words from his brother filling the room.

"What's wrong, Nora?" Eugene stepped through the door, another bag in his arm. "Well I'll be." A smile split Eugene's face and he set the bag on the table, wrapping his arms around Max and Eleanor.

"I was just telling Jessie what a Christmas miracle it is to have Max home," Sam said.

"Yes it is." Eleanor wiped her eyes.

The following day was Christmas Eve and the family piled into the car for the evening church service followed by dinner at Uncle Tommy's. At the church, Jessie scanned the room for Virginia. He waved when he saw her Aunt Mary and made his way to her.

"Merry Christmas," he said when he reached her side.

Mary smiled. "Merry Christmas to you. I suppose you're looking for my niece."

"Yes, ma'am."

"I'm not sure if they are going to make it tonight or not. I see your brother's home, though."

Jessie tried to contain his disappointment at hearing Virginia may not be here. "Yes, he came in yesterday."

"I'm sure Virginia will be sorry she missed seeing you and your family."

Jessie rejoined his own family and took his seat as the music started. They sang carols and the pastor read from the book of Matthew about the birth of Jesus, but

Jessie wasn't paying attention, he was wondering what had kept Virginia and her family away.

"It's so good to see you." Uncle Tommy gave Max a hug and slap on the back when they arrived for dinner. Sally and Tommy Jr. were dressed in matching red shirts and bounced up and down on the couch. Jessie could tell they were trying to contain their excitement and that they didn't understand why so much attention was being focused on Max.

"Sally, why don't you sit next to me," Jessie offered as they made their way to the tables. She hurried to the chair next to him and took a seat.

"You look very pretty tonight," Jessie complimented her.

"Thank you," she whispered.

"Max, why don't you do the honors of carving the turkey tonight?" Uncle Tommy handed the large knife and fork to him.

"I don't know." Max tried to refuse, but Uncle Tommy insisted.

Max nodded. "I'll do my best."

When the bird was sliced and plates had been filled, they all joined hands and Eugene stood to pray. "Dear Lord, we thank you for sending your Son to save us from our sins and we thank you for bringing Max home to celebrate this special day. We pray that you will keep him safe when he returns to the Army and that you will bring him home to us once again."

"What's the Army?" Sally whispered in Jessie's ear.

"It's kind of like a job, but it is very dangerous."

"Why does Max have to go to a dangerous job?"

"I wish I could answer that, Sally, but sometimes we have to do things we don't want to do."

Jessie watched his family, sensing the undercurrent of anxiety that tempered their laughter. He picked at his food and tried to follow the conversation between his cousins and his brothers, but his thoughts were on Max and where he would be in four days' time.

"Can't you stay just a few more days?" Eleanor clasped Max's shoulder. Jessie could tell she was trying not to sound desperate, but the strain showed in her eyes.

Max took his mother's hand, giving it a squeeze. "Everything's going to be alright."

Eleanor pulled Max into a tight hug. Jessie saw her lips moving as she whispered into Max's ear. He nodded and stepped back from her embrace. "You boys stay out of trouble."

"You too," Sam replied with a salute.

CHAPTER FORTY-NINE

Transitions

February 26, 1966

"I can't believe the *Gemini* program is almost over." Jessie rubbed his hands together trying to warm them against the morning chill.

"A lot has been accomplished in a short time, though." Dr. Weston rocked on the balls of his feet.

Jessie nodded. "Sure does seem like NASA is learning faster. At this rate, maybe we can make it to the moon in another two years."

"There's still a good deal of work to do," the doctor cautioned.

Jessie knew his friend was right and the outcome of today's mission would be an indicator of what was to come with the new *Apollo* program. "What do you think of this new Saturn rocket?"

Dr. Weston gazed across the lightly rippled river. "From what I've gathered, it's quite powerful, and that's what we'll need to get all the way to the moon — power."

Jessie grinned. "I wish I could see one close up. They must be huge."

"I bet the space museum we've been hearing about will have all of the different rockets on display one day. Won't that be a sight?"

"You really think so?" Jessie thought about the few rockets he'd seen down by Patrick Air Force Base in Cocoa Beach and grew excited at the idea of being able to walk among the Redstone, Atlas, and Saturn rockets that were paving the way to the moon.

"I do. We're making history."

Jessie flinched with a shiver, unsure if it was the cold or his excitement. He zipped up his jacket, tucked the radio in the crook of his arm, and shoved his hands into his pockets. "Looks like the weather is going to cooperate today. Hopefully there won't be any more delays."

"I almost forgot to tell you. There is going to be an opening on the launch abort team. One of the doctors is moving to Colorado and I'm one of five being considered to replace him."

Jessie turned to his friend, not surprised to find him beaming. "That's great! I know they're gonna pick you."

Dr. Weston shrugged. "The competition is tough, but I should know in a few more weeks."

"That would be so cool."

"You just think it will get you closer to the astronauts."

Jessie dipped his head.

The doctor chuckled. "No reason to be embarrassed. That's one of the reasons I want the job myself. It would make me happier than you know to be able to introduce you."

"Thanks, doc." Jessie looked up at his friend.

"You're a good kid, Jessie. I wish I could have had a son like you."

"I'm sorry."

Dr. Weston shook his head. "No need to be. Martha and I made peace with not being able to have kids a long time ago." The doctor locked eyes with Jessie. "Since meeting you, though, I almost feel, well, like you are a surrogate son."

If a brisk wind had blown through at that moment, Jessie would have fallen over, his body had gone so rigid. "I don't know what to say."

Dr. Weston waved in dismissal. "I probably shouldn't have said that."

Jessie massaged his temples with the thumb and middle finger of one hand for a long minute, as he always did when trying to understand thoughts and emotions rushing through him, as if he could slow them down. "No, it's okay." Jessie spoke slowly, allowing his thoughts to catch up. "With Max gone, I've felt kind of lost. The only times I haven't really felt alone are launch days when I've been able to see you."

Jessie let his words drift on the wind for several seconds before continuing. "You know things have never been great with Pop. Even though he's been home almost a year and seems to be sober, I still don't trust him. Not the way I trust you."

"I don't want to replace your father, Jessie. I hope you know that."

"Sure, I know." Jessie gave a sly smile. "I don't think you're my mama's type anyway."

They both laughed and Jessie relaxed, understanding that his friendship with the doctor had grown deeper in a matter of moments.

Jessie turned his gaze back across the water and a plume of fire, larger than any he'd seen before raced into the sky. The higher the rocket rose, the brighter the fire seemed to burn.

"Looks like *Apollo* is off to a good start," Dr. Weston cheered.

"Yes, it does."

CHAPTER FIFTY

Space Emergency

March 17, 1966

"I guess I don't have to ask if you're going to be watching the docking operation this evening." Virginia grabbed Jessie's hand as soon as he joined her on the walkway.

Jessie nodded, reliving the launch of *Gemini 8*, hours earlier. The previous day's delays had been worked out and now he couldn't wait to see the capsule dock with the Agena Target Vehicle.

"Maybe I could come over to watch it with you." Virginia batted her eyelashes and Jessie felt his heart leap. It was the first time she'd asked to be a part of his space obsession.

"Sure," he replied, giving her hand a squeeze. "You could stay for dinner too. Mama won't mind."

"I have to do a couple of chores, but I should be done by four thirty."

"What I wouldn't give to be inside that capsule right now." Jessie looked up to the clear, blue sky, wondering what continent the astronauts were looking down on at that moment.

"Is there ever a time that you don't feel that way?"

Jessie returned his gaze to Virginia then leaned over and brushed his lips across her cheek. "When I look at you, I almost forget about space."

Virginia frowned. "I guess almost is better than not at all."

Jessie sighed. "Forgetting about it completely would be like forgetting to breath. Isn't there something you care about so much it keeps you awake at night?"

Virginia looked away. "Not really."

Her answer surprised him and he got the impression she was embarrassed so he tried to lighten the mood. "Not even the Beatles?"

A tiny smile tugged at the corner of her mouth. "An appreciation of their music doesn't mean I want to be a musician myself."

"Maybe you should. I love listening to you sing in church."

A train whistle sounded behind them. Jessie pulled Virginia closer to the tracks. "Have you ever jumped a train before?"

"Of course not. Why would I?"

"Come on, it's easy. We'll ride down to Knox McRae and hop off." Jessie laughed as Virginia's eyes widened. "We do it all the time."

The engine passed, followed by several empty flats, then dozens of boxcars, stretched as far down the tracks as he could see. He pointed at one of the cars as it crept by. "See the ladder on the back there? Jump up onto the first rung."

Virginia shook her head.

"Watch." Jessie waited until the next car slid by and reached for the ladder. His right foot and hand touched the metal at the same instant. He grinned back at Virginia then jumped off five feet farther down the tracks.

"How do you do that without being terrified?"

"What's to be scared of? It's barely moving."

"But if you slip, you're still going to be crushed."

Jessie gave a dismissive wave and held out his hand. "Come on. Give it a try."

Virginia hesitated, but Jessie could see the curiosity lurking deep in her eyes. Three more cars passed before she took a step toward him.

"Get ready for the next car. One, two, three, jump!" Jessie watched her leap for the ladder and followed a second later. He wrapped his free arm around her and held her close as they rode. He could feel her trembling and leaned forward to whisper in her ear.

"Okay, in a minute we're going to jump off, you first, then I'll follow."

Virginia gave a slight nod and Jessie counted it down. Virginia dropped to the ground. As soon as she was clear of the train, Jessie leapt free and jogged back to her.

She looked up at him, her eyes bright. "That was exciting. Don't ever make me do it again."

Jessie sat down beside her to wait for the rest of the train to pass. "I knew you'd like it."

"It was the most terrifying thing I've ever experienced. You and your brothers must be out of your minds to do that all the time."

"I guess I shouldn't tell you the stories about wrestling gators then."

Virginia shook her head vigorously and stuck her fingers in her ears, causing Jessie to laugh so hard his sides hurt. "You still want to come over to watch the *Gemini* dock?"

Virginia seemed to consider this for a long minute before reaching up to caress his cheek. "If I want to be part of your world, then I need to have a better understanding of it. I'll be there."

Jessie helped her to her feet, feeling himself fall just a little bit harder for this girl.

Two hours later, Jessie and Virginia were seated on the couch in front of the television, watching the evening newscast. Sam was in his room studying, Ricky was working at the grocery store, and Eugene wasn't home yet.

Eleanor sat in her rocking chair, sewing a button onto a shirt. "I'm so happy you came by, Virginia,"

"Thank you, ma'am. I appreciate you letting me stay for dinner."

"Do you follow the space program as closely as Jessie does?"

"No, ma'am, I can't say that I do, but I know how important it is to him so I thought maybe I should learn more about it."

Jessie thought he saw his mother give a slight nod of approval. He wanted to put his arm around Virginia, but restrained himself. The few times he'd been to her house, she'd kept him at arm's length and by her current place on the couch, she seemed to want it that way here as well.

A commercial for Lucky Charms cereal faded out and the distinctive voice of Walter Cronkite filled the room. Jessie turned all of his attention to the television. The top story was about a submarine locating a missing American hydrogen bomb off the coast of Spain, followed by several stories on the war in Vietnam.

Jessie felt his stomach tighten as the number of casualties was reported. He tried to remember how long it had been since their last letter from Max. Had he mentioned where he was or where he was headed?

He felt something soft on his hand and glanced down to see Virginia had placed her hand on his. He raised his eyes and recognized the look of concern on her face. He turned to his mother and found her head down, concentrating on the tiny stitches she was working on, her hands trembling.

For a full ten minutes, reporters droned on about the war effort before going to a commercial break. Jessie didn't laugh at the commercial with a skating clown who falls and a hamburger goes flying through the air. He didn't even get excited at the commercial for Tang that showed how the *Gemini* astronauts prepared the powdered drink. However, he did relax his tense muscles when he recognized an image of Cape Canaveral.

"This morning, NASA had another successful launch," the reporter announced. "*Gemini 8* roared into space with astronauts Neil Armstrong and David Scott onboard. The mission of Armstrong and Scott was to dock with the Agena Target Vehicle that was launched yesterday from launch complex fourteen, as well as conducting extra-vehicular operations. We have confirmed that Armstrong was able to successfully complete the docking operation just minutes ago and hope to have video footage for you by the end of the broadcast."

Jessie couldn't believe they hadn't shown the docking in real time. How could he share the excitement and anticipation with Virginia, when they finally did get to see it, if they already knew the mission had been accomplished? Part of the thrill was not knowing what was going to happen.

"Sounds like another good mission," Eleanor said.

"What was the point of the docking?" Virginia asked. "Are the astronauts transferring to this other vehicle?"

Jessie shook his head. "NASA needed to see if docking could be accomplished in space. The Saturn rockets that will be used for the *Apollo* program are massive, but they aren't big enough to send up the capsule, land on the moon and return."

"So why don't they just make the rocket bigger?"

Jessie gave an inward chuckle at Virginia's lack of understanding. "Bigger rockets cost a boatload of money and need more technology. You remember the announcements about the *Apollo* program a few years ago?"

Virginia shook her head.

"NASA laid out what the plans were for the program. A bunch of what they said was about the things they still needed to study, but emphasized the need for a second vehicle for the actual landing, based on time and cost considerations." Virginia's blank expression told Jessie he wasn't getting through to her.

"We have breaking news from Cape Canaveral," the television anchor announced. Jessie's head shot up.

"We've just received word that Neil Armstrong has disengaged the *Gemini* capsule from the target vehicle after experiencing violent yaw and tumble. Upon disengaging, the *Gemini* capsule went into even more roll until the astronauts engaged the reentry control system. Mission control has cancelled the planned spacewalk and all other objectives of the mission and the astronauts will return to earth later tonight."

Jessie was stunned. He heard the ancient springs of the rocking chair squeak as his mother stood. He glanced at her then at Virginia. They each placed a hand on him; Eleanor on his shoulder, Virginia twining her fingers through his, and he felt the disappointment and frustration leak out of his body.

CHAPTER FIFTY-ONE

Social Changes

June 12, 1966

"Come on boys," Eleanor called from the kitchen. "We're going to be late."

Jessie shoved his feet into his dress shoes, grimacing as his toes pinched. He eyed Ricky's shoes, still sitting at the end of the bed. Before he could get up to try them on, Ricky strolled in, still running a comb through his thick hair.

"Better hurry up. Mama doesn't sound happy." Jessie bolted out the door leaving Ricky to finish getting ready. A bowl of eggs and a plate of bacon waited on the table. Eugene placed his cup of coffee by his plate before pulling out his chair and spooning out some eggs. Jessie accepted the cup of coffee Eleanor offered and took a spot on the other side of the table.

The living room fan whirred on high, but the room was still hot and sticky. It was definitely going to be a scorcher. Jessie loosened his tie, counting the minutes until he would be free to remove it completely.

"Where's Sam?" Jessie mumbled.

"Don't talk with your mouth full." Eleanor gave him a stern look. "He ate while you were in the shower. It would be nice if you boys got up a little earlier, so we aren't always in a rush."

Ricky appeared and grabbed a handful of bacon. Eleanor gave an exasperated shake of her head. "What?" Ricky asked.

"Just sit down and eat." Eleanor headed toward her bedroom.

Jessie emptied his plate and took it to the sink. When he turned around, Sam and Eleanor emerged from the hall. He noticed Sam wore a dark blue shirt and an orange tie, already showing pride in his new school, the University of Florida. He'd be heading to Gainesville in a few weeks to start his first semester of college. Jessie winked at his brother and fell into line, out through the front door.

Every window in the church was open and hand-held fans were being waved back and forth with such vigor that Jessie thought the place might just take flight, and still the heat pressed down on them. The hymns were sung with less enthusiasm than usual, which the preacher must have sensed because they only did three before he let them sit down and he started his message.

"Our community is on the brink of change. The space program is growing, creating hundreds, perhaps even thousands of new jobs, which I praise God for. I believe this growth will be a good thing; that it will bring in families with new ideas, new skills, and hopefully a longing to serve the Lord. But I'm not naive. Folks who have lived here all their lives, well, some of them are going to struggle with the coming changes, the increase in population, adjusting to different cultures, and the need for more government."

Jessie caught movement out of the corner of his eye and cocked his head to see Eugene tense at the pastor's words. Eleanor patted her husband's leg and he clasped her hand. Jessie thought about the changes his family had endured. Could they make it through anything else?

"We won't just be seeing new faces, though. Desegregation is taking a big step this fall, when the black students at Gibson High School will be merged into the student body at Titusville High. We need to begin praying for those students now."

Murmurs broke out around the church. Jessie guessed, like himself, they hadn't heard about the school merger either. What did that mean for him and his brothers? They didn't know many black kids, mostly those back on the island who had come out to help harvest oranges. Even then he hadn't really had a chance to get to know them.

The pastor raised his hands to quiet the congregation. "This merger isn't something to get upset about. In fact, it's long overdue. We have an opportunity here, with the children in this church, to set an example when the school year starts."

The pastor's eyes roved the congregation, pausing now and then. When the pastor's gaze met Jessie's, he wanted to shrink away. What could he do to set an example?

"We have students in this room today, not as many as I would like, but we will revisit this again closer to the beginning of school, students who can make a difference." The pastor stepped off the elevated stage area, onto the main floor of the church.

"In this room are athletes, tutors, and musicians, who will have the chance to offer their hand in friendship to the black students. They are going to be just as unsure of the situation as you are. They are going to have preconceived ideas of how they will be treated poorly, how teachers will be harder on them, how coaches will want to use them."

Eugene stood. "I'm sorry, pastor, but I'm not comfortable with this kind of talk."

The pastor stood still, twenty feet from Eugene. Jessie tensed, expecting the worst. The pastor bowed his head, slightly, and closed his eyes. When he looked up again and opened them, there was no anger on his face, only peace.

"I understand, Eugene, but do you think that Jesus wants us to keep our country segregated? Didn't he send His disciples out into *all* of the world before He ascended to heaven?"

Eugene shifted his weight from one foot to the other. He looked down at Eleanor and along the pew at each of his boys. Jessie met his gaze and saw the turmoil in his father's eyes.

Jessie didn't know what the pastor meant when he talked about Jesus sending out His disciples, but he also didn't understand why blacks and whites were kept apart. He'd never even questioned it. That was just the way it had always been. Sure he knew about slavery and the Civil War, but that was a hundred years ago, what did that have to do with today?

Eugene leaned forward, placing his hands on the pew in front of him, and looked at the pastor. "You know I am new in my faith and there is much I still don't understand."

The pastor nodded. "Even those who have walked with God for many years are struggling to understand the changes happening in our country. We are in a war that is taking so many of our young boys. We are tearing down cultural barriers that have been in place for more than a century. Things that have been believed in for generations are being challenged. Many wonder if we are entering the end times."

"I don't know if I would go that far," Eugene interjected.

The pastor steepled his fingers in front of his chest. "I agree. I believe there is much more that will happen before the end comes, but that doesn't mean the times aren't frightening to many believers. Now, we need to draw strength from the scriptures, we need to seek God's will, so that we may face these fears, and love one another as God has instructed us to."

"Let us love one another, for love is of God," Eugene replied as he sank down into his seat, his hands still grasping the pew before him.

"Yes, First John, chapter four, verse seven. It goes on to say 'everyone who loves is born of God and knows God'. I want to ask you a question, Eugene, and I want you to know I'm not judging or criticizing you in any way." The pastor paused until receiving a nod from Eugene. "Why did you feel uncomfortable with my call to extend a hand of friendship to the black students?"

Eugene looked at the ground, but Jessie could see the furrow of his father's brow, the tightening of his jaw. "Honestly, I don't know." Eugene lifted his head. "My father taught me to steer clear of the colored folks. Whooped my hide when he found me kicking a ball with a couple of them."

"That is what I mean when I talk about long held beliefs being challenged." The pastor turned to face the rest of the congregation. "If you are challenged to let go of the belief that the blacks should be kept separate, what other beliefs that you have clung to may be wrong as well?"

Jessie saw heads nodding around the room.

"I say, if the beliefs we are clinging to are not found in the Bible then we need to reevaluate them. Many things in our lives have been handed down from generation to generation. When our country was made up of mostly farmers, we planted our crops the way our fathers had. When we became more industrialized, we often went into the same professions as our fathers. In our homes we place the Christmas tree in the same spot each year, we organize our kitchens like the kitchen we grew up in."

The pastor smiled, his lips parting just enough to show a row of perfectly straight teeth. "Ladies, how many of you give your children Castor Oil anytime they have a sniffle?" A chuckle rose from the ladies along with a groan from their children. "These are the traditions that we have turned into beliefs. Many of us have traditionally, probably even unconsciously, kept ourselves separated from the blacks in our communities. I don't know that it's the government's place to tear down this wall, but I will admit I'm ashamed that, as your pastor, I haven't done more to bring unification here in Indian River City."

CHAPTER FIFTY-TWO

Crossing the tracks

August 22, 1966

The chirp of crickets and vibrating rattle of katydids filled the humid pre-dawn air. Jessie and Ricky trudged along the railroad tracks, delaying their return to school as long as possible. Jessie didn't know what to expect of the new school year, with Gibson High and Titusville High having been merged. The schools were only separated by the railroad tracks, but before today, it might as well have been an ocean. The black kids at Gibson didn't interact with the white kids at Titusville, but that was all about to change. With the population of the two schools being integrated, Jessie and Ricky would both have classes in the Gibson building

"I wish Mama would let me drive Max's buggy to school," Ricky moaned.

"When did you get too good for walking?" Jessie shot back. The buggy Max had received for his eighteenth birthday had sat on the side of the house, barely touched since he'd left for the war.

"It's not good for it to just sit there, though. The battery's gonna die and the tires are gonna rot."

Jessie nodded, conceding his brother's points. "Maybe we should talk to Mama and Pop about it. Even if we don't drive it to school every day, taking it out on the weekends would be good."

Ricky grinned. "We could drive down the beach with a couple of girls."

Jessie tried to imagine Virginia having to climb into the back seat, her hair flying in the wind, beach chairs strapped to the flat bed where a trunk should have been. "I don't know how many girls we could talk into riding with us. It's not much to look at."

"It's got an engine and four wheels, what more does it need?"

Jessie gave his brother a hearty slap on the back. "Don't you know by now, girls want more than boys do? They expect cars to have doors and roofs. The buggy doesn't have either."

"I've seen plenty of girls riding around in convertibles."

"Not when it's raining. They ride with the tops up then. What do you think is going to happen if we are out in the buggy and it starts raining?"

"It's just a little water," Ricky replied, but his tone let Jessie know he'd won.

They walked the next several blocks in silence. Jessie saw a crowd gathered in the middle of the road as they approached the school. He picked up his pace to see what was going on. Alan Welty stood in front of JT Crawford and Dave Wheeler. The three bullies leered at a half dozen black boys.

"I don't care what the school says, I ain't sitting in the same class as any of you," Alan bellowed. "Why don't you just turn around and head back to your own school?"

JT and Dave sounded cries of support for their leader, echoed by three or four other students. Jessie glanced around, recognizing each of the other ten white students. A few looked sheepish at Alan's display and started to drift away.

A tall, skinny boy with a shaved head and thin goatee, who seemed to be the leader of the black students, stepped forward. "What are you gonna do about it?"

Alan raised his fist and shook it in the boy's face. The skinny one smiled, revealing perfect white teeth, and gave a tiny nod. Three other black boys came forward, one short and squat, the other as big as a refrigerator, but Alan didn't back down.

"I got a class to get to, so why don't you move out of my way?" the skinny boy demanded.

Alan scowled and moved to slug the black boy, but his hand was caught in mid-swing and the skinny boy landed his own punch on the side of Alan's face. In seconds, JT and Dave were engaged. Jessie watched with delight as Alan was knocked to the ground.

"We should help Alan," Ricky whispered.

Jessie turned to his brother in disbelief. "I was just thinking we should help the new kid. Didn't the pastor tell us to extend a helping hand just a few weeks ago?"

"I don't think this is what he meant."

"Why not? They're new to our school, they've engaged the bully, shouldn't we show them some support, let them know that we aren't all the same?"

Jessie could see his brother considering this, but before Ricky could reach a decision, the fight was over. JT and Dave limped away, while Alan lay in a ball on the ground, arms wrapped around his head.

"Anyone else want some of this?" the skinny boy called out, sending most of the remaining spectators scurrying toward their classrooms. Alan stumbled to his feet and slunk off toward the gymnasium.

Jessie stepped up to the boy. "I'm Jessie Cole. You've got some nice moves."

The skinny boy sized Jessie up. "I'm Broderick, but you can call me Bo."

"Good to meet you, Bo. The guy you wailed on was Alan Welty. He crowned himself king of the school back in first grade, from what I gather." Jessie hooked a thumb at Ricky. "This is my brother Ricky. I got two older brothers too, but they've graduated. We've been the only ones, since we came to town, to stand up to Alan and his little thugs."

Bo brushed some dirt off his shirtsleeve. "Maybe between you boys and my crew, we can teach him a lesson he won't forget."

Jessie glanced at the two guys behind Bo. They weren't even winded from their skirmish. He flicked his gaze back to Ricky who gave an imperceptible shake of his head. "When's your lunch period?"

Bo pulled a crinkled piece of paper out of his pocket and showed it to Jessie.

"Same as ours. Why don't you guys sit with us in the cafeteria? We'll send the message to Alan and his goons that you have friends here."

"That's all? Sitting together at lunch?" Bo rolled his eyes. "That ain't gonna do nothing."

"You'd be surprised how fast news will spread about this fight, and if kids see us together they'll know we've teamed up. Alan is hard-headed, but I think he may get the message without us having to whip him anymore."

"If you say so, but if he comes within five feet of me again, I'm gonna beat him so hard he won't even remember his name."

"What year are you in?" Jessie asked Bo as they started walking toward the gym.

"Sophomore. You?"

"I'm a junior, Ricky's a senior."

"Fletch is a senior too." Bo pointed at the refrigerator-sized boy.

The boys talked about the teachers they had assigned, Jessie giving insight into those he'd already had, and Bo sharing about the teachers at Gibson. Before they separated, Jessie made sure his new friends knew where they were headed for the first few classes and pointed out the cafeteria.

"See you at lunch." Jessie waved as Bo jogged toward a doorway.

"I don't think this is a good idea," Ricky worried.

"We're extending the hand of friendship, just like the pastor said." With a grin, Jessie ducked into his own classroom, leaving Ricky alone with his anxiety.

CHAPTER FIFTY-THREE

Apollo 1

January 27, 1967

Dishes clattered as Jessie and Ricky cleared the dinner table. Jessie rubbed his stuffed belly and released a loud burp that drew a scowl from Eleanor.

"Excuse me." He tried not to smile.

"Can we watch *Tarzan* after the kitchen is cleaned up?" Ricky returned the butter to the refrigerator before turning around with hope in his eyes.

"May you," Eleanor corrected. "I suppose so." She scrubbed a plate then handed it to Jessie to rinse and dry.

Ricky wandered back to his bedroom while Jessie helped finish the dishes. Eugene clicked on the television as the evening news report was ending.

"Are you still enjoying ROTC?" Eleanor asked, letting the water out of the sink and shaking her hands dry.

"I guess," Jessie shrugged. "If Mr. Smith hadn't pointed out the head start it would give me to become a test pilot, I would never have considered it."

"I'm proud of all you've done to pursue your dream." Eleanor ruffled his hair. "You are growing up so fast."

"It's all I can do to keep up in some of my classes, though." Jessie blew out a loud breath. "Chemistry is really kicking my butt."

Eleanor laughed. "You'll be a whizz at it by the end of the year."

"I hope so." Jessie checked the clock. "I'm going to go write Max a letter before we watch TV."

"Okay, honey. Send him my love."

Jessie nodded and ambled down the hall to his room where he found Ricky flipping through an old comic book. Jessie opened a notebook to a clean sheet of paper, found a pencil, and licked his lips, trying to decide what to say. Max had been gone for almost two years, sending home a handful of letters, some to the whole family, some to just Jessie. In the family letters Max was brave and confident for their mother's sake, but in the personal ones, he confided in Jessie about some of the horrors he'd seen. Jessie hated writing about life back home, as if nothing had changed since Max's departure, but that is what Max had asked him to do.

Hey Max,

I hope this letter finds you well. It's only a couple of weeks until the first launch of the Apollo rocket. We are getting closer to the moon every month now it seems. Remember Bo, the guy that I wrote about a few months ago, who had the fight with Alan at the beginning of school? Hanging out with him really seems to be keeping Alan in check. He hasn't bothered Ricky or me at all.

Virginia is doing good. Can you believe we've been dating for a year? You mentioned in your last letter that you have become buddies with a chaplain over there. What's he like? How can he still believe in God in that hellhole?

"Jessie, sweetie." Eleanor stepped into the bedroom with Eugene close behind. Her face was wet with tears and Jessie's heart stopped, certain his brother had been killed.

She wiped the back of her hand across her eyes. "There's been an accident." Her voice trembled and broke.

Eugene kneeled in front of Jessie, placing a hand on his son's shoulder. "There was a fire during the *Apollo* test."

Jessie felt his throat close up, stymying his cries of disbelief. "Grissom?" He managed to whisper.

Eugene shook his head somberly. "All three of them were dead in seconds. Your friend, Dr. Weston, just called and told us."

"Where is everyone?" Ricky called. "*Tarzan* starts in ten minutes."

Jessie heard Ricky's footsteps stop outside the bedroom door for only a second before rushing into the room.

"Is it Max? Did something happen?" Ricky demanded.

Eugene stood to face Ricky. "No, it's not Max. There was an accident at the Cape."

"What happened?" Ricky stammered.

"All we know right now is a fire broke out during a test," Eugene repeated. "Dr. Weston has a friend who works out there, who called to tell him about it. The astronauts died quickly, but several of the workers out on the pad who tried to open the capsule were badly burned as well."

Jessie dropped his head into his hands and Ricky sat next to him. "I'm sorry, Jess. I know how much you looked up to Grissom."

Jessie eyes lifted, holding back the tears threatening to spill down his cheeks, remembering the promise he'd made in that first dream with Grissom. *I won't doubt.* Jessie repeated the words over and over to himself, his resolve growing each time. Gradually, he straightened his back, lifted his head, and blinked back the tears. With a deep breath, he stood and made eye contact with his mother and father.

"Grissom wouldn't want us to mourn this loss." Jessie's voice grew stronger as he spoke. "We will carry on and honor his memory by never giving up."

Jessie held Eugene's gaze after he finished speaking and thought he saw a flash of admiration in his father's blue eyes. Eugene clapped him on the back, then pulled him into a tight hug.

"You are going to make a fine astronaut, son," Eugene whispered into Jessie's ear.

A shot of pride coursed through Jessie. He hadn't realized how much he'd craved his father's support.

"So, are we going to watch *Tarzan*, or what?" Jessie stepped back from his father and offered a weak grin.

"We don't have to," Ricky offered.

"Maybe it will be good to take our minds off everything," Eleanor proposed.

"If you're sure that's what you want to do." Ricky stepped toward the door at Jessie's nod.

Jessie left the room last, taking a moment to catch his breath. His parents and brother were settled on the couch when he joined them and chose a spot on the floor in front of the television. He watched the story of a gunrunner and two assassins trying to kill Tarzan, but his thoughts were focused on Grissom and on how the fire would affect the space program. By the time the show ended and the *Man from U.N.C.L.E* started, Jessie was convinced the fire was going to deal a devastating blow to the goal of reaching the moon before the end of the decade.

Jessie rolled over and sat up. "I'm gonna go to bed early."

Eleanor reached out for him as he walked past her chair. He bent down and kissed her cheek. He knew Ricky would stay up until the show finished and so he would have some time alone. When he saw the unfinished letter on his bed, he took up his pencil again.

> *Today there was an accident at the Cape. Gus Grissom, Ed White, and Roger Chaffee are all dead. I'm stunned. Things have been going so well. How could this have happened? When Mama came in to tell me, Ricky and I both thought she'd had news about you. I'm glad it wasn't you that died, but I can't believe Gus is gone. You think the government will shut down the program? Ask your chaplain friend how God could let so many good men die in such terrible ways.*
> *Mama sends her love.*
>
> *Stay Safe,*
> *Jessie*

CHAPTER FIFTY-FOUR

Max's Injury

May 15, 1967

School was winding down for the summer. Jessie couldn't believe that in a few more days Ricky would officially be a high school graduate and Sam would be coming home from his first year of college. Virginia walked by his side, along the familiar route home.

"Are you going north for the summer again?" Jessie hoped he didn't sound as forlorn as he felt at the thought.

"I'm not sure. Mother hasn't mentioned it."

"Your dad hasn't been traveling as much this year has he?"

Virginia shook her head. "He's only been on a dozen trips. Last year we barely saw him. I've heard him talking about getting a different job. I don't know if mother would be happy if he was home all the time, though."

"Really? Back when Pop wasn't living with us, and as much as I didn't want him to come home, I know it made things easier for Mama."

"Yeah, but your father was only away for a few months. Your mother didn't have a chance to build her own life, get used to having things done her way. Now, when father is home, there is always this tension. Mother almost seems to be looking for things he is doing wrong." Virginia stopped and tugged on Jessie's hand.

Jessie noticed apprehension clouding the blue eyes he loved so much. He reached up to tuck a lock of hair behind her ear. "Don't worry, we won't be like that," he assured her.

"How can you say that? You are going away to college and then you'll be in the Navy. You'll be gone just as much as father."

"But I already do everything you tell me to." Jessie chuckled.

"It's not funny." Red spots colored Virginia's cheeks.

"Are you saying you don't want me to go to college or into the Navy? You know if I don't then I'm certain to be drafted." Jessie had to restrain himself from yelling, feeling his hands curl into fists. He relaxed his fingers and took a deep breath.

"I don't want you going to war, you know that, but…" Virginia looked away, her hair falling like a curtain across her face.

"Why are we worrying about this now? We still have another year of high school before anything is going to change. Who knows what will happen between now and then." Jessie cupped Virginia's chin in his hand and gently turned her to face him. "I love you and that's all that matters."

She kissed his palm, reached for his other and started walking again. Before they turned the corner onto her street she stopped and wrapped her arms around Jessie's neck, leaning in close for a lingering kiss. Jessie tried to pull her closer, but she broke the connection and backed away. She looked him in the eyes and he was sure she was going to say something, then she turned and ran down the street.

Bewildered and breathless, Jessie didn't know if he should run after her or not. He took a step toward the house, hesitated, then turned toward home. He had a shift at the grocery store that evening he needed to get ready for.

He entered the house and found Ricky at the table eating a peanut butter sandwich, a tall glass of milk before him. The peanut butter jar and bread were still open, so Jessie reached for a couple of slices and made his own snack.

"You working tonight?" Ricky mumbled through a mouthful of bread.

"Yep, you?"

"Nope. I have one more final to study for."

"How's it feel to be graduating?"

Ricky lifted his glass and took several gulps of milk, followed by an appreciative sigh. "That hits the spot." He wiped at his milk mustache with the sleeve of his shirt. "I guess it feels good."

Jessie registered the lack of excitement in his brother's tone. "You're worried about the draft, aren't you?"

"Of course I am. We can't afford to send me to college and we know my grades didn't earn me any scholarships. Maybe if I'd played a sport I'd have had a chance for some money." Ricky shrugged. "I guess we just wait and see."

"Sam was lucky to get a full scholarship," Jessie agreed.

Ricky laughed. "Lucky? There was no luck about it. He was the Valedictorian, for crying out loud. He probably could have gone to any college he wanted."

It had been a long night. He must have loaded more than a hundred grocery bags into cars and Jessie wanted nothing more than to crawl into bed. He walked past the neighboring houses, the flickering light of the televisions illuminating their windows, like every other night. The familiarity was comforting after the argument he'd had with Virginia and his talk with Ricky. Maybe everything wasn't changing, after all, these houses were still the same. When he reached his own home, light streamed out of both the kitchen and living room windows, but the television wasn't flickering. His steps slowed when he recognized Uncle Tommy's car parked on the side of the road.

Jessie crossed the front porch and pushed through the front door. Eugene and Uncle Tommy sat at the table with cups of coffee. Jessie could hear Ricky in the bedroom with Sarah and Tommy Jr., but didn't see any sign of his mother.

"Hey, Uncle Tommy." Jessie noticed the coffee cups were still almost full, but they weren't steaming as he would have expected if they'd just been poured. He looked at the percolator and saw the burner it sat on was turned off.

"Take a seat, Jessie," Eugene directed.

Jessie could tell by the weariness in his father's tone this wasn't going to be good. He pulled out a chair and sat down, perching on the edge.

"Max has been injured." Eugene didn't try to soften the blow.

Jessie felt his chest tighten, like when he dove down deep into the river, staying under for as long as possible. He looked from his father to his uncle for a cue on how to react. Both men were stone-faced, their lips drawn tight.

Jessie steeled himself for the only question that mattered. "Is he coming home?"

Eugene gave a slight nod. "In a few weeks. He's on his way to the Brooke Army Medical Center in Texas."

Jessie was confused by the grimness of his father's words. If Max was coming home then everything was okay, right? Why doesn't Pop seem happier, though?

"He won't have to go back, will he?" Jessie studied Eugene's face.

"I don't know."

Jessie noticed how carefully Eugene picked his words. "What aren't you telling me?"

Eugene's shoulders slumped even more, his head dropping to only inches above his coffee cup. He let out a ragged breath and scraped his hair back with one hand before making eye contact with Jessie.

"We don't know much, but from things we've gathered, he's in bad shape. We'll have to wait and see."

Jessie didn't like the sound of that and still felt Eugene was holding out on him, but decided not to push. Maybe he didn't want to know the whole truth, not yet. He scraped his chair back and stood up.

"It's been a long day. I'm gonna get a shower." Jessie paused as he passed his father, and placed a hand on his back. It felt awkward, offering support to the man he'd spent most of his life hating. Even after the past two years of improving relations, the bitterness was still there, deep in his soul.

Jessie shut the bathroom door and leaned against it, thoughts of what could have happened to Max flashing through his mind. The television news carried pictures of soldiers returning home missing arms or legs, some had been burned so badly their families barely recognized them. Would they know Max when he came home? Ricky had turned eighteen the month before. Would he be called to take his brother's place?

CHAPTER FIFTY-FIVE

Max Comes Home

July 24, 1967

Aplane buzzed overhead, unseen through the patchy gray clouds. Jessie rocked from side to side, by the aging Bel Air, sweat trickling down his temples. Eugene pulled the front door of the house closed and approached the car, his steps slow and weary. Jessie was certain no one had gotten much sleep the night before, anxious for Max's return. The pass provided by the Army to access Patrick Air Force base was only valid for two people, and it had been decided Jessie would accompany Eugene.

"I'll have a nice dinner ready for you as soon as you get back," Eleanor had assured them as they left.

Jessie sat in the passenger seat, his feet beating impatiently against the floor while his father fumbled with the keys. The engine sputtered several times and Eugene revved the gas when it finally burst to life. Jessie thought he might pull his hair out as they crept past the neighbors, until finally reaching US 1.

Wind blew through the open windows as they picked up speed along the narrow road. Jessie watched the landscape pass the window, wishing they were returning to their island home or heading to the beach for a launch.

The car slowed as they approached the bridge across the Indian River.

"How much farther?"

"Not far." Eugene's eyes never left the road, but he reached over to pat Jessie's leg, which had started shaking up and down with nervous energy.

Jessie made a conscious effort to stop it, placing his hands on his knees and pressing down hard. He closed his eyes and thought about the strain of the past two months; Max's rare phone calls from the Army hospital, the lack of information about his injuries, the frustration at not having enough money to go see him.

Another thirty minutes passed before they reached the guard station and Eugene presented the Army letter, giving them authorization to be on the base. The guard gave them directions and opened the gate.

Eugene followed the road and turned into a parking lot by a plain looking building. He cut the engine and pulled a baseball cap down low over his eyes. Jessie jumped out of the car, bouncing from one foot to the other as if the concrete burned his feet. Eugene moved slowly, shifting his weight out of the car and holding onto the door frame until his legs were steady beneath him.

Unable to wait any longer, Jessie started zigzagging through the cars to the long building. He reached the door and turned to look for his father who was still two rows away, head down, plodding in a straight line. Eugene pulled the door open and the pair stepped into a cavernous room, the far wall completely open onto an expanse of tarmac. A pair of F-106 "Delta Darts" were parked at the far edge of their view. There were several families holding American flags and crudely written signs of welcome.

One young woman caught Jessie's attention, a baby on her hip and a blonde-headed toddler tugging on the hem of her dress. Her hair was in a perfect coiffure, her dress neatly pressed, and her shoes shone like new, but her face was pale and drawn. Unlike the other families, she didn't seem happy to be here. Jessie got the impression she dreaded seeing the person coming off the arriving flight. He watched as she bounced the baby up and down several times when it started to cry. She batted at the toddler's hand when he pulled on her dress too often, but her gaze never left the tarmac beyond the building, where the passengers would arrive.

Fifteen minutes later, a bus pulled up and men started trickling out the front door. Some limped, some wore slings around an arm, and some hobbled on crutches. There was a pause in the flow and Jessie waited anxiously, his eyes straining to see through the bus windows to pick out Max, but they all looked the same in their worn uniforms and crew cuts. He watched as a man set a wheelchair by the door before climbing the steps and returning a minute later with another man in his arms, his legs mere stumps ending at his knees.

Jessie felt his stomach tighten, heard his father's sharp intake of breath. The crowd around them seemed to go silent all at once, every eye watching as the wheelchair was pushed toward them. When the man was wheeled closer, Jessie relaxed, realizing for the first time he had grabbed his father's hand. He let go and shoved his hand into his pocket. It wasn't Max.

A shrill cry broke the silence and Jessie turned to see the pale mother, a hand over her mouth and her eyes wide as the wheelchair rolled toward her. The man's face was ashen and tears rolled unashamedly down his face. He reached his arms up and the woman placed the baby in them. He cradled the child who immediately started screaming. The toddler hid behind his mother's legs, peeking around at the disfigured man. The woman gently pulled the child out in front of her, knelt down and whispered something. The child looked from her to the man, gave a shake of his head and buried his face against his mother's shoulder. The woman in turn leaned over and rested her head in the soldier's lap.

Jessie averted his gaze, knowing he'd witnessed a personal moment that would stay with him forever. He turned, studying all of the faces, but didn't see his brother. He looked back out to the bus and saw two people descending its stairs.

They both wore camouflage fatigues hats pulled low over their faces, but Jessie knew without a doubt that one of them was Max. Jessie started to run to his brother, but paused when he noticed Max place his hand on the other man's shoulder as if for support.

Jessie felt his father behind him, placing a hand on his own shoulder. Jessie braced himself and trained his gaze on the approaching men. Thirty seconds later, Max stood before them.

"Mr. Cole, and let me guess," the soldier who had led Max to them touched his chin as he studied Jessie, "you must be Jessie."

"Yes, sir," Jessie whispered. Clearing his throat he stepped forward. "Welcome home, Max." His words came out strong, but his knees felt weak. When Max raised his head, Jessie felt his father's grip on his shoulder tighten.

The right side of Max's face was burned, leaving scarlet, puckered skin, and his eye was covered by a gauze patch. His left eye was intact, and darted from side to side trying to focus. Jessie felt his stomach rise into his throat and had to swallow hard to keep from losing the meager breakfast he'd picked at before leaving home.

Eugene stepped forward and extended a hand to the soldier standing beside Max. "Thank you for helping my boy." His voice trembled.

"It was my pleasure." He gave Max's arm a squeeze. "Take care of yourself, Max."

The soldier stepped aside and Eugene touched his son's arm. Jessie saw Max flinch at the change in touch. "I just need someone to follow."

Eugene placed Max's hand on his shoulder and led him out of the building. Jessie fell in behind.

At the car, Eugene helped Max into the front seat. All of the stories Jessie had been so excited to share with his brother seemed irrelevant now. What could he say? Had Eugene known this was the condition Max was in? Why didn't he warn me? Jessie didn't know if he was grateful or angry that he hadn't known from the start that Max would never be the same.

The front door flew open as soon as the Bel Air's engine cut off, Ricky and Sam rushing out to greet them. Eleanor stood in the doorway, wiping her hands on her worn apron. Jessie stepped out of the car and opened the door for Max, touching his arm to provide guidance. Max turned so he could plant both feet on the ground before standing up. Jessie saw Ricky and Sam screech to a halt the instant Max faced them, their eyes wide.

"Come on, give me a hug." Max opened his arms, waiting for his brothers to come to him. Sam approached first, clasping Max in a tight hug.

"It's good to have you home." Sam slapped Max on the back before stepping aside to allow Ricky his turn.

Ricky hesitated, his gaze flitting from Sam to Jessie. Jessie gave Ricky a stern look and a subtle motion with his thumb to get moving. Ricky shuffled forward, not looking at Max's face, and looped one arm around his brother's shoulder, offering a half-hearted side hug.

"I must look pretty bad for you to be so quiet." Max spoke softly so only Jessie and Ricky could hear.

"No uglier than before you left." Jessie poked Max in the ribs.

Max threw his head back with a loud guffaw, then felt around until he found Jessie's face. "I see you still aren't shaving, baby face."

Jessie batted Max's hand away. "Virginia happens to like my baby face."

Max smiled. "I bet she does. Let's go inside, it's hot out here."

"Can't be any hotter than the jungle you came from," Sam chirped.

Max's smile faded and he nudged Jessie forward. Jessie glared at Sam as he guided Max to the front door. Max stopped two feet short of it and inhaled deeply.

"Mama," he whispered.

Eleanor crossed the gap between them, enveloping Max in her arms, burying her head in his shoulder. Jessie stood to the side watching as Max stroked her back and whispered something in her ear. Eleanor nodded and after another minute stepped back, her hands running down along Max's arms. Grasping one of his hands, she pulled him into the house.

CHAPTER FIFTY-SIX

Max's Story

July 24, 1967

Jessie followed Max and Eleanor inside, his mouth watering despite the knot in his stomach. Every fan was running at full speed, pushing the aroma of pot roast, carrots, potatoes, and black eye peas throughout the house. Max let out a groan of delight.

"I haven't had a decent meal in two years. I hope there's enough left for you guys once I've finished eating." Max felt the back of a chair, struggled to pull it out from the table, and dropped down into it. He swiveled his head around, as if taking in his surroundings. Jessie thought he saw Max's undamaged left eye meet his own, but Max's head continued to move around the room.

Eugene, carrying Max's duffel bag, passed through the kitchen and living room without a word. Jessie heard the door open to Max and Sam's room, before Eugene returned a minute later. Jessie stood in between the living room and kitchen, unsure what to do. There were so many things he'd planned to show Max when he got home; pictures of Virginia, the new knife he'd gotten for his birthday, the .22 pistol he'd saved a year to buy. How could he show them to Max now?

"Come on, why's everyone so quiet? I expected to be bombarded with stories about girls or the wonders of college life. Tell me what's been going on? Have you met any of the astronauts yet, Jessie?"

Ricky's nervous laugh embarrassed Jessie and gave him the courage to move to the kitchen table to join his oldest brother. With a loud scrape, Jessie pulled out a chair, straddling it with his chin on the back, ignoring his mother's annoyed look.

"No, I ain't met them yet, but Dr. Weston did and he told me all about it."

"You still see him?"

Jessie thought back to the first launch, after Max had left for training, the troubled *Gemini 6*. He remembered Dr. Weston's confidence that Jessie would fly on one of the rockets and that Max would be home for Christmas.

"We saw every launch until…" Jessie swallowed hard. "Until the fire. I ran into him a couple weeks ago, though."

"So, what did the good doctor tell you?" Max asked.

"He got to meet Jim McDivitt and Gordon Cooper. They were at a restaurant down in Cocoa Beach. Dr. Weston said they were the nicest guys, didn't mind folks stopping by their table. Took them two hours to eat their dinners between all the visitors they had. Doc waited until they were finished eating to introduce himself and then he paid for their meal."

"Did he tell them about you?"

Jessie could barely contain himself now, forgetting about Max's injury and diving into his story.

"He sure did, and you won't believe what they said."

"Don't keep me guessing, what did they say?" Max leaned forward in anticipation.

"They said they were going to see if they could get us passes for a launch!"

Max gave a long whistle. "And did they?"

"Not yet, but it was only two weeks ago. That's why I hadn't written to you about it yet. I'm sure he'll hear from them any day now. Maybe you can come along too, and—" Jessie stopped abruptly.

"I'd like that." Max lifted a hand and moved it in front of him until he found Jessie's head resting on the back of the chair. "The doctors aren't sure if I will regain full sight in my left eye, but I can still enjoy the launch. You can talk me through it, and I'll be able to feel it, hear it. If we are close enough, maybe I can even smell it. You wouldn't believe how good my sense of smell has gotten, but I believe God can restore my sight, I just have to be patient."

"I'm sorry, Max. I didn't mean to—"

"Forget about it. I'm glad you were talking to me like nothing has changed. I don't want everyone to baby me and treat me like I'm different."

"Wait, you said you believe in God." Sam leaned across the table to join the conversation.

Max turned his head toward his brother's voice. "Surprised, professor?"

Sam grimaced at the nickname. "A little."

"It took me a long time, but some of the things I've seen, well, it's hard not to believe."

"Hard not to believe?" Jessie nearly screamed the words. "I've seen the news, the things that are happening over there, how can God let that happen?"

Eleanor arranged the bowls of food on the table before making up a plate for Max. The other boys filled up their own and waited for Eugene to bless the food.

Max smiled at the end of the prayer. "I wish you could meet Chaplain Foster. He got me through some tough times." Max turned to Jessie. "You may have seen him. He was in a wheelchair."

The image of the little family around the soldier with no legs made Jessie's breath catch in his throat. "That was the chaplain you wrote about?"

"Yep. He told me he was going to meet his daughter for the first time. Did you see a baby about eighteen months old?"

Jessie nodded.

"I'm assuming that is a yes?" Max smiled then fumbled with his fork. It took him a minute to figure out where everything was on his plate, but when he bit into the pot roast he gave a contented sigh.

"Yeah, the baby screamed when he took her in his arms. There was a little boy too, maybe three or four."

"That would have been his son, John. Foster talked about him a lot." Max's face clouded and he scooped up some black eye peas and potatoes. "He was more upset about not being able to teach John how to play football than anything else when he found out he'd lost both his legs."

Jessie's mouth felt dry and he licked his lips. "What happened?" Jessie felt Ricky punch him, heard Sam hiss at him, and saw Eleanor glare at him from her spot by the stove. The only person who didn't seem interested in remonstrating was Eugene, who merely pushed the meat and vegetables around his plate.

Max seemed to sense the tension in the room and gave a half-hearted chuckle. He scraped the last of his carrots and peas onto his fork, chewed them up and pushed the plate back. "It's alright, guys. There are some things I don't want to talk about, but I can give you the highlights of what happened to me and Foster."

"Max, you don't have to." Eleanor reached across the table and clasped Max's hand. Her eyes were moist.

"I know, but…" Max's lower lip trembled and Jessie watched his brother swallow several times, his Adam's apple rolling up and down. "There are things they should know, in case…"

"In case any of them have to go over there too," Eugene finished. Jessie turned to his father who pushed his own plate back, despite having barely touched it. His face was grim as he studied his eldest son.

Max nodded and took a deep breath. "We'd been hiking through the jungle nonstop for two days. There'd been no sign of the North Vietnam Army, which made most of us more nervous than usual, but a few guys started to relax, crack jokes, make noise." Max paused, the corner of his eye twitching.

"Foster and I were in the middle of the snaking column, barely able to stand up, we were so tired. I thought about falling out of line and catching a few minutes of shut-eye but Foster kept me going. It must have been close to midnight when the Lieutenant called a halt. Too exhausted to even take my pack off, I dropped to the ground right where I'd been standing. Next thing I knew, I was being dragged into the trees."

Max swiveled his head toward Eleanor. "May I have a glass of water, please?"

"Of course." Eleanor gave Max's shoulder a squeeze and returned with a tall glass of water. After setting it on the table, she reached for Max's hand and guided it to the glass. Max took a long drink before continuing.

"I could hear gunfire and yelling, but it was so dark I couldn't tell where the fighting was. Foster told me everything he knew, which wasn't much. He'd only woken up a few minutes before dragging me off.

"From what he'd been able to piece together, the front of the column had unwittingly stopped less than fifty feet from a village held by the NVA. Once our boys settled in, the enemy crept up and attacked, barely making a sound. We found out later that one guy woke up just as the knife was coming down on him and was able to sound an alarm before he was stabbed in the throat. If he hadn't, who knows how many more of us would have been killed."

Jessie shifted his gaze from Max to his mother and saw her shiver. Ricky and Sam sat on either side of Max, their bodies turned so they could focus on him. Ricky's elbow was on the table, his hand propped under his chin, but Sam's palms were on the edge of the table, almost as if holding onto it for dear life. Max took another drink of water, some trickling out the side of his damaged mouth.

"When the guys up front awoke and started fighting back, the Vietnamese didn't turn back; they kept on coming, like they thought they couldn't be killed. The sound of gunfire moved down the column waking more guys up, but everyone was confused. Foster said he saw a couple of the guys ahead of us get shot by some of our own troops farther back. That's when he started dragging me off the path into the woods.

"By the time he'd caught me up, the whole platoon was in chaos. Muzzle flashes and tracers lit up the darkness all around us, but no one really knew what was going on." Max shook his head. "It was like all of the training we'd had went out the window. Foster and I slipped through the trees and found a Platoon Sergeant trying to settle the boys down. I don't know how much time passed before the shooting stopped. The Sergeant found the closest radio operator and called in to the firebase we'd been heading to. The remaining enemy forces seemed to have pulled back, but we knew they were only preparing for another attack.

"Foster and I partnered up with some other guys in a circle with our backs to each other to keep watch on all sides. Just before sunrise, I saw movement. You wouldn't believe how well those guys could disguise themselves. You could watch for hours and see nothing but clumps of tall grass, rocks, and trees, then a clump of grass would seem to move, such a small amount you were sure it was a trick of your eyes. Half an hour later that clump of grass was running at you with a rifle aimed at your head.

"Anyway, I whispered to Foster that I thought I saw something and he said he had too. Our little band prepared for battle, attaching bayonets to our rifles, making sure our extra magazines were handy. As the first rays of sunlight cut through the darkness, we found hundreds of NVA rushing toward us from a clearing seventy-five yards away. We dropped to the ground and started firing.

"Hours passed before there was a lull. The LT gathered everyone, to start collecting the injured and dead. We loaded them onto helicopters that had been called in and watched them fly off, dodging enemy fire. When they were all gone, the LT ordered us to move.

"We made it to a wide valley where we came under heavy fire. We tried to retreat, only to find we were surrounded. The radio operator was calling in coordinates for an air strike, but we were being overrun and running out of ammo." Max felt around the table until his hand wrapped around the half-empty glass of water. He lifted it to his mouth and drank what remained. Eleanor reached for the empty glass and moved to the sink to refill it.

"Thank you." Max took the glass placed in his hand and drank some more.

Jessie rubbed his face and realized he was sweating.

Max cleared his throat and resumed his story. "By the time darkness came, we were exhausted, huddled behind the few rocks or tree stumps the valley offered, or dug into shallow trenches. The fighting died down, but no one dared close their eyes. Someone got spooked and tossed a phosphorus grenade that exploded only feet from me." Max touched his burned face. "Foster dug the burning shrapnel from my cheek. While he was bandaging me up, another grenade went off and Foster went down. I couldn't see anything, I could only hear his screaming." Max's voice broke and he covered his face with one hand.

"Enough." Eleanor pulled Max's head against her chest and buried her face in his cropped hair. Jessie watched her shoulders rise and fall in ragged breaths. Eugene stood, placing one hand on Eleanor's back, the other on Max's shoulder, pulling the two close to him. Jessie saw his father's lips move in whispered words reserved for Eleanor alone.

"You must be tired from your trip. Why don't you go lie down for a while?" Eugene stepped back and helped Max to his feet. Max nodded and allowed Eugene to lead him across the kitchen and into the hall.

CHAPTER FIFTY-SEVEN

Adjustment

July 24, 1967

J essie remained with Ricky and Sam, his gaze glued to the table as he tried to imagine the scene Max had described. The Cole boys had found themselves in some tight spots, threatened by alligators, panthers, even a bear once back on the island, but those all seemed like childish games now. Jessie had seen stories on television about the war, heard about the protests, but this was the first time he realized how terrible things were in Vietnam. He relived the details of Max's story, his fists clenching tightly.

"Sam, you can sleep in my bed tonight." Ricky scratched at a spot of dried mustard on the table.

Sam shrugged. "We'll see. Max might not want to be alone."

Jessie stood up, the legs of his chair scraping loudly, drawing a sharp look from his mother. He left by the front door, careful to keep it from slamming and disturbing Max. Once outside he sprinted into the darkness.

The smell of a charcoal fire teased Jessie's nose and made his stomach growl. Max was the only one who'd eaten much. He'd practically inhaled his meal. Jessie felt a twinge of guilt for running off without helping clean up. He shifted his course, moving parallel to the edge of the forest for half a mile, then turned south, emerging three blocks from Virginia's.

He crossed the street and moved past houses with lights in the front windows, the sound of televisions and radios wafting from their open windows, and that scent of charcoal fire growing stronger. He turned onto Pritchard and passed two houses before standing in front of Virginia's. Not much had changed since that first day he'd walked her home.

The robin's egg blue had faded some in the Florida sun, the shutters were starting to peel, but the boxwoods were still neatly trimmed and the white Chevy Impala still sat in the driveway. Between his work schedule and Virginia's volunteering at the hospital, they hadn't seen each other in over a week. Jessie ran a hand through his hair, hoping he didn't look as wild as he felt.

He had only taken three steps toward the door when it opened and Virginia stood in the glow of the light from the living room. She wore a dark brown dress, a pale blue belt cinched tight around her tiny waist. Her hair was pulled back in a ponytail and her feet were bare. Jessie looked into her eyes and felt his own feet moving faster until he stood only steps from her.

"Jessie, are you okay?" Virginia's eyes met his and he recognized the apprehension in them.

Jessie stepped closer and pulled her into his arms, burying his head in her neck. She smelled of jasmine and orange blossoms, still so fresh even at the end of the day.

"Is there someone at the door?" called a woman from the back of the house.

"It's Jessie," Virginia replied, pulling him into the house. Jessie followed her into the kitchen where her mother and father were still seated at the dinner table.

Mrs. Benson smiled and stood when they entered. "It's good to see you, Jessie. Have you eaten dinner? There is plenty left over if you are hungry."

"I appreciate it, Mrs. Benson, but no thank you. May I talk with Virginia for a few minutes?"

"Of course. Why don't you two go sit in the living room. George and I will clean up in here. Won't we, dear?" and gave her husband a sharp look.

Jessie thought he saw Mr. Benson frown, but he started to gather up the empty plates and carry them to the sink. Virginia tugged on Jessie's hand and the pair moved back to the living room, settling onto the couch.

"What's wrong?" Virginia leaned in and touched his face, her finger's tracing a line across his jaw. The motion made Jessie think of Max's damaged face and how no woman would ever want to touch it. He reached for Virginia's hand and pulled it away.

"Max came home, but…" Jessie didn't know how to begin to describe Max's injuries, how angry he was that they had been caused by his own platoon, or how helpless he felt.

"How bad is it?" Virginia lowered her eyes and Jessie was grateful. He couldn't look into her gentle soul and tell her the truth.

"He's blind." Jessie decided not to go into details. Not now. There would be time for that later.

Virginia gasped, causing Jessie to flinch. "That's awful," she whispered.

Jessie wondered what she would say if he told her the rest, that Max looked like a monster out of a cheap horror movie.

"How's he taking it?"

Jessie shrugged. "He has a little bit of use of his left eye and seems to think there's a chance it will improve."

"Why only one? Couldn't they both get better?"

Jessie's stomach lurched. He swallowed hard against the knot rising in his throat. He'd put on a good front with his family, unwilling to let Max pick up on any trace of his horror, but now he felt like he was suffocating.

"Jess?"

He blinked and turned his gaze upon Virginia, her creamy skin so perfect and smooth. He cupped her cheek with one hand and pulled her close. He nuzzled her cheek, her nose, her eyes, marveling at how soft they all were. Virginia giggled and tried to meet his mouth, but Jessie pulled back.

"I don't ever want to forget how you look right now."

A tinge of pink flushed Virginia's cheeks and she reached a hand up to brush at a stray lock of hair. Jessie clasped her hand and pulled it away, moving closer to her. She nestled her head on his shoulder and he rested his cheek on her forehead.

"Max is never going to be the same," he whispered.

"This war has changed us all," she agreed.

CHAPTER FIFTY-EIGHT

Last Year of High School

September 9, 1967

J essie shuffled across the hall to the bathroom, barely awake until he splashed several handfuls of cold water onto his face. He was already three weeks into his senior year and knew he had to get serious about making plans for life after graduation. He dressed quickly, threw a sandwich and some fruit in a paper bag, and was out the door before anyone else was awake. An orange line lit up the horizon, growing brighter with each step he took toward the river. By the time he reached the water's edge, the sun burned into his eyes as he trained them on the Vertical Assembly Building, nearly a year old now, a black silhouette against the flaming sun. It had been eight months since the *Apollo* fire, without a single launch. Even with this new building and launch site finished only a few months before, he feared the space program would die before he had a chance to be a part of it.

A seagull fluttered across the river letting out a plaintive cry, as if expecting Jessie to toss a tasty morsel into the air. It made him remember the girl who'd had her bag of chips stolen that time at the launch. Hard to believe that was only two years ago.

The seagull drifted above him a moment longer, then, with a flap of its wings, moved down the shore. Jessie gazed across the river until a car horn behind him broke his concentration. He turned to see Randy in a sparkling new '67 Mustang.

"Nice ride," Jessie commented as he jogged up to the passenger window.

"Early graduation present." Randy reached across the car and pushed the passenger door open. "Hop in."

Jessie ducked in. "Early is right. Your folks must be pretty sure you aren't going to screw things up this year."

Randy chuckled. "I've had straight A's since I was in third grade. I'd have to work pretty hard to not graduate."

Jessie felt his face redden. "Right, I forgot you were a genius."

This made Randy laugh even harder as he revved the engine and pulled back onto the highway. Jessie leaned his head out the open window, the wind whipping at his face, his hair, that he'd allowed to grow long over the summer, flapping wildly. The mile ride ended all too soon when Randy pulled into a parking spot, right in front of a half dozen girls.

Jessie watched his friend unfold himself from the low seat and swagger toward them. He saw a couple giggle as Randy approached. Jessie scanned the grounds for Virginia, but when he didn't see her, made his way toward Randy.

"Which one of you fine young ladies would like to take a ride with me after class?" Randy was asking as Jessie approached. Another round of giggles rippled through the girls. Randy leaned close to a cute blonde in a lime green mini skirt and a sleeveless white top. Her boots made her two inches taller than Randy, but he didn't seem to mind. "How about you, Tammy? Wouldn't you like to take the Mustang for a spin?"

Tammy batted her eyes, her gaze darting around her circle of friends, finally stopping on Randy. "I might consider letting you drive me home, if you play your cards right."

Jessie suppressed a smile at the way she played with Randy. *Boy, am I glad I don't have to go through that with Virginia.* He turned to look for his sweetheart once again and caught a glimpse of her on the far side of the courtyard. Without a word, Jessie peeled away from the group, taking long strides to meet Virginia. He slipped an arm around her waist and kissed her.

"Good morning," he whispered when their lips parted.

"Good morning to you. What brought that on?"

"I was thinking about how lucky I am to have you." Jessie nodded toward the group he'd left. "Randy is trying to get one of those girls to go out with him."

"He's the smartest guy in our class. I don't think he'll have much trouble getting a date."

"The brand new Mustang he drove up in probably won't hurt his chances any either, but I'm still glad I don't have to worry about flirting anymore."

"I wouldn't mind you flirting with me a little." Virginia rested her head on Jessie's shoulder as they walked toward their first class.

"Maybe I can flirt with you on the way home this afternoon." Jessie gave Virginia's waist a squeeze before releasing her and following her through the classroom door.

Randy came flying into the room seconds before the bell rang and dropped into the seat next to Jessie.

"How'd it go?" Jessie whispered, out the side of his mouth.

Randy gave a thumbs up signal before opening his textbook and turning his attention to the teacher. Jessie knew better than to try to continue the conversation during class. He'd have to wait until lunch to get the details.

The weather was so beautiful, Jessie was sure he'd find his friends eating lunch outside so he bypassed the cafeteria. He found Randy and a couple of other guys sprawled on the ground, faces tipped up to the sun, and plopped down beside them.

"So, who gets the honor of riding with you this afternoon?" Jessie asked.

"Tammy, of course." Randy bit into his sandwich. "Was there any question she'd say yes?"

"I didn't hear her say so," Jessie countered.

"You should have stuck around. She was practically begging me to take her home."

Jessie shook his head in disbelief. "If you say so."

"You doubt it?"

Jessie held up a hand. "I didn't say that. I'm sure you played your cards right."

Randy's eyes narrowed, then he relaxed and laughed. "Yeah, I guess you could say that. I have to drive her sister and one of her friends home too."

"So you got three for the price of one," Jessie teased. All of the guys laughed and the conversation turned to the new Mustang.

As lunch wound down, Jessie balled up his empty lunch bag and tossed it into a nearby garbage can. "Hey, you think I can borrow your car to take Virginia out sometime?"

"I don't know. I'll have to ask my folks."

"I promise to be careful. She gets so embarrassed when I take her out in Max's car."

Randy shook his head. "You and your brothers did a great job fixing that old buggy up. She should be impressed with what you've done."

"Yeah, but she complains about her hair getting messed up."

"Girls. They just can't appreciate a good thing." Randy tossed his own bag into the trash and gathered up his books.

Jessie whistled on his way back to class, looking forward to seeing Virginia again in a couple of hours.

CHAPTER FIFTY-NINE

Launches Resume

November 9, 1967

A light breeze brushed against Jessie's skin, causing goose bumps to rise along his arms. In his excitement he hadn't thought about bringing a jacket. He stood at the front of the crowd gathered to watch the first launch since the *Apollo 1* fire, which also happened to be the first from one of the new launch pads and the first to use the Saturn V rocket system. Jessie knew it wasn't a manned flight and the orbit would last less than ten hours, but he still felt butterflies in his stomach and could tell those around him did so as well.

Several radios played the countdown, creating an echoing effect down the coastline. Jessie focused on the nearest of the broadcasts and kept his eyes glued to the opposite side of the river. His breaths became more shallow as the seconds melted away until the broadcaster announced ignition and lift off. He bit into his bottom lip until he saw the plume of fire and smoke rising into the air and the rumble of the powerful engine rolled across the water to batter the anxious spectators.

Cheers and clapping filled Jessie's ears. He released his lip and added his own voice to the cacophony until the spacecraft disappeared from sight. As the crowd drifted back to their cars, Jessie looked around for Dr. Weston. He hadn't been able to reach his friend before the launch, to make arrangements to meet, but hoped he might still run into him. He saw two burgundy Impalas similar to the doctor's, but when he approached them, found neither belonged to Dr. Weston. A look at his watch told Jessie he was already late for school, so he abandoned the search and darted across the street.

"Nice of you to join us, Mr. Cole," his English teacher greeted him with a cold stare, as he tried to sneak in the door.

"Sorry," Jessie mumbled and sank into the nearest chair.

"As I was saying, you will all be writing a term paper that will count for fifty percent of your grade this semester."

Jessie gave an inward groan and pulled out a piece of paper to take notes. After his summer of being grounded to the house a couple years ago, he'd found some books that he'd enjoyed reading, but still didn't see any need for writing papers. He wasn't going to be writing great works of fiction or deconstructing classic literature when he got into the space program.

On the edge of his paper, he started doodling a rocket lifting off, surrounded by stars and planets. The ringing of the bell startled him from his daydreams and he gathered up his books, only mildly ashamed he'd missed the entire lesson.

"Did you catch the launch?" Virginia slipped her hand into Jessie's and fell in step beside him.

"Of course." Jessie gave her a look that he hoped conveyed his shock at her even having to ask, but he appreciated that she had.

"How unhappy was your teacher that you were late?"

"I wish Mr. Smith were my teacher for these morning launches. He gets it."

"Of course he does. He's a math and science guy."

Jessie didn't respond, thinking about the paper his English teacher had assigned them. He was supposed to write five pages on where he saw himself in five years. He'd been focused on what he needed to do after graduation, whether to try to go to college or join the military; unsure which path would give him the best shot at becoming an astronaut. Could he be in astronaut training in five years?

"What are you thinking?" Virginia asked.

"About this paper I have to write. English teacher wants to know where I see myself in five years." Jessie turned to look at Virginia and saw her lips twitching at the corners as if she was trying to contain a smile.

"Do you see me in your five year plan?" she asked.

"A few months ago we were arguing about staying together, but lately things have been great."

Virginia looked away and Jessie was sorry he hadn't assured her that of course he saw her in his future. Students were ducking into classrooms, leaving them practically alone in the hall.

Virginia released his hand. "I'll see you after school."

Jessie watched her walk to her own classroom, her hips swaying like a palm tree in a gentle breeze. He let out a loud breath and raked his fingers through his hair. Girls. When was he ever going to understand them?

CHAPTER SIXTY

The Term Paper

December 1967

"Well done, Mr. Cole." The English teacher walked up and down the rows of desks, returning the term papers. Jessie stared at the A+ on the paper she placed on his desk then looked up to see her nodding her approval. He'd spent days working on that paper and had been proud of his work, but he hadn't expected an A+. He'd brought his grades up in every class except English, in which he'd held a steady C average.

The teacher moved on up the aisle and Jessie flipped through the pages, noticing several comments in that ubiquitous red pen. He smiled to himself thinking about using such a big word. Maybe he had been learning more than he thought after all.

"I was happy to see that some of you have big dreams for your futures." The teacher had returned to the front of the room and her gaze swept over the students. "Of course, you all have to pass this class before you can chase those dreams, so why don't you open up your books to chapter twenty-one."

There were chuckles along with the rustle of turning pages. Jessie tucked his paper into his tattered folder and flipped to the chapter, feeling more engaged and more determined to do well. The class went by faster than ever before, the ringing bell surprising him.

Virginia fell into stride beside him. "You look happy. Did the teacher like your paper?"

Jessie nodded. They hadn't talked about the paper or Jessie's vision of the future since the day of the assignment. Jessie had broached it that afternoon, but Virginia had changed the subject.

"I got an A+."

Virginia gave his hand a squeeze. "That's great."

Jessie knew she meant to be encouraging, but it felt forced. He hadn't let her read it before he'd turned it in, and wasn't sure he wanted her to read it now. What if his vision didn't match hers?

"My family is going to Boston for Christmas. My aunt Sherry isn't doing well."

There she went changing the subject again. "Is she going to be all right?"

"I don't know. I can tell mother is worried, but she hasn't said much."

"Maybe you will have a white Christmas. I'd like to see snow once."

Virginia's face brightened. "It's beautiful. We were up there for Christmas when I was seven or eight. I remember spending all day outside, building snowmen and making snow angels."

"Sounds like fun. When are you leaving?"

"The day after school gets out. We'll be there for the whole break."

"You think we can go out Friday before you leave, so I can give you your gift?"

"I'll check with mother." Virginia leaned forward and gave Jessie a peck on the cheek. "See you later."

Before Jessie could say anything more she was halfway to her class.

"Cole, are you coming?" Randy called from the door to their math class.

Jessie trudged to the doorway. "Why are girls so hard to understand?"

Randy guffawed. "Why're you trying to understand them? That's a waste of time. You just need to get yourself a hot car like mine and the girls will be falling all over you."

"I don't want more girls. I can barely handle the one I got."

"The problem is you only got one. You haven't been playing the field, allowing them to compete for you."

"I don't know how they haven't all ganged up against you yet." Jessie gave his friend a lopsided grin.

Randy replied with a nonchalant shrug. "What can I say? They love me."

Jessie admired his friend's confidence, but couldn't imagine dating more than one girl at a time. "Whatcha doing over Christmas break?"

"Not much. I think we're spending a weekend at my uncle's place down in Miami. You got plans?"

"Nah. I'll probably just pick up extra shifts at the grocery store."

The science teacher shut the door behind them, ending the boys' conversation. Jessie opened his book and tried to focus on the lesson. This was usually one of his favorite classes, but he found himself distracted by thoughts of Christmas and Virginia's trip.

After the final bell rang, Jessie shuffled through the throngs of students, head down, deep in thought. Virginia's news about leaving as soon as school was out had really thrown a wrench in his plans. He'd picked out a necklace he wanted to get, and worked out exactly how many shifts he would need to work to afford it. Now he was losing a week of work time and so had to find a way to come up with the extra money.

Virginia was waiting beside the gym, her hair fluttering in the breeze. Jessie gazed at her, wondering how he'd been lucky enough to get her to fall in love with him. She held her books in one arm and slipped the other through his. They walked in silence for the first block.

"Have you sent in any of your college applications yet?" Virginia asked.

"I sent in a few right after school started. There's a couple I still need to finish, but they aren't my top choices. Have you?"

"Not yet. Mother has been hounding me about it, but I'm not sure where I want to go." Virginia's steps slowed.

Jessie stopped and watched her chew on the inside of her bottom lip. He knew she only did that when she was worried. He reached out to touch her chin tenderly. "What's bothering you?"

Her jaw stopped working and she lowered her eyes. "What if we don't go to the same school?"

Jessie hadn't really thought about that. His top schools were mostly in Florida, but there were a couple out of state. He knew all of the colleges the current astronauts had attended. He knew which ones had ROTC programs where he might be able to get a scholarship. But he wasn't even sure what Virginia might want to go to school for. He felt a pang of guilt that he'd never thought to ask her.

"I love you and nothing is going to change that."

The corner of Virginia's mouth twitched a little. "What if I don't want to go to college?"

"That would be fine with me, but you are so smart, why wouldn't you? You could be anything you want."

"That's what my parents say too. I'm not saying I don't want to go, I'm just not sure."

The couple started walking again. The sound of a train horn floated on the wind and they moved a few feet further from the tracks they were following.

"I don't want to hold you back, Jessie. I know how much you want to be an astronaut and I don't want you to limit your school choices because of me."

Jessie felt that stab of guilt again. Purdue University, up in Indiana, had made his top five without a single thought of leaving Virginia behind. "I don't want to hold you back either. It's not fair for you to wait around here while I go to school."

"What do astronaut wives do, other than worry their husbands will be blown to bits?"

Virginia's words cut into Jessie bringing him to an abrupt halt. He looked into her wide eyes and saw the look of regret. The locomotive engine chugged past them, the whistle sounding shrilly, the ground beneath them rumbling.

"I'm sorry." Virginia swatted at a tear that sprung to her eye.

"You don't want me to be an astronaut, do you? Is that what this is really about?"

Virginia shook her head fervently. "That's not what I meant. I know how much it means to you and I want you to be happy."

"You just don't want to be married to me if that is what I am doing, right?"

"I didn't say that."

"NASA doesn't want the astronauts to blow up either. The *Apollo* fire was a terrible accident and they take even more precautions now." Jessie eyed the train creeping by. There were still ten cars, each the perfect way to escape this conversation. He could jump onto the ladder and roll away from Virginia, hop off when he reached the edge of town and lick his wounds. Maybe Randy had the right idea about girls after all.

Jessie looked back at Virginia. Her lips trembled and her eyes were watery. He stepped toward her and pulled her into his arms.

"I'm sorry," she whispered into his chest.

Jessie stroked her hair in reply. He had some serious thinking to do.

CHAPTER SIXTY-ONE

Broken Hearts

December 15, 1967

The mirror was clouded with steam that Jessie had to wipe away with his damp towel. When he could see himself, he dropped the towel on the floor and reached for a comb. He parted his hair to the right, then the left, then combed it forward, unhappy with any of the styles. He should have stopped for a hair cut after school one day. He didn't want Virginia to go away for the holidays with an image of him in such a scraggly condition. Pounding on the door made him jump.

"Come on. Other people need to use the john."

Jessie unlocked and opened the door to find Max leaning on the doorjamb, his new eyeglasses askew on his damaged ear and nose. "I have to finish getting ready for my date."

Max tousled Jessie's hair. "You're a mess."

Jessie batted his brother's hand away. "I am now. Thanks a lot."

Max chuckled. "Let me in, I'll only be a minute."

"Yeah, okay." Jessie stepped out and wandered into the kitchen where Eleanor was stirring a pot of chili.

She glanced over her shoulder when Jessie pulled a chair out from the table. "You're going to brush your hair aren't you?"

"I was trying to when Max ran me out of the bathroom." Jessie ran his fingers through his hair, pulling the long locks down over his eyes.

"You need a haircut."

Jessie swept the hair out of his eyes. "How old were you and Pop when you got married?"

Eleanor set the spoon on a small plate, covered the chili pot, and wiped her hands on her apron before turning around to look at Jessie. "I was eighteen, he was twenty. Why?"

"Are you sorry you got married so young?"

Eleanor pulled out a chair and sat across from Jessie. "There have been a few times when I've wondered if we should have waited. It was the middle of the war and Eugene could have been sent overseas at any time. A lot of couples got married right before the young man shipped out and many of them never came home."

Jessie noticed the distant look in her eyes and guessed she was remembering days his parents never talked about around the boys.

"It's not very different now I guess. Boys are still going off to war." Eleanor reached across the table for Jessie's hand. "We won't have to worry about that with you, though. You're going to college and then on to the moon."

Randy was true to his word and got his father to agree to loan the Mustang to Jessie for the night. At six o'clock Jessie was waiting outside when Randy pulled up in front of the house. Randy left the car running when he slipped out of his seat.

"Be careful with her," Randy admonished.

"You want me to drop you back at your house?"

"Nah. I'm going to walk to Cutters and meet some friends. One of them can take me home later."

"Thanks again. I owe you one."

Randy gave a dismissive wave. "Get outta here. You don't want to keep your girl waiting."

It took less than three minutes to reach Virginia's. Jessie looked in the rearview mirror, straightened his tie, and pushed the door open. The front porch light was already on, creating a yellow glow in the fading twilight. Jessie only had to wait a few seconds after knocking.

Mrs. Benson opened the door with a warm greeting. "Come inside, Jessie. Virginia will be ready in a couple of minutes. Would you like some hot chocolate?"

Jessie followed Mrs. Benson into the living room. "No, thank you, ma'am."

"That's a nice car," Mr. Benson turned from the front window of the living room as Jessie was taking a seat on the couch.

"It belongs to one of my friends. He let me borrow it."

Mr. Benson nodded and settled into a green and black paisley print wingchair. Mrs. Benson took a spot on the opposite end of the couch from Jessie.

"What are your plans for the evening?" Mrs. Benson asked.

"Dinner at the Riverview Restaurant and then a movie. I'll have Virginia home by eleven."

"I suppose she told you we are leaving in the morning for Boston."

"Yes. I'm sorry to hear your sister isn't well. I hope she's better soon."

"I appreciate that, but I don't think she has much longer." Mrs. Benson's eyes clouded. "I haven't mentioned that to Virginia and I would appreciate it if you didn't either. I don't want to ruin her last evening with you."

"Of course, I won't say a thing." Jessie was surprised by the seriousness of Virginia's aunt's condition, but something else about Mrs. Benson's words worried him as well. He didn't have a chance to consider this before Virginia appeared in the doorway.

She wore a blue dress that was fitted at the top, accentuating her great figure, then flared out in a short skirt he imagined would twirl up should they go dancing. Her hair was held back with a matching blue headband, allowing him a clear view of her creamy ivory face.

Jessie stood. "You look amazing."

"Thank you." Virginia's eyes flitted to her mother.

"You're beautiful, sweetheart," Mrs. Benson confirmed. Virginia crossed the room, dropped a kiss on her mother's cheek, then her father's.

"Are you ready?" Virginia held out a hand to Jessie.

"Have a good time," Mrs. Benson called as the couple moved toward the door.

Virginia reached for a coat hanging by the door before stepping outside behind Jessie. She shrugged it on then gasped. "Whose car?"

Jessie couldn't help grinning. "Randy's."

"He's not coming with us, is he?"

Jessie laughed. "Of course not. He let me borrow it for the night."

Jessie opened the passenger door and helped Virginia in, making sure her dress was tucked inside before shutting the door. He rubbed his hands together, the air turning colder with the growing darkness.

The ride to Riverview Restaurant was filled with small talk about preparations for Virginia's trip and the exams they'd taken that day. Jessie could feel sweat on his palms, unsure if he was nervous about driving Randy's car or the gift weighing heavily in his coat pocket.

Jessie turned into the parking lot and took a full turn around it, trying to decide if he should park close to the entrance or at the edge, so there was less chance of the car getting scratched. He finally opted for somewhere in between. Randy had been driving to school for three months and no one there had scratched it. Surely it would be okay tonight. He hurried around the car to open the door for Virginia. They entered the restaurant hand in hand, greeted by a girl not much older than them.

"Good evening. Table for two?" The girl pulled two menus from a box by the door. Without waiting for a response, she led them through a large room filled with conversation and laughter, stopping at a small table near the back of the restaurant.

Jessie pulled out Virginia's chair and helped her scoot close to the table then took his own seat. The waitress handed them each a menu, spieled the specials, something about trout and twice-baked potatoes. Jessie and Virginia each ordered a Coke before the waitress left them to study the menus.

"What looks good to you?" Jessie asked.

"The trout and potato she mentioned sounds good."

Jessie nodded. "I think I want the dozen shrimp. I wonder if I can get the twice-baked potato with that instead of french fries."

The waitress appeared and confirmed that Jessie could do the switch, and assured them their order would be out as quickly as possible. In the meantime, she left them a basket of hot hush puppies. Jessie watched Virginia spear one of the fried dough balls with her fork and proceed to cut it into bite-size pieces. He considered following her lead, but that wasn't his style. He plucked one from the basket, broke it in two and popped half into his mouth.

"What are you doing during the holidays?" Virginia asked.

"I asked to pick up some extra shifts at work. I may go hunting with my brothers. Sam will be home tomorrow."

"I'm sorry I won't get a chance to see him this year. I like his stories about college."

"He sure does love talking about it." Jessie took a drink then finished the other half of his hush puppy. "I'm glad he's enjoying it, though. Not like there was any question he would, but it's still nice to see him so happy."

"What about Ricky? Do you think he will decide to go to school?"

"Nah. He's happy working with Pop, clearing land for new construction. He and Max have been talking about starting their own construction business. Max didn't spend much of his pay from Vietnam and Ricky's been saving up, so they may have enough money to start something small."

"Doesn't he worry about getting called for Vietnam?"

"We don't talk about the war." Jessie dabbed at the corners of his mouth with his napkin. He hadn't told her about the nightmares Max still had at least twice a week or the fainting episodes Ricky had started having a few weeks back. Dr. Weston had said Max may never stop having them and Ricky had an appointment with the doctor the first of the year.

The waitress returned with two plates. "Is there anything else I can get you?"

Jessie looked to Virginia who shook her head. "I think we are good for now," he replied.

Virginia cut into the flaky, white fish, placing a bite on her fork. Jessie watched her enjoy the first taste, her face brightening. He reached for the ketchup, squirted a dollop on his plate and proceeded to swoop shrimp through it, biting off their tails.

Virginia giggled.

"What?"

"I love that you aren't afraid to enjoy your food."

Jessie looked at the pile of shrimp tails and his greasy fingers. He thought about the dainty way she always ate and felt ashamed. He reached for a fresh napkin and wiped his hands then picked up his fork.

"No, don't stop. I didn't mean to make you self-conscious."

Jessie hesitated, but held onto the fork, deciding to focus on his potato for a while.

"Will you write to me while I'm in Boston?"

"It's only two weeks."

Virginia frowned. "I know, but won't you miss me?"

"Of course. Only, by the time I write and get it in the mail, you will be practically home."

"You're right. It was a silly question." Virginia lifted her Coke, blocking Jessie's view of her face.

Jessie finished his potato and kept his fork for the remaining handful of shrimp. He turned the conversation to Virginia's aunt and enjoyed listening to her stories of past visits. It was obvious she liked her aunt a great deal and wished she lived closer.

"Which movie would you like to see?" Jessie asked as they waited for their check.

Virginia folded her napkin in a precise square and placed it under her empty plate. "Why don't we skip the movie and go to the river?"

Jessie couldn't believe his ears. Going to the river meant going to make out. He had buddies who went to the river every weekend and he'd heard their stories. He knew how many of them had gotten to third base there and even a couple of home runs. He and Virginia hadn't even gotten to second base yet.

"I told your parents we were going to a movie."

"I'm not in the mood for a movie and you have such a nice car tonight."

Jessie hoped Virginia didn't see his hands trembling as he pulled some money from his wallet to pay the bill. He helped her on with her coat before they stepped outside and he took a deep breath, and once in the car, listened to the quiet purr of the engine to calm his racing pulse.

They passed the fishing pier and rolled over the bridge on the beach road, leaving the city lights behind. On the far side, Jessie could make out the outlines of several cars already parked along the shoulder. Their noses faced the water, lights off, radios playing.

Jessie turned onto the shoulder, found a spot a little way past the last car in the row, dropped theirs into park and killed its lights. The radio played a Rolling Stones song, the beat of the drum matching Jessie's own heartbeat. He turned to face Virginia, who was reaching into her coat pocket.

"It's not much, but…" She handed him a small box wrapped in red and green plaid paper.

He took it and opened one end, pulling out the box. When he opened the lid he found a rocket-shaped Christmas tree ornament with his name painted on the side. He lifted it from the box and draped the thin loop of string around the end of the rearview mirror. Jessie watched it swing back and forth for a few seconds.

"It's perfect," he assured her, pulling her closer and giving her a long kiss.

"My turn." Virginia held out her hand expectantly.

Jessie pulled a box from his pocket, its snowman wrapping paper seeming childish in this setting. He handed it to her and watched her face as she meticulously removed each piece of tape, never tearing the paper. She lifted the lid of the white box, her eyes growing wide as she pulled a gold chain from it, a small heart pendent resting against her wrist.

"It's beautiful," she whispered.

"Turn around, so I can put it on you."

Virginia handed the necklace to him, turned and lifted her hair off her neck. Jessie reached around her, allowing the pendent to drop onto her chest and fumbled with the clasp for a full minute.

"There. Now let me see."

Virginia turned back to face him. "Thank you, Jessie."

"You are the most beautiful girl in the world."

Virginia leaned forward, took his face in both her hands and kissed him. It was a long, deep kiss that conveyed more longing than Jessie had experienced with her before.

"Let's move to the backseat," she murmured against his ear.

"Are you sure?" Every fiber of his being screamed at him for hesitating.

Instead of answering, Virginia pulled herself between the two front seats, into the back and extended a hand to Jessie.

He gazed at her, his eyes searching hers. "This isn't right."

She reached forward and caressed his face. "Yes it is."

Jessie reached for her hand and kissed her fingers. "I should take you home."

Her face drained of color. "You don't want to?"

"Not in the back of someone else's car. Not like this." Jessie couldn't believe what he was saying. Every other guy here tonight was probably getting lucky and he was saying no, but this wasn't like Virginia. Something wasn't right. "Why do you want this now?"

"I thought…" Virginia's lips quivered. "You got Randy's car and the necklace." Tears splashed on her cheek.

"I wanted to give you a nice night before you left so you would have good memories while you were in Boston."

"What did you write in your English paper about your life in five years?"

"What?"

"Why didn't you let me read the paper? Was I in it?"

"Of course you were." Jessie sighed.

"Then why didn't you let me read it?"

"Because I didn't know if you had me in your five year plan." He rested his chin on the back of his seat. "I haven't really known where we stand for the past year. I've told you that but you change the subject."

Virginia tucked her legs under her, the skirt of her dress splaying out all around her. "Mother thinks I should've been dating other boys instead of tying myself to you all through high school. She married dad right out of school and I think she regrets it now. She worries the same will happen with us."

"Is that how you feel too?" He could see her jaw moving and knew she was chewing on her lip, but he didn't try to stop her.

"I don't know." She said it so softly he could barely hear it, but he saw the doubt in her eyes.

"And yet you were ready to…" Jessie waved at the backseat. He had to grit his teeth to keep from screaming. None of it made sense.

Virginia went to church and believed all of the stuff the pastor talked about. Even though Jessie hadn't bought into it all, he knew the pastor wouldn't be happy if they'd had sex tonight. He was pretty sure his parents would be disappointed as well, but that wasn't what had stopped him. It was the thought that Virginia was so willing to give all of that up without any seeming hesitation, but now she was saying she wasn't even sure they should still be dating. The contradictions made his head hurt.

Jessie turned to face the steering wheel, the rocket swinging with the movement of the car. He wanted to grab it and throw it out the window. "Get back up here. I'm taking you home."

"Jessie." Virginia touched his shoulder, but he shrugged her off and started the engine. Virginia climbed back into the front seat, smoothing her dress around her as Jessie backed up and peeled out onto the street.

CHAPTER SIXTY-TWO

Lunar Module Test

January 22, 1968

Outside the classroom window, Jessie could see the bright blue sky, not a cloud in sight. His leg bounced anxiously against his desk as he glanced at the large clock above Mr. Smith's head. He stared at it unblinking, willing the seconds to tick off faster.

"Mr. Cole?"

Jessie dragged his gaze away from the clock and met Mr. Smith's eyes.

"I know you're excited for the launch this afternoon, but would you please stop beating on your desk?"

Jessie's leg stopped. "I'm sorry, Mr. Smith."

The teacher resumed his lesson and Jessie tried to pay attention, but all he could think about was the launch. He was disappointed it was another unmanned mission, but he knew there was still testing to be done on the new vehicles that were needed to make a moon landing. The unmanned missions may not be as glamorous as those with astronauts onboard, but they still fascinated him.

This mission would give NASA the chance to test remotely the ascent and descent propulsion systems of the lunar module. The idea of a man, sitting in the Mission Control Center, pushing some buttons that would transmit signals into the spacecraft miles above the earth was almost as thrilling to him as the idea of riding in the spacecraft himself.

The final bell rang and Jessie shot out of his seat, barreling past the other students. He crossed the parking lot before a single car door had been opened and reached the street in thirty seconds. He jogged down the road, past the Howard Johnson to a small clearing on the edge of the river. Dr. Weston waved from the edge of the crowd.

"I was afraid you weren't going to make it," Dr. Weston greeted Jessie with a hearty handshake.

"Me too." Jessie took a minute to catch his breath. "Where are we at, in the countdown?"

"They've been holding for a while. You know how it is."

Jessie nodded and followed Dr. Weston through the crowd, closer to the water for a better view. A nearby radio played a slow song by The Beatles that made him think about Virginia. He tried to push the thought away, unwilling to darken this day. Farther away he could hear a voice he recognized from the many launch broadcasts he'd listened to and motioned for Dr. Weston to follow him. They moved closer and listened to the reporter talk about the objectives of the mission, but there was nothing new on the unexpected hold.

"Why don't we go back to my car and sit down? It could be a while."

"Yeah, okay." Jessie's anticipation was flagging as he started to worry the flight wouldn't happen today.

When they reached the Impala, Dr. Weston hopped onto the trunk and leaned back against the window. Jessie followed suit, the warm metal and glass feeling good against his back.

"We haven't seen each other in a few months. How have you been?" Dr. Weston asked.

"All right, I guess."

"Are you still dating that pretty redhead? What was her name again?"

"Virginia." Jessie paused. "I don't know what's going on with that."

Dr. Weston rolled his head to the side. "You want to talk about it?"

Jessie didn't turn to face his friend. Instead, he followed the path of a seagull circling overhead, hoping it wasn't planning on dropping any gifts on him. "She's finishing the school year in Boston."

"Really? Why's that?"

Jessie closed his eyes, and the letter he'd received at the end of Christmas break appeared on his eyelids as vivid as the day it had arrived.

Dear Jessie,

There's so much I want to tell you and I don't even know where to start. I know I made things difficult the past year and I hope you can forgive me. I'm sorry for the way I acted before Christmas and hope you will one day understand how thankful I am for the respect you showed me.

I don't know why I never told you, but my parents have been separated for five months. I think my father had an affair, although mother won't discuss it with me. Father would be at the house when we knew company was coming, putting on a show that all was well. I think that is a large part of why mother wanted us to come to Massachusetts. Aunt Sherry is sick, I didn't mean to imply she isn't, but not as bad as I had thought. Mother and I are going to stay here for a while. We've made arrangements to have my school records transferred so I can finish out the year here.

I don't expect you to wait for me. You have grand dreams and I never wanted to hold you back. Follow your heart to the moon and know I will be cheering you on.

Much Love,
Virginia

Jessie opened his eyes and gave a sideways look at his friend. "I think she dumped me."

"I'm sorry to hear that."

"I don't know what I did wrong."

"You're young and these things happen. Not everyone marries their high school sweetheart."

"How did you and your wife meet?"

Dr. Weston chuckled. "She was my high school sweetheart."

"Oh great." Jessie felt his heart sink even further. He looked across the river, hoping to see rising smoke and fire, but only saw a dozen boats spread out across the river.

"We didn't get married until after college, though. We actually broke up the summer after high school. We went to different colleges, and didn't meet again until the summer before I started my internship. There's not much free time during a medical internship, but she and I would go out every couple of weeks. When I started my residency, we decided to get married. I figured if she could put up with the crazy hours I was working, then she must be the girl for me." Dr. Weston paused and adjusted his sunglasses. "Plus, I never really got over her."

"Virginia and I had a fight before she left for Christmas break, and there were a few other arguments over the past year. I really didn't know where I stood with her, but when she chose to stay in Boston," Jessie shrugged. "I guess that says it all."

"Have you decided which school you're going to?"

Jessie was grateful for the change in subject. "Did I tell you I was offered scholarships to Purdue and Embry-Riddle Aeronautical Institute?"

"That's wonderful," Dr. Weston exclaimed, rising to a sitting position.

Jessie sat up also and tried to meet his friend's eyes through his dark sunglasses. "I know Purdue is a good school, especially for engineering, but I don't know if I could stand being that far away from the action. Think how many launches I would miss. Embry-Riddle is up in Daytona; I could even see the launches from there if I couldn't get away. And, it has both Navy and Air Force ROTC programs I could choose from."

"I've heard good things about Embry-Riddle. Either school would be a great choice."

"I have to make my decision in the next couple of weeks."

"Whichever one you choose, I'm proud of you, and I'm sure your folks are too."

"Thanks, Doc. What's been going on with you?"

"Not too much. The wife and I did take a trip back to Kentucky for Christmas. You wouldn't believe how popular I was when the town found out I'm living here now. Everyone wanted to know how many astronauts I had met and if any of them were my patients. I was afraid to tell them that I am on the team that is on call for the manned launches, in the event of an emergency."

"Well, you haven't been on the team long." Jessie winked at his friend. Dr. Weston had jumped at the chance of replacing an on-call surgeon who was moving out of state. The medical team was at the ready in the event of an abort on the launch pad, or shortly after takeoff, to attend to the astronauts. Fortunately, the team hadn't been needed yet.

"By the way, I finally got permission to bring you out for the next manned launch."

"No way!" Jessie jumped off the trunk of the car and pulled the doctor into a bear hug.

The doctor laughed. "I don't know when exactly it will be yet."

"That's okay. Just knowing it's a possibility is enough."

"Sure, you say that now, but if this launch doesn't go, it could be months, maybe even a year before they have another manned mission."

"Nah. I believe they're getting the hang of this. Plus, we gotta get to the moon soon if we're going to meet President Kennedy's challenge."

As the hold grew longer, many of the local spectators gave up and went home, but the out-of-towners opened up their ice chests and fired up their grills. The smell of hamburgers, hot dogs, and grilled onions filled the air, making Jessie's stomach rumble. The waterfront took on the atmosphere of a Fourth of July picnic, with children throwing Frisbees or footballs, while the adults tended the grills or mingled over the cans of beer and bottles of soda.

"The countdown has started again!" someone yelled. There was still an hour to go, but the crowd kept one eye on the river and the other on their dinners. Soon the grills were closed, a haze of smoke lingering on the still air, while seagulls circled, searching for abandoned tidbits. Jessie faced the looming Vertical Assembly Building, trying to discern which launch site the rocket sat on.

As the sun sank behind them in a brilliant orange ball, a similar orange glow lit the eastern horizon as *Apollo 5* lifted off, leaving behind a massive plume of billowy white smoke. The crowd cheered and toasted with their metal cans and glass bottles. Jessie felt Dr. Weston's hand on his shoulder, but didn't take his eyes off the rising rocket. If all went well, they would be one step closer to landing on the moon.

CHAPTER SIXTY-THREE

Return from Embry-Riddle

December 20, 1968

The first semester of college was winding down and Jessie was excited to be going home for Christmas. He stuffed some clothes into his duffel bag, slung it over his shoulder, and ran downstairs to meet his ride. He'd met Mark his first week at Embry-Riddle. Mark was a junior, but he didn't look down on the freshman the way some of the other guys did. When Jessie found out Mark loved the space program and was hoping to become an astronaut as well, he knew he'd found his new best friend. The boys spent most of their free time together and Mark shared the things he'd learned, advised Jessie on the best teachers, and helped him choose his classes for the next semester.

With sandy brown hair, blue eyes, and a tan, athletic body, Mark was a favorite of the local girls. When Jessie and Mark went out on the weekends, the girls seemed drawn to him. Jessie didn't mind that he didn't have the same all-American hero look. Between studying and ROTC drills, he didn't have time for girls.

Mark leaned against the hood of a blue Thunderbird, wearing loose jeans, a black long sleeve t-shirt, and sunglasses. He waved to Jessie, rolled off the car, and opened the small trunk. Jessie tossed his bag inside.

"Thanks for the ride."

"No problem, I go right by Titusville on my way home."

"Are you going to be around for the launch tomorrow? Maybe we could get together."

"It's going to be an early one. I may only be able to make it out to Fort Pierce beach." Mark started up the car and pulled away from the curb, waving at a group of guys as they passed.

"If you don't mind sleeping on the couch, I'm sure you'd be welcome to spend the night with us."

"You think it would be okay with your folks?" Mark glanced at Jessie.

"I don't see why not. Mama is always telling us to be kind to those less fortunate, and I'd say having to watch the launch from a hundred miles away makes you less fortunate."

Mark slowed the car at a stoplight, laughing so loud the pedestrians on the sidewalk turned to stare. "I love the way you think, Cole."

"You come inside when we get to my house and I assure you Mama won't be able to say no."

An hour later, Jessie directed Mark through the streets of his hometown. Mark parked on the side of the road in front of the small house and for a moment Jessie had second thoughts about inviting his friend inside. Jessie tended to forget Mark's family was rich. His car was the only outward sign of his status.

Mark interrupted Jessie's thoughts. "I wish the folks where I live would get together and decorate like this."

Jessie looked around and realized all of the houses were decked out for Christmas. With the approaching dusk, lights were already lit, some of the places with nativity scenes on the lawn. He returned his attention to his own house and saw a rocket, three feet tall, and wrapped in Christmas lights, on the edge of the porch.

"We have some great neighbors," Jessie agreed.

The boys stepped out of the car and walked up the driveway.

"Neat rocket. Did you build it?" Mark asked.

"No, I've never seen it before." Jessie opened the front door. "I'm home," he called.

The kitchen and living room were empty, but Jessie could smell lasagna in the oven. Eleanor came down the hall, clipping a pair of earrings on.

"Welcome home, sweetheart." She opened her arms and Jessie stepped forward and gave her a hug.

"This is my friend, Mark." Jessie stepped back and introduced his companion.

"Nice to meet you, Mark. You'll stay for dinner won't you?"

"Actually, would it be okay if he spent the night?" Jessie gave his best sad puppy face. "He wants to see the launch tomorrow and he lives all the way down in Fort Pierce."

"If you're sure your folks won't be disappointed at not seeing you tonight." Eleanor smiled. "Why don't you give them a call?"

"Thank you, ma'am. I'm sure it will be fine, they aren't expecting me until tomorrow anyway, but I'll give them a call, let them know where I am."

Eleanor showed him the phone before hooking Jessie's arm and walking with him into the hall. "Is that the boy you mentioned at the beginning of the year?"

"Yeah, he's a good guy. He's really helped me get settled in and he wants to be an astronaut too."

"I'm glad we can do something for him then." Eleanor gave Jessie's arm a squeeze and kissed him on the cheek. "Your brothers should be home soon."

"Sam will be home tonight?"

"Apparently he only had one class today and finished at noon. He caught a ride with some friends coming out to see the launch. They should be here in an hour or so."

"Where's Max?"

"He had to run out to the bank. He'll be home for dinner."

Jessie could hear Mark wrapping up his phone call. "Where did the rocket out front come from?"

Light danced in Eleanor's eyes. "You'll have to wait till everyone is home to find out."

"Come on," Jessie begged. "I know it wasn't Sam, and Ricky doesn't give the space program a second thought anymore."

"Your folks are okay with you staying?" Eleanor asked as Mark hung up the phone.

"Yes ma'am. They are going out to a party tonight anyway."

Jessie thought Mark sounded upset, but before he could say anything, the front door opened. Eugene entered, breathing heavily and dragging a Christmas tree.

"Gene, let the boys help you with that," Eleanor scolded, rushing across the room to her husband's side. Jessie followed and relieved his father of the heavy tree.

"Did you get the biggest one on the lot?" Jessie called over his shoulder, noticing the tree holder waiting in the corner of the living room.

Mark picked up the trunk and the two managed to set it in place, Mark tightening the screws around its trunk while Jessie tried to hold it straight. Fragrant pine needles showered the floor, drawing a weary sigh from Eleanor.

"I thought we'd discussed this, Gene, and we weren't going to get a real tree this year." Eleanor opened the pantry, grabbed the broom, and started sweeping up the mess.

"It's not every Christmas we send men to orbit the moon, Nora." Eugene's voice was filled with a boyish excitement that Jessie didn't recognize in his father. "Hi, I'm Eugene Cole." He held his hand out to Mark.

"Mark Schmidt. I go to school with Jessie." Mark took the offered hand.

"Good to meet you. Any friend of Jessie's is welcome here. Are you staying for dinner? Nora makes a delicious lasagna."

"He's going to spend the night and watch the launch with me in the morning," Jessie interrupted.

"Wonderful. Have you seen a launch before?"

"Yes, sir. Mostly from down south, but I've been fortunate enough to make it out to Cocoa Beach for a few launches. Jessie tells me seeing it from right here across the river is almost as good as being out at the VIP viewing area."

"I can't compare the two myself, but I guess, with all the traffic we get here, it must be a good spot."

"Gene, sit down," Eleanor coaxed, stepping forward with a glass of water.

Eugene took the water, taking a long drink. "I'm fine, Nora, stop fussing over me."

Jessie studied his parents and noticed the anxious look his mother wore. *What has happened that has her so worried? I should have been better about writing or coming home. I don't know what's been going on the past four months.*

"You mind if I show Mark around town before dinner?" Jessie hoped he could remove his friend from the awkward tension in the house.

"Sure, just be back in an hour." Eleanor took the glass from Eugene and refilled it.

Jessie motioned for Mark to follow him outside.

"Is everything okay with your dad?" Mark asked when the door was closed.

"I have no idea. I'll find out what's been going on when Max gets home."

"He's the brother who got injured in the war, right?"

Jessie nodded. "You mind if I drive?"

Mark tossed the keys across the car. "Any chance we'll run into an astronaut here?"

"I doubt it. They usually hang out in Cocoa Beach. Maybe we can cruise down there after dinner."

"Yeah? That would be cool." Mark rolled down his window and stuck his head out. The rising moon cast a silver glow on the glassy river, the VAB and launch pad black silhouettes on the opposite bank.

Hundreds of cars were already parked along the side of the road, in anticipation of the launch. Jessie found an open spot and stopped the car.

"I can't believe how many people are already here," Mark marveled.

"Yeah, they sleep in their cars so they can have a good view. Of course, I always get out here while they are still sleeping and stake my claim." Jessie winked. "You're gonna have to get up mighty early tomorrow."

"It'll be worth it."

The boys walked to the edge of the water, standing in silence for several minutes. Jessie thought about how many times he'd stood on this shoreline watching rocket launches, the goal of the moon a seesaw of successes and failures. Tomorrow, if all went well, they would be closer than ever before. They just might make Kennedy's goal before the end of the decade.

"We should probably get back." Mark broke the silence, turning from the view that represented the future for both boys.

Jessie reluctantly turned back to the car. "Sorry about the stuff between my parents."

"Forget it. That was nothing compared to my house."

Jessie heard the same disappointment in Mark's words as he'd heard after the call to his parents. What did rich people have to argue about? Virginia's parents had never seemed very happy and now Mark's family apparently had issues too. Since Eugene had gotten sober and kept a steady job, Jessie couldn't remember a single argument between his parents, even though he knew there were concerns about paying the bills.

The table was already set when Jessie entered the front door. Ricky bounded off the couch to greet his brother and eagerly welcomed Mark.

"What kind of planes have you gotten to fly?" Ricky asked when he heard Mark was studying for his pilot's license as well as a degree in mechanical engineering.

"Cessnas mostly, one Piper Cub. I only have a couple hundred flight hours."

"What about you, Jessie, are you learning to fly?"

Jessie laughed. "Not yet. I still have a lot to learn on the ground first."

"Hey, Jess." Max and Sam entered the living room. Jessie introduced Mark and they all took seats around the table. Eugene said a prayer and the boys dug into the pan of lasagna.

"This is wonderful, Mrs. Cole," Mark complimented.

"Thank you, Mark." Eleanor offered an appreciative smile.

"Nora is a great cook." Eugene patted his belly, which appeared larger than Jessie remembered.

"I didn't realize how much I missed home cooking," Jessie mumbled around a mouthful of food.

"It's good to have all my boys home." Eleanor looked around the table, smiling at each of them.

Conversation turned to the events of the past few months, Sam and Jessie telling them all about their studies, Ricky filling them in on the new construction going on throughout the county. After the dishes were cleaned up, Mark went out to the car to grab his bag and Jessie pulled Max into his bedroom.

"What's going on with Pop?" Jessie asked.

"What do you mean?"

"Mama was worried about him when he brought the tree in earlier."

Max nodded. "She's been fussing over him a lot lately. They haven't said anything about why, but I did overhear them talking one night. There's some concern about his heart. I guess he's been having some pain and went to the doctor last month."

"Are they doing anything for it?"

"I think they gave him some pills. Mom gets upset whenever he exerts himself too much. She's had Ricky mowing the yard and taking care of some of the other things around the house."

"He doesn't seem too worried about it."

Max shrugged. "He's never been one to worry about his health."

"True."

"Your friend seems nice."

"He is. I'm not sure I would have made it through the semester without him. My classes were tough and ROTC is much stricter than in high school. He really helped me balance things." Jessie stood up and straightened the bedspread. "Hey, where did the rocket out front come from?"

Max chuckled. I was wondering if you'd noticed. "You'll have to ask Pop about that."

"Why won't anyone answer me about this?"

"Answer you about what?" Eugene popped his head in the bedroom. "We're going to watch *A Charlie Brown Christmas,* you going to join us?"

"Where did the rocket on the porch come from?"

"Do you like it?"

Jessie nodded.

"Good. Come on, shows starts in a couple of minutes." Eugene headed back down the hall.

"Pop got it?" Jessie asked.

"He built it," Max patted Jessie on the shoulder, "for you. Let's go watch TV."

CHAPTER SIXTY-FOUR

Apollo 8 Launch

December 21, 1968

"Wake up, it's time to go." Jessie leaned close to Mark's head and shook his friend.

"What?" Mark rubbed his face.

"The launch is in two hours," Jessie whispered.

Mark's eyes shot open and he kicked off the blanket. "Give me five minutes to brush my teeth."

"I'll give you ten if you brush your hair too," Jessie teased.

Mark rummaged in his bag for his toothbrush and a comb before darting to the bathroom. Jessie filled a thermos with coffee, thankful his mother had at last been able to get an electric coffee pot from the department store where she worked. By the time Mark returned, Jessie had packed a bag with his traditional early morning launch snacks; peanuts, oranges, and a chocolate bar for each of them. For a moment he was transported back to the tree house on the island, Max and Sam removing the same snacks from their pockets as they waited for Alan Shepard's historic trip to space, seven and a half years ago.

"Ready?" Mark reached for the jacket he'd left hanging on the back of a dining room chair.

"Yeah." Jessie picked up a thermos, grabbed his bag, and opened the door. "You want to drive?"

"We're going to walk. It's less than a mile and the car will be a hindrance." Jessie pointed to the beach chairs leaning against the side of the house. "Grab those."

Mark picked them up and the pair set off through the breaking dawn light.

"You weren't kidding." Mark's mouth gaped in awe when they reached US 1. The field before them was filled with cars, traffic already pouring in from Orlando and other inland cities.

"I told you it gets crazy." Jessie weaved through the slow moving vehicles, ignoring the horns and occasional shouts from frustrated drivers.

Some of the spectators who'd spent the night in their vehicles were starting to emerge, stretching and groaning in discomfort. Jessie made his way to the farthest point on the shore and motioned for Mark to set up the chairs. Mark looked around at how the area had changed overnight as he placed them down.

"You want some coffee?" Jessie uncapped the thermos and filled a cup. "I put some sugar in in."

"Thanks." Mark took the cup and sipped at it. "I've heard the news reports about all the people that come out for the launches, but seeing it like this really puts it in perspective."

"Wasn't there a crowd at the launches you saw from Cocoa Beach?"

"Probably, but we stayed in a hotel on the ocean and watched from the balcony. My parents would think it beneath them to be part of a crowd like this." Mark gave a mischievous grin. "They'd flip if they saw me here now." His grin widened. "I wish I had a camera."

"There are plenty here." Jessie looked around for an early bird hoping to catch a photo of the sun rising behind the launch site. "Over there," Jessie pointed at a man a dozen feet away, in a floppy hat, his sweatshirt stretched tight across his drum-like stomach.

Mark went over in a flash, pulled a bill from his pocket and offered it to the man who nodded and followed Mark back to the chairs.

"Get together and say cheese," the man instructed, lifting the Polaroid camera.

"No, this direction." Mark pointed toward the growing chaos behind them.

"You don't want the Cape in the background?" The man frowned.

Mark shook his head, giddy with delight. Jessie threw an arm over his friend's shoulder and stepped back so the photographer could get in front of them.

"Take a couple more steps back," the photographer instructed. "Good, now smile."

The flash exploded, leaving Jessie with floating lights before his eyes for several seconds. The camera spit out a four by four square, which the photographer handed to Mark. "You sure that's the picture you want?"

"Definitely." Mark gingerly pulled back the film to reveal the image of the boys in front of all the cars. "I can't wait to show this to my family. Thank you," Mark shook the man's hand.

Jessie smiled at Mark. "You are probably the only person out here who thinks the crowd is just as cool as the launch," and returned to his chair where he clicked on his radio. "You want something to eat?"

Jessie handed Mark an orange before pulling out his pocketknife, to score the skin of his own.

"I can't believe how calm you are," Mark commented between bites.

"This is the easy part, no real danger yet, still plenty of time for the mission to be scrubbed. Once we get within thirty minutes, that's when I can barely sit still."

"Why didn't your brothers come?"

"Max is the only one who is still interested in the program, but with his vision so limited now," Jessie shrugged, "it's hard on him."

"Sam seems like a smart guy, I can't believe he isn't interested."

"Sam is more interested in history that's already happened, than history in the making."

"T-minus thirty-nine and we are go for our countdown for the *Apollo 8* mission to the moon at this time." Jessie recognized Jack King's voice from the radio. He pulled a bandana from his pocket, wiped his hands and face clean from the sticky orange juice and tossed the skin into the bushes.

"Here we go." Jessie rocked back and forth in his chair, feet tapping the ground in anticipation.

The boys listened to the newscast as it commented on the backgrounds of the men chosen for this mission, the experience they represented and the families who would celebrate Christmas without them this year.

"I'm glad the weather seems to be holding out," Jessie said.

"Me too, I was worried it would be scrubbed when they were talking about fog last night."

"I'm sure my folks wouldn't have minded you staying another day."

"Is there any coffee left?"

Jessie refilled Mark's cup and handed it to him. "You want to drive down to Cocoa Beach when the traffic clears out? Neil Armstrong and Buzz Aldrin are in town, maybe we can spot them."

Mark looked up from his cup. "Sure, I don't have to get home at any special time."

Jessie's ears perked up at the change in voices on the radio. Jack King was back on, announcing T-minus five minutes. Jessie jumped from his chair and raised a hand to shade his eyes. "Are you ready for this?"

Mark stood as well. "More than you can imagine."

Even after seeing more than forty rocket launches, Jessie's stomach still clenched, his heart still raced as the countdown ticked on. He crossed his fingers behind his back, the same way he had for all but one of the launches, and waited until he saw the fire rising in the sky, announcing lift-off.

"Oh wow," Mark exclaimed as the rumble reached them. "Wow, wow, wow."

"Awesome, isn't it?" Jessie grinned so big his cheeks hurt. "One day that's going to be you and me going up there."

"That day can't come soon enough."

CHAPTER SIXTY-FIVE

The Book

December 21, 1968

Jessie waved as Mark pulled away. They hadn't spotted Armstrong or Aldrin, but they'd had a good lunch and spent a couple of hours on the beach. Jessie was sorry to see his friend go, worried about the depression that had come over him as time for his departure had neared.

"Did you have a good time?" Eleanor looked up from a magazine when Jessie entered.

"We did." Jessie wandered into his bedroom and found a package waiting on his bed.

"What's this, Mama?" he asked, carrying the package into the living room.

"I don't know, it came in the mail this afternoon. I didn't recognize the return address."

Jessie looked at the handwriting on the brown paper for the first time and felt his heart stop. He would have recognized that script even without the Massachusetts return address.

"Is everything okay?"

"Yeah," Jessie replied without looking up from the box. "Do I have time to run an errand before dinner?"

"As long as you are back by six."

Jessie grabbed the key to Max's buggy and stepped outside into the golden light of sunset. He set the package in his lap, keeping one hand on it all the way out to the fishing pier. The pier was unusually empty, the only sounds were the ticking of the hot engine and water slapping against the pylons in the wake of a passing boat. He pulled at the corners of the paper, slipping his fingernail underneath the tape, removing the wrapping without a single tear. He removed the box lid to find a book. *Gemini! A Personal Account of Man's Venture into Space* the title exclaimed above the photo of an astronaut in a space capsule, the author's name above the title, Virgil "Gus" Grissom.

Jessie's hands trembled as he opened the front cover and found a piece of stationary with purple lilacs printed on the top and bottom.

> *I saw this and thought of you. I hope you don't already have it. It's been a long time since we last talked or exchanged letters. My parents' divorce was final a couple of months ago. Mother went back to Florida to pack up our things and ran into your mom. She said you were doing well.*
>
> *Merry Christmas,*
> *Virginia*

Jessie read the note several times before folding it up and flipping the pages of the book, pausing to look at the photos. He reached the end and read the epilogue, written by the book's editor, telling how Grissom had finished the rough draft just weeks before his death and that the finished product had been completed with the help of his wife. Jessie didn't know which hurt more, the memory of losing his hero or the ache in his heart Virginia's note revived.

At home he went straight to his room, ignoring his mother's questions, slamming the door behind him. He took the note from Virginia out of the book and tossed it in the garbage can at the end of his bed. He paced back and forth, the book clenched in his hands.

"What's wrong?" Max's head appeared around the edge of the door.

Jessie stopped pacing, held up the book, then plopped onto his bed.

"Um, you know I can't read that far away, right?"

"Virginia." Jessie blew out an exasperated sigh.

"Oh." Max stepped inside and stood at Jessie's bed. "What happened?"

"She sent me a book. Gus's book."

"That was nice. Why are you so mad?"

"We haven't spoken in seven months. I haven't seen her in a year. Why did she send this now? What does she want from me?"

"Maybe she doesn't want anything. Maybe she was just trying to be nice. She knew he was your hero, didn't she?"

"Of course she did."

"And she knows how hard you have had to work for every penny you've ever had, right?"

"Yeah."

"Why is it so awful that she sent you the book then?"

"She's never coming back. Her parents are divorced and her mom is living in Boston. I suppose she is too since the package came from there."

"Did you think she was coming back?"

"I don't know." Jessie rubbed his eyes and pinched the bridge of his nose. "Maybe I did. Doesn't really matter. I'm too busy to worry about her now."

"Again, what's the problem?"

Jessie gave a half-hearted laugh and sat up. "You think you got life all figured out, don't you?"

"Nah." Max shook his head. "I know better than anyone how life throws you a curve ball and you gotta adjust. That's all this is, a curve ball. She's not coming back, you don't have time for her, let it go. Focus on the future. There's too much to live for to allow yourself to get stuck in the past."

Jessie looked at his brother, surprised at how Max could still convey deeper meaning with just the good half of his face. He knew Max was telling him to let go of their childhood, of his resentment toward Eugene, just as much as he was telling him to let go of Virginia.

"How many times do I have to tell you, the stuff with Pop is over? I've moved on."

"Have you told *him*?"

"He knows. It was an unspoken thing."

"Are you sure he knows?"

Something about the way Max said it made Jessie's spine tingle.

CHAPTER SIXTY-SIX

First Lunar Orbit

....

December 24, 1968

The television was on from early in the morning until late at night for the next three days. Jessie never strayed far, anxious for the next update from CBS news on the progress of the *Apollo* crew. Early Christmas Eve morning he curled up on the floor in front of the set, with the volume low, his cassette recorder positioned next to the television speaker. Walter Cronkite let the nation know the spacecraft was approaching the far side of the moon, then played a recording of Jim Lovell describing the moon as they saw it when they reached lunar orbit, just before five that morning.

Jessie watched in awe as Dr. Eugene Shoemaker, a geologist and astronomer, pointed out, on a map of the moon, the locations Lovell was describing. Cronkite went on to explain the difference between the time it takes the spacecraft to orbit the earth, about an hour and a half, versus orbiting the moon, about two hours. Jessie said a silent thank you to Mr. Smith for giving him the solid base in physics that made it so easy to understand the news anchor's explanation.

"Turn it up some." Eugene's sleepy voice startled Jessie, causing him to hit his head on the edge of the television console. "Are you okay?"

Jessie clutched his head, biting his tongue against the sharp pain. He didn't feel any blood against his fingers and slowly nodded. He could hear his father's bare feet scrabbling into the kitchen. A second later he heard the freezer open and ice cubes being scooped out of the tray, then Eugene returned with a bag of ice wrapped in a dish towel.

"Here, put this on."

Jessie took the bag of ice and held it against the throbbing knot rising on his scalp.

"I didn't mean to startle you." Eugene sat on the edge of the couch, looking down at Jessie.

"It's okay. I couldn't sleep and didn't expect anyone to be up this early."

"I was having trouble sleeping myself. When I heard footsteps, I figured it must be you. What's the update?"

"They made it to the moon a couple hours ago and they are approaching the far side where there will be loss of radio contact for thirty-five to forty minutes."

Jessie turned back to the television where an animated simulation of the spacecraft's orbit around the moon was being played out.

"I never thought I'd see this day," Eugene leaned forward and patted Jessie's back, "but you didn't have any doubts, did you?"

Jessie remained focus on the television, listening to Walter Cronkite describing the breakfast the astronauts were having. He chuckled to himself when he heard they were having bite-sized cinnamon toast cubes, so there wouldn't be crumbs floating around the capsule. He remembered the story of John Young handing Grissom a corned-beef sandwich during their *Gemini 3* mission, the bread crumbling when he took a bite. I guess it's a good thing Young pulled that prank, Jessie thought. They even used what they learned from that to make space travel better.

"Speaking of breakfast, would you like some eggs?" Eugene pushed himself off the couch.

Mission Control broke in to announce loss of signal was expected within the next five minutes. Jessie looked over his shoulder at Eugene. "Sure, four scrambled would be good."

An exchange between Mission Control and the spacecraft was broadcast, confirming last minute details before the loss of signal. Jessie sat up, his long legs crossed Indian style, knees bouncing as he watched the inching progress of the simulation.

"Yes," Jessie whispered when Cronkite talked about how perfect the launch had been, needing only minor course corrections over the past two days to get the *Apollo* crew into lunar orbit.

"Why are you up so early?" Eleanor's slippers scratched across the floor as she entered the living room.

Jessie didn't take his eyes off the television. "They're about to go behind the moon."

"Want some eggs, Nora?" Eugene pulled the egg carton from the refrigerator and set it on the counter. Jessie could hear him fumbling in the cabinet for a skillet and adjusted the volume of the television.

With loss of signal, Mission Control announced they were going to play back the recording of the first words from the astronauts when they reached lunar orbit. Jessie clasped his hands together, grateful for the replay of the moment he'd slept through.

There was a report from the spacecraft of their position and acknowledgement from Mission Control. Mission Control was then going to play the recording of Jim Lovell's description of the moon, but Cronkite broke in, advising they had already shared that and that there would be a commercial break. Jessie let out a frustrated groan.

"Your eggs are ready." Eleanor set a plate on the table.

"Why don't you let him eat in the living room?" Eugene suggested.

Jessie glanced over his shoulder, surprised by the offer. His parents believed civilized people didn't eat anywhere except the dining room table. His parents exchanged a long look, then Eleanor nodded and carried the plate and fork to Jessie.

Jessie hesitated before reaching up to accept them. "Thanks."

He ate his eggs, losing interest in the broadcast as they went to a previously recorded interview with an astronomer and physicist in England. He sopped up the last bit of egg with a piece of bread and stood to return his plate to the kitchen.

Eugene and Eleanor sat at the table, sipping coffee. Jessie collected their empty plates as well and turned on the hot water, pouring a generous amount of dish soap into the sink.

"Don't worry about that, I'll clean up." Eugene pushed back his chair and started to stand.

"It's going to be awhile before they regain radio contact. I need to do something to help the time pass."

Eugene sat back down. "In that case, would you mind pouring us some more coffee?"

Jessie wiped his hands on his pants and turned to gather their cups. "You know it takes two full hours to orbit the moon?"

"I didn't. That's interesting." Eugene accepted the refilled cup and set it on the table.

"The families of those men must be going out of their minds right now." Eleanor spooned some sugar into her cup and stirred it in slowly.

"They are smart guys and they have the best spacecraft out there. They're going to be fine." Jessie returned to washing the dishes, one ear tuned to the news.

"Still, things can go wrong. Are you sure you want to be an astronaut?"

Jessie set the last plate in the drainer and let the water out of the sink. His mother's words cut deep, reminding him of Virginia's comment about astronaut wives hoping their husbands aren't blown up. Was that all women thought about, the dangers rather than the excitement? Didn't they understand the laws of physics the engineers who designed the rockets and spacecraft had overcome to get this far?

Jessie rested his hand on the edge of the sink, took a deep breath, and turned to face his mother. "I've never wanted anything more in my life, you know that."

He saw the anguish in his mother's eyes, much like the look he'd seen when Max received his orders to report to Fort Benning.

Eugene reached across the table and touched her hand. "You have to support him on this, Nora. He got himself into college, all expenses paid, and he's following the path he set out on as a little boy. His dream isn't any less valuable than Sam's."

"But Sam isn't planning on playing with explosives or leaving the planet God put us on."

Eugene glanced at Jessie then back to Eleanor. "There is danger everywhere. Any of the boys could be hurt or killed right here in town. Jessie has never lived in fear and I'd hate to see him start to now, just to give you some peace of mind."

Jessie stood in silence, struggling to accept his father standing on his side of this debate.

Eugene stood and slipped an arm over Jessie's shoulder. "You better get back to the news, sounds like they are coming out of the darkness."

Eugene's touch brought back a flash of memory. The night of the *Apollo 1* fire, the admiration in his father's eyes, the hug, the whispered words, "You are going to make a fine astronaut, son." Had Eugene been on his side since that night? Jessie's gaze flicked across the room to the television.

"It looks like Cronkite is back on." Jessie returned to his worn spot on the linoleum and sank to his knees.

Jessie spent most of the day in front of the television, following the progress of the lunar orbits, capturing every communication between the flight crew and Mission Control on his cassettes. For the first time he was grateful for not having a girlfriend, which had freed up his finances so he could afford the recorder and tapes.

"We are going to the five o'clock Christmas service at church, do you want to stay here?" Eleanor asked.

Jessie turned from the television. "I can go with you. They have a few more orbits before they perform Trans-Earth Injection."

Eleanor gave him a blank look and Jessie smiled. "Before they conduct the maneuvers that will put them on their path back home."

"Oh, okay. Be ready to leave in thirty minutes."

With a last look at the television, Jessie rose. He picked out a clean red shirt and black pants, got a shower, and spent ten minutes trying to style his hair. When he emerged, he found Ricky waiting at the door.

"You haven't taken a shower in two days and you decide to take your sweet time now?" Ricky pushed past him and slammed the door.

"What's his problem?" Jessie asked, wandering into Max and Sam's bedroom.

"Who knows, he's always been the moody one," Max replied.

Jessie laughed. "Ricky the moody one, not you?"

"I was never moody," Max protested before joining in the laughter. "Things certainly have changed."

"Yeah," Jessie agreed. "I'm starting to think they have."

"You going to church with us?"

"I am. I think maybe I'll say a prayer for the astronauts to have a safe return. Do you think God will hear me?"

"Do you believe in Him now?" Max shifted on the bed.

"Maybe. After seeing the pictures the astronauts have sent back from space, I'm starting to think there might be a higher power."

"I guess that's a start." Max sighed.

CHAPTER SIXTY-SEVEN

In the Beginning

December 24, 1968

T he church was decorated with green garlands and red velvet bows, and a manger sat at the front of the sanctuary, filled with straw and a baby doll wrapped in a white blanket. The Cole family filed into their usual pew and took their seats only minutes before the choir entered. Jessie joined in the singing of Christmas hymns, "Joy to the World", "O Come All Ye Faithful", and "Away in a Manger". During the singing his eyes roved the pews around them until he realized he was searching for Virginia, then he dropped his gaze to the floor, only looking up when the pastor stepped to the podium.

The pastor read the Christmas story from the book of Luke. When he came to the end of the chapter, Jessie sat up straighter.

"How do you suppose Mary might have been feeling during the months of her pregnancy, when people probably looked down on her for being pregnant before she was married? I'm sure there were some who said very hurtful things to her, but when her son was born, the shepherds came to her from great distances, telling her about a choir of angels appearing to them to announce the child's birth. These words must have been a salve to her heart, maybe even a reminder that God knew she was honorable, and that was what was truly important."

Why these words resonated so deeply in Jessie's heart he didn't understand. Did it matter to him if God found him honorable? Had he done anything in his life not to be found honorable? He worked hard; he treated most people he encountered well. What did God consider honorable?

A stabbing pain in his shin pulled Jessie from his thoughts. He looked up to see Ricky standing, trying to get past him in the pew. The service was over and worshipers were talking in the aisles or flowing out the door.

"Sorry." Jessie stood and moved down the empty pew. Turning to the door, he caught sight of Virginia's Aunt Mary. He looked away and hurried out the door before she saw him.

A nearly life-size nativity scene was set up on the church lawn. Jessie wandered over to it, studying the craftsmanship of the woodcarving and the delicate details of the hand-painted figures, then his gaze traveled up to the black sky. There was too much light around the church to allow him to see the stars, but he could see the moon, waning from the new moon it had been five nights before. He wondered where the *Apollo* spacecraft was and if he'd be able to make it out as it passed the lighted half of the moon.

"Come on, Jessie," Eleanor called.

In the backseat he rested his head against the cool glass of the window and closed his eyes. He knew when they got home they would each get to choose one gift to open, saving the rest for Christmas morning.

Ricky chattered about which one he thought he wanted to open. "The big box surely is tempting, but last year Max faked me out by putting a small compass in a giant box."

"You've gotten a lot of use out of that compass, though, haven't you?" Max chortled as he made his way from the car to the house.

"I'm going to make some hot chocolate. Why don't you boys go get changed then we can open your gifts." Eleanor retrieved a carton of milk and filled a saucepan halfway.

The boys changed and gathered around the table. Eugene uncovered a coconut cake and cut them each slices. "This may be your best cake yet, Nora."

"Yeah, really good, Mom," Max agreed.

"Who wants to open the first present?" Eleanor asked.

"Me, me." Ricky jumped up from his chair.

"Why don't we let someone else go first this year? How about you, Sam?" Eleanor placed a medium-size box on the table in front of him, which he picked up, shook several times, then ripped into its wrapping paper.

He removed the lid to reveal a large book. His eyes lit up as he pulled it out and thumbed through the pages. "This is great. I've been wanting to read this. Thanks."

"Boring," Ricky derided.

"Jessie, how about you next?" Eugene reached under the tree to retrieve a square box.

Surprised by its weight, Jessie ripped the paper free and lifted the lid of the box to find a pair of binoculars. He reached in and gingerly pulled them free of their tissue paper padding. He looked up to find everyone waiting for him to say something.

"These are awesome, but how did you afford them?"

"We all chipped in." Eleanor smiled. "We wanted you to have the best view of the moon launch possible."

"Thank you," Jessie whispered.

Max and Ricky opened their gifts and once again Ricky was hoodwinked by the size of his own gift, receiving only a lump of coal in a box big enough for a pistol.

"It's just not right," Ricky shook his head. Jessie looked at Max, knowing this would be an ongoing tradition for years to come.

"Why don't we all watch the broadcast from the *Apollo* crew together?" Eugene suggested.

They settled into their customary seats while Jessie turned on the television. An image of the moon through the spacecraft window appeared on the screen, the voice of Major William Anders narrating what was being shown; the dark crater Picard, the Sea of Fertility, cracks and craters, the Sea of Tranquility. The image was small, a whitish-grey blob that reminded Jessie of a paper airplane, surrounded by the darkness of the spacecraft.

With the approach of lunar sunrise, William Anders announced that the crew had a message for all the people back on earth. Jessie could feel the attention of his family intensify. Major Anders started reading from the first chapter of Genesis. Even Jessie recognized the words.

"In the beginning God created the heaven and the earth. And the earth was without form, and void; and darkness was upon the face of the deep. And the Spirit of God moved upon the face of the waters. And God said let there be light and there was light. And God saw the light, that it was good: and God divided the light from the darkness."

There was a pause before Jim Lovell took over the reading. "And God called the light Day, and the darkness He called Night. And the evening and the morning were the first day. And God said, Let there be a firmament in the midst of the waters, and let it divide the waters from the waters. And God made firmament, and divided the waters, which were under the firmament from the waters which were above the firmament: and it was so. And God called the firmament Heaven. And the evening and the morning were the second day."

Commander Frank Borman continued. "And God said, Let the waters under the heavens be gathered together unto one place, and let the dry land appear: and it was so. And God called the dry land Earth; and the gathering together of the waters He called Seas: and God saw that it was good. And from the crew of *Apollo 8*, we close with good night, good luck, a Merry Christmas, and God bless all of you - all of you on the good Earth."

The transmission from the spacecraft ended and Walter Cronkite's image filled the screen. Jessie felt tears on his cheeks, but didn't wipe them away.

"That was beautiful." Eugene's gravelly voice betrayed his emotion more than the quiet sniffs of Eleanor. Jessie looked over his shoulder at his family, even Sam and Ricky appeared moved.

Jessie pushed himself off the floor. "Merry Christmas," he whispered before grabbing his binoculars and ducking out the door.

Outside, he wrapped the binocular strap around his hand, holding them close to his chest as he swung across the ditch into the woods. The wilderness they had roamed was rapidly diminishing, but their fort had yet to be touched. Jessie picked his way through the familiar underbrush until he reached the front door. The wall had fallen down in several places and one of the huts was gone, but the towering structure Eugene had helped build was still standing.

Jessie climbed to the second floor, stood in front of the large window and peered up at the moon. It looked the same as it always had but he felt he knew it better now. He glanced around the room, strewn with dead leaves, wood shavings, spent shell casings, and an abandoned bird nest. He raised his new binoculars and trained them on the moon. Their magnifying power made it appear close enough to touch, but didn't reveal the spacecraft orbiting its surface.

"In the beginning, man blew up a bunch of rockets, until he made one so strong it would land a man on the moon."

CHAPTER SIXTY-EIGHT

Moon Launch

July 16, 1969

Even before the sun rose, the air was still and hot. Jessie crept through the house, careful not to wake anyone. He collected his binoculars, a thermos of cold water, a bag of snacks, and tucked the waiting beach chair under his arm, then strolled to the end of the street, whistling the "Star Spangled Banner".

Fifteen minutes later he arrived at the river. The light of the new moon reflected off the roofs of cars packed so close together the doors could barely open. Jessie passed a gleaming Mustang and a beat-up Malibu, peeking into their windows at the sleeping occupants. He set his chair in his usual place at the very edge of the shore and settled himself without a sound.

A mild breeze blew across the river, causing the water to lap softly against the rocks below his feet. He rested his head on the back of the chair, closed his eyes and tried to imagine what Neil Armstrong, Buzz Aldrin, and Michael Collins were doing at this very moment.

With his eyes still closed, he sensed a subtle shift of shadows as the sun peeked over the horizon. He lifted his eyelids a fraction to watch the fiery ball rise, its golden rays stretching across the river. Behind him, people started stirring, the springs of the cars groaning as they shifted, door hinges squealing, and loud yawns of protest against the early hour.

Jessie didn't turn around, but did pull a small radio from his pocket, already tuned to his favorite channel. He planned to focus on nothing but the launch pad directly across from him.

Launch time was still four hours away, but as more people slipped from their cars, the air crackled with anticipation. He took long, deep breaths, inhaling the scents of fresh cut grass, rotting seaweed, and sausages being cooked on a nearby grill. A hand settled on his shoulder, startling him from his imaginary walk-through of the launch sequence. Jessie turned and found his father looking down at him.

"Do you mind if I join you?" Eugene asked, waiting for Jessie's nod before setting his own chair in the damp grass.

"How did you know I was here?"

Eugene gazed across the river. "This isn't just a big day for the country, it's a big day for you. I figured you'd want to have the best seat possible." Eugene turned to face Jessie. "I'm sorry Doc Weston couldn't get you into the VIP viewing area like he did last year. Is he on call for this launch?"

Jessie nodded. "I knew it was a long shot. There are so many family and friends who want to be a part of this, and of course all the reporters. I appreciate he even tried." Jessie gestured toward the grey structure in the distance. "This ain't half bad, though."

Eugene glanced around at the crowd growing about them. "Looks like a lot of other people think so too."

"You know the launch isn't until nine thirty, right?"

"If I waited until then to get out here, we wouldn't have a chance to talk."

Jessie wasn't sure he wanted to talk this morning. He didn't want anything to mar the memory of this day.

Eugene shifted, the metal frame of his chair creaking. "I don't know if I've told you how proud I am of you. You may not be the first in the family to go to college, but you had to work the hardest for it. Sam was always smart; he gets that from your mother. Once you decided you wanted to be an astronaut you put your whole heart into it and got yourself a scholarship."

"I couldn't have done it without Mr. Smith tutoring me." Jessie remembered the day his teacher had broken up the fight with Alan and his goons, then later offered to tutor him. In so many ways that day had been a turning point. Jessie glanced at his father and saw him frown.

Appreciating the help of another man probably makes him feel bad, Jessie thought. Well, it's the truth, and it's something he'll just have to live with.

"I'm proud of you for choosing the Navy ROTC program at school too. I know it must have been a tough choice."

Jessie held back a snort. Tough choice was an understatement. Going Navy had meant following in Eugene's footsteps, even if only a tiny bit, but since the program in high school had been Navy sponsored, it had seemed logical to continue that path at Embry-Riddle. He had seriously considered changing to the Air Force program but having the three years of Navy ROTC behind him from high school had given him the push to stay the course.

"It made sense to stay in the Navy program." Jessie reached for the thermos at his feet and poured half a cup of water. He drank it slowly, hoping the conversation would die with his silence. The unspoken truce between them had lasted this long by not digging up the past.

"I hope your mother and brothers get out here before the crowd gets much larger. They won't be able to find us if they don't."

Jessie hadn't bothered waking any of his brothers, knowing their interest in the space program had waned. Sam was more absorbed than ever in his books, his third year of college now behind him. He'd come home from school six weeks earlier and spent most of his time reading or out exploring the old Indian mounds they'd played on as kids. Ricky and Max had started their own construction business earlier in the year and already had contracts on two new hotels.

"I didn't think they would be coming." Jessie craned his neck to look through the milling throngs, toward the highway.

Eugene laughed. "This day will go down in history, Jess. I don't have any doubt that this mission will be a success."

Jessie's body tensed. He'd followed every single launch since he was five years old, every explosion, every satellite, every test, every success and failure. Not once had he uttered a word of confidence that all would go as planned. More often than not there were issues or delays.

"You have no idea what you are talking about." Jessie had to force the words out through clenched teeth. He saw Eugene's smile fade.

"I didn't mean to upset you. I thought…"

Jessie shook his head, cutting his father off. "I don't want to talk about it anymore. Let's just sit and wait."

Peter, Paul and Mary's song "Leaving on a Jet Plane" drifted into the silence between them. Jessie couldn't help but smile. He relaxed his tense muscles, stretched his legs out in front of him, so that his feet dangled above the water, and closed his eyes. The sun was now above the looming VAB and felt warm on his skin. In another hour he knew he'd be sweating, but right now it was just right.

By eight o'clock the crowd had swelled to thousands, the excited chatter of young and old alike filling Jessie's ears. He scanned the faces for anyone he might know, but everyone seemed to be from out of town. It was thrilling to be part of such an enthusiastic gathering and yet he felt a longing for the old days, climbing on the roof of their little house on Merritt Island and watching the rockets with his brothers.

"What do you know about the guys flying this mission?" Eugene broke the silence that had reigned over them for the better part of two hours.

Jessie could tell his father every detail ever printed about the astronauts. Jessie sighed. Max was right, it was exhausting trying to be mad at Eugene all the time, and he was the only one in the family who seemed to care about the significance of this day.

"Neil Armstrong, he's the Commander. He and Grissom went to Purdue at the same time. Armstrong was in the Naval Air Cadet program and called to active duty two years after he started Purdue. He flew in the Korean War, then returned to finish his degree in aeronautical engineering." Jessie felt his heart start to race with excitement as he spilled out more details on each of the astronauts.

"Did you know there was another guy named Michael Collins who was a leader in the Irish rebellion back in 1920, or somewhere around then? Sam told me about it. I don't think this Michael Collins is related though. He's the command module pilot, so I hope he doesn't feel rebellious and leave Neil and Buzz down on the moon."

Eugene chuckled. "Slow down, catch your breath. We have plenty of time for you to catch me up on everything I need to know."

Jessie thought about this a minute, bent down for his thermos, poured another cup of water, then nodded. "You're right. There's a lot you need to know. Let's start with an overview of the *Mercury* program."

"Whoa, do we need to go back that far?"

"The story goes back farther than that, but I didn't want to bore you with the general missile tests and the shame of the Russians getting a satellite into space before us. And, well, I don't know what you know or remember from *Mercury*. You were…"

"I was kind of out of it, I know." Eugene pulled the baseball cap off his head and ran his hand over the few strands of hair still clinging to his scalp. "I did some reading after the fire, though, found out a bit of what the space program had been working toward."

Jessie fumbled with the thermos lid, nearly dropping it in the grass. "You did?"

"You had such a conviction that the way to honor the memory of those men who died was to carry on and never give up. I knew I hadn't instilled that kind of courage and determination in you and wanted to know more about those who had." Eugene dropped his gaze to the ground. "I knew you kept news articles in a box under your bed, and I would sneak in to read them when you went to work in the evenings."

Jessie stared at his father. "What was the name of the capsule that Grissom and John Young flew in?"

"*Molly Brown* of course. Grissom thought of it because of the incident with the hatch on his *Liberty Bell 7* blowing early and sinking that capsule."

"Who completed the first EVA?"

"You mean the first extra-vehicular activity or spacewalk? Ed White." Eugene looked up, his eyes twinkling, challenging Jessie to ask him more.

"What happened the first time there was a rendezvous and docking?"

"The *Gemini* capsule started spinning out of control. This Armstrong fellow managed to get it back under control."

"What was the maximum height for a *Mercury* astronaut?"

"You got me there."

Jessie nodded, accepting his victory. "Five feet, eleven inches. I was worried when I had that growth spurt. They raised the maximum to six feet for *Gemini*."

"I don't remember reading that in any of your news articles."

Jessie shrugged. "Maybe Dr. Weston told me, I don't remember exactly."

"I'm surprised we haven't seen him out here."

"He's on call in case there is an emergency abort." Jessie held up a hand to cut Eugene off. "Don't say it. It won't be fine until they are in orbit and even then there are dozens of things that can go wrong."

"Maybe we should say a prayer then."

Jessie opened his mouth to protest, but then nodded and closed his eyes.

"Dear Lord, we pray for your hand of protection on the astronauts today. We pray for guidance and wisdom to the men in the control center. We pray that the rocket and spacecraft were made with skilled hands and reviewed by eagle eyes. We pray for a mission that goes as planned and that all three astronauts will return to us safely. We thank you for this creation you have given us and the intelligence that has brought us this far in our space journey. Lord, keep your hand of protection and guidance on Jessie as he studies to follow in the footsteps of these brave individuals. Thank you for giving me the chance to be here today to experience this moment with my son. In your holy name I pray, Amen."

Jessie opened his eyes and noticed the people around them had grown quiet, hats had been removed, and many heads were bowed. In a rippling motion, those heads raised and whispers of amen could be heard. Several men made eye contact with Jessie and nodded.

The buzz of conversation resumed, but Jessie remained silent. He leaned back in his chair, shading his eyes against the bright sun. He tried to count the boats dotting the river, but was distracted and lost track. He turned his gaze on the grey tower across the river that supported the *Saturn V* rocket they were all waiting for, but he still couldn't focus.

"T-minus thirty minutes," someone shouted.

Jessie turned on the radio he'd placed by his feet. There were a dozen other radios playing, but he liked having the control of choosing his favorite broadcaster. The familiar voice calmed his rattled thoughts and he felt himself slip into the trance-like state he entered before every launch, in tune with the whispers of the wind and the announcer's voice, everything else fading away.

"They're interviewing Arthur C. Clarke," someone announced.

Jessie turned up the volume, intrigued to hear a writer talking about how the space program was a good investment. The experiments the astronauts did on their missions didn't get a lot of coverage, and had seemed like low priorities up to this point. With longer missions possible, there would be more chance to experiment and learn how things act differently in space. Maybe they would find new cures for diseases.

"We're at ten minutes and counting, aiming for a planned lift-off at thirty minutes past the hour." The broadcaster announced before giving a detailed account of what was to come at launch, telling those who may have never seen a launch before about the water dumped into the fire trench area before launch, to help reduce the vibrations and noise from the engines, how ignition takes place in the five engines at eight to ten seconds before lift-off, providing seven and a half million pounds of thrust.

The voice went on to explain about Max Q, at around one minute and twenty one seconds, when the rocket reaches the maximum dynamic pressure it can sustain, one of the most dangerous parts of the launch. Jessie knew it all well; his lips moved in silent recitation of the steps the crew would go through before reaching orbit.

The broadcast went to commercial and Jessie rose from his seat. The countdown was down to four minutes when the commercial ended. The voice of Jack King in launch control replaced the broadcaster. King announced the firing command coming in and the automatic sequence.

"T-minus three, we are go with all elements of the mission at this time. We're on an automatic sequence as the master computer supervises hundreds of events occurring at this time." King explained about the members of the launch team in the control center monitoring red line values, such as temperatures and pressures, ready to call out anything that would cause a deviation in the plan.

Jessie felt his chest tighten; he tried to take deep breaths, to slow the slamming of his heart against his chest. King's voice continued to keep the millions of people watching around the world appraised of the progress of the rapidly diminishing minutes to lift-off.

"Twenty seconds and counting, ten, nine, eight." Jessie took a deep breath and held it, his fingers crossed behind his back. "Five, four, three, two, one, zero, all engines running. Lift-off, we have a lift-off, thirty two minutes past the hour."

Fifteen seconds later the rumble shook the ground beneath Jessie's feet followed by the roar of the engines. The windows in the cars rattled and cheers erupted. The plume of flame rose through a thin veil of clouds. Jessie released his breath when he heard the report that they had reached Max Q and all was good. When the first stage separated, he uncrossed his fingers. When he heard the report from Armstrong that the engine skirt and launch escape tower had separated, Jessie at last allowed himself to join in the cheers.

Four minutes into launch and the spacecraft was a mere speck in the vast sky, traveling at almost eight thousand miles an hour. Many of the onlookers returned to their cars, probably hoping to beat the rush back to the highway, but Jessie wasn't moving until he heard that the second stage had separated and the third had activated without fail. At nine minutes they got word that staging and ignition was confirmed. Jessie gave a sigh of relief and turned to his father.

'Eugene's face glowed and tears glistened on his cheeks. Their eyes met and Eugene smiled.

Jessie nodded. "I forgive you."

CHAPTER SIXTY-NINE

Moon Landing

July 20, 1969

S unday morning, Jessie had to be roused from a deep sleep. "It's time to get up, Jessie. We're going to be late to church." Eleanor shook his shoulder.

"Do I have to go?" Jessie grumbled.

"Yes." Eleanor stood and walked to the door. "We're leaving in fifteen minutes so you better get moving."

Jessie threw back the blanket and stumbled into the bathroom. He gave his teeth and hair a half-hearted brushing and dressed in the only set of clothes hanging in his closet. He was still rubbing sleep from his eyes when he entered the kitchen ten minutes later and poured a cup of coffee.

"You don't have time to drink that," Eleanor warned.

Jessie tipped the cup up and filled his mouth with the hot liquid, burning his tongue and stinging its way into his stomach, the pain jolting him to action. "What are we waiting on? Let's move."

Eleanor rolled her eyes and picked up her purse. Jessie called "window" and waited for Ricky to scoot to the middle of the car's back seat before taking his own spot and shutting the door.

The service felt like it lasted for years, Jessie's leg anxiously bouncing, drawing critical looks from his mother. He would make a conscious effort to control it only to have it start again a few minutes later.

"I'm going to walk home," Jessie announced after the service when Eleanor started to join a circle of women.

"I'll only be five minutes," Eleanor assured him.

Eugene tilted his head toward the door. "Go on. If she's really done in five minutes we'll stop to pick you up."

Jessie bolted out the door before his father could change his mind. He untucked his shirt and unbuttoned the cuffs, rolling the sleeves up to his elbows. A hot wind blew in his face, causing him to squint against the stirred up sand. Once he was in the house, he turned on the television before changing from his dress clothes into a pair of shorts and a t-shirt. In the kitchen, he swiped an apple from the fruit bowl, along with a bunch of grapes, and dropped down in front of the television.

He flipped through the channels, checking out the news reports on each of the three networks. There were still two hours before the moon landing and Jessie was as antsy as a child waiting for his first visit with Santa Claus. He heard a car pull up outside and tried to guess who would be first through the door, but instead, there was a knock. He rose, peeked out the window, and found Uncle Tommy and his family waiting on the porch.

"Hey, Uncle Tommy." Jessie opened the door and gestured for them to come in. "How are you all?"

"We're good. Where are your folks?" Tommy asked.

"They haven't made it home from church yet. Mama went to talk with some of the ladies and you know how that can go."

"We thought we might watch the moon landing with you." Aunt Donna held up a picnic basket. "I brought some fried chicken, potato salad, and baked beans."

Jessie inhaled deeply when she lifted the lid and the smells filled the room. "Why don't you put that on the counter. They should be home soon."

Donna placed it by the stove. "Sally, why don't you and your brother find something to do outside?"

"Ah, Mom, do I have to?" Sally complained. "I don't want to mess up my hair."

"Yes, the fresh air is good for you, just look out for cars." Donna opened the door and shooed them outside.

"This must be an exciting day for you, Jessie." Uncle Tommy pulled up his pant legs as he took a seat on the couch.

"Yeah, but the waiting is killing me."

Tommy laughed. "We've waited eight years, a few more hours isn't going to kill us."

The door opened and Ricky entered, followed by Tommy Jr.

"Tommy, good to see you," Eugene bellowed when he entered. Tommy rose and the brother's shared a brief hug.

"I hope you don't mind us stopping by. We thought it would be nice if we could all watch the landing together."

"Of course, it's a fine idea."

"I brought some food," Donna offered. Jessie noticed his mother's tense expression relax and knew she'd already started worrying about what she was going to feed everyone.

"That wasn't necessary, Donna, but thank you." Eleanor set her purse on a table by the door. "Would you like to help me get lunch together?"

Donna nodded and the women stepped into the kitchen. Donna unloaded the picnic basket and Eleanor pulled containers of food from the refrigerator, emptying some into pots to be reheated on the stove. The words they shared were too quiet for Jessie to hear. It took them twenty minutes to heat the food and arrange it in a buffet style.

The family piled their plates high; the Cole boys and their cousins were seated at the table while their parents took their plates into the living room. The volume on the television had been turned down so they could talk, but Jessie kept his eyes glued to the picture for any sign of the upcoming landing. By two o'clock the dishes were stacked in the sink, the few leftovers packaged up and put in the fridge, and everyone was seated around the television, waiting in anticipation.

Two hours later, the screen showed the surface of the moon and one leg of the lunar module as Armstrong and Aldrin descended. Walter Cronkite and astronaut Wally Shirra added some commentary on the speed of the lunar module, moving at seven hundred sixty feet per second, the slowest man had ever flown in space, but mostly they let the communication between the astronauts and Mission Control speak for itself.

The clarity of the transmissions and the video astounded Jessie. Goosebumps covered his skin when he heard the go for landing, but then his stomach tightened only a second later when the lunar module broadcast a 1201 alarm. Mission Control quickly gave a go on it. The astronauts reported their rate of descent, dropping from five thousand two hundred feet to three thousand in seconds, yet the video they were providing looked like they were barely moving.

Two thousand feet, sixteen hundred, fourteen hundred, 1202 alarm. Jessie squeezed his crossed fingers together even tighter. Five hundred forty feet, four hundred feet, three hundred. The image changed to what Jessie guessed must be a view from the command module, showing the lunar module inching toward the surface of the moon. It looked like something out of a *Star Trek* episode or an alien invasion movie, and yet it was real.

One hundred feet, seventy-five, sixty seconds of fuel remaining, thirty seconds of fuel, engine stop.

"We copy you down, Eagle."

"Houston, Tranquility Base here, the Eagle has landed."

"Roger, Tranquility, we copy you on the ground. You got a bunch of guys about to turn blue, we're breathing again."

Jessie let out his own breath and heard the others in the room do the same, followed by excited cheers. Exchanges between Mission Control and the astronauts about the preparations for the moonwalk filled the next several minutes with little commentary from Cronkite and Shirra.

Jessie stood and stretched his tense muscles. "It's going to be hours before they actually exit the vehicle."

"That was incredible," Eugene murmured.

Uncle Tommy looked at Jessie. "If someone had told me, when I was your age, that we would land men on the moon, I would have thought they were crazy. By the time you're my age, I wouldn't be surprised if we have explored the farthest reaches of the galaxy. I'm proud of you for wanting to be part of that."

Jessie felt self-conscious with all eyes on him. "I haven't done anything yet, but I will do my best to make you all proud of me. Right now, I think I'm going to go for a walk."

Jessie left the house without any destination in mind. He wandered through the diminishing forest, past the crumbling fort, across the railroad tracks and cut through a construction site. He relived every second of the landing as he walked, and then went back to the beginning, remembering how disappointed he'd been with Alan Shepard's first brief entrance into space. It was hard to believe it had only been a little over eight years, and so much had happened. More than twenty men from the United States had flown in space, some more than once. The race between the Americans and the Soviets had often seemed lost, yet it was America that had come out on top. What new frontiers would be opened to him by the time he finished school? The possibilities seemed endless.

The smell of dry seaweed slowed Jessie's steps. He looked ahead of him, across the river to the towering building that had become an iconic symbol of the Kennedy Space Center. He looked behind him at the narrow two-lane road that led into the heart of Orlando, which would be filled with cars once again in a matter of months when the next *Apollo* launch was scheduled. Jessie was sure after today's success the crowds would be even larger than before.

CHAPTER SEVENTY

Moon Walk

July 20, 1969

J essie returned home to find his family gathered around the dinner table. The leftovers had been reheated, but there was still so much excited chatter, that the food was barely touched. Jessie grabbed a piece of chicken and caught Max's attention before heading for the back door. Max joined him on the back porch a minute later. Jessie sucked the last piece of meat off the chicken bone before throwing it into the trees behind the house.

"That was pretty cool," Max said as he took a seat in one of the old beach chairs.

Jessie nodded. "You remember Alan Shepherd's launch, back when we were on the island?"

"Yeah, you weren't too happy it was so short." Max chuckled. "Who would have believed eight years, two months, and fifteen days later we would land on the moon?"

"You counted it out?"

Max shrugged. "What do you think it will be like when they get out and start walking around?"

Jessie felt his heartbeat quicken. "I don't know. I wonder what Buzz and Neil are thinking right now. You think they have time to appreciate just how awesome what they have done is, and are about to do?"

"I think they've probably been dreaming of this moment as long as you have." Max leaned his head back on the chair and Jessie did the same. The sun had fallen behind the trees and darkness would be upon them in another hour.

"What time do you think they will actually leave the lunar module?" Max asked.

"I dunno. Maybe we should go back inside so we don't miss it." Jessie studied the sky, lit by the gold and pink hues of sunset, then pushed himself out of his chair.

Most everyone had returned to the living room; Sam and Ricky could be heard talking in one of the bedrooms, while Sally and Tommy Jr. remained at the kitchen table, playing cards. Max took a spot on the couch next to Uncle Tommy and Jessie found his regular place on the floor.

Jessie hadn't realized how comfortable it could be spending time with his parents and his brothers, without the weight of anger, resentment, bitterness, or confusion hanging over him. He'd thought he'd let the past go many times before, but it wasn't until he'd said those three small words on launch day that he'd finally felt completely free.

His thoughts turned to his friend Mark from Embry-Riddle and wondered if he was watching with his own family. I'll write him a letter tomorrow, Jessie thought.

The hours passed and the excitement of the landing faded as eyes grew tired. Conversation turned to politics, race riots, and the hippie movement, but remained far from the lingering war in Vietnam. They had all been relieved when Ricky failed

Rebekah Lyn

his draft physical due to a heart murmur and poor vision. He'd started taking medication and his fainting spells had become rare.

Jessie was shuffling around the kitchen, nibbling on a piece of bread when the phone rang. He reached for the receiver, wondering who would call so late. "Hello?"

"Jessie, is that you?"

"Yes." Jessie tried to place the voice.

"It's Dr. Weston. Are you watching the television?"

"Hey, Doc. Yeah, we're watching, but nothing much is happening."

"Only you would think that," the doctor laughed.

"You know what I mean, they aren't outside yet."

"But they *are* on the moon. You youngsters always want more."

Jessie knew the doctor was teasing and chuckled. "I suppose you're right. Did you and your wife see the landing?"

"Of course. I was calling to see if we might come over to watch the moon walk with you."

Jessie couldn't believe he hadn't thought to invite the doctor over for the whole event. He'd been so caught up in his own excitement, he hadn't thought about anyone else. He put his hand over the phone and called to his mother. "May Dr. Weston and his wife come over?"

Eleanor turned and studied Jessie for several seconds. He was sure she was going to say no, but then she nodded and rejoined her conversation.

"Come on over, Doc. Sorry I didn't think to invite you earlier."

"I suspect you've been a bit focused. We'll see you soon."

The clock in the kitchen moved past ten. Chairs had been pulled into the living room for the Westons, just before they arrived, and several pots of coffee had been brewed to help everyone stay awake. The CBS News was showing a simulation of the astronauts in the lunar module and all they were doing to prepare for their first excursion on the moon. Jessie felt his excitement reignite as he listened to the words of Mission Control and the astronauts as they confirmed steps and completed radio checks. Then, in a flash, the picture changed from simulation to live video on the moon.

The picture was upside down at first, but rotated seconds later, and then a shadow moved and Jessie heard one of the men on television say it was a foot coming down. Jessie rocked back and forth on his knees, his hands clenched together in a tight ball.

Neil Armstrong reported in that he was at the foot of the Lunar Excursion Module ladder and Jessie thought his heart might explode.

"That's one small step for man, one giant leap for mankind," Armstrong said as he took the final step off the ladder.

The living room erupted in celebration. Everyone was on their feet, hugging and dancing, but Jessie moved closer to hear the words from the television. He listened intently as Armstrong described the surface as fine and powdery. He remained in awe as Armstrong reported moving around was easier than in their simulations.

The black and white video showed shadow and light for several minutes, before an x-ray type image appeared, making it harder to tell what was happening and leaving only the words from Mission Control, the astronauts, and the news team to explain what was taking place. Walter Cronkite gave a recap of what had happened and what had been said in those first few minutes on the moon, while Armstrong inspected the LEM and the conditions on the surface.

Jessie felt a hand on his shoulder and looked up to find Dr. Weston and Eugene standing over him. Both men wore large smiles. Jessie glanced back at the television, but Armstrong had stepped out of view to collect some samples. Jessie stood and accepted the warm hugs from his father and his friend.

"Thank you for letting me be part of this historic moment with you and your family," Dr. Weston said. "I look forward to the day when we are cheering you into space."

Eugene reached for the doctor's hand. "Thank you for being such a good friend to my boy."

Jessie watched the two men who had exerted such vastly different influences over his life shake hands, brought together through his own love of space. He glanced back at the television in time to see Buzz Aldrin drop from the LEM ladder onto the moon. Jessie knew that this night would hold memories of more than one historic event.

"Martha and I better head home," Dr. Weston said.

"But you'll miss the rest of the walk," Jessie said.

"Only a few minutes. They are supposed to be out for a couple of hours." Dr. Weston stifled a yawn. "I'm sure glad tomorrow is a Saturday. I don't think any of my patients would appreciate me falling asleep during their appointments."

Jessie smiled. "I'll stop by and see you before I head back to school."

"You better. I miss our little chats." Dr. Weston shook Jessie's hand and moved to collect his wife.

Aunt Donna and Uncle Tommy woke Sally and Tommy Jr. and guided them out the door a few minutes later. The house was then quiet except for the reports from the television. Eleanor rubbed at her eyes.

"You can go on to bed," Jessie offered. "I'll turn everything off when this is over."

Eleanor kissed Jessie on the cheek. "I'm happy it's going well."

Eugene followed Eleanor down the hall, leaving Max and Jessie alone. "You mind if I stay up with you?" Max asked.

Jessie shook his head and the boys returned to the couch, leaning forward to make out the pictures as Aldrin and Armstrong moved around. The two brothers sat in silence, watching and listening.

"I wish they'd keep the camera still," Jessie said, several minutes later. "It's making me sick watching that bright spot move around so much."

"It's gotta be hard for them to maneuver in those gloves. The work gloves Ricky and I use took forever to get used to. I imagine theirs are even more bulky."

"Look at that," Jessie whispered as the camera was turned around and the LEM came into focus, with Buzz Aldrin standing in front of it. Then the camera moved again, providing images all around it, the sunlight reflecting bright white off the lunar surface.

"I can't believe it's already been an hour," Max said when a voice from Mission Control provided the update.

"Do you think Gus is able to see all of this?" Jessie turned from the television to face his brother.

"I hope so," Max replied, turning his good eye to meet Jessie's gaze.

"I wonder if his family is watching."

"I can't imagine anyone not watching this." Max smiled.

Just then they could hear chatter between Houston and the *Columbia* command capsule in which Michael Collins was still orbiting the moon, waiting for his colleagues to return. Houston control provided him an update on the events taking place below him, mentioning that he was the only person who didn't have television coverage of it all. Jessie admired the man for his sacrifice and his response that it didn't matter. A moment later, Aldrin and Armstrong unfurled the American flag. There was some struggle to plant the flagpole in the surface of the moon, but once it was secured, the astronauts took turns taking photos of each other next to the flag.

Jessie smiled when Aldrin started to move around, almost as if he were dancing. His movements conveyed sheer joy as much as experimentation, and the old longing ached deep within Jessie's heart to be up there with them.

Mission Control interrupted, calling both astronauts into the camera's field of view and announcing that the President of the United States was on the phone for them.

"That's a mighty long distance phone call," Max joked.

"Aint it, though?" Jessie agreed.

The picture on the television switched to a split screen showing President Nixon sitting in the Oval Office on one side and the astronauts on the other. Jessie nodded as the President expressed his pride in the astronauts, then immediately felt humbled by the President's words, of how, at that moment, everyone on the earth was united in pride for their accomplishment. This wasn't just a success for America, but for all mankind.

A little after one in the morning, with Aldrin and Armstrong safely back inside the LEM, Jessie stood and clicked off the television. "Thanks for staying up with me." He gave Max a playful punch on the arm.

"I wouldn't have missed it." Max pulled Jessie into a hug. "It's gonna be strange when Ricky and I move out next month."

"I'm happy the business is going well for you two, though." Jessie's gaze ran over Max's face, one side still scarred, but less frightening. The glasses he wore to help with his remaining eye had a dark lens to cover the empty socket on the other side. "I'm proud of you for not giving up when things looked bad."

"It's God who gave me the strength to keep going. Anything is possible when you trust in Him."

The brothers walked down the hall and parted at their bedroom doors. Jessie crossed the dark room and switched on the lamp by his bed. A small pool of light fell on his side of the room and he glanced toward Ricky's bed, to make sure he was still sleeping. Without making a sound, Jessie slid out the worn box from under his bed and removed Grissom's book and his treasured piece of rocket debris.

"We didn't give up, Gus." Without changing his clothes, Jessie crawled into bed, still clutching the book and the metal, and fell fast asleep.

Acknowledgements

Writing this book has been a real treat for me. I grew up watching the Space Shuttle launches and will admit I got to a point where I took the program for granted. The research I did to learn about how it all started gave me a deep respect and appreciation for the ingenuity and dedication of those early pioneers. I met a number of people who provided great insight into the history of Titusville and Indian River City as well as first hand stories of families who were removed from Merritt Island to make way for the Kennedy Space Center. Many thanks to Joan Harper and the volunteers at the North Brevard Historical Society and Museum for allowing me to go through old newspapers and taking time to share your own stories of life in the Titusville during the 1950s and 1960s. Thank you Shane at the County Records office for taking the time to go over county maps with me and your assistance with the CD of aerial photos from the time period. Best of luck to you in your own writing endeavors; you have some great stories to share.

I wanted to be as accurate as possible when telling Max's story of Vietnam and must thank Bill Fanning for his openness about his own experiences. Joe Malcolm, Craig Garner and Nathan Twigg provided additional military consulting. I thank them all, not only for their feedback and guidance, but for their sacrificial service to our country.

As part of my research I had the chance to take a tour of the original launch sites located on the Cape Canaveral Air Force Station. I am so thankful I did this tour when I did as it was suspended only a few weeks later due to sequester. I hope that these tours will one day resume so others may be as inspired as I was. You can see a video from my tour on my YouTube channel.

None of my books would be possible without the efforts of my beta readers, Pam, Sharon, Jeanette, DiVoran, and Onisha. Thank you ladies for your insight and eagle eyes. I can't say enough about my wonderful editor Clive Johnson. Working with Clive was a pleasure and helped me see many aspects of the story in a different light. I appreciate his patience and the guidance he provided to help me grow as an author.

Finally, I must thank my family. My mom has provided me more support than I could ever ask for, reading endless drafts, feeding me when I was in the zone, and keeping me on task once the writing was finished. Writing this book drew me closer to my father and I enjoyed hearing his stories of growing up in Indian River City much like Jessie and his brothers. Without the support of my parents I would never have pursued writing as fiercely as I have over the past four years and I will always be thankful for them.

You may also be interested in reading some of the books I studied to get the details just right. They include: *A history of Kennedy Space Center* by Kenneth Lipartito, *Brevard: On the Edge of Sea and Space* by Elaine Murray Stone, *History of Brevard County, Volume 2* by Jerrell H. Shofner, *Moon Launch! A History of the Saturn-Apollo Launch Operations* by Charles D. Benson, *Memories of Merritt Island* by Gail Briggs Nolen and my two personal favorites, *Live from Cape Canaveral: Covering the Space Race, from Sputnik to Today* by Jay Barbree and *Gemini! A Personal Account of Man's Venture Into Space* by Virgil "Gus" Grissom.

Keep reading for an excerpt from the next book in the Jessie Cole trilogy, *Destiny's Call.*

Destiny's Call

CHAPTER ONE

April 11, 1981

Jessie Cole stood and retrieved his duffel bag from the plane's overhead compartment. Even seated near the front, he had to wait five endless minutes before he could exit. The moment he entered the terminal he saw his mother. Her eyes lit up when they met his and he hurried to meet her. She pulled him into a tight hug and her unique scent filled his nostrils. It was sweet and reminded him of wildflowers.

"It's so good to have you home."

"It's good to be back." Jessie scanned the other faces in the crowd. "Where's Pop?"

"I'm right here."

Jessie turned to see Eugene Cole lumbering toward them, his six-foot-three frame appearing hunched and his blue button-down shirt hanging loose on his shoulders. Eugene closed the gap between them and Jessie extended his hand. Eugene took it, but instead of a handshake, tugged Jessie into a hug.

Jessie and Eugene hadn't seen eye-to-eye on many things. In fact, Jessie had hated the man for most of his childhood. Things had started changing after their family had been forced to leave their home on Merritt Island when the space program needed more land for the burgeoning rocket program.

Eugene hadn't taken the move well and it had led Jessie's parents to separate for several months. When Eugene moved back in with the family, he'd seemed different—stopped drinking, started going to church, and the beatings had stopped—but Jessie hadn't trusted the change.

On the night of the *Apollo 1* fire, though, Jessie's heart had started to soften. Astronaut Gus Grissom had been his idol, and his death knocked the wind out of Jessie, but he'd put on a brave face, believing that's what Gus would have done. That night, Eugene had told Jessie he'd make a fine astronaut one day. It was the first time Jessie could remember his father saying anything positive to him. Over the next several years, a tentative relationship grew between father and son, but there was always a whisper of doubt in the back of Jessie's mind.

"You feeling all right, Pop? You look like you've lost weight."

"I'm right as rain," Eugene assured him.

Jessie continued to study the older man. *I'll have to talk to Max later.* "Let's get going, then. I'm starving."

Eleanor Cole smiled. "I thought you might be. I have some sandwiches and sodas in the car."

Jessie followed his parents out of the terminal to the parking lot. Eugene opened the door of a midnight-blue Chevy Malibu and Eleanor slipped in. Jessie reached for the back door, spotting the cooler as soon as he slid inside. He opened it and pulled out an ice-cold Coca-Cola and a stack of sandwiches wrapped in aluminum foil. His stomach rumbled as he peeled back the foil.

The drive from Orlando to Titusville took almost an hour and Eleanor filled the car with details of all that had been happening in town since Jessie's last visit.

"Look over there," Eleanor said, pointing to a swathe of freshly cleared land. "That's one of the sites Max and Ricky are developing."

Jessie looked out the window and realized he wasn't sure where they were. "Where are we going?"

Eleanor looked over her shoulder and grinned. "I thought we'd take you to see our new house. We move in next month."

"You're moving?" Jessie felt like he'd been punched in the stomach. Losing his boyhood home on the island had been hard, but he'd believed it was for a worthy cause. He enjoyed trying to guess if one of the rocket launch sites now sat where the house had been, but to lose the house they'd moved to in town seemed wrong somehow.

"It's one of the houses Max and Ricky's company is building, and it's gorgeous."

"It's too big for the two of us," Eugene grumbled.

"I want to have plenty of room for Jessie and Sam to visit, and hopefully they'll be bringing little babies along, too." Eleanor turned back to Jessie, and he saw the question in her eyes.

He'd made it clear to her after finishing graduate school that he didn't have any plans for marriage until he'd become a test pilot. When he was accepted into test pilot school, she'd started counting the days until he would find a wife and settle down.

"I told you, Mama, I don't have time to meet women. I spend as much time in the air as possible. I want NASA to take me seriously."

Eleanor shook her head. "I don't know who I worry about more, you or Sam."

"Why are you worried about Sam?"

"He's always heading off to some God-forsaken place that no one's ever heard of looking for lost civilizations. Last year he almost died from an infection after cutting himself on some rocks. It took the team he was with four days to get him to a city large enough to have a hospital."

Jessie scratched his head. "I hadn't heard about that. The snake bite on the dig in Algeria was a bit scary, though."

The color drained from Eleanor's face. "He was bit by a snake?"

"You didn't know?" Jessie gave his mother a sheepish grin.

"I think I prefer not knowing what you boys are up to. When I heard about that business in Iran back in seventy-nine, I just knew you were going to be sent over there to fight. I don't understand why you had to volunteer for the military after what happened to Max in Vietnam."

Jessie sighed. This was an argument he'd had with his mother more than once since graduating from Embry-Riddle. She hadn't seemed to mind when he'd received a free education through the Navy ROTC scholarship. Now that he was repaying the debt by serving his country, she brought up the dangers at least once a year.

Eugene took one hand off the steering wheel and reached over to Eleanor. "Let it be, Nora. He's a man now and has big dreams. We have to support him and let him know how proud we are."

Eleanor turned so she was facing Jessie and reached out to touch his cheek. "I am terribly proud of you."

"I'm sorry I make you worry. There are some dangerous aspects to my job, I know, but I'm good at what I do."

"We're here," Eugene announced as he brought the car to a stop, a hint of relief in his voice.

A truck pulled up behind the Malibu and honked its horn. Eugene stepped out of the car and waved. Jessie opened the door for his mother then turned to see Ricky and Max climbing out of the truck. He ran around the car and barreled into Max, the oldest of the four brothers.

Max and Jessie had endured the bulk of Eugene's beatings as kids, a shared experience that had bonded them tighter than the other brothers. Every day Max had spent in Vietnam, Jessie had felt as though a part of himself was missing. Wrestling his brother to the ground, he wondered if Max felt the same way now that Jessie was the one off playing soldier.

"You two aren't ever going to grow up, are you?" Ricky's voice brought the tussle to an end.

"Hey, Rick, how are you?" Jessie said, spinning around to him and brushing dirt from his clothes.

"I'm glad you're home, little brother." Ricky tried to reach up and give Jessie a nuggie, but Jessie ducked out of his reach. "Cecilia and the kids are looking forward to seeing you. Little John told me last night he wants to be just like his Uncle Jessie when he grows up."

Jessie grinned. "Mom says this is one of your projects. Are you trying to make Sam and me look bad by giving our folks a new house?"

"They aren't giving it to us," Eugene interjected.

Ricky shook his head. "We tried, but you know dad. He's too proud to accept charity."

"It's not charity," Max said. "If they hadn't let us keep living at home those first years after we started the business, we'd never have been able to afford the risks we took. The risks paid off, though, and now we wanted to give something back."

To hear Max talking about giving back to their father made Jessie even prouder of his brother. Max had been the first to start letting go of the anger and resentment toward Pop. Now it seemed as though there had never been a dark side to their relationship.

"Come on, let's give you the tour." Max led the way and Eleanor slipped her arm through Jessie's.

Max and Ricky explained the structural details while Eleanor described each room as she envisioned it once she had everything moved in. Eugene followed at the back of the pack without saying a word.

"It sure is a change from the places we grew up in," Jessie said at the end of the tour. "But I'm glad I came back in time to stay at the old house one more time."

"It's a good thing NASA decided to finally launch their Space Shuttle," Ricky said. "You may never have come home again if they'd dropped the program."

"I come home when I can."

Max placed a hand on Jessie's shoulder. "We know how hard you're working and the limited time you get away from the navy. I'm glad the timing worked out for you to be here for the launch."

Jessie nodded. "Me too; makes me think there might be a God out there listening to my prayers."

"You boys are coming over for dinner tonight, aren't you?" Eleanor asked when they'd reached the cars again.

Max nodded. "Yes, ma'am. Wouldn't miss it."

"Everything should be ready by six; let me know if you're going to be late."

"See you tonight," and Jessie waved at his brothers before ducking into the car.

CONNECT WITH REBEKAH LYN

I hope you enjoyed reading this book and would appreciate a brief review on whichever book site you prefer. I'd also love to get to know you. Here are my social media coordinates:

Friend me on Facebook: www.Facebook.com/AuthorRebekahLyn

Follow me on Twitter: @RebekahLyn1

Subscribe to my blog: www.RebekahLynsKitchen.wordpress.com

Follow me on Pinterest: http://www.pinterest.com/itsrebekahlyn/

Visit my website: www.RebekahLynBooks.com

Youtube: https://www.youtube.com/user/AuthorRebekahLyn/videos

Amazon, Barnes & Noble, iBooks, and Smashwords.com